RECKLESS TRUTHS

Lost Kings MC #21

AUTUMN JONES LAKE

RECKLESS TRUTHS
LOST KINGS MC #21
Copyright 2022 Autumn Jones Lake
All rights reserved
Digital ISBN: 978-1-943950-72-0
Paperback ISBN: 978-1-943950-77-5
Hardback ISBN: 978-1-943950-80-5
Cover Design: Shanoff Design
Editing: Creating Ink
Proofreading: Julie Barney

ALSO BY AUTUMN JONES LAKE

THE LOST KINGS MC™ SERIES

Slow Burn (Lost Kings MC #1)– *Free ebook!*

Corrupting Cinderella (Lost Kings MC #2)

Three Kings, One Night (Lost Kings MC #2.5)

Strength From Loyalty (Lost Kings MC #3)

Tattered on My Sleeve (Lost Kings MC #4)

White Heat (Lost Kings MC #5)

Between Embers (Lost Kings MC #5.5)

More Than Miles (Lost Kings MC #6)

White Knuckles (Lost Kings MC #7)

Beyond Reckless (Lost Kings MC #8)

Beyond Reason (Lost Kings MC #9)

One Empire Night (Lost Kings MC #9.5)

After Burn (Lost Kings MC #10)

After Glow (Lost Kings MC #11)

Zero Hour (Lost Kings MC #11.5) - *Free ebook!*

Zero Tolerance (Lost Kings MC #12)

Zero Regret (Lost Kings MC #13)

Zero Apologies (Lost Kings MC #14)

White Lies (Lost Kings MC #15)

Swagger and Sass (A Lost Kings MC Novella) - *Free ebook!*

Rhythm of the Road (Lost Kings MC #16)

Lyrics on the Wind (Lost Kings MC #17)

Diamond in the Dust (Lost Kings MC #18)

Crown of Ghosts (Lost Kings MC #19)

Throne of Scars (Lost Kings MC #20)

Reckless Truths (Lost Kings MC #21)

Rust or Ride (Lost Kings MC #22)

...and many more to come!

GLOSSARY OF CHARACTERS AND TERMINOLOGY

The Lost Kings MC™ World © Autumn Jones Lake

All the secrets are about to be unleashed! Reckless Truths really can't be read as a standalone. Chapter One starts during the events of After Glow (Lost Kings MC #11) But if you haven't read the series in a little while, I hope this glossary helps you out! Obviously, I can't cover *every* detail here or we'd be reading a million word glossary instead of a few pages!

THE LOST KINGS MC: UPSTATE, NY ("EMPIRE," NY)

- **President:** Rochlan "Rock" North. Leader of the Upstate NY charter of the Lost Kings MC.
- **Sergeant-at-Arms:** Wyatt "Wrath" Ramsey. Protector or enforcer for the club.
- **Vice President:** Blake "Murphy" O'Callaghan. Murphy was the road captain up until *White Lies (Lost Kings MC #15) He's now the Vice President.*
- **Treasurer:** Marcel "Teller" Whelan. Handles the money and investments for the club. Engaged to Charlotte.
- **Road Captain:** Dixon "Dex" Watts (newly appointed to the position in *White Lies*)

- **Grayson "Grinder" Lock:** The former sergeant-at-arms of the New York charter. We saw a little about his relationship as Rock's mentor in *Wheels of Fire (Hollywood Deoms #3)*. We first "met" him in *Corrupting Cinderella (Lost Kings MC #2)* and have seen him a few other times throughout the series, most recently in *Zero Regret (Lost Kings MC #11.)* He has been mentioned throughout the series by the brothers as they looked forward to his release from prison. He was voted in as the SAA for the downstate charter in *Throne of Scars*.

THE LOST KINGS MC: DOWNSTATE, NY ("UNION" NY)

- **President:** Angus "Zero" or "Z" Frazier. As of *Zero Apologies (Lost Kings MC #14)*, Z is the president of the Downstate, NY charter of the Lost Kings MC.
- **Vice President:** Logan "Rooster" Randall
- **Sergeant-at-Arms:** Grayson "Grinder" Lock as of *Throne of Scars*.
- **Treasurer:** Hustler
- **Road Captain:** Jensen "Jigsaw" Kilgore

THE LOST KINGS MC: PORT EVERHART, VA

- President: Cypress "Ice" Caldwell
- Vice President: Farmer
- Sergeant-at-Arms: Pants
- Treasurer: T-Bone
- Road Captain: Wings

THE LOST KINGS MC: DEADBRANCH, TN

- President: Digger
- SAA: Squiggy - as of *Throne of Scars,* Steer is the new SAA.

OTHER LOST KINGS MC MEMBERS

Cronin "Sparky" Petek: Sparky is the mad genius/hippie stoner behind the Lost Kings MC's pot-growing business. He is rarely seen outside of the basement, as he prefers the company of his plants.

Elias "Bricks" Serrano: We have seen Bricks and his girlfriend Winter throughout the series. He's one of the few members who does not live at the clubhouse.

Sam "Stash" Black: Lives in the basement with Sparky and helps with the plants.

Thomas "Ravage" Kane: We've gotten to know Rav and his snarky humor a little bit better in each book. Ravage is a general member who helps out wherever he is needed.

Sway: Former president of the downstate charter of the Lost Kings MC. We've seen Sway and his wife Tawny off and on in the series since *Strength From Loyalty,* usually annoying Rock in some fashion. He was shot in the head in *Zero Tolerance* and Z took over as president downstate. Sway and Tawny disappeared after a raid of the downstate clubhouse in *Throne of Scars* and have not been seen since.

Hoot: We've seen glimpses of him since *Slow Burn* when he was a lowly prospect. He finally got his full patch, but still gets a lot of the grunt work.

Birch: We also met him as a prospect. He's been voted as a full-patch member but shares in a lot of the grunt work with Hoot.

Priest: The Lost Kings MC's national president. We first met him and his wife, Valentina, in *After Burn.* He played an important role in *Zero Tolerance* and *Zero Apologies.* Recently, he appeared in *Diamond in the Dust* and *Throne of Scars.*

Malik: A prospect for the Lost Kings MC. Helps out at Crystal Ball. Owns the Lucky Duck pawnshop in Ironworks.

THE LADIES OF THE LOST KINGS MC

Hope Kendall North, Esq.: Nicknamed *First Lady* by Murphy in *Corrupting Cinderella (Lost Kings MC #2),* Hope is the object of Rock's love and obsession. Their daughter is named Grace after Rock's mother.

Trinity Hurst Ramsey: Wrath's angel. Former caretaker of the club. She now has her own photography and graphic design business. She is married to Wrath, fiercely loyal to the club, and best friends with Hope.

Heidi "Little Hammer" O'Callaghan: Murphy's wife and Teller's little sister. Heidi just graduated from college and works at Empire Med. Murphy officially adopted her daughter, Alexa Jade.

Charlotte Clark, Esq: Teller's sunshine. Often credited with taming the brooding treasurer of the Lost Kings, Teller.

Lilly Frazier: Z's brave and devoted siren. The new queen of the Lost Kings MC's downstate charter. One of Hope's best friends. Z and Lilly's son is named Chance.

Shelby Morgan: Rooster's sassy little chickadee. Country music singer from Texas. We first met Shelby in *Swagger and Sass*.

Serena Cargill: Former downstate club girl. At one time, she was broken-hearted over Murphy. We first met her in *Strength From Loyalty*, got to know her better in *White Heat* and *More Than Miles*. She has appeared here and there in the series since then. Mistreated by Shadow, the former VP of the downstate charter, we have not "seen" her since *Zero Regret*.

Swan: Lost Kings MC club girl and dancer at Crystal Ball. Swan has found a new calling as the yoga teacher for the old ladies of the Lost Kings MC and is slowly moving away from dancing at Crystal Ball.

Willow: Bartender at Crystal Ball, but once or twice we've caught her sneaking in or out of the basement with Sparky.

Tawny: Sway's ol' lady. The former "Queen B" of the downstate charter of the Lost Kings MC.

Anya Regal: Porn princess of the Lost Kings MC, Virginia charter.

OTHER RECURRING CHARACTERS RELEVANT TO THIS STORY

Carter Clark: Charlotte's goofy, often inappropriate, younger brother. He lives in a guest house on Charlotte and Teller's property. He helps babysit the club's kids sometimes and started a job tattooing with Bronze. He also works for Rock at his custom bike shop.

Bianca - Carter's friend, not girlfriend. We think.

Mercy - Charlotte's friend.

Russell "Chaser" Adams: President of the Devil Demons MC in Western NY. (*The Hollywood Demons* series contains his story.)

Mallory "Little Dove" DeLova-Adams: Chaser's wife. Daughter of mafia boss Anatoly DeLova.

Angelina Adams: Mallory and Chaser's daughter

Remington "Ruthless" Holt: Owns "The Castle" with his best friend, Griff. It's an underground fighting ring Murphy used to participate in. We've seen him most recently in *White Lies and Lyrics on the Wind*. Remy is the caretaker of his younger sister, Molly. He is currently considering forming a support club to the Lost Kings MC with Griff, Eraser, and Vapor.

Griffin "Stonewall" Royal: Remy's best friend and business partner. We saw him most recently in *Lyrics on the Wind*.

Eraser: Owns Zips, a racetrack near the Lost Kings MC territory. Married to Ella.

Roman "Vapor" Hawkins: The book *Renegade Path* is his story. We first met him and his wife, Juliet, in *After Burn*.

Jake Wallace: One of Wrath's business partners in Furious Fitness. Jake has appeared off and on throughout the series since *Tattered on my Sleeve*. He sometimes holds self-defense classes for the ladies. He's the younger brother of Sullivan Wallace, whose story can be found in Warnings & Wildfires.

Anatoly DeLova: Mallory's father. Leader of Russian mafia. Sometime business associate of the Lost Kings MC.

Dawson Roads: Famous (fictional) country music singer in the Lost Kings MC world. He's been mentioned here and there since *One Empire Night,* but we didn't "meet" him until *Rhythm of the Road.*

OTHER MCS: FRIENDLY CLUBS:

Devil Demons MC: Based in Western NY. Long-time friend of the Lost Kings MC. Their clubs are intertwined and share a lot of history. More of this is explored in the *Hollywood Demons* series.

Wolf Knights MC: Mostly an ally of the Lost Kings. Runs Slater County but has had a number of shake-ups in the last few years. Whisper is their current president. Claimed to be dissolving their charter and turning Slater County over to the Lost Kings but we haven't seen them fully exit the area yet.

Iron Bulls MC (From the *Iron Bulls MC* series by Phoenyx Slaughter): Southwestern outlaw club. Meets up and does business with LOKI once in a while.

Savage Dragons MC (From the *Iron Bulls MC* series by Phoenyx Slaughter): Texas outlaw club.

ENEMY CLUBS:

Vipers MC: Used to run Ironworks until the Lost Kings took over that territory. Still active in other parts of the country.

South of Satan MC: Vermont MC who has stirred up trouble for LOKI in the past. Members Thumbs and Sticks appeared in *Beyond Reason.* Other members of SOS caused trouble in *White Lies.*

LOST KINGS MC TERMINOLOGY

LOKI: Short for LOst KIngs

War room: Where the Lost Kings hold "church."

Property patch: When a member takes a woman as his old lady (wife status), he gives her a vest with a property patch. In my series, the vest has a "Property of Lost Kings MC" patch and the member's road name on the back. The officers also place their patches on the ol' lady's vest as a sign that they always have her back. Her man's patch or club symbol is placed over the heart. Rock's patch is a crown. Wrath's is a star. Murphy's is a four-leaf clover. Teller's is a dollar sign. Z's is the letter Z. Rooster's is a rooster wearing a crown. As a joke, Wrath gave Rock and Hope a "product of" patch for baby Grace. Maybe it will catch on as more kids are born into the club? We'll see.

PLACES IN THE LOST KINGS MC WORLD

I use a mix of real and imaginary names to describe the places in my series. Again, I bend and shape geography to my needs as this is a *fictional world that I have created.*

Empire, NY: The territory run by the Lost Kings MC upstate charter. This is a fictional version of Albany, NY, the capital of New York State. Many of the Lost Kings MC's businesses are located in and around Empire.

Slater, NY: Loosely based on Schenectady County. Until recently it was the Wolf Knights MC's territory. The Lost Kings MC will be taking control of Slater.

Ironworks, NY: Loosely based on Rensselaer County (Troy, NY). In the beginning of the series, it was run by the Vipers MC. It is now considered territory of the Lost Kings MC.

Union, NY: A fictional area two hours south of Empire, NY, where the "downstate" charter is located.

Crystal Ball: The strip club owned by the Lost Kings MC and one of their legitimate businesses. They often refer to it simply as "CB." Located in Empire County.

Furious Fitness: The gym Wrath owns. Often just referred to as "Furious." Located not far from Crystal Ball.

Strike Back: Owned by Sullivan Wallace but members of the Lost Kings MC have worked there in the past.

Johnson County/Johnsonville: Fictional area where Heidi grew up. About an hour west of "Empire." Where Strike Back Gym, The Castle, and Zips are located. Possibly the new home of a Lost Kings MC support club? We'll see!

Zips: Racetrack owned by Eraser where all the illegal gambling/racing in the area happens.

The Castle: Formerly a juvenile detention center. The building is now used to house the underground fighting ring run by Remy and Griff. Murphy used to fight here. Other LOKI members also blow off steam in the cage here from time to time. Located in the middle of nowhere, NY, it once-upon-a-time housed Griff, Vapor, and possibly Teller during their "troubled youth" days.

Kodack, NY: Another *fictional* NY area located in Western New York. Somewhere near Buffalo, perhaps. This territory is run by the Devil Demons MC.

Empire Medical Center: Local hospital where all the Kings receive medical treatment. Heidi also works there now.

OTHER MC TERMINOLOGY

Most terminology was obtained through research. However, I have also used some artistic license in applying these terms to my romanticized, fictional version of an outlaw motorcycle club. This is not an exhaustive list.

Cage: A car, truck, van—basically anything other than a motorcycle.

Church: Club meetings all full-patch members must attend. Led by the president of the club, but officers will update the members on the areas they oversee. (Some clubs refer to the meeting room where they hold church as the "chapel." My club refers to it as their "war room."

Citizen: Anyone not a hardcore biker or belonging to an outlaw club. "Citizen wife" would refer to a spouse kept entirely separate from the club.

Cut: Leather vest worn by outlaw bikers and adorned with patches and artwork displaying the club's unique colors. The Lost Kings' colors are blue and gray. Their logo is a skull with a crown. The *Respect Few, Fear None* patch is earned by doing time for the club without snitching. *Brother's Keeper* patches are earned by killing for the club. *Loyal Brother* is for a brother who's spent more than five years with the club.

Colors: The "uniform" of an outlaw motorcycle gang. A leather vest, with the three-piece club patch on the back, and various other patches relating to their role in the club.

Fly colors: To ride on a motorcycle wearing colors.

Muffler bunny or "bunnies": A girl who hangs around to provide sexual favors to members. Old ladies in my series will sometimes refer to them as "friends of the club," depending on the girl in question. Some clubs refer to them as club whores, patch whores, or cut sluts. These terms are not regularly used in my series. Sometimes simply referred to as a "club girl."

Nomad: A club member who does not belong to any specific charter, yet has privileges in all charters.

Old lady/ol' lady: Wife or steady girlfriend of a club member.

Patched in: When a new member is approved for full membership.

Patch holder: A member who has been vetted through performing duties for the club as a prospect or probate and has earned his three-piece patch.

Road name: Nickname. Usually given by the other members.

Run: A club-sanctioned outing, sometimes with other chapters and/or clubs. Can also refer to a club business run.

I'm sure I'm forgetting something! But that should get you started!

DEDICATION

For the true Lost Kings MC family.
My readers who kept asking me when certain secrets would be exposed.
Reckless Truths is yours.
Just remember, you asked for this.
Let the secrets be revealed...

PROLOGUE

Crossed Paths

MARCEL - AGE TWELVE.

IN AND OUT.

The guy said it should take no longer than five minutes. And he'd pay me fifty bucks.

In and out. Grab the lockbox the bikers keep stored in the garage and…well, I hadn't thought it through much more than that.

All I knew was fifty dollars would buy a lot of groceries.

My mother hadn't been home in days. Any food we'd had was long gone.

I'd be fine. School lunch got me through the day. But even if I were able to sneak some of it home to my baby sister, it wasn't stuff I thought she should eat.

Besides, Blake's mom wasn't much better than my own—which meant there were three mouths to feed at my house. Blake didn't expect me to take care of him. He pulled his weight in other ways. Heidi was good, but there was only so much watered-down cereal I could feed the kid.

There was no way I'd tell anyone my mother had disappeared. I

1

couldn't risk Heidi being taken away. This wasn't the first time Mom had taken off. Eventually she'd show up.

At least I hoped so. There was always the possibility she'd run off just like my dad had a couple years ago.

It was up to me.

I'd already raked every last leaf in the neighborhood for a few dollars. I'd tried asking the creep who lived across the street if he needed any help around the house. Instead he'd told me about the bikers who'd stolen some stuff from him and offered me fifty bucks to get it back.

He was probably lying, but I really needed that cash.

Blake and I had narrowly missed taking a ride in a cop car after shoplifting food from the Price Chopper the other day. It'd be a while before I'd try to steal from there again.

"You got her?" I asked Blake, nodding to Heidi who was busy playing with a stuffed pony Blake had given her earlier. I hadn't asked where he got it from. It made Heidi happy and that was all I cared about.

"Yeah." He puffed out his chest. "I got her, but you sure it's a good idea?"

"You got a better one?"

He shook his head, shaggy red hair falling over his forehead. Heidi climbed up on the couch next to him, waving a book in his face to get his attention.

"I'll be right back." Not a promise I was sure I'd be able to keep, but I said it anyway.

It was only late September, but the evening air had turned brisk. The wind kicked up and I wrapped my knock-off Carhartt jacket around me tighter. Not that it did much good.

"Kid!" the creep across the street called, waving me over.

"What?" I snapped, eager to get this whole thing over with.

"You got a weapon?"

"Fuck no. I'm not plannin' to run into anyone."

"Well, just in case, take this." He handed me a cheap hunting knife way too big to fit in any of my pockets.

"Where the fuck am I supposed to put this?" I handed it back and he shrugged. "Where's this box again?"

"In the garage."

2

"Yeah, I got that. *Where?*"

"Either in the metal cabinet or under the wooden workbench." He held his hands roughly twelve inches apart. "It's a gray metal box about this big. Silver handle."

"How am I supposed to get it open?"

"You're not. Just bring it back."

This whole plan stunk.

He reached out, clamping a hand over my shoulder, squeezing enough to make me wince, but I didn't move a muscle or show any fear. "You get caught, don't mention my name, understand?"

"Sure." I barely knew the guy and I sure as fuck didn't have any warm, fuzzy, loyal feelings for him. But I wasn't planning to get caught, so I kept my mouth shut.

"You're gonna need something to get in that garage," he said, looking around on his front porch. He returned and handed me a stubby screwdriver.

"That works." I slipped it in my pocket and walked back to my house to grab my bike. I'd taken any reflective bits off earlier and Blake had helped me spray the shiny parts with matte black paint. Good way to get hit by a car, but I was hoping it'd help me stay off the radar of the guys I was plannin' to rob.

I pedaled slowly, considering how to approach this job. Wondering what was in the box that had this guy willing to break into a garage owned by a bunch of bikers. Well, *he* wasn't willing to do anything. He was sending a kid to do his dirty work. Figuring, what? The bikers wouldn't be pissed to find me breaking in and stealing their shit? I had no illusion they'd go easy on me if I got caught.

Then don't get caught.

Easier said than done.

In and out.

The parking lot for the strip club Crystal Ball was packed. The muffled thump of dance music throbbed through the air. Now, *that* was a place I'd rather sneak into. The garage next door, not so much.

The bikers that hung out there were scary.

But I needed that money. *In and out.* That's all I had to do. I'd be quick. Then I could stop and pick up some groceries on the way home.

The building next door to the strip club was dark, although a truck

3

and a couple motorcycles sat in the parking lot. I hadn't determined what exactly went on in that building. Other than loud parties, lots of motorcycles, and half-naked chicks every weekend, the place seemed vacant. The garage behind it was usually full of bikers coming and going.

Tonight, the garage was dark and locked tight.

First, I circled the building. El Creep-o said I might be able to get in through one of the windows. Since they were high up and only about six inches wide, the odds of that seemed slim.

The front doors had a simple lock, which shoulda been my first clue that breaking in was fucking stupid. But I pried it loose with the screwdriver. Even then the door wouldn't open all the way. Good thing I'd come instead of Blake. He might've been two years younger than me, but he was twice as wide and never woulda fit through the narrow opening.

Once inside, I cursed that I'd forgotten a flashlight. I was the worst burglar ever. I stepped carefully, holding my arms out in front of me. First thing I collided with hurt like hell. From the cool metal and solid feel, it must've been a motorcycle that bruised the shit out of my shin.

Thankfully, I didn't knock it over.

I located the metal cabinet and said a prayer that the stupid box was inside. Risking a petit larceny charge at Price Chopper was looking better and better.

The doors creaked, as if calling out for help. I slid my hand over the dust and grime on each shelf. Something sharp sliced into my index finger.

"Fuck." I jammed my finger in my mouth, the tang of copper hitting my tongue. My other hand brushed up against something smooth, cool, and box-like. I grabbed it. I could barely see the damn thing, but it felt like what I was looking for. I didn't try to open it. Probably needed a key. But since El Creep-o hadn't asked me to retrieve one, I didn't bother looking.

Tucking the box under my arm, I turned.

And stopped dead in my tracks.

Two of the scariest bikers I'd ever seen stood just outside the open doors. One was at least seven feet tall and as wide as a mountain. The other, not much shorter and almost as broad. Both wore scowls that

4

were too terrifying to look at directly. Mountain man had long, fuck-you hair down to his shoulders and tattoos on arms that were bigger than my entire body. They both wore heavy shit-kicker boots that were probably about to kick the shit out of me.

How long had they been watching me fumble around in the dark?

The answer didn't matter.

I was worm food.

One of them reached inside and flicked on the overhead light, blinding me.

My hand flew up, shielding my vision. I squinted, afraid if I closed my eyes for even a second, they'd chop me into pieces.

Rock

"What the fuck is that?" Wrath gestured toward the garage, drawing my attention away from the back door of Crystal Ball.

You'd think we'd have the area lit up better. But there wasn't a person in Empire who didn't know this property belonged to the Lost Kings MC. You'd have to be suicidal to break into our garage.

I squinted into the darkness and barely made out the shape of a bicycle propped up against the side of the garage. A tall, skinny shadow fiddled with the lock on the double doors. It was a pretty flimsy lock, but like I said, no one should be breaking into the building.

Wrath chuckled, the sound more frightening than light-hearted coming from him. "It's a kid. Let's go scare the shit out of him."

"Wait," I said, throwing my arm out to stop him. "Let's see what he does first."

After the kid slid inside the doors, we crossed the parking lot. Wrath, stealthy as usual, slipped the lock off the doors and opened them wider. He smirked at me as we watched the kid bumble around in the near darkness.

The kid grabbed something out of the metal tool closet where we kept all sorts of parts and tools, including a lockbox that held no more than a couple hundred dollars. He didn't bother with any of the tools—just the box. How the hell had this scrawny boy even known about it?

I guessed we'd find out.

He turned and froze. Wrath reached out and casually flicked the overhead light on, startling the kid. The lockbox clattered to the ground as he threw his arm up to shield his eyes.

"What'cha doin', lil' buddy?" Wrath asked. He crossed his arms over his massive chest and aimed his stony glare at the kid. I elbowed him in the ribs, but he seemed to be taking his role of "bad" biker seriously and didn't relax the threatening pose. It'd be up to me to play "nice" biker—a role I wasn't all that familiar with.

"Didn't anyone ever tell you it's rude to touch another man's tool chest?" I asked.

The kid blinked and glanced at the metal cabinet. "Actually, it's more of a tool *closet.*"

"Funny guy," Wrath said, sounding less than amused.

"What's your name, kid?" I asked.

He opened his mouth and closed it.

"Don't lie to me either," I warned.

"Spit it out or we'll beat it outta ya," Wrath added.

The color drained from the kid's face, but he squared his shoulders and faced us head-on.

Brave little shit.

"Marcel," he finally said.

I swept my gaze over him. Jeans short enough to show off bony ankles, worn sneakers, ill-fitting threadbare jacket. Chin lifted in defiance. "How old are you, Marcel?"

"Twelve."

I raised a brow. Tall for his age. More than that, he was awfully young to be headed down the sort of path that would get him killed.

Without a doubt, if our president had been the one to catch him, Marcel would have been in the middle of a beating by now. Ruger wouldn't care about the kid's motivation for stealing, his age, or finding out who sent the kid to rob us. There were no gray areas for Ruger. No thought behind his decisions. Our president was a disappointing mix of reactionary violence, cruelty, and stupidity.

"Shouldn't you be home watching cartoons?" Wrath sneered.

Marcel didn't answer, but his jaw tightened and he dropped his gaze to the ground.

"Where you from, Marcel?" I asked.

"Couple blocks away."

"Who told you to break in here?" Obviously, the kid didn't come up with this half-assed plan on his own.

He hesitated, scraped one scuffed toe of his sneaker over the concrete floor, then shook his head. "I'm not a snitch."

Normally, that was a quality I admired. Silence was a requirement to be a Lost King. In our world, snitches ended up in ditches.

I took a step closer. "You don't have a choice this time, kid."

Was it an older brother who'd put him up to it? His father? A member of one of the two rival MCs in the area?

"All right," Wrath said, stepping forward and sizing the kid up. "Been looking for a new speed bag for the basement. You're about the right size."

I smothered a laugh.

Marcel lifted his head. His gaze darted to Wrath, perhaps assessing how serious the threat was. I adopted a similar pose to Wrath's. Arms crossed over my chest and an unforgiving, relentless stare down, assuring him the threat was indeed very real.

He ran a hand over his short blond hair before he seemed to make a decision. "This guy who lives across the street."

At least it wasn't a relative.

"We need a name, kid," I prompted. While I had no love for rats, I admired Marcel's bravery.

"I think his name is Keith."

Next to me, Wrath snorted. "Keith the tweaker?"

Marcel lifted one bony shoulder. "That explains a lot," he mumbled.

"How'd you get involved?" Wrath asked.

"I needed the money. He offered me fifty bucks if I brought the box to him."

"You need fifty bucks that bad?" I asked.

He set his jaw in a firm, defiant line.

"Come on, kid," Wrath snapped. "We haven't decided if you're gettin' a beatdown or we're calling the cops."

That brought his head up, but not for the reason I thought.

"Please don't call the cops," he pleaded in a soft voice devoid of his earlier defiance.

I tilted my head toward Wrath. All six feet, six inches and two-hundred-eighty pounds of him. "You'd rather take a beating from *him* than a ride downtown?"

It wasn't a fair question. Either way, I had no intention of calling the cops.

Marcel flicked his gaze at Wrath and scowled. "No, but I can't afford to be at the police station all night. Or—never mind."

"Or what?" I pressed.

He finally met my stare. Strain and exhaustion lingered in the haunted depths of his eyes. "I can't afford to have CPS called. So just do what you gotta do."

"Okay," Wrath said, stepping forward.

I grabbed his arm, holding him back. "Where're your parents?"

Marcel sighed and rolled his eyes. "Don't know. Dad split last year. Mom's been away for a couple days."

"If the state takes you, at least you'll get fed," Wrath said.

Marcel started shaking his head before Wrath finished.

Something wasn't right. I tapped Wrath's elbow and we waited in silence for the kid to spill.

Marcel seemed to be weighing his options. From my vantage point, I had to admit, they were all pretty shitty.

"I can't get separated from my sister," he finally answered. "She needs me."

Well, fuck if that wasn't the one thing the kid could say that would flick Wrath's kill switch to *off*. He lifted his chin. "How old is she?"

"Almost two."

"Ah, Christ." I ran a hand through my hair. "Who's with her now?"

"My buddy."

"What'd you need the money for?" I almost feared the answer. Desperation made people do reckless things.

Marcel balled his fists and stared at the floor. "Groceries."

Admitting that cost him. He was a proud kid. I respected that.

"You got any other family?"

"My grandmother, but she lives about forty-five minutes away, and Blake needs me too."

"That's your buddy watching your sister?"

"Yeah."

"How do I know you're not full of shit?"

Marcel lifted his head, a spark of insolence returning to his eyes. "Guess you don't."

I chuckled and pointed to the box still on the floor. "Give it to me."

He hurried to pick it up. Slowly, he handed it over, as if he expected me to lash out.

The lock on the box hadn't worked in years. I flicked open the box and shuffled through some cash, pulling out a few bills. I handed the box to him. "Put it back where you found it."

While he did that, I jerked my chin toward the parking lot, and Wrath followed me outside.

"You got the keys to the cage?" I asked.

"Yeah. Why?"

I glanced inside the garage. "I'm gonna give him a ride home."

He cocked his head. "Why? You plannin' to adopt him? Thought you didn't want kids?"

"Very funny. I like him. Think he'd make a good prospect in a few years."

Understanding sparked in his eyes. "You wanna start stacking the club with people loyal to you."

"Loyal to *us*," I corrected. We both knew our current president had to go. In the few years since Ruger had taken over the MC, our quality of life had gone to shit. He didn't value any of the qualities that had drawn me to club life—loyalty, honor, brotherhood. The reasons I'd brought Wrath and our friend Zero into the club. The things my mentor, Grinder, had taught me club life *should* be about. Eventually, Ruger would get one of us killed. "I'm looking at the bigger picture here."

"He's not a coward, that's for sure." Wrath glanced inside again. "He puts on a few pounds of muscle and works on that scowl, he could be your mini-me. We can call him 'Rock Junior.'"

"Just give me the damn keys, wiseass."

He finally pulled the keys out of his pocket and handed them over. "I'll follow you."

"Have a chat with Keith. Make sure the message sticks this time."

An evil smile lit up his entire face. "My pleasure."

"Well?" Marcel asked from the doorway.

He stood there, feet shoulder-width apart, chin lifted, arms loose at his sides. Like if he was going down, he'd at least try to get in a few punches. My admiration for him grew. He was scared shitless, if the sweat on his forehead was any indication, but brave.

"Grab your bike and follow me."

Wrath took off for his Harley and Marcel followed me without question. At the club's old Ford truck, I stopped and gestured for Marcel to throw his bike in the back.

"Where are we going?" he asked before lifting the bike.

Smart kid. "I'm gonna take you home and see if your story's true. Then I'll decide what to do with you."

"I'm not lying," he muttered.

Yeah, I didn't think he was. Still wanted to keep him on his toes. The last shred of morality I possessed wouldn't let me beat a twelve-year-old kid bloody. But I had no qualms about scaring the shit out of him for trying to steal from us.

"Get in and shut your mouth," I said with not much heat behind the order.

He hurried around to the other side and flung the door open.

"This is a sweet truck." A note of excitement perked up his voice. "It's a classic. You could fix it up really nice, you know," he said, running his hand over the dashboard.

I pointed to the clubhouse in front of us. "We're a motorcycle club, not a pickup truck club."

He shrugged. "They're cool too, but motorcycles don't have four-wheel drive. What ya gonna do in the winter?"

I bit my lip to hold back my laughter. "Put your seat belt on, you little knucklehead."

He gave me directions to his house. It turned out it wasn't far from where I'd grown up. "How long you lived here?"

"Long enough. It sucks."

I snorted. "You do all right in school?"

"When I go, yeah. That's my house," he said, pointing to a short, pockmarked driveway.

I followed him inside the house and stopped when we entered the living room.

Even though I figured Marcel wasn't lying, seeing the two kids zonked out on the couch together tightened my chest.

The boy was as tall as Marcel but rounder and baby-faced. With his red hair and larger frame, they probably weren't related. It made Marcel's dedication to his friend even more interesting.

"Shit," I muttered, backing out the door. Marcel followed me.

"So?" he demanded.

"Get in the truck. I'll take you to get some food."

He didn't move. "I tried to steal from you."

"I'm aware."

His gaze ping-ponged from the truck to his house.

"You can call it a loan if it makes you feel better."

That worked.

The trip to the store was a quick one. Marcel carefully selected basic items—milk, eggs, peanut butter, jelly, bread, butter, hot dogs, boxed mac 'n' cheese, cans of chicken, tiny bottles of apple juice—nothing fancy. Most of it seemed to be for his sister. He didn't try to fleece me or buy the normal junk food a twelve-year-old kid might want. His approach to shopping was more adult than Wrath's or Zero's. Somehow that depressed me even more.

After my mother died when I was little, my father fully embraced the lifestyle of a deadbeat dad, frequently leaving me alone or with random women. I didn't have any siblings to care for. By the time I was Marcel's age, I was chasing girls, not pretending to be the adult of the household. I'd had a charmed childhood compared to what Marcel seemed to have been through.

Back at the house, I followed him inside with the groceries. We set everything on the kitchen table. Then he went to check on his sister.

The other two kids were still curled up on the couch together.

"Blake," Marcel whispered. "I'm back."

Slowly, the redhead blinked and sat up, careful not to disturb the tiny dark-haired bundle curled next to him.

"Marcel? Are you okay?" He rubbed his eyes. "What's going on?" His gaze darted to me and his eyes widened when he took in the black leather cut I wore. "Shit. You got caught?" He positioned himself in front of the little girl, as if he thought I posed a threat, and he wanted to protect her.

If I *was* a threat, the gesture would have been futile. But since I wasn't, his attempt to protect the little girl was sweet. Heartbreaking even.

11

I glanced down at Marcel. "That's your sister?"

"Heidi, yeah."

"You're Blake?" I asked the little ginger bodyguard.

He nodded.

"All right." I nodded at Marcel and stepped into the hallway. A heavy sigh eased out of me. Maybe a good citizen would've called some agency and reported the obviously neglected kids. That wasn't going to be me. The three of them would get split up for sure. I'd known enough kids who'd gone through the system to know sometimes it was worse. Never mind the fact that bikers didn't handle problems by calling in the cops.

Instead, I reached into my pocket, curling my fingers around the money I'd stuffed in there earlier. "Take this."

Marcel's eyes widened. "Why?"

"For giving us the tip about Keith."

At the mention of the guy's name, Marcel's mouth twisted.

"Don't worry. He won't be sending you on any more jobs. Wrath's having a chat with him now."

"Oh."

I glanced around for a piece of paper, but all I found was a stack of textbooks on the dining room table.

"What's your favorite subject?" I asked.

"Math. I'm good with numbers."

Willing to steal or not, I could tell he wasn't the sort of kid who would accept handouts.

I flipped open his math book and scribbled my number on the inside. "You need something, call me. I'll put you to work."

"Okay."

Before leaving, I gripped his shoulder and gave him one last stern look. "Stay out of trouble."

He rolled his shoulders back and lifted his chin, a hint of his earlier boldness returning. "I'll do my best."

CHAPTER ONE

Teller

THE TRUTH IS A PAINFUL WEAPON. IT BURNS, CUTS DEEP, AND CAN SCAR you for life. Eventually pain fades, blood washes away, but the truth remains. Dirty, savage, mocking truth you can't escape.

Blood never lies.

Thank fuck I'm not the father of Inga's kid. None of my brothers are. Best news we've gotten since the porn star who used to dance at our strip club—and bang our president from time to time—decided to sue almost all of my MC brothers to determine the paternity of her son.

DNA doesn't lie.

It's been a tense couple of weeks while we waited for the results. One where I enjoyed needling Rock a little too much about how he's responsible for bringing this fuckery into our lives.

I pull out my phone and send Charlotte a quick text.

Me: Not the father of the porn star's baby. None of us are.

I stand and push in my chair, ready to celebrate.

"Teller, can you stay for a minute?" Hope's soft voice is a mix of urgency and sadness. This lawsuit was the last thing she needed to deal with while she's pregnant. Last thing Rock needed when all he seems to want to do is hover around his wife. Talk about a helicopter parent. He's a helicopter husband. Hell help their poor kid. These two first-time parents probably won't let their baby out of their sight.

Murphy claps my shoulder and leaves the war room. I drop back into my seat, curious but not alarmed that Hope asked me to stick around. Maybe she wants to talk to me about planning Heidi's wedding or something.

Hope winces and Rock jumps to his feet, guiding her into Wrath's chair.

"Are you okay?" I ask.

"I'm fine." She squeezes her eyes shut and takes a deep breath. "The lab discovered something else. I, uh, don't understand the why of it, but they tested the samples against each other... Gosh, I don't even know—"

Cold fear stabs through my stomach. "What, Hope? Are we sick or something? You're freaking me out."

Rock reaches over and grabs my hand. To shut me up? Or reassure me that everything will be okay?

Tears rain down Hope's cheeks. Pregnant or not, she's not prone to crying around us. Not even when Wrath used to get his jollies off trying to terrorize her away from the club. Today, she's shaking and taking deep sips of air.

"There *was* a match," she finally says.

"Who? Are we related to someone famous or something?" What kind of testing facility did she send us to? They were only supposed to take samples to match to Inga's kid. Did they put us in some national database? Shit, did those tests link us to a past crime or something?

Rock slowly turns and stares at me. Is he running down the long list of club enemies we've disposed of over the years too? We're always so careful getting rid of the bodies.

"Rock?" Hope's strained voice twists my heart. I'll take the fall for whatever they want to pin on my president. He can't be in jail when he has his first kid coming in a few months.

"They matched. You two. Teller's your...Teller's your *son*."

"What the fuck?" I jump out of my chair so fast, I lose my balance, crashing into the wall behind me. "What are you talking about, Hope? That's not even possible. That's crazy."

Being matched to a past crime is more plausible than Rock being my father.

Rock sits there, staring into space. A complete non-reaction. Like

Hope just announced she was going to take a nap instead of blowing up our entire lives.

"Are they sure?" he asks in a dazed tone.

"They tested it a few times…" Her quivering voice is a mix of misery and embarrassment. She shouldn't be the one delivering this news. Some doctor in a lab coat who has no connection to us should be telling us this. So I could grab him by the throat to choke off this outrageous lie. "Because of the age difference, they tested it a few times."

"Rock, that's insane," I protest. For fuck's sake, he's barely twelve years older than me. "That can't be right." I wait a beat, searching for some sort of response. Anything at all. But Rock's useless, lost chasing his own internal demons. I turn toward Hope. "How is that possible?"

She struggles to get out of her chair and rounds the table, approaching me slowly.

"How?" I ask again.

She pulls me into a warm, comforting hug. "I don't know." Her soothing voice and the familiar floral scent clinging to her hair calm me for a second. But the awkward angle has to be uncomfortable for her. I pull out the chair next to me to get her off her feet. She glides her soft, warm hand over mine and squeezes.

"Rock." I add a sharper bite to my tone to get his attention. "Did you know my mother?"

He lifts his gaze and snorts. "Apparently."

"How—I mean, I didn't think you ever met her…" I can't recall a single time Rock and my mother were face-to-face, let alone… Once I found the club, I kept that part of my life a secret. I had something that was mine and didn't want to share my new family with the mother who'd failed me in so many different ways.

"Has to be Tina," Rock mutters. "My dad used to pay this girl in the neighborhood a couple bucks to watch me when he was gonna be out overnight."

My heart stops cold. *Tina.* "My mother hated her name," I whisper, shaken down to my soul. This is *real*. Rock's my father. "Her middle name was Christina… Sometimes she went by Tina, even though my father refused to ever call her that."

"I never…knew that."

Why would he? I didn't give a lot of thought to my mother's weird hang-ups around her name. I was too busy trying to make sure Heidi was fed and cared for, and that my mother's creepy boyfriends stayed the fuck away from my baby sister.

Rock clears his throat and sits forward. "I never met her when you started hanging around the MC. Saw her from a distance once or twice. But that had to be thirteen or fourteen years later. When Wrath and I hired people to search for her after she took off, we used her real name."

"When…I had the issue with my mom and, you know, her boyfriends sniffing around Heidi, I told Lucky and Grinder. They're the ones who had a chat with her. I wonder if she would've figured it out if I'd told you instead."

Rock's solemn gray eyes widen and fill with shock. "Why didn't you tell *me*?"

"I was embarrassed."

"You have nothing to be embarrassed about with me, Marcel."

The shame that clings to me from my past never ends. "I always suspected Heidi and I didn't have the same father. Figured that was why my dad took off after she was born…But maybe he realized *I* wasn't his. My grandmother always implied I was a bastard. That's supposedly why she hated me so damn much." I stop my random word vomit and jam my fingers through my hair. This is fucking unreal. All this time…I've known Rock for so long. We've done…shit. "I have to get out of here." I stand, careful not to knock into the wall again.

"Rock," Hope pleads.

Fuck, what if they tell Heidi? Try to break the news to her gently before I have a chance to wrap my brain around this first? She craves family so much. It would break her heart to find out we're half-siblings. Not to mention, she thinks of Rock as a father figure. "Please, don't say anything to anyone. Especially not Heidi."

"Of course not," Hope says, hurrying to my side. She throws a scowl at Rock as she passes him. "But where are you going? Please don't go off when you're this upset."

"I just need to go for a walk in the woods, Hope. That's all." I'm not sure that's where I'm headed, but I need to tell her something so she doesn't worry.

In a daze, I step into the living room.

"Everything all right, welterweight?" Wrath rumbles from his usual spot on the couch.

He's so solemn, concerned, even. It's not like Wrath. He loves busting my nuts way too much. Does he know?

"I'm fine." I hurry outside to get away from him.

Rambunctious voices spill out of the garage. Fuck. I can't reach the trail to the woods without someone seeing me. Frozen in place, I stare into the wide-open overhead doors. My gaze lands on Murphy in the back corner, talking to Dex.

What am I going to say?

I retreat into the relative safety of the clubhouse. Ignoring Wrath, I return to the war room and knock on the door, then open it. Rock and Hope seem tangled in an uncomfortable conversation. Might as well make it full-throttle awkward. "Hey, can we talk for a second?"

Rock waves me in without answering. Hope pushes herself out of her chair. "I'll leave you two—"

"You don't have to go, Hope." I'm torn between wanting her to stay and act as a buffer and not wanting her to hear any more gory details about my sordid beginnings.

"No, I think you two should talk alone. If you need me, I'll be right out there."

Somehow, I find that comforting. On impulse, I grab her as she reaches for the door. She leans into me, curling her arms around my waist and hugging me again. Why couldn't I have had someone more like *her* for a mother?

Ooof, if I said that out loud, she'd probably kill me.

"He already loves you so much, Teller. This doesn't change anything," she whispers against my ear.

Sweet Hope with a comforting lie. "Thank you, Hope."

The door closes behind her with a soft click.

"Come here, knucklehead." Rock opens his arms wide.

I snort at the nickname, then stare at him, unsure I want any physical contact at the moment. My hesitation doesn't deter Rock. He pulls me in close. It's awkward as fuck. The urge to shove him away burns through my arms.

"What do we do?" I mumble.

Instead of answering, he pushes me toward one of the chairs, then pulls his closer to me. "What do *you* want to do?"

What do I want to do? I'm a grown-ass man who just had his entire history rearranged. "Fuck, I don't know." I scrub my hands over my face, searching for an answer that will make sense. "Can we take the test again? I want to... I want to be sure before..." The lab fucked up once already. What if this is all a big mistake? There has to be something I can do to regain control of my life.

Rock opens his mouth like he wants to say no, but then nods. "I'll ask Hope if she can schedule it for us."

Poor Hope. I've been kind of shitty to her in the past—*thank you, mother issues*—but I've grown to love and respect her a lot. And now, she'll probably resent the fuck out of me.

"Christ, we've joked about you being Dad for years." And don't all those jokes Murphy and I made sound a lot different now.

"Well, I knew who Murphy's mother was, so I'm definitely not his father too."

Murphy's the one who deserves to have Rock as his father. Not me.

I push the thought away. "You think Carla knew and that's why she was always such a bitch to us?"

Rock blinks at the mention of his ex-wife. "I think she was just jealous of anyone else who had my attention."

"Hope's not like that," I say. "Shit, this is the worst timing. You're finally about to have your first kid and now this. Christ, this is so fucked up. Do you want me to leave? Take off for a while so I'm not in your face?"

"What the fuck for?"

"I don't want to be in the way or fuck stuff up for you guys when this is supposed to be—"

"Stop right there. You're not in the way. You're my son."

It still sounds so unnatural, no matter how hard Rock's trying to normalize this situation.

"The question you should be asking is are you ready to be a big brother again when you're about to settle down and have your own family?" Rock seems to be reaching for a light, kidding tone but I'm not feeling it.

The reminder that Charlotte and I have our own secret we've been waiting to share punches me in the stomach. Then there's the reminder of all the shady things I had to do as a kid to keep Heidi safe. That won't be an issue with Rock's kid...my little sister. "Yeah, at least I won't have to break into garages and steal shit to feed the baby waitin' at home for me. You sure you're having a girl? I don't know if I can handle another little hellraiser like Heidi." Aw, fuck. *How am I going to explain this to Heidi?*

"I don't want to explain this to Heidi right now," I say. She's matured a lot in the last few years, but the damage done by our family always lingers, waiting to rise from the ashes and cause chaos. "I can't tell you how many times she said she wished you were her dad when she was growing up. Things are going good for her. I don't want to—"

"I get it," Rock says.

"And I don't want to say anything to Murphy either. There's no point making his life awkward by keepin' stuff from Heidi." That's only one of many reasons I want to keep this from my best friend.

"You gonna talk to Charlotte?" he asks with a bit of presidential authority creeping into his tone.

Hell, Charlotte's the *only* person I want to talk this over with. "She won't say anything."

"Good." His gaze turns distant. While wallowing in my own confusion and worrying about everyone else, I haven't given a lot of attention to how Rock is handling this. "Are you okay, Rock? This must be really fucking weird for you."

He lets out a sad laugh. "It's such a long time ago."

"But you remember what happened?" I ask. Not that I want details.

"Some of it," he answers carefully, as if he's concerned it's the nitty-gritty story I'm after.

I'm done. I slap the table. "I'm sure I'll have more questions for you. Right now, I want... I don't know."

"Whatever you need. I'm always here for you."

And that right there is one of the only truths that matters. "You're one of the few people who've always been there for me, Rock. I don't think I've ever really thanked you for that."

"You don't have to thank me for anything. I'm proud to have you as my son. You need to know that. So whenever, if ever, you want to tell anyone and go public—I'm leaving it up to you."

That's an awfully big decision with many possible consequences that he's thrown in my lap.

Go public.

An uncomfortable sensation crawls over my skin. No one can know about this. For now, the truth about my paternity needs to remain a secret.

But in the back of my mind a red warning light blinks.

Secrets always have an expiration date.

CHAPTER TWO

Charlotte

THE RUMBLE OF MARCEL'S BIKE ECHOING DOWN OUR DRIVEWAY DRAWS ME out of the house and onto the front porch. As soon as he parks, I rush down the stairs to meet him.

"Happy not-the-father day—" The silly greeting dies in my throat. A heavy cloud of despair seems to surround Marcel. Fear thrums through my veins. "What's wrong?"

He drops his head for a second, then turns and faces me. "Let's go inside."

My stomach cramps with apprehension. He said the test cleared him. None of the Lost Kings fathered that woman's kid. "What—"

He curls his cold fingers around mine. "Please. I need to talk to you."

"Okay." I rub my palms over his hands in an effort to warm his skin. His lips pull into a half smile.

"I'm fine, Sunshine."

Dreading whatever he has to tell me, I follow him into the house. He stops in the kitchen and flips the faucet on, pouring a glass of water and drinking it in a few quick swallows.

A thousand questions scream through my brain but somehow, I remain calm on the outside, waiting patiently.

He sets the glass on the counter with a soft clink and jerks his chin toward our kitchen table.

My hard wooden chair scrapes against the tile as I pull it out and slide onto its unforgiving seat. "You're scaring me, Marcel."

"Sorry." He leans over and kisses my forehead. "I'm a bit rattled."

"I can see that. Talk to me."

Instead of sitting at the table, he curls his fingers over the back of his chair and leans on it like a crutch. "I don't even know where to start. It's so absurd."

Marcel's stood by my side through some of my darkest moments. There is nothing we can't handle together. "I'm right here," I say.

Finally, he turns his troubled teal eyes my way. Someone or something hurt him. My inner demon prepares to come out swinging. To decimate whoever caused the man I love an ounce of pain.

"Rock is my father."

Individually, I know what all those words mean. Lined up in that order, they don't make any sense. "Says who?"

"The lab. Well, Hope read the lab results to us."

"How is that even possible?"

His lips quirk again. "That's what I said."

"No, Marcel. Seriously, how is that even possible? He's not...old enough to be your father." *Is he?*

"Well, apparently all those jokes Grinder used to make about Rock trying to romance every fucking woman he met as a kid were based in truth." A hint of anger seeps into Marcel's voice as he recounts the bits and pieces he learned from Rock.

"Whoa." When he finishes, I sit back and blow out a breath. My temples throb. "Your mother—"

"Is even more of a foul bitch than I'd thought," he finishes, aiming his glare at the wall.

"Uh, not that I don't agree, but someone who would...do that with a kid she was babysitting..." I suppress a shudder of revulsion. "Combined with how cavalier you told me she was about Heidi's safety, it's possible she was abused herself."

He slowly slides his gaze my way. "I'm not real interested in defending her right now."

"I'm not defending her. I'm trying to make sense of the situation."

"There's no making sense of this."

"What did Heidi say?"

He stares at me as if I've lost my mind. "I didn't tell her. I'm not going to tell her. Or Murphy. No one can know. Not right now."

I stare right back. "How exactly is that going to work?" I cross my fingers in front of my face. "You and Murphy are tight. I'm pretty sure the two of you communicate by telepathy sometimes. And Heidi? You *have* to tell her—"

"No. She's so close to finally graduating. She's supposed to be planning her wedding. This will... I don't know how it will land with her. I won't be responsible for ruining things when she's finally on the right track."

Heidi's much more resilient than he gives her credit for. But the secrets I'm hiding from my own brother resurface. Out of love and my desire to protect him at all costs, there are some truths I won't ever share with him. I'm out of arguments. "Okay. I understand. What about Hope and Rock, though? Murphy and Heidi are living at their house. That's going to be difficult."

"Hope's a lawyer. She's used to keeping things confidential."

"Yeah, *client* matters. Not family."

"She promised me she won't say anything until I'm ready. And I trust her."

"All right. So what's your plan? Announce it after Heidi's wedding?"

"I haven't thought that far ahead."

Obviously. I don't know how the hell Marcel thinks he can keep this quiet for so long. But in one afternoon, his entire world has been rocked. If he needs me to lie to get through this, I will.

"We'll tuck this secret away and pretend nothing has changed." I wince at how sarcastic that sounds.

But if Marcel caught the disbelief that crept into my voice, he doesn't react. "Thank you."

I'd walk through fire to ease Marcel's suffering. But it still twists my heart in complicated ways. I love Heidi like she was my own little sister. Lying to her won't be easy. Murphy too. Sometimes, I feel closer to him than my own brother.

It's not my decision to make. For now, I'll keep the truth hidden.

Even though I know secrets this painful can't stay buried forever.

CHAPTER THREE

Teller

MILES AND MILES OF HIGHWAY STRETCH BETWEEN EVERYTHING I LOVE AND me. Charlotte, the eternal sunshine in my life, understood why I needed to get away. To clear my head. Or maybe find some answers.

The man I grew up believing was my father, the man who abandoned my family before I was a teenager, was nothing to me. No tie or connection at all.

In a strange, cruel twist of fate, the man I considered a surrogate dad and who I respect more than anyone else in the world is not only my MC president—he's my father. Not family by choice, like I always thought. *By blood.*

Did my mother know who my real father was?

Rock would've been awfully young when they had their…what the fuck do you call a nineteen-year-old woman who fucks an eleven-year-old kid? Christ, my mother was much more screwed up than I ever imagined. Had she already been in a relationship with my fake dad at that point? Or did she hurry to find someone more suitable to take care of her and her unborn spawn?

So many questions and no one to ask. My grandmother's dead—since she hated me with a borderline crazed passion, I assume she always suspected something was off about my paternity. My mother? Even if I located her worthless ass, I doubt she'd have any useful insight to share. And I don't want to do anything to bring her into my life, or God forbid, my sister's life.

When will the mistakes of our parents stop haunting us?

Heidi needs to focus on finishing college, taking care of her daughter, and planning her wedding. She's been robbed of enough of life's milestones. Is a peaceful graduation and wedding too much to ask?

Heidi's feelings may be a convenient reason to postpone sharing the news, but she's not my only motivation.

Who am I? Not Marcel Whelan, the name I've known my whole life. Now it feels wrong and mismatched.

North. Marcel North. Does that sound any better? I asked Charlotte to marry me not that long ago. What name do I want to give her? What name do I want our children to have?

The big green sign up ahead signals my exit is approaching. I flick my blinker on and guide my bike to the right. I've managed to put almost three hundred miles behind me and it still doesn't feel like enough.

It's been years since I've ventured this far north. Nothing looks the same. I slow my bike at the Rainbow Bridge checkpoint. My record was clean enough to allow me to visit Grinder in prison for years without any issue. Crossing the border into Canada should be a breeze.

The stone-cold border patrol officer scans my passport. In a bored tone, he asks, "Business or pleasure?"

Neither. "Pleasure."

He rakes his gaze over me but his expression remains unreadable behind mirrored sunglasses. "Enjoy your stay." He flips my passport closed and hands it to me.

I tuck my identification into my breast pocket and take off. Traffic's light but bottlenecks as the road narrows. The constant balancing to keep my bike upright while we stop and go keeps my mind occupied.

Why here?

Something lured me across the border. What?

Flashes of a long-ago family trip fire in my memories. Heidi hadn't been born yet. It was just the three of us. Not-my-Dad, Mom, and me. A weekend trip to visit Mom's family. A sister? Cousin? A vague memory of pestering not-my-father about going over the falls in a barrel rises to the surface. Even then, I had an unhealthy fascination with the limits of my mortality.

I've made my peace with a shitty upbringing. Made a life for myself. The Lost Kings MC is the only family I need. Found the woman I want to spend the rest of my life with. Why am I chasing answers that don't even matter?

Physically exhausted, I find the first hotel that looks bedbug free. Mentally, my mind's still spinning. I check my phone and find dozens of texts from Murphy, Heidi, Rock, and Charlotte.

Guilt crawls over my skin. I don't want them to worry, but I can't talk to Murphy or Heidi right now. The fear that I'll let this secret loose before I'm ready to deal with the consequences holds me hostage.

An irrational anger with Rock followed me all the way here, so I don't want to talk to him either.

I send Charlotte a message and let her know that I'm okay and where I'm staying, then shut off my phone.

CHAPTER FOUR

Charlotte

"I won't be gone much longer, Sunshine. Promise."

I stare at the calendar on my desk and slash lines through the days Marcel's been gone. How many more?

"Sunshine, you there?" he asks.

His warm voice doesn't soothe me the way it usually would. "Just be careful, okay?"

"I will," he assures me.

My emotions are so tangled, it's hard to concentrate on the file in front of me after we hang up. The day's already off to a rough start. After the bombshell news Marcel received, and his abrupt trip out of town to cope with the life-altering revelation, work has seemed impossible.

I should've gone with him.

Except, he didn't ask me to.

And I didn't push.

At least Marcel isn't the father of Inga's baby. *I* might have had to skip town if *that* test had come back positive. If I don't try to find the silver lining in this whole mess, I'm going to lose my marbles. Marcel didn't father a stripper's baby—that's the upside.

Rock and Marcel are father and son. It's too complicated to put it in the good news or bad news column.

Quickly, I sort through a stack of mail, a chore I hate. My struggling solo law practice doesn't have the funds to hire even a part-time secretary. Not for the first time, I consider the offer from one of my law school classmates to join his high-end firm. At least then someone else would open my mail.

Bills, bills, advertisements, and a notice from the Johnsonville family court that I stop to add to my calendar. A shady company offering to add me to their directory of "distinguished" lawyers for the measly sum of five-thousand dollars. Next, a reminder that I need to fulfill my continuing legal education requirements. I set that one aside. Maybe I can talk Hope into taking a class with me after she has the baby. Who am I kidding? She checked out of anything legal-related the second she found out she was pregnant. I brush my hand over my stomach. Maybe I'll get to do the same soon. Hope's friend Mara will probably go with me, and I scribble a note on the letter to remind myself to ask her.

The familiar thump-creak of someone prying open the front door to the building reaches me. The sticky lock always catches and makes it hard to open the door. It finally groans whooshes open. I tip my head up and concentrate on any familiar sounds. Postman delivering a package? Nope, he'd call out to get my attention.

Potential client?

Uncle Chuck stopping by to deliver some inane threat?

Silence.

It can't be Uncle Chuck. He's on the road and out of my business. He and Marcel seem to have come to some sort of biker understanding that I'm under the protection of the Lost Kings MC and no longer the concern of the Wolf Knights MC.

The door thumps closed and heavy footsteps clomp over the thin hallway carpet.

A chill slithers along my neck.

Quick and silent, I slide out of my chair, grab my heavy red stapler, and hurry to my open office door. I peer around the corner.

Rock's in the small waiting area, staring at the box of toys I keep in the corner to entertain my younger clients. My gaze slides over the back of his leather cut. The blue and gray Lost Kings MC patch. Discolored, faded, and well-worn from years of life in the club.

Why would he come to my office? He's never been here before. That

I know of. His vice president *did* place surveillance cameras in my apartment, though. Maybe Z and Rock bugged my office at some point.

Fear edges down my spine. Is the secret of Rock and Marcel's true relationship one Rock wants to keep hidden for good? In some weird, twisted biker way, it could be used against Rock by rival clubs. Maybe he still doesn't trust me.

Stop it.

I've spent plenty of time around Rock and the rest of the MC. Rock isn't a threat.

"Mr. North—uh, Rock. My, uh, what are you doing here? I thought you were headed out of town. Is everything okay?" Damn, why I can't I get my voice under control?

He turns away from the toy box, the hard lines of his face softening. As if he's trying to coax a frightened kitten out of hiding, he holds up his hands. "Have you heard from Marcel?"

Really. Marcel hasn't touched base with Rock yet?

I drop my gaze and nod.

"Can we talk for a minute?" Rock's voice drops to a low, hypnotic rumble. "If you have the time."

"Oh. Of course." Finally, I wrestle my fear into submission and force a quick smile. He's worried about Marcel, not here to murder me. "Come on back into my office."

His bulky size emphasizes how small the hallway is, and he shoots a glare at the ceiling that hangs low enough to tickle his scalp. I turn but hear the whisper of his leather cut against my bright yellow walls as he follows me.

"Have a seat." I gesture toward one of the chairs in front of the desk and take the other one, turning it so we're facing each other. "What's on your mind?"

What a stupid question. He's not here for legal advice.

"So, you heard from him? He's okay?"

Damn you, Marcel. "Yes. He didn't call you?"

He pulls out his phone and checks the screen but his expression remains impossible to read. "Teller talk to you before he took off?" he asks, tucking his phone into his pocket.

"About the paternity test?" Duh, why else would he be here? "About you and him? Yes. He told me."

"I thought he was okay. But then he just left."

I may not know Rock all that well but the note of hurt in his voice rings true. "I think he felt bad… He was worried he caused Hope to have problems." Hope had gone to the hospital with Braxton Hicks contractions shortly after telling Marcel and Rock about their true relationship. No matter how much Hope had tried to assure Marcel the two events weren't related, he didn't buy it. It was the final push Marcel needed to take to the highway.

"Charlotte, I'm worried about him. Nothing more. I want to make sure he's okay."

Get a grip, Charlotte. "He's okay. Honestly, Rock, as long as I've known him, he's always"—I hesitate, trying to find the most honest and least offensive way to phrase this—"looked up to you. Thought of you as a father."

"Obviously, I don't deserve that."

This is a far different conversation than I ever expected to have with Rock. Feeling more confident, I give him my honest opinion. Thoughts I've already shared with Marcel. "From the stories he's told me, I think you do. He's always said you're the only person he's been able to count on. You're the one who steered him in the right direction. Made sure he finished school. Kept him out of trouble. Gave him the ability to take care of his sister. Nurtured his business sense. Those are all things he's told me were because of *you.*"

Rock's jaw twitches as he seems to digest my words.

"If it wasn't for you, he wouldn't have been able to take care of Heidi," I repeat.

Finally, his lips twist into a wry smile. "He ever tell you how we met?"

Something about trying to steal from the club. It's a miracle Marcel's even alive to tell that story. "Just bits and pieces."

"He was a brave kid. Risking his life to take care of his sister and his buddy."

"Murphy?" *Who else?*

"They were inseparable long before I met them."

"Marcel's a good man, Rock. Maybe you didn't know he was your son, but you raised him well." I hope he understands I mean every word.

"Thank you, Charlotte. Appreciate that." He stares at me and I force myself not to flinch under his penetrating gaze. "You're good for him."

"I hope so."

"When did he call you? What did he say? He tell you where exactly he is?"

Although I don't think Rock's here to hurt me, I still want to protect Marcel. If he doesn't want to be found right now, by Rock or anyone else, that should be his choice. "He called about half an hour before you showed up. He didn't really give me any details, but he said he's fine."

"You know where he is?" he asks again.

Damn. What is it about this man that makes it impossible to lie? *He* should have been a lawyer. "Niagara Falls. I'm not sure why he went there. I offered to meet him."

"But he wants to be alone?"

"Yes." I gesture to the pile of papers on my desk. "I would've taken the time. Whatever he needed." I hope Rock knows I didn't choose work over Marcel.

"It's not you, hon. He needs to be alone and sort it out. Maybe when he gets back, you two could take off together for a bit."

That would be nice. "I hope so."

"Everything okay with the house?"

The question has the flavor of fatherly concern, and for the first time it hits me, really hits me, this man isn't just Marcel's MC president—he's going to be my father-in-law. "It's fantastic. He's in his country-boy element. He and my brother were discussing buying baby chicks and building a coop." My voice falters. Why am I rambling about chickens? "Before the news."

"If you need something while we're gone, don't be afraid to call Murphy or Z."

"I will."

He stares at the stack of files on my desk. "You ever deal with a case like this?"

"Like this?" A long list of the cases I've handled spins in my mental filing cabinet. Nothing seems to match. "An adult discovering paternity? Not quite. Children, one or two teenagers. But not an adult."

"How does it work out?"

Holy shit. My earlier unease returns. What do I say that won't offend him? "It's hard. If the father already has another family, sometimes his first reaction is denial for fear of angering his wife or losing his family."

"Marcel doesn't have to worry about that. Hope already treats him like a...younger brother."

"Yes, but you're getting ready to have a baby. I think he's worried this has lessened that experience for you somehow. To find out you're already a father."

"It hasn't lessened anything," he insists. "I'm worried he's pissed that I didn't figure it out sooner."

The admission frees me to give my honest assessment. "Sometimes the children are angry. They feel abandoned. But I don't think Marcel feels that way at all. I think he's almost...embarrassed? He already has no love lost for his mother, and this only multiplies that hatred." And oh, how I understand Marcel's hatred.

"Shit, yeah. I don't blame him there. But I can't really blame *her* either. I doubt she knew. If she was with someone else..."

I refuse to point out that Marcel's mother took advantage of Rock. Nice to me or not, he's still a biker. Giving any indication that he's a victim in the situation won't be received well. "You must've been a kid yourself," I say.

"Not *that* much of a kid, apparently." The dark humor coloring his words reminds me so much of Marcel.

"Don't take this the wrong way..."

"Speak freely, Charlotte. You're not going to offend me."

I'd like to believe him, but life experience has taught me to be careful with my "smart mouth," as my uncle always called it. "I know you're rather...stoic and don't share your emotions. Especially with the brothers. Your role as their president doesn't really afford you that luxury."

His gray eyes widen and he nods slowly, encouraging me to continue.

"What do *you* want?" I ask.

He doesn't even hesitate. "I want to make things up to him."

"Rock, there's nothing you can do about the past. But going forward, I think if you want to develop this...new relationship, you're both going to have to be honest with each other about your expectations and emotions surrounding being father and son."

He blinks as if I'd slapped him.

My body tightens with fear. Maybe I said too much.

Slowly, he stands. "Thank you for letting me drop in on you unannounced."

I stand as well. "Anytime." Did this conversation help or hurt the situation?

Either way, it's only the beginning of what's to come.

And nothing will ever be the same.

CHAPTER FIVE

Teller

A FINE SPRAY OF MIST COATS MY FACE AS I STARE AT THE RUSHING waterfalls. As a kid, I'd been awed by the powerful display of nature. As an adult, I still find it hypnotizing. Although now I have a much better appreciation for how dangerous the plummet to the churning waters below would be.

My phone pings, and I pull it out to check the text.

Rock: We're riding out for a meet at the Demons' if you want to join us.

Maybe Rock's struggling with the news as much as I am. He doesn't refer to me as knucklehead, fuckwit, or any of the other charming nicknames he's given me over the years. His text almost sounds *apologetic*.

Or maybe I'm reading too much into a simple sentence.

Either way, I don't answer, something that gives me a perverse amount of pleasure.

My streak of rebelliousness is replaced by guilt.

As much as I hate admitting it, Rock was one of the only people I could count on when I was a teenager. Not-my-dad was long gone. My mother was useless and eventually, she also disappeared. My grandmother kicked me out of her house at the first opportunity. The club was all I had. Rock protected me, gave me work, and encouraged me to finish school. It's embarrassing to admit how much I looked up to him and wanted to be like him in so many ways. Murphy and I both did.

As Rock's mentor, Grinder also took a special interest in my well-being. He was someone I felt comfortable talking to about my mother's slimy boyfriends. Wrath and Z supervised me and looked out for me when Grinder and Rock went to prison. Once Rock got out, I did everything possible to help him clean up the club and turn it into a true brotherhood. A family.

I've fucked around on this fruitless "finding myself" adventure long enough.

I turn away from the waterfalls and lean against the railing. Absently, I run my hand over my thigh, the scars that are my constant reminder that life is short and painful.

Whatever my new relationship is with Rock, he's still my MC president. I can't keep ignoring his texts and not expect an ass kicking when I finally return.

I take my time, stopping at a tourist-trap store to pick up a few things for Charlotte. Hated telling her that I wanted to be alone on this trip. She's been more than understanding.

The ride to the Demons' compound takes a while. Haven't been out here since last fall before our trip to Nationals.

Before my world was turned upside down.

At the gate to the Demons' clubhouse, two prospects nod and wave me in. I recognize Rock's bike and a few others from my club. A relieved breath eases out of me. At least they're still here.

Inside the clubhouse, it's quiet. A few ol' ladies are at the bar, talking. My gaze lands on one with long blond hair. Chaser's wife. Mallory notices me and her face brightens. After speaking a few quick words to the others, she slides off the barstool to greet me with a warm smile.

"Teller! Welcome," she says. I accept a quick embrace from her. "Rock said you were running a bit behind the others."

Guess Rock was confident I'd show up.

"Good to see you, Mallory," I answer, without any excuses for my late appearance.

She turns toward the closed chapel doors. "They're all at the table." Her tone indicates she has no plans to interrupt the club to announce my arrival. Fine by me. Her father-in-law, Stump, isn't one of my favorite bikers, so skipping a meeting he's leading doesn't bother me one bit.

Instead, I take a seat at the bar with Mallory. A girl behind the bar bats long eyelashes at me as she pushes a glass of ice water my way. "Will you be sticking around for the party later?" she asks in a low voice.

Next to me, Mallory rolls her eyes. "Easy, Tracy. This one's spoken for."

"Shame." The girl flips her hair over her shoulder and saunters away.

The corner of my mouth quirks. Mallory's awfully ballsy.

Mallory returns the smirk. "You're not the cheating type."

She's right, but I'm still amused. Not many ol' ladies have the stones to get involved in a biker's personal business. "You know me that well, huh?"

She shrugs and sips her drink. "How's Charlotte?"

"Good." Mallory's only met Charlotte a few times, but I'm not surprised she remembers her name.

"And Heidi? She's getting married soon, right?"

The mention of my sister stabs right through my chest. "She is." I search for a way to move the conversation somewhere else. "Dylan's busting his ass at Wrath's gym, but how's Angelina doing?"

She brightens at the mention of her children. "Angelina's home with us for a little while."

I can't remember what her daughter does, so I just nod. "That's nice."

"Mallory," an older woman rasps. "Where the boys at?" She grasps the edge of the bar and rakes her gaze over me.

Mallory lifts her chin toward the chapel. "At the table."

"Why didn't you send this one in?" She stares holes through my chest.

"Stump didn't want to be interrupted." Mallory waves her hand at the chapel doors. "But by all means, Doe. Go ahead."

Such a diplomatic way to tell the old woman to fuck off. I smirk into my water glass and take another sip.

Doe shuffles closer and runs her gaze over me again. "You're the treasurer, huh?"

"We've met before," I remind her.

"You all look the same."

I raise an eyebrow. "Treasurers or Lost Kings?"

Her wrinkled face splits into a grin and she wags a finger at me. "A wiseass, huh?"

"Always."

"Don't go hittin' on Mallory, you hear me?" She jerks her head toward the chapel doors. "Anyone ever tell you the story of how your prez waltzed in here as a cocky teenager and tried to bag Mal? Right after she and Chaser got engaged."

"Stop it, Doe," Mallory says with more heat in her voice than I've ever heard from her. "That's not quite how it happened."

"The hell it ain't," Doe says, unruffled by the vice president's ol' lady scolding her in front of me.

My stomach turns. I've actually heard this story before. Then, it was a hilarious anecdote about my president acting like a dumb, horny teenager once upon a time. Now, it feels more tragic than amusing.

Out of the corner of my eye, I catch red spreading over Mallory's cheeks. "That was a lifetime ago. We're all older and wiser now."

Doe shrugs and slaps my shoulder before shuffling away.

"I'm sorry about that," Mallory whispers. "I hope she doesn't go running around telling everyone that story this weekend. I doubt Rock will appreciate it."

"He'll live." I study her more closely. "In a way, it's an interesting piece of history between our clubs."

She snorts. "I guess you could say that." Her gaze shifts to the kitchen doors and then the chapel again. "I knew Wrath's wife when she was a little girl too. So in some ways, Lost Kings will always be extended family."

Rock has always worked hard to maintain a good relationship with the Demons. I assumed it was for territory reasons but maybe they were more personal.

The doors creak open and members spill out of the chapel. I brace myself for questions from my brothers.

Like a good hostess, Mallory walks me over to Rock when he emerges, then takes off.

"Where you been, welterweight?" Wrath thumps me on the back hard enough to knock the wind out of me. *Fucker.* "You missed all the fun."

"Yeah, sorry about that."

He slaps me again and wanders away.

Relieved Rock and I are alone, I turn to him. "Can we talk?"

The whole way here, I thought about what I wanted to say. Maybe visiting another club isn't the most ideal spot to air out these old skeletons, but here we are.

"Yeah. Let's go outside." Rock jerks his head toward the front door.

I squint at the sunlight and slip on my shades. Our boots crunch over the pavement as I follow him to the side of the clubhouse. Several small brick buildings dot the property way back by the tree line. I make out a few Devil Demons standing guard in front of one. That can't be good.

Rock stops at a picnic table. I climb on top of it and sit my ass down, resting my feet on the bench. Rock tests the bench before stepping up and sitting next to me.

"Where you been?" he asks.

"Canada."

He stares at me but I don't offer up any details. "Find what you needed?"

"No."

"Charlotte's worried about you."

I run my hand over the back of my neck, forcing myself not to tell him to stay out of my business. "I talked to her."

"Murphy's worried about you."

"Talked to him too."

"You didn't answer *my* texts or calls."

This *dad* shit's gettin' old real quick. "I'm here, aren't I?"

Several emotions seem to flicker over his face. Annoyance—I'm used to that one. Frustration—seen that one before too. Sympathy—that's a new one, and I'm not a fan.

"I'm worried about you," he says.

"What are we supposed to do, Rock?" What the hell does he expect from me? How does this change our relationship going forward? First we were hangaround and mentor. Then brothers. Treasurer and president. Now father and *son*? "Am I supposed to call you Dad?"

"If you want to, yes." He elbows me in the ribs. "Shit, you and Murphy have been doing it for years anyway."

How the hell am I ever going to share this with Murphy? The one person I've never kept secrets from. "Yeah."

We sit there, staring at the ground until I can't stand another second of the silence. "Shit, just when I think I can't hate my mother any more, something else happens."

"She's...something."

My stomach churns thinking about my mother and Rock. It's too gross and wrong to contemplate. At least in my early memories, before things turned to shit, my parents had seemed to care about each other. "Did you love her?"

What a stupid question to ask him.

Rock doesn't call me out. No, his eyes bug, like he's trying to digest the question without choking.

"Never mind. You were a fucking kid." I slide my gaze toward him again. "Did you like her at least?"

He blows out a relieved breath, like this question isn't as tricky. "Yeah. I liked her a lot. Looked forward to her coming over. Before we got involved, I mean."

Involved. That has to be the most delicate term I've ever heard Rock use for *fucking.*

"My father fell apart after my mom died," he continues. "He earned the money, and she took care of me. That was their arrangement. So, he didn't know what the fuck to do without her. I missed her so much. Cried a lot. He really had no patience for that."

"Jesus, Rock." The flowers he leaves on his mother's grave for her birthday every year make so much sense now. My *grandmother.*

"He drowned his own sorrows in alcohol. Made him a fucking asshole, and I resented the hell out of him. Really fucking hated him when he started trying to replace my mother with any woman who gave him a passing glance."

Good Christ, the only thing that could make this worse would be finding out that Rock's father—my *grandfather*—took a turn with my mother too. "He and my mother didn't...?"

"No. Fuck no," he answers quickly. A little too quickly for my taste. "Not that I ever knew." He closes his eyes, like he's desperately trying to claw back fuzzy memories.

"He'd take me to bars and shit," Rock continues. "I was nine, maybe ten, so he'd make me stay in the car. Got so cold one night, I tried walking home. Ended up getting picked up by the cops. I wouldn't tell them anything, but they didn't need my words once he showed up. Narrowly missed going to jail and having me taken away. After that, he asked one of the neighborhood girls to come watch me. Don't remember her much except she kicked me in the teeth with a fuckin' wooden clog one night." He stops and taps his front teeth. "Split my lip. Never saw her again."

"On purpose?"

"Nah, I was probably trying to look up her dress or something."

I burst into laughter. "Sounds about right. Go on."

The smile fades from his face. "Tina was next. I think she worked at the gas station..."

"That makes sense. I remember her telling me about her first job selling cigarettes before she was old enough to buy them. It's why I was always so adamant about Heidi not working when she was in high school."

"I was always impressed with you for the way you looked after her."

I can't take the guilt of thinking about my sister during this conversation. "I didn't mean to interrupt. Go on," I encourage him.

"He paid her to stay with me while he went out whoring and drinking. I didn't mind. It was better than being in the back seat of the car until last call. We'd play video games, watch cartoons, normal shit." Rock pauses. "I met Grinder maybe a year later. Started hanging around the MC when I could. Told my dad I didn't need a babysitter anymore. But she'd still come around."

"Was your dad still paying her?" I'm not sure why that matters. Does it make things better or worse?

"Probably. I never asked."

Memories of stories I heard at the MC early on flood my brain. "I remember you joking about seducing your babysitter when you were a kid. Fuck, I even remember Grinder joking about it. Never thought you were talking about my *mother*."

"That's not on you, Marcel. That's me. And her. It has nothing to do with you."

What the hell kind of bullshit is he trying to sell me? "It has *everything* to do with me. You think she knew?"

"It's not an excuse, but I was a kid. I never thought—"

"Jesus, Rock. I don't blame you. I can't believe she roped my father..." Embarrassment and shame swallow the rest of my words.

"What do you want, Marcel? What can I do to make this better?"

Make this better? There's no way to do that. I want to shake off every bit of my "family" that I can. "How would you feel...? Would you...?" I take a deep breath. "I want to take your last name."

Rock stares at me, surprise darkening his eyes. "Yeah. Yes. Absolutely." His voice picks up speed and enthusiasm. "There's nothing I'd like more."

How will I explain that to everyone? Shit, Wrath already calls me Rock's mini-me. They'll think— "Not now. I still gotta figure out a way to explain this to Heidi, and I don't know how you feel about telling the club."

"I'll tell them right fucking now." Rock's body jerks as if he's ready to run into the clubhouse and shout out the news. "No hesitation. None, Marcel."

Too much, too soon.

CHAPTER SIX

Teller

"Sunshine, I'm home," I call out as I step into the house. It's unusual for Charlotte not to meet me at the door.

Unless she's waiting in our room with a surprise. The thought of her sprawled out on our bed in some sexy outfit propels me up the stairs. Every inch of our old farmhouse has been remodeled but the old stairs still creak in certain spots. There's no sneaking up on Charlotte unless she's in the shower or maybe asleep.

The bedroom's dark. As my eyes adjust, the faint shapes of a dresser, nightstands, and our bed fall into place.

She has to be home. Her car was in its usual spot. Unless she's at Rock and Hope's. Or she's visiting her brother.

A soft sniffle breaks the silence.

"Char?" I push the door open wider and slide my hand along the wall, searching for the light switch.

"Don't," she says in a hoarse whisper.

"What's wrong?" I cross to the bed and find her wrapped in a ball of blankets. "Hey, are you sick?"

"No."

Cold fear strikes me in the chest. *Our little secret.* The news we haven't shared with anyone yet. It was too soon.

"Tell me." I need to know, even if I'm afraid of what she's going to say.

Instead of words, she grips my arm. "I got my period while you were gone."

"Shit."

"I went to the doctor—"

"By yourself?"

Her face screws into a scowl. "They told me miscarriages are common this early." The bitterness in her voice fades. She sniffles. "They acted like I was ridiculous for even coming in and sent me home."

"Fuck. Are you serious?"

She groans and curls up even tighter.

"Are you in pain?"

She hums a noise that I interpret as a *yes.*

"Should we go to the hospital? Or another doctor?" I need to do *something.* Wrap my hands around the neck of the doctor who so callously sent her home and squeeze really hard. How could I be off wallowing like a pussy when my girl was going through this alone?

"Did you tell anyone? Call someone to go with you?"

"No," she groans. "Hope's close to her due date. And I didn't think I could see Heidi right now."

"Charlotte." I sigh and stand. "You should've called me. I would've come back right away."

"Don't go," she pleads.

"I ain't going anywhere, Sunshine." I strip off my clothes and tug on the blankets. "Scoot over."

She slides a few inches away. Enough for me to ease my big frame onto the mattress and pull the covers over us. Her skin's hot against my fingers. "Are you all right?"

"No. I'm not okay at all."

"I mean…" Fuck, why am I asking her stupid questions? I skim the back of my hand over her cheek and against her forehead. She's warm but not feverish. At least, I don't think so. "Are you sure we shouldn't go to the hospital?"

"I'm sure." A little softer she adds, "Just hold me."

Those three simple words burrow deep and threaten to shatter my heart. I slide one arm under her body and pull her close, curling myself around her in an attempt to protect her from the world. "I'm sorry I wasn't here, Sunshine."

"It's okay." She sighs and turns to face me. "Probably better that you weren't. You might've punched the doctor for being mean to me."

I lean in and kiss her forehead. "Can't promise I'm not going to hunt her down later."

"How'd it go?"

"What? My ride?"

"You stopped to see Rock, didn't you?"

That's the last thing I want to talk about now. "I'll tell you about it later."

"No. Please. I need...to hear your voice. Tell me about your trip. Take my mind off of...things."

My throat's so tight, I can barely speak. "First, do you need anything? Advil? Water? Food?"

"No, just you."

I kiss the top of her head and run my hands over her back. "Like I said on the phone, I went to Niagara Falls."

"Canadian side or American?"

"Canada."

"Really? What made you cross the border?"

I hesitate, not sure if I can put it into words that'll have any meaning. But that's why Charlotte and I work so well—she always helps me make sense of the most absurd situations. "I couldn't stop thinking about this trip I took with my parents...uh, my mother and her husband, when I was a kid. Before Heidi."

"BH, huh?"

"Yeah." I chuckle.

"I bet you were so cute when you were little... I was hoping... I wanted..." Her voice breaks.

"Shhh. It's okay." I lean closer and rub my forehead against hers. "I was a scrawny daredevil who scared the shit out of my parents because I kept asking about going over the falls in a barrel."

The silly memory does the trick. A quick chuckle spills from Charlotte, her warm breath sliding over my neck. "Go on," she encourages.

"We visited my mom's cousin or aunt. I vaguely remember sitting in her kitchen drinking loganberry juice."

"Ooo, I remember that stuff. It was so good. My dad used to bring us home loganberry syrup whenever he went up there on a run."

"You're in luck. I brought you home a bottle."

She squeezes me again. "You're the best fiancé."

Pleasure that I did at least one thing right fills me for a second, then evaporates. "No, I'm not. I should've been here, Char—"

"Knock it off and finish your story."

This woman. God damn, I love her.

"Everything's changed so much, I barely recognized anything. Couldn't find the house. Who knows if I was even looking in the right place?"

"What were you going to do if you found it?"

I huff out a quiet laugh. "I didn't think that far ahead."

"Marcel," she whispers, running her fingers through my hair. Her touch soothes and reassures me, even though she's the one who needs comforting.

"I spent some time staring at the falls and thinking over my life. Unfortunately, no good answers came to me."

"It's going to take a while to get comfortable. Your whole identity has been shaken."

"I still love *you* no matter what," I say. She needs to understand that nothing about this revelation changes how I feel about her or our future together.

"And I love you," she repeats.

That's what I needed to hear. "Will you love me more or less as a North?"

She pulls back and blinks at me. "Are you thinking of taking Rock's last name?"

"Yeah," I admit quietly, shifting my gaze to the nightstand. "I floated the idea when I saw him at Chaser's place."

"And?"

"He seemed receptive."

"I'm sure he was. He cares about you a lot, Marcel. This is eating him up too."

Something in her voice sets me on edge. "What makes you say that?"

"He…uh, came to talk to me at my office. He was worried about you."

"He came to your office?" I repeat slowly, not liking the sound of that at all. Her experience growing up around an MC wasn't always warm and fuzzy. Given the current situation, my MC prez showing up out of the blue probably scared the shit out of Charlotte. "What'd he do, waltz in your front door?"

"Yes. Scared the hell out of me at first," she admits. "I wasn't sure how he felt. If he wanted to keep it quiet or he was worried about the club finding out."

"And?"

She pauses and seems to consider her words. "I think he feels…guilty."

"Why? It's not his fault."

"I think he's worried about…losing you."

That's new. Hell, my parents were all too eager to get *rid* of me. "No one's ever been afraid of losing me before."

"*I* worry about losing you." She struggles to sit up.

"Easy." I pull her into the safety of my arms again. "I'm sorry I took off."

"I understand." She blows out a long breath and traces her fingers over my chest. "It was hard to explain to Murphy though. Heidi's been busy so she didn't question your absence too much, but Murphy was out of his mind worried. Not to mention how pissed he was that Rock wouldn't let him go on the run."

Shit. "What am I going to say to Murphy? It might actually be harder to tell him than Heidi." While we don't spend lots of time getting deep in our feels, he's always thought of Rock as a father figure. More than I even did. "At least I *had* a dad for a while. He didn't. If anyone should've been Rock's son, it should've been Murphy."

She sighs. "To be honest, I considered that too. Neither of you are great at expressing emotions." She slants a look at me. "Not only am I worried he'll lose his shit if the news upsets Heidi, I'm worried that once it sinks in how the dynamics have changed, he'll take it harder than she does."

My natural instinct is to jump to Murphy's defense. He's a tough fucker who's endured plenty of shit. There isn't another person I trust more to have my back. But I just confessed that I'm worried about the same thing. "The guy I thought was my dad was an asshole who left us. But at least he *was* there for me in the beginning. I have some decent memories, like that trip, and—"

"Going hunting." Her lips tip into a smile.

"Yeah, that too. But Blake didn't have *any* of that. He had an addict mother who caused constant chaos for him. He has zero fun family-trip memories."

Her eyes shine with unshed tears. "No wonder he's so determined to be the perfect husband and father."

For a brief moment, I see things without the cloud of my overprotective big brother nature obscuring the situation. "You're right."

"Daaaamn," she teases, drawing out the word.

"Knock it off. I admit you're right more than anyone else in my life."

She shakes with laughter against me. "God, Marcel. You're the only person who could make me laugh right now."

"Good." I kiss her forehead again. "All I want to do is make you happy."

Her laughter dies. "I'm so sorry."

"You don't have anything to apologize for."

"What if I did something to cause—"

"No." I cut that off immediately. "Don't go there, Charlotte. It happens. We knew that. That's why we didn't want to share the news yet."

"I know." She takes another deep breath. "Keep talking to me. Tell me about the rest of your trip."

"Nothing much to tell. I walked around. Spent a lot of time watching the falls. Tried so hard to remember more about my parents but it's like time covered everything in cobwebs."

"You had to have been young."

"Eight or nine when we took that trip, I think. The memories I have are actually good, and that doesn't seem right considering all the bad that came after."

"No person is one hundred percent good *or* bad, Marcel. Even if they ultimately failed you, it's okay to acknowledge there were some positive moments."

"But it all seems so fake now. I feel sick that I called him Dad for so many years."

"It's on *them*. Not you. You're innocent in all of this."

"So is Rock, when you get down to it. Not only was he a kid, but she never told him about me." I clench my jaw so hard my teeth ache. "But I can't help being, I don't know, *angry* with him for some reason."

She reaches up and runs her fingers through my hair. "I think that's a normal reaction. Even if it's not fair or rational. Try to be aware of it and remember this is hurting him too."

"I sound like a whiny pussy, don't I?"

"I think you mean whiny *ball sack*." She grins at me. "But no, I don't think you're whiny at all. It's a huge shock. Complicated by the fact that you have no one who has more details to ask." She pauses again. "Have you thought about tracking down your mother to ask her?"

"Fuck no."

"All right." She presses her palm against my chest. "I don't blame you."

Pure love pulses though me. "Tell me what I can do for you, Charlotte. Please."

She ducks and rubs her forehead against my chest, lightly kissing over my heart. "What you're doing."

"Do you want to talk to someone? Someone besides me?"

"No." She snaps her head up so fast she hits my chin. I wince as my teeth slice into my tongue. "Don't tell anyone. Please. Promise me."

"Why?"

"Hope's about to have a baby. I don't want her to feel bad or guilty. And I don't want everyone talking about it or pitying me."

Even though anything our club family said would be out of love or concern for us, I understand what she means. "All right."

"Thank you." She kisses along my jaw. "What can *I* do to help you?"

"For now, I don't want to say anything. Rock understands. It sounds like an excuse, but Heidi's so close to finally finishing school, I don't want this to derail her again. And I want her and Blake to have their wedding without this overshadowing the whole affair."

"You think once Murphy's settled into married life, he'll handle it better?" Charlotte asks in a hushed voice.

"Maybe." I lift my shoulders.

"I know you'd never do anything to hurt either one of them," she assures me. "Maybe it will be good for you to take some time to get your head and heart around it too. Before revealing the truth."

I grunt in semi-agreement as the copper tang of blood from my bitten tongue fills my mouth.

Truth is rarely revealed without pain.

CHAPTER SEVEN

Teller

THE GRAND RE-OPENING OF FURIOUS FITNESS SEEMS TO BE A SUCCESS. Couldn't be happier for Wrath and Murphy. Unfortunately, I've been avoiding Murphy most of the afternoon.

My phone pings, and I pull it out of my pocket.

Z: Hope went into labor. At Empire Med with them.

My new little sister's on her way.

Me: Everything okay?

Z: Get your ass down here and keep me company.

I snort and shove my phone in my pocket. "Looks like Grace is making an early entrance."

"I saw them hurry out before." Charlotte glances toward the back of the gym. "I was wondering where they went. Is Hope okay?"

I pull my phone out and check again. "Don't know."

Wrath actually seems rattled when he stops to talk to us.

"What's wrong with you?" I ask.

He tears his intense stare away from the side door that leads to the parking lot. "I'm worried about Hope."

"Was she in pain?"

He turns and scowls at me. "She was about to drop a baby. I'm guessing it hurts like fuck."

"Rock's probably freaking out. Z just told me to get my ass down there."

"Trin's there. I'll head down when we close up here." He slaps my shoulder and walks off.

Charlotte's quiet, staring at the floor. Her bottom lip trembles slightly. I slide my hand over hers. "You all right?"

"Yeah. No. I'm worried about her too. You better get going. Z will need company so he doesn't drive Rock nuts."

"You're sure you don't mind?"

"I have that case…I…" Her voice trails off.

"Hey, I get it." She still hasn't recovered from our loss. "Drop me off at the hospital. I'll catch a ride home later."

Relief spreads over her face. "Are you sure? I want to be there and see the baby. I'm just not…"

Over losing our own baby. "I know, Sunshine," I say in a low voice. "Come here." She leans in and I kiss her cheek. "It's okay."

THE SLIDING doors of Empire Med whoosh open and I brace myself. After spending so much time in the hospital after my accident, I'm not exactly a fan. The smell, bright lights, and squeaky tiles all set my nerves on edge. What am I even doing here? Won't I be in the way? Z's not a child; he doesn't need me to entertain him in the waiting room.

The labor and delivery ward takes forever to find. I breathe a sigh of relief when I spot Z sitting in a chair, tapping on his phone.

"What's up?" I ask, kicking my foot against his outstretched legs.

He tucks his phone away and grins up at me. "Hey. Glad you finally showed up. I'm bored silly."

"No nurses to romance?"

"Not yet."

"I fucking hate hospitals," I grumble, falling into the chair next to him.

His smile falters. "Shit, brother. I'm sorry. I'm only fucking around. You don't have to stay."

"Have to now." I cock my head toward the window. "Charlotte dropped me off and went home."

Z's head jerks up and he stands. "How's she doing?"

At first, I think he's asking me how Charlotte's doing. But nobody even knows about our loss.

Then I follow Z's gaze to Rock stalking down the hallway toward us. His face is pinched with worry. "She's doing good." He holds up a small paper cup. "They sent me for ice chips." His gaze lands on me. "Hey. Thanks for coming. Afraid there's nothing exciting to report yet."

His voice is stiff and formal. Did he think I wouldn't be here? Of course I want to see my new baby sister.

Painfully aware of Z's presence, and the way his sharp gaze shifts between Rock and me, I choose my words carefully. "Yeah, no problem. Anything I can do, Prez?"

A small shift or twitch at the corner of his eyes suggests he's disappointed. Did he expect me to call him Dad in front of Z or something?

"Nah, you two might as well go home and get some sleep. I'll text when Grace is here and it's okay to visit."

Z shifts his weight, peering over Rock's shoulder. "Can I see her to say goodbye? Wish her good luck or something?"

Any other time, Rock would probably threaten to punch Z for trying to intrude, but his face transforms into a more relaxed smile. "No." He reaches out to squeeze Z's shoulder. "I'll tell her though."

Trinity walks up behind Rock and taps him on the shoulder. "Here." She passes him another paper cup that seems to be full of ice.

"Thanks, Trinny. You heading home?"

"Unless you want me to stay?"

"Nah, I'll let you know when something exciting happens."

"Can I catch a ride with you?" I ask Trinity.

"Yeah, sure."

I wait a beat until Z and Trinity are near the elevator, then pull Rock to the side. "Do you want me to stick around? Is there anything I can do for you?"

"No, I think it's going to be a while. Go home." He hesitates. "Come back tomorrow, though?" he asks, as if he hates imposing on me.

"Hell yeah. I'll come sooner if you need me to. Just call."

He tilts his head and holds out his arms. I reach in and hug him. "I'll be back. I can't wait to meet my new little sister," I say against his ear.

"Thanks," he rasps, patting me on the back with his free hand.

"You coming?" Z calls out.

I slap Rock's shoulder one more time, then turn and catch up to Z.

"Is Charlotte okay?" Trinity asks. "She seemed quiet at the party."

"Yeah. Big case she has coming up this week," I answer quickly. It's true but not the only thing bothering Charlotte lately.

I wish to hell Charlotte would let me say something to someone. I get why she doesn't want to tell Hope. And guilt follows me all day, every day, that she's not comfortable talking to Heidi. She's gotten close to Trinity, though. And I think Trinity might understand.

But I made a promise to Charlotte and I won't break it.

THE NEXT MORNING, I head to the hospital. Alone.

Should've known Wrath and Trinity would be there first. I roll my eyes at the ridiculous *product of* patch Wrath and Z had made for Grace.

Rock's holding Grace close to his chest like she's the most precious thing he's ever seen.

After Wrath and Trinity leave, I ask if I can hold Grace, looking to Hope, then Rock for permission.

My new little sister screams and punches her fists in the air.

"Do you want to say hello to your big brother?" Hope tickles her daughter's cheek.

My breath catches and I stare at Hope for a second. She hasn't once tried to make me feel like shit or even hinted that she hates this new role I have in Rock's life. She seems to have accepted it easier than Rock and I have.

Rock stands slowly, cradling Grace in his arms. He slides next to me and carefully passes the tiny little bundle into my arms.

She's light and so perfect.

"Hi, baby Grace," I whisper, staring at her sweet little face. She blinks up at me. "I've already been through this before. So I know all the little sister tricks."

She coos and gurgles.

Hell help us all. I'll do anything to keep her safe.

"She's really beautiful, Hope."

"Thank you."

I pass her back to Rock. What do I even say? Emotion swells in my chest. I want all good things for Grace. I already know she has two parents who will love and protect her. But I'll also always be here to protect her. Do better for her than I did for Heidi.

I'm happy for my president...my MC brother...my *father*. "Congratulations...Rock." I can't call him Dad. It would ruin this moment for him.

The hospital door pushes open and Heidi appears.

Guilt threatens to drown me. Like I've betrayed her by having all this love for another sister.

Murphy follows her inside, carrying Alexa.

I glance at Hope, and she nods at me.

As Murphy introduces Alexa to Grace, I nudge Heidi with my elbow. "I'm going."

"Now?" She stares at me. "We just got here."

More guilt rains over me. But I give her a casual shrug in return.

I need to leave. *Now.*

Heidi opens her mouth as if she's about to protest again, but Alexa shouts, "Mine!"

Heidi's attention is drawn to her daughter, giving me the chance to escape.

In the hallway, I close my eyes for a second.

The hospital scent fills my nose and propels me toward the exit.

CHAPTER EIGHT

Teller

MURPHY: YOU WON'T BELIEVE WHO'S BACK.

Back where?

I haven't even finished typing out a response when the loud buzz of Murphy's bike echoes down my driveway.

"The fuck?" I grumble, tossing off the covers and sliding to the edge of the bed.

Behind me, Charlotte groans and burrows under her pillow. I glance at the clock on my nightstand, then reach over and nudge her leg. "It's almost noon, Sunshine."

She answers by yanking the covers up higher. It's been almost three months and she still seems to be in a funk I can't shake her from.

"I'm going to see what Murphy wants and start breakfast."

"Okay," she murmurs from somewhere underneath the comforter.

I hurry to jump into a pair of jeans and snag a T-shirt, throwing it over my shoulder on my way downstairs. Murphy's heavy footsteps thump over the porch outside. I twist the deadbolt and open the front door before he has a chance to knock.

"What's up?" I ask, stepping aside to allow him in while yanking the T-shirt over my head.

"Christ, I would've waited five seconds for you to cover yourself." He shields his eyes with his hand. "No one needs to see that mess this early in the afternoon."

I'm not in the mood to be baited. "You're free to leave." I turn and head toward the kitchen, confident he'll follow.

The door clicks closed and he's quiet for a few seconds while he stops to leave his boots by the door. Out of respect for Charlotte, not me.

Even though my back is facing the entrance while I start the coffee, I sense his energy behind me. Eager. Brimming with excitement to be the first one to share some news.

Not wanting to give him the satisfaction of my interest—yet—I don't say anything while I add water to the coffee maker.

"Did you get my text?" He steps next to me and flings open one of the cabinet doors and grabs a coffee mug, plunking it on the counter.

"Who said you could have my coffee?"

"Pfft." He opens the refrigerator and rummages through it for a carton of creamer. "You're low on half-and-half."

"You *could* bring some with you one of these days, you know. Since you help yourself to it often enough."

"That *would* be nice of me, wouldn't it." He sets the container on the counter.

I peek out the kitchen window. The chickens are running loose again. I'll have to get them in a minute. "Where's Heidi?"

"At Rock's." He waves his hand in the direction of the clubhouse. "Guess who's back?"

"Back where?"

"Here. In New York."

"The Jets."

"What? No." He shakes his head, his frustration with me obvious. "They're a terrible team anyway. Jersey can have 'em."

My mouth quirks. Time to throw him a bone. "All right. Who?"

Now it's his turn to fuck with me. He lifts his chin. "Why's your coffee maker so fucking slow?"

I take an exaggerated look around the room. "Does this look like a Starbucks to you?"

"No. I'd have some coffee in my cup by now if it was."

"Doubtful," I mutter, searching for two more mugs. "All right, so what has your panties in a bunch this morning? Tell me. I'm dying to know who's back in the great State of New York."

"Lilly."

Well, fuck. My hand stops mid-air and the cup I'm holding clatters onto the counter. "Seriously? Where's she been all this time?"

"Don't know. But..." He takes a long, dramatic pause. "She didn't return alone."

"She married or something? Z won't be thrilled." I'm already losing interest in this conversation. Lilly couldn't have made it clearer that she didn't want to be Z's ol' lady when she ghosted his ass. Why anyone, except Hope, gives a shit about her return is beyond me.

"He'd probably prefer *that*," Blake says. "She has a kid."

"*A kid?*" A sick feeling settles in my stomach. "Or *Z's* kid?"

He wags his finger in my face. "Ding, ding, ding!"

I slap his hand away. "Knock that off." Jesus, who knew being business partners with Wrath would mean Blake would pick up so many of his annoying habits?

"Hope said the kid looks just like Z. She arranged for Z and Lilly to meet up at the park. Lilly didn't deny it, I guess."

"Damn." Z's gotta be hurting over this. "How old is the kid?"

Blake shrugs. "I dunno. Whenever we saw Lilly last, minus nine months?"

"That's so fucked up."

"Yup. I saw Z just before he left, and he seemed rattled." He shrugs. "I gave him one of our car seats just in case."

The more details he gives, the sicker I feel. It's too close to my own situation. Or maybe it's nothing like my situation. Z's kid is young enough that he won't remember not having his dad in his life the first few years, whereas I've got thirty-some years of parental damage to unpack. Either way, it leaves a sourness burning in my stomach.

"What's he going to do?" I ask.

"Get to know his kid, I guess." He shrugs. "You know how he felt about her."

"Did Hope know about the kid?"

"No way." He immediately shuts down that question. "She's hopping mad about the whole thing."

"She probably feels guilty. Z wouldn't have met Lilly if it wasn't for her."

He cocks his head. "Not cool. You better not say that to Hope, either."

"Why? Is Rock gonna deck me?"

"No, I will."

I give him a quick shove sideways. "Love to see you try, brother."

"Now, boys, what did I tell you about fighting before coffee?" Charlotte shuffles into the kitchen and yawns.

Blake runs his concerned gaze over Charlotte's bathrobe and sleepy appearance. "Are you okay?"

"Late night." She reaches up and ruffles her hand over Blake's hair. "What's up, my ginger twinny?"

He chuckles and runs his hands through his hair, trying to straighten the mess Charlotte made of it.

"He sped over here to share some hot gossip like a little ol' church grandma," I say, pouring coffee into her cup.

"Ooo." Charlotte accepts the mug and adds creamer. "Do tell."

"Lilly's back," Blake says.

"Hope's friend? The one Z liked?" she asks.

"Yup." Blake reaches for the coffeepot but I bat his hand away. "She's got a kid too. Z's."

"Daaamn." Charlotte's eyes meet mine. I quickly lift one shoulder. "That's rough."

"Wonder how that will go over with Stella?" I snicker into my coffee cup. "Z's little porn-star girlfriend doesn't seem like the motherly type."

Charlotte smacks my arm.

"I doubt Z gives a shit." Blake shrugs. "Rav said Z had two bunnies in his bed last night."

"Gee, can't imagine why Lilly left," Charlotte mutters.

"Nah, he wouldn't be nailing two chicks a night if Lilly had been here," Blake says with confidence. Hell, maybe he's right. Doesn't explain or excuse what Lilly's done.

"Hope won't want to touch that custody case with a ten-foot pole. I can find someone for Z if he needs it," Charlotte offers.

I squeeze her shoulder. "Let's wait and see what happens." I don't want Charlotte involved in some nasty custody battle, even if it's to help one of my brothers.

Her mouth quirks as if I'd said the quiet part out loud. "So, Hope could represent *you* when you were trying to get custody of Heidi, but I can't represent Z?"

The way this woman reads my mind is downright scary sometimes. "Not the same thing."

She glares at me.

Blake grins from ear to ear. "I love you two."

CHAPTER NINE

Teller

THE WIND IN MY FACE ISN'T AS ENJOYABLE AS I USUALLY FIND IT. BONDING with my brothers over a long run can solve a lot of problems. Not today. The open highway as we ride downstate doesn't bring the peace it normally does. Not for any of us.

The low thrum of fear settles into my gut. Someone shot the president of our downstate charter. Sway took a bullet to the head and somehow survived. Whether I think Sway's a sleazeball or not, he's still a brother.

Was the shooting personal? Or club-related?

My gut keeps saying it's personal. Sway's fucked over a lot of people. But maybe I'm just trying to rationalize away the danger.

I stare at the back of Rock's cut, then Z's. Murphy's riding next to me and Wrath behind us. All the Upstate officers in one neat formation. Easy pickings.

Fuck. Thinking like that will get us all killed. The whole point of us riding down is to flip a middle finger at whoever shot Sway and show them we're not scared.

I've had enough club-related near-death experiences to maintain a healthy amount of fear on this trip. Instead of enjoying the scenery, I study the vehicles around us, searching for anything out of the ordinary.

The gun in the holster hugging my side offers some reassurance. I'll go down shooting to protect my brothers.

We pull into the Union County Hospital parking lot and find a place to line our bikes up close to each other. A quick scan of the garage and surrounding lot reveals a few clusters of motorcycles and large black SUVs.

Inside, the hospital's full of brothers from Sway's charter. Rock jerks his chin toward the waiting room, indicating Murphy and I need to park our asses there. Fine by me.

"Fuck," Murphy breathes out. His gaze lands on Downstate's VP. "What's he all twitchy for?"

"Probably hoping he won't have to do any extra work."

Murphy snorts. MC brother or not, neither of us are fond of Shadow.

An hour later, the atmosphere changes. Brothers stir and stand at attention. A murmur goes through the crowd.

"Well, damn." Murphy nudges my elbow. "How'd Priest make it up here so fast?"

I cock my head and catch sight of our national president. "Should I be insulted that Priest didn't come visit me in the hospital?" I ask in a low voice.

"No, you should be thankful. Rock's probably spitting nails."

I let out a humorless laugh. Rock hates anyone, even the national president—hell *especially* the national president—in our business.

"Guess we're not invited to *that* conversation," Murphy says, tipping his head toward the glass window that looks out on the hospital hallway. I turn in time to catch a grim-faced Rock, Z, and Priest walking toward the parking lot with Wrath and the national enforcer following behind.

"Good," I grumble.

Murphy settles into his chair, clasps his hands over his stomach, stretches out his legs, and closes his eyes.

"Are you seriously napping?" I mutter.

"Yup," he answers without opening his eyes.

I pull out my phone and text Charlotte to let her know we've arrived in one piece.

A thump to my right pulls me away from my phone. Murphy's elbow jabs my side as he bolts upright.

"Ow, ya fuck," Murphy growls. "What'd you kick me for?"

Jigsaw grins down at us. "You two assholes can't say hello?"

Murphy's foot lashes out, delivering a quick blow to Jiggy's shin. "Hello, asshole."

"Hey, Jiggy." I stand and hold out my hand to him. "Didn't see you when we came in. How you been?"

"Dark times, my brother." He clasps my hand and pulls me in, slapping my back. "Dark times."

"No shit." I lean closer. "Club have *any* idea who shot him?"

Jigsaw's usual maniacal grin fades. "No."

"Everyone else okay? Clubhouse—"

"Is on lockdown." Jiggy turns slightly, checking out the crowded, biker-filled room. "You coming by later?"

I glance at the hallway. Still no sign of Rock or Z. "Looks that way."

There's a bit of a commotion at the door. Shadow and a few others are called into the hallway by one of Priest's guys.

"I'm sure *that's* going to be a fun time," Murphy mutters.

Jiggy shifts on his feet, almost as if he's anxious about something. Unnerving as fuck, since this dude's usually the one *causing* the anxiety in anyone he turns his scary eyes on. "I suppose Priest's going to appoint an interim president for us," he says.

Fuck, I hadn't thought that far ahead yet.

"Doesn't look like you're going to have a chance to vote on it either," Murphy says.

I elbow his arm and shoot him a shut-the-fuck-up look. Pecking order says Shadow should be named the temporary president while Sway recovers. But from what I remember, Priest isn't real fond of Shadow.

"You think it's gonna be Shadow?" I ask Jigsaw. Might as well go the direct route, instead of dancing around the topic.

Jiggy glances over his shoulder quickly, then shrugs, as if he doesn't care one way or another. But I doubt that's true.

He doesn't trust *us*.

The history between Upstate and Downstate is rough. But Jiggy transferred from our Washington charter with Rooster a few years ago.

He wasn't around when all the bad shit went down. Still, I'm sure Sway talks plenty of shit about us, especially Rock, and some of that must've colored Jigsaw's opinion.

It doesn't take long for Priest to make a decision. Z will be the temporary president of Downstate until Sway recovers. Rock's quick to order Murphy and me to stick around and watch Z's back.

Priest wants to put on a show to announce Z's new role. Although I already met with Rock, Z, Wrath, and Murphy earlier, I stop by Rock's room before heading to the chapel.

"Anything you want me to do at the meeting?" I ask, dropping into a chair at the small table in the corner.

"Watch what you say before we go in," Rock warns me. "I don't know if everyone's aware Z's staying on as president. Let it come from Priest."

"Got it. Anything else?"

Rock raises an eyebrow. "What brought on this bout of helpfulness?"

"Yeah, yeah." I blow out an annoyed breath. "I'm over it. I understand why you want Murphy and me to stick around. For fuck's sake, I said we'd go look at a house to rent. What more do you want from me?"

"I want you to be careful. We still don't know who shot Sway. I'm not happy about *any* of you being down here right now," he rasps.

The heaviness in his voice prompts me to set aside my feelings and study Rock closer. Circles ring his eyes, the kind that hint he was up all night worrying, not enjoying other nocturnal activities.

"I'll be on alert," I promise.

"Blend in as much as you can while you're here," he suggests. "Get to know some of the younger brothers better. See where their heads are at. Are they loyal to Shadow? Will they try to undermine Z?"

"Doubt anyone will come out and say that."

He cocks his head. "No shit, knucklehead." He runs his fingers over his lips in a zip-it gesture. "Close your mouth and open your ears. Use your gut feeling to guide you. I trust your opinion."

Pride sputters through me and I sit up straighter, determined not to let him down. "I'll be listening."

"Good." He stands and slaps my shoulder. "Now, get out of my room."

Laughing, I step into the hallway and send Murphy a text.

Me: Meet outside chapel?

Murphy: Already there.

I stalk through the maze of hallways, noting the grungy carpet under my boots. Can't even tell what color it is anymore. Red? Brown? A far cry from the gleaming hardwood floors of our Upstate clubhouse.

Blake's waiting at the end of the last hallway that leads into the main room.

He lifts his chin. "What's up?"

I cast a quick glance around the area. Downstate brothers are clustered by the open chapel doors. Priest and brothers from our Mississippi charter are close to the front office. I glimpse Z's wide shoulders in that inner circle.

This is really happening.

"I just want to stick together."

"As if I'd go in there without you." He slaps my shoulder and steers me toward the chapel doors. Downstate brothers are already filing into the room.

I jerk my head to the right. "Let's blend in."

Rock and Wrath end up near the head of the table. I catch Rock's eye and he nods. Last of all, Priest enters with Z following.

I lean closer to Murphy. "Z looks like he's being marched to his death," I say low enough for only him to hear me.

He grunts in response and slides lower in his chair.

"Thank you for having us." Priest runs his shrewd gaze over every brother seated at the table. "Awful thing when a brother's almost taken out this way. I know this has been a rough time for everyone."

Understatement.

Downstate brothers sit forward, hanging on Priest's every word.

"As you know, our brothers from Upstate have been here offering support and protection. I've asked their VP, Zero, to stick around and take over as president until Sway recovers."

Boom, there it is.

Ripples of conversation reverberate around the room. I study each brother closely, searching for signs of hostility. Smoke—a brother we all have questions about—grumbles and glances down at his lap.

Murphy elbows me and from the corner of my eye, I catch his chin tipping toward the other end of the table. Standing behind Z, Shadow's watching with a dead-eyed glare.

Well, we knew he was trouble too.

I resume my study of the other brothers. Jigsaw—alert and interested. Rooster, nodding and frowning at the same time. Hustler just looks confused. And after I went over the club's books this morning, I'm not surprised. Steer's relaxed against the back of his chair, almost like he's relieved he wasn't asked to step from the SAA role into the president's position.

Now that he's lobbed the grenade at everyone and given us time to absorb the shock, Priest taps his knuckles against the table to regain our attention. "I hate even saying this, but if at some point it looks like Sway isn't going to make a full recovery, then we'll discuss other options." He glances over and smirks at Rock. "I know Upstate isn't pleased about losing their VP, so this isn't a permanent arrangement. Right now," he adds.

Rock's expression remains steely and calm, although his eyes narrow slightly. He gives Priest a curt nod but doesn't respond.

Z flicks his gaze to the ceiling and my chest squeezes. He's in an awful position.

"Now, even though it's temporary, we need to make it official," Priest says, waving his hand at Z for him to stand and approach.

A sick sensation slithers through my stomach. Murphy and I both lean forward.

Priest crooks a finger at Rock, silently asking him to join Z. Blink hands Priest a knife and Priest hands it to Rock.

"Holy shit," I breathe out.

"You gotta be kidding," Blake murmurs.

Priest's message to Rock seems obvious. *I call the shots.*

Z's never coming home.

I push the thought away and concentrate on the scene unfolding in front of me, hating every second of it.

Rock doesn't hesitate. He accepts the knife from Priest without a word. Then neatly slices Z's VP patch off his cut.

I close my eyes, feeling the imaginary sting of the knife against my own flesh.

This is so wrong.

I was there when Z was given that VP patch. I was still a prospect, so my vote wasn't counted. But I remember the day well. After all the struggles and hardships our club had gone through, we'd found our way to a true brotherhood. Z's my brother and one of my best friends. This is excruciating to watch but I sit still because sharing each other's pain is what brothers do.

Rock hands the patch to Z and says something to him that I can't hear. Forcing Rock to be the one to take Z's patch seems like the ultimate *fuck you* from Priest.

"What the fuck?" Murphy breathes out.

"Congratulations," Priest announces, as if this is something to celebrate instead of mourn. He slaps a small patch in Z's hand. Then, to pour salt in our fresh wounds, he hands Z a "Downstate" bottom rocker.

Z stares at his hands for a few seconds.

Everyone in the room stands and claps. Heart pounding, I rise and join them. I catch Wrath's eye at the other end of the table, and he shakes his head.

The warm welcome from his new charter seems to shake Z out of his shock. His mouth slips into a fake smile. "Thank you for welcoming me with open arms during such an uncertain time. As everyone knows, our two charters go way back, and I'm honored to lead Downstate through this rough patch until Sway recovers."

Nice try, Z, but you're going to be wearing a Downstate rocker.

Sway might have taken the bullet to the head, but it's *my* club that's getting torn apart.

CHAPTER TEN

Charlotte

MARCEL'S BEEN DOWNSTATE, HELPING Z SORT THROUGH THINGS FOR weeks while Sway's in the hospital recovering. I want to be a good ol' lady, support the club and all that, but I miss him. Heidi and I have gone downstate almost every weekend to spend time with the guys and help Lilly adjust to her new role as the president's ol' lady. But now I'm behind on work and need to catch up.

I'm obsessing over my notes for an upcoming trial when the front door to my office opens. My gaze jumps to my calendar. No appointments.

"Sunshine, I'm home!"

"Marcel?" I jump out of my chair and hurry around my desk. I'd kicked off my heels earlier and my tights stick to the carpet as I run.

In the hallway, I stop and stare.

Marcel's long legs eat up the distance. He crashes into me somewhere in the middle. He lifts me against his body, holding me tight.

"Are you really home for good?" I murmur against his bristly cheek.

"Fuck, I missed you so much," he whispers. His lips collide with mine. I curl my arms around his neck and melt into him.

"Missed you too," I whisper. "I hate sleeping without you next to me."

"Is that all you miss?" His mouth quirks as he sets me on my feet.

"No." I wrap my arms around his waist, unwilling to release him even for a second. "I miss that soft snoring you do when you're *really* sound asleep."

"I don't snore."

Laughing, I push him away. "Seriously, are you home now?"

"Yeah, Sunshine. Z has his crew under control. If I stay any longer, it's gonna start to undermine him."

"True." I lace my fingers with his and pull him toward my office. "It was good for Downstate to see how much you guys support him, but eventually they'll wonder if he can handle it or not."

He squeezes my hip. "You always get it."

"Bikers aren't all that hard to understand." My mouth quirks. "Respect few, fear none, covers a lot of different situations."

His snort of amusement fills the hollow space in my chest, and I hug him again. "I'm so happy you're home. My brother will be happy to see you too."

"Yeah? He wasn't relieved I wasn't around to corrupt his tender mind?"

"No." I flash a quick smile. "Well, maybe."

"I owe him. He was a big help to Heidi and Lilly. I think Lilly's upset he won't be coming down to help out anymore. Chance is going to miss him too."

We cross the threshold into my office. I close and lock the door behind us.

Marcel's mouth twitches at the corners. "What are you doing?"

"Welcoming you home."

"Take your clothes off for me."

"Here?" I play with the silk bow of my blouse. "Now?"

"Here and now." He steps closer and leans against my desk. "Right here in front of me." He kicks one of my chairs to the side and points to the floor.

An excited shiver races over my skin. The heat in his eyes. The gruff commands. In my office, in the middle of the day. It's almost too much. Still, I take my time sauntering close to the spot he pointed out. Can't give him what he wants too soon.

"Stop trying to tease me, Charlotte."

I tug at one end of the silk bow at my neck. "You have a lot of nerve."

"Yeah, about nine inches of it." He palms his crotch and his mouth slides into a cocky smirk.

"You barge into my office in the middle of the day, expecting a striptease?"

"I expect much more than a tease, Sunshine." He raises one blond eyebrow, challenging me to continue.

One by one, I slip the buttons loose, watching his face. The way his teeth sink into his bottom lip flips my stomach.

"Good." He drags out the word until I feel it sliding over my skin. "That's nice."

I slide the blouse down my shoulders and drape it over the back of a chair.

"Very nice," he praises.

"Are you planning to stand there and watch me all day? Or are you going to actually do something?"

His nostrils flare. I'm poking the right buttons

"Get on your desk."

"What?"

He walks me behind the desk and pushes me until I'm perched on the edge of it. His hands slide under my skirt, hiking it up around my waist. "You won't be needing these." He strips my tights off, carefully rolling them down my legs, and sits in my chair.

I reach behind me and slide my papers and notepads to the side, then hop all the way onto the desk.

"Nice." Marcel pushes my skirt higher, hooks his fingers in my panties, and drags them down my legs, dropping them on the desk. "Scooch back."

My bare butt sticks to the glossy wood top but I inch back until he's satisfied.

"Lie down."

He curls one hand around my calf and guides one of my feet to the edge of the desk, then the other. "Spread wider." He touches my knees, gently parting them.

"Fuck, I've missed having your pussy in my face." He grins up at me.

"You have a lot of mornings to make up for." I reach down, running my fingers through his hair, scraping my nails over his scalp.

He closes his eyes and shivers with pleasure. "I do. Gonna have you bouncing on my dick every chance I get."

"No bunnies bounced on you, right?" I ask quietly.

His eyes pop open. Hurt, anger, and surprise all flicker over his face. "Don't even fuckin' joke about that." He grips my thighs harder and leans in to slowly flick his tongue over my clit. "I don't think I'm going to let you come now. Or at all."

"That's mean."

"So was your question."

Feeling too raw and vulnerable spread out before him, skirt up around my waist, bottom half on display, I struggle to sit up.

He rises, placing his palm against my sternum, and presses me down on my desk. "Where do you think you're going?"

"Let me up."

"No."

Oh, Jesus. I shouldn't be this turned on right now. The fire in his eyes, the harsh rasp of his voice, his big hands pinning me in place. All of it ratchets up my desire.

He leans over me and nips my earlobe. "If you want to be restrained, just ask me nicely. Don't say things to piss me off."

"I didn't mean to," I whisper. I should apologize but can't form the words.

"I'm still not letting you come." His gaze searches the area behind me. "You have another outfit here?"

"Yes—"

He stalks behind me and picks up my discarded blouse.

"What are you doing?"

"Quiet."

Somewhere, my brain says I should be outraged.

He jerks my blouse under my body, working it to my shoulders, then tangling it around my arms. "What are you doing?" I twist and try to sit up again.

"Don't. Move."

"I'm stuck."

"I know." He flashes an evil grin and twists the blouse, further trapping me.

"What are you doing?" I repeat.

Holding onto the material, he squats down.

I strain and twist my head, trying to see what creative torture he's planning. The material yanks tighter, leaving me open and at his mercy.

"Are you tying me to my desk with my own clothes?" Shock and outrage squeeze my voice high.

"Looks like it." He scoops my underwear off the desk and shoves it in my mouth. "It's messy but it'll hold you for now."

"Marcel!" I mumble, shaking my head and spitting damp lace from my lips.

He strokes his fingers over my breasts and down my stomach as he returns to the other side. "I like you like this."

"I don't." *Liar, liar, pussy on fire.*

He smirks. "Sure you don't." My chair squeaks as he sinks into it. He rolls it closer until his breath puffs over my legs. His rough hands caress my thighs. "You should see how wet you are."

He runs his fingers down my center, then holds them in front of my face. "You don't have to say anything. I have all the evidence I need, counselor."

I turn my head and snort-giggle into my armpit.

There's a click and a buzz. Something tickles right above my clit. My body jolts but I can't go far.

"Not so funny now, is it?" Marcel says, slowly rolling whatever toy of torture he brought with him over me.

"Where did you...whose is that?" I squirm, trying to see what he's using.

He flicks the vibrator off. "It's *yours*. You left it at the house. Whole way up here, I was planning how I wanted to use it on you. Never expected you'd ask if I'd been banging bunnies while I was downstate."

"I'm—"

He flicks the vibrator on again, drowning out my apology. Every time, just as I'm close to release, he stops. I try to be sneaky and not make a peep. But he just *knows* when I'm close.

"You're so beautiful spread out like this." He brushes his fingers over my stomach. "It almost hurts to look at you."

His hot mouth comes closer. My breathing stops as he slowly licks my clit, then sucks. I spread my legs wider, begging him to devour me. Wishing I wasn't tied down but loving it at the same time.

He slides one of his hands up and pinches my hard nipple. I arch my back and moan.

I'm panting and trembling all over, pushing up against the edge again. Maybe this time he'll—

He stops.

I jerk my hips and cry in frustration.

"Aw, what's wrong, Sunshine?" He rounds the desk again, wagging the vibrator in his hand. My desperate eyes follow his every move.

"Does this hurt?" He traces his fingers over my arms.

"No."

"Good." He unzips his fly and frees himself.

I lick my lips.

"You've got the idea," he encourages. The head of his cock nudges my mouth and I open wide, sucking enthusiastically.

He groans and watches me intently. "Good girl."

The angle's awkward. Uncomfortable but not painful. He seems to understand and cradles my head with one hand, taking the pressure off my neck.

With his other hand, he flicks on the vibrator, leans over me, and slides it between my legs.

"Keep sucking. Don't you dare stop," he warns.

I moan and cry around his huge cock as he slides the vibrator back and forth over my clit. The setting is too low to do anything other than leave me anticipating *more, more, more.*

I deep throat him with enthusiasm, the odd angle making it somehow easier to take more of him into my mouth.

He pushes the vibrator inside me and I gasp, choking on him.

"Easy." He pulls back. "You like that?"

My hips rock up to meet the vibrator.

He clicks it off.

I whine and thrash on the desk.

Breathing hard, he pulls out of my mouth and flashes that evil smile again. "Aw, were you close, Sunshine?"

"Yes!" I wiggle my hips, trying to find relief.

He leans over me and flattens his palm, lightly smacking right over my clit.

"Oh my God!" My body twitches.

He returns to the other side and pushes his cock deep inside me.

"Yes." I wrap my legs around him, trying to draw him closer. Out of my mind with the need for release, I circle my hips, trying to meet every one of his thrusts.

He flicks the vibrator on again, pressing it to my clit.

"Oh. More."

"Nope." He flicks it off. "That's all you get."

He repeats the same exquisite torture several times.

My orgasm flutters closer. I bite my bottom lip and slow my movements, circling my hips in exaggerated motions. Waves of bliss pulse down on me.

"I'm—"

"Go ahead, Sunshine." He clutches my hip but doesn't interrupt my flow. "You earned it."

I want to respond but I'm too busy having an out-of-body experience. Every nerve ending sings with pleasure. He drags his hand to my stomach and up over my ribs. I roll my hips faster, dizzy with anticipation. So close. He strokes his thumb against my collarbones. I tilt my head to the side.

"Is that what you want?" he rasps.

Pleasure coils tighter through me. "So close."

He grips my throat, gently squeezing. Colors burst behind my eyes as I'm finally, blissfully thrown over the edge. I wrap my hands around his powerful forearm and grind against him harder.

"That's my girl," he grits out through clenched teeth. "Don't you ever think I'd let someone else ride my cock."

"Mine," I whisper.

"That's right, Sunshine," he rasps. "Come for me."

Tears leak from the corners of my eyes. The orgasm hits me like an explosion. Waves and waves wash over me.

"Thank you," I chant again and again.

He groans but I'm barely aware of his release. The pleasure stretches into something timeless I can't quite grasp as it goes on and on.

Marcel quickly unties me. Tingles race into my limbs as he frees me from the ruined blouse and cradles me in his arms. He sits back in the chair, holding me secure.

He studies my neck, kissing every couple inches.

"What's wrong?" I whisper.

"Nothing." He drops a kiss in an extra-ticklish spot, and my shoulders jerk. "I don't want to leave any marks on you."

Always so rough but gentle. "No? You don't want everyone to know I belong to you?"

"I have better ways to brand you than bruises, Sunshine." He runs his hands over my arms. "Do they hurt? I shouldn't have left you tied at that angle for so long."

I open and close my hands a few times. "I'm fine. A little lightheaded from the supernova orgasm."

He rumbles with laughter. "Supernova? I like that. I'm going to make you wait more often."

"I wanted to kill you and fuck you senseless every time you cut me off." I snuggle against him. We're a naked heap in my office, sweaty and breathing hard.

"I'm so happy you're home," I whisper.

"Me too."

I hope you never have to leave again.

CHAPTER ELEVEN

Teller

AFTER OUR *SUPERNOVA* AFTERNOON AT CHARLOTTE'S OFFICE, WE HEAD home and I'm able to finally sleep in my own bed.

The next morning, I head to the clubhouse. Hope's the first person I run into.

"Teller! Rock said you were sent home." She reaches up and hugs me.

"For good." I glance over her shoulder, my gaze landing on Grace in her bouncy seat. "Can I say hi to Grace?"

"Of course." She squeezes my arm. "Actually, would you mind watching her for a few seconds? I need to run out to the garage."

"Sure." I'm actually relieved to have a few seconds alone with my baby sister.

"Thanks. I'll be right back."

"No hurry. We'll be fine." I unbuckle Grace and gently lift her up. "I missed you, little nugget. Look how big you've gotten." I brush the tip of my index finger against her cheek.

All the shit that happened while I was downstate gave me plenty to think about when it comes to my life. The mistakes I've made. The desire to do better going forward.

"I'll do a better job protecting you, little sister," I whisper. "You can always come to me if you need something. Even if you're afraid to tell your mom and dad. I promise to listen."

"You always listened to me." Heidi's soft voice breaks the quiet in the room.

My heart jumps. How long has she been here? I tip my head up and find her at the bottom of the staircase watching us. "Where'd you come from?"

"Upstairs."

"Where's Alexa?"

"In the kitchen with Auntie Trinity."

I shift Grace into the crook of my right arm and move into the corner of the couch. "Join us."

"Hi, baby," she coos, leaning over and running her index finger over Grace's arm. She smiles at me. "Did I interrupt an important conversation?"

It's too uncomfortable to hold her gaze. "Not at all."

She settles next to me and leans against my arm. "You always listened to me, Marcel."

I should've known she wouldn't let that go. "No, I didn't. I listened through my own filter. I never *heard* what you were really saying."

She rests her hand on my knee and squeezes. "I'm older now than when you patched in to the club, Marcel. And I have a better understanding of how hard things must've been for you after Mom skipped out and Grams made you leave." Her voice falters. "Nothing you or anyone else can say will ever, ever convince me that you're not the best brother who's ever walked this Earth."

I almost choke on the weight of all the ways I've failed her and all the things I'm hiding from her. Would she still feel the same way if she knew the truth?

"Thanks." I force a smug big brother smirk onto my face. "You're pretty cool too…for a little sister."

She rolls her eyes. "Are you home for good now?"

"Looks that way. Blake won't be down there too much longer," I assure her.

She nods. "He's helping the guys renovate the clubhouse. Can I hold her?" She sticks her arms out, and I pass Grace over.

"Oh," Heidi sighs. "She's the sweetest when she's sleeping. Those six a.m. alarm calls are murder, though." She laughs and kisses Grace's forehead.

Should I tell Heidi about Rock and me *now*? The words try to line up on my tongue but I bite them back. "You're not upset Alexa isn't the baby of the club anymore? She held the title for a while."

Heidi lifts her head to scowl at me. "Of course not." She rocks Grace gently. "I love her too much. Besides, Alexa's literally being spoiled by Trinity right now." A wicked smile curves her lips. "And I'll be honest, spending time with Grace makes me want another baby so badly."

"Worry about finishing school."

She clucks her tongue and rolls her eyes at my harsh tone. No matter how old we get, our brother-sister dynamic will always be present.

"I *am*," she huffs. "But I *like* being a mom too. There's nothing wrong with that."

I let out a deep sigh. "No, there isn't."

She stares at me with wide eyes, as if my agreement shocks her. "What about you? Don't you and Charlotte have baby fever yet?"

The teasing question hits me in the gut. I feel like a damn deer on the highway with a tractor trailer's high beams lighting me up while it speeds toward me.

"Marcel?" Heidi touches my arm and hands Grace to me. "I was kidding."

"Huh? Yeah, no. We'll get there."

Her forehead crinkles as she studies me. "I think you and Charlotte will be really great parents."

"Yeah," I answer. "I hope so."

She frowns again.

CHARLOTTE

I can't catch my breath.

Marcel holding Grace with Heidi by his side is the sweetest picture.

His two sisters.

Guilt chases away my melancholy. It's been months. So much has happened, and Heidi still has no idea who Grace really is to Marcel.

"Hey, guys," I call to get their attention.

Marcel glances up and his expression softens. "Hey, Sunshine."

How ironic that he calls me sunshine when I always feel so warm and loved under his gaze. "Hey. Hope said you were with Grace."

I approach slowly, like he's cradling a rattlesnake instead of a baby. One of Grace's fists escapes her blanket, and I can't help smiling.

No matter how sad I am for my own loss sometimes, my heart fills with love. "Can I hold her?"

"Yeah," Marcel rasps. We haven't spoken about our miscarriage since the night he came home and I told him about it. The desperate need to do *something* to make it better claws at me every day.

Heidi hops out of her seat and offers it to me.

"Thanks," I murmur and sink onto the couch.

She grins and opens her mouth, then frowns and closes it. Was she about to tease me about having baby fever, like I overheard her doing to Marcel a few minutes ago? Is my Grim Reaper face what stole the question from her lips?

"Hey, baby girl," I whisper as Marcel hands Grace to me. "Everyone's loving on you today, huh?"

She smacks her little lips and blinks at me.

"I gotta run." Heidi leans over me to peer at Grace one more time. "Just wanted to see the little peanut before I head to class."

"Hey." Marcel captures Heidi's hand. "Kick some ass today."

"You know it." She dips down and pops a kiss on his cheek, then scurries toward the dining room.

"Did you two have a good talk?" I ask without looking away from Grace.

"Not about what we should have." He gently runs his hand over Grace's curls. "I wanted to but with Blake still not here, it seemed like the wrong time."

"I don't know that there will ever be a perfect time for that talk."

"Probably not."

The front door opens and closes. "I'm so glad you're here, Charlotte. I feel like I haven't seen much of you lately," Hope says. "Thanks for watching her, Teller."

"No problem," Marcel says.

Rock follows her inside but his gaze slips from his son to his daughter. "How'd she behave for you, knucklehead?"

"She was perfect."

As if Grace senses her parents have returned, she scrunches up her little face and wails.

"Shh, it's okay. I've got you," I whisper.

"Aw, I'll take her, Charlotte," Hope says.

I'm not ready to relinquish Grace yet, but I can't exactly keep Hope's baby hostage, either.

Rock's glued to Hope's side as she takes Grace to the couch opposite us. He's the kind of attentive father I know Marcel will be...eventually.

Hopefully.

One day.

Panic increases my heart rate. Sweat pops across my forehead.

I have to get out of here.

I glance at Marcel. *Please, let's go.*

He nods.

"We're heading home." Marcel stands and takes my hand, pulling me off of the couch. "Unless you guys need anything?"

"Nah, we're good." Rock touches Hope's shoulder, then approaches us. "Thanks for staying with her."

"No problem." Marcel curls his hand around mine, the warmth easing my tension. "You need anything, call me."

"Thank you, Teller," Hope calls.

"You got it."

"Good to see you, Charlotte," Rock says. "Work keeping you busy?"

Heat floods my cheeks and I can't meet his intense eyes. "Almost more than I can handle," I answer. The excuse seems weak.

"That's good, though, right?" His eyes crinkle at the corners.

"Sometimes."

Once we're finally outside, Marcel pulls me closer. "You all right?"

"Just tired." *Emotionally exhausted* is closer to the truth.

"Want me to get the ATV?"

"No, I like walking through the woods with you." Maybe it will give me a chance to burn off all this sadness.

"Charlotte," he says once we're a good distance from the clubhouse. "Do you think maybe it's time you talk to someone?" His words and tone are gentle but firm.

"No. I'm fine."

"You looked like you were ready to burst into tears."

"I got a little choked up seeing you and Heidi and Grace together..." Damn, that's a tired excuse. I wasn't trying to change the subject and pile more guilt on his shoulders. But he doesn't seem offended.

He just squeezes my hand and continues guiding me through the maze of trees, branches, and piles of leaves. "I'm glad I didn't say anything." He blows out a thoughtful sigh. "She loves Grace, and I don't want to be the reason she ends up resenting her or something."

That sounds like another lie he's told himself. But I'm not exactly in a position to point that out.

Excuses, excuses. We're both full of them.

CHAPTER TWELVE

Charlotte

"You ready for tonight?" Marcel calls out a few seconds before appearing in our bedroom doorway.

"Almost," I mutter between curled lips. I swipe a few more careful strokes of dark red gloss along my bottom lip. I actually feel...happy tonight. More excited for a night at the clubhouse than I've been in a long time. Rooster and Shelby have returned from her tour. Everyone from the Downstate charter should be visiting. It's going to be fun. I need fun.

Marcel groans. "What are you trying to do to me?" He steps behind me, resting his hands on my hips. In the mirror, he seems to tower over me. He leans closer to brush a kiss against my neck. "You know I can't resist that color on you."

I hold the tube in front of his face. "This is different. It's a gloss, not a matte lipstick. Melted Poppies, not Unicorn Blood."

"As if it matters." He hooks a finger in my hair and slides it out of his way, dropping a kiss in the dip between my neck and shoulder. "It's hot as fuck and makes me want to do dirty stuff to you."

A bolt of electricity crackles down my legs. "I don't think we have time for dirty stuff. Maybe just stuff." Somehow, I keep my voice steady and carefree.

"I always have time for you." He dips down and slides his hands under my bathrobe, over the outsides of my thighs.

The tube of gloss falls out of my hands, clattering onto the counter. My legs tremble from the sensual tickling of his rough hands against my skin. I curl my fingers over the edge of the sink. Otherwise, I might melt into a puddle.

"That's it. Hold on," he encourages. His fingers brush my hips. "No underwear. I like that."

"Well, not yet, I—"

"Shh." He brushes more soft kisses over my shoulder. "How are you feeling? Ready for family dinner night? It's going to be complete chaos now that everyone's back home from the tour."

"I was looking forward to hearing all the crazy stories from the guys. Jiggy's version of events is always somehow hilarious and creepy."

"Very true."

I inhale a shaky breath, keenly aware of Marcel's hand creeping over my thigh. "But I could be convinced to stay home."

"Why not do both?" He squeezes my hips and spins me to face him. Heat floods his eyes. He lifts me and sets my butt on the counter.

My heart squeezes. How is it possible to never get tired of looking at this man? I reach up and run my fingers through his thick blond hair, staring into the intelligent teal eyes that have captivated me from the moment we met. "What's your secret?"

He lifts his eyebrows. "To?"

"Getting more handsome every day."

The fierce expression on his face softens. "Handsome?" He tugs at the knot in the belt of my bathrobe.

"Sexy. Definitely sexy."

"And?"

"Fuckable. Extremely fuckable."

Satisfaction curls his lips. "I live to please you, Sunshine."

He finally works the knot loose. I shimmy my shoulders and let the robe fall open. My skin warms where his gaze falls on my body.

The look of appreciation in his eyes burns hot as ever.

"Now that you have me naked—"

"Not quite." He tugs the robe from my shoulders and off my arms. "That's better."

"It seems unfair that you're not." I tease my fingers along the edge of his belt buckle.

"Take what you want, Sunshine." His lips tilt into a cocky line.

I slick my tongue over my lips as I work his belt loose, slide down his zipper, and ease his jeans over his hips. I curl my fingers around his cock. Hard and hot. He hisses as I squeeze and stroke his firm flesh.

I flick my gaze up and he's watching me, expectant, with loving eyes. He cocks an eyebrow, challenging me. Using his body to brace myself, I slide off the counter, landing on the soft bathroom rug. He backs up a step to give me room.

"What're you up to, Sunshine?"

"I want a taste." I open my mouth and lightly swipe my tongue against the head of his cock. He breathes out a curse and burrows his fingers into the messy knot of curls piled on top of my head.

For a few minutes, that's all I do—taste him. Soft, teasing kisses and slow licks, enough to excite but not satisfy. His legs shake each time I open my mouth as if I'm planning to take him all the way in.

He lets out a laugh that's somewhere between frustrated and vengeful. "Sunshine, you're playing with fire."

I bat my lashes as if I have no idea what he's talking about. I squeeze him tighter and take another long, slow lick.

His hand tightens in my hair. He brushes me away. "Hands behind your back."

I fight to keep my lips from curling into a smile as I slide my arms behind my back, grasping each elbow with the opposite hand to thrust my breasts up the way he likes.

"Why so naughty today?" He grips his cock and lightly taps my bottom lip. "Open for me."

I tease my tongue past my lips and against his cock.

"No," he rasps. "Open. All the way."

My red-hot desire to please him can't be restrained. I open wide and close my mouth around him, sliding as much down as I can until he hits the back of my throat.

"That's it." His body and voice tremble. "Good girl. Keep going."

My happy hum pulls another shuddering gasp from him. He thrusts into my mouth and I relax, letting him set the pace.

Throbbing with my own need, I release my elbows and slide one hand between my legs.

His wild thrusts stop. "Don't you fucking dare touch yourself. Mine."

I whine a pleading noise.

"No." He tugs on my hair. "Suck."

The ache between my legs intensifies.

I grip his hips, pulling him closer.

"That's it," he encourages. "Gotta pay for teasing me."

If that dirty, affectionate smile on his face is my reward, I'm more than happy to pay the price.

"Fuck." He groans and tugs my hair, pulling me off of him.

"What are you doing?" I squeal as he lifts me off the floor and spins me to face the vanity. "I almost bit off your dick."

He snorts a laugh. "You're the only person who makes me lose control."

"You seem pretty in control to me." I meet his eyes in the mirror. Blotches of pink stand out all over my chest, neck, and cheeks.

"Look how pretty you are. All pink from ears to nipples." He traces his fingers over both places and I close my eyes. "So excited just from sucking my cock?"

"Yes."

"Open your eyes. Brace your hands against the counter."

"Marcel." I wiggle my behind, bumping into his erection, leaning forward, trying anything I can to get him inside of me.

But my man won't be rushed. He slides his hand between my thighs, going straight for my clit. He gently flicks his thumb against me and I squirm.

"Like that, don't you?"

"You know I do." Good God, every part of this man is talented when it comes to working my body. He increases the pressure slowly until I'm squirming.

"Marcel, please," I beg.

"Shhh," he whispers against my ear. "Don't come yet."

"I...I don't think I can...I need more...oh my God."

He stops.

I cry out in frustration. "Why?"

An evil chuckle flows past his lips. This is his favorite game of torture. Taking me right to the edge. Mine, too, even if I'm not in the mood to admit it.

"Please?" I shift on my toes, eager to release the tension inside me.

"That's all you've got? Please?"

Bastard. "Please let me come."

"You're beautiful." He traces one finger along my neck. "I'm a lucky man."

"Why?"

"Because I get to fuck you for the rest of my life."

Sweetness burns through my frustration. "I'm the lucky one." I rub my thighs together, desperate to relieve the ache. "Usually. You're extra sadistic tonight."

"Maybe." He brushes his lips over my shoulder. "I love watching you squirm."

His arms band around my waist and he lifts me, carrying me into the bedroom. "Get on the bed and spread out for me the way I like."

I can't scramble onto the mattress fast enough. There's no hesitation as I rest my feet flat and spread my legs wide.

"God, you're a beautiful sight." He falls to his knees like he's about to pray at the altar of my body. "Come closer."

I inch near the edge of the bed and he yanks me the rest of the way, burying his face against me. The same maddening dance starts a second time. Slow heat races over me. Tension tightens my muscles. Butterfly-light kisses turn into harder licks and sucks.

"Tell me what you want," he murmurs against my skin.

"Make me come. Please."

He slides one finger inside me, turning it and rubbing gently at the spot that sets my legs quivering.

"How?" He raises an innocent eyebrow and rubs harder. "Like this?"

"Do you need me to draw a treasure map?" I reach down and use two fingers to expose myself. "Your tongue on my clit always works wonders."

He shakes with laughter, his shoulders bumping my thighs as he swoops in, wraps his lips around my clit, and sucks hard.

"Fuck!" My hips shoot off the bed.

He thrusts a second finger inside me, quickly pumping them in and out while his mouth devours me with hard, fast, open-mouthed kisses.

The sharp, sweet snap of pleasure breaks me open. The exquisite pulses of bliss transport me to another plane.

I'm still tingling and twitching when he pulls away.

There's no time to protest. He falls over my body and enters me in one quick thrust.

"Oh! Jesus." My eyes fly open, and I find him inches from my face.

"No, just me," he says in that maddening way that's equal parts smug and sexy. He hooks his arm under my thigh, spreading me open. "You can take it. You just came so hard. You're so, so wet."

"Yes, but you're still so, so big."

He seems to smother a smile and leans in, brushing his damp lips against my neck.

His movements slow to a gentle rock of his hips. "Better?"

Fire races over my skin. "Yes," I whisper.

"Love having my cock buried in you, Sunshine."

"Finally." I lift my legs higher, locking them around his waist.

He rests his forehead against mine. We're nose to nose, and I don't need any light in the bedroom to see the desire shimmering in his eyes. "So impatient tonight."

"You're just that good."

He unwraps my arms from around his neck and pins them over my head. The slow, gentle waves of bliss turn sharper. Underneath him, I squirm and wriggle. He groans and shifts his hold on my wrists. Freeing one hand to press my hip into the mattress, he drives into me deeper with each thrust.

"Yes, yes, yes," I chant over and over.

His lips curl, like he has teasing words for me, but pleasure seems to steal them right out of his mouth. His breathing turns ragged. Eyes close.

"Eyes on me, Marcel," I whisper, borrowing one of his favorite lines.

"Fuck." He stares at me, his body jerking and shaking against me. He grabs my hips with both hands, thumbs digging into my flesh, until he finishes.

Breathing hard, he rolls to the side, landing next to me. He finds my hand, curling his fingers around mine.

"I don't think I can move," I whisper.

He slowly turns, a smile playing over his lips. "Did I finally fuck the sass out of you?"

"Never." I pop a kiss on his cheek and sit up. He curls his arm around my waist, dragging me back down on top of him.

"We'll be late," I warn him, snuggling into his warm embrace.

"Don't give a fuck," he murmurs into my hair.

No one seems to notice our later-than-usual arrival at the clubhouse. Why would they? Rooster finally patched Shelby. After her passionate speech to thank the brothers who added their patches to her cut, I'm confident she'll fit right in.

The festive atmosphere at the clubhouse continues into dinner. For the first time in a long time, I feel completely connected to the celebration as we all choose our seats at the long dinner table.

"Everyone, welcome our newest patched ol' lady!" Trinity grabs Shelby's hand and lifts it high in the air.

Shelby ducks her head and laughs, embarrassed, I think, from all the extra attention. Endearing since she's used to performing in front of huge crowds.

"Thank you, guys," she says in her soft Texas drawl.

I rest my head on Marcel's shoulder. "Poor Shelby. I hope someone's going to take the attention off of her tonight."

"No such luck. They'll razz Rooster all night long."

"She always has a sweet way of deflecting the guys and their little barbs."

He studies Rooster and Shelby for a second. "Yeah." He almost seems conflicted but I don't have a chance to ask him about it.

When it's time, we hustle to the buffet. Around these guys, it's grab your dinner early or starve.

While we're waiting in line, Marcel brushes my hair to the side and kisses my shoulder. "You must be starving after the way I worked you over."

My skin tingles from his touch. "I am."

As we're finishing dinner, Heidi leans into me. "Hang onto my brother for a second, will you?"

"Huh?" I grab my napkin and dab my mouth, but she's already standing and tapping her fork against a glass.

Shelby slides down in her chair until just her chin's above the table. Poor thing must be bracing herself for more teasing. I try to give her a reassuring smile but her gaze is focused on her plate.

The chatter at the table barely dies down.

"Fuckers," Murphy grumbles. He stands and slaps his hands together. "Settle the fuck down. My wife has news to share."

My lips twitch at the proud note in his voice when he says *my wife*. Their wedding wasn't the perfect event they'd envisioned. They were just happy to finally be married.

Now that they have everyone's attention, Murphy nods to Heidi and takes his seat again. He curls his arm around her legs. "Go ahead."

"What the fuck now?" Marcel grumbles next to me.

"Shh." I smile up at Heidi, eager to hear whatever she plans to announce.

She rests her hand over her stomach, and my smile freezes.

Oh, no.

Be happy for them, no matter what.

Don't you dare ruin this.

"We're having a baby!" Heidi shouts.

"Congratulations!" Lilly squeals and runs to Heidi's side.

Sour jealousy I can't wish away burns at the back of my throat. I'd finally started to forget my loss and feel normal again.

Be happy for them.

Just try to be happy.

Smile. Congratulate them.

I can't do this. Not tonight. Not now.

I quietly push my chair back.

"Hey." Marcel grabs my hand. "Are you okay?" he whispers.

"No." God, I need to get out of here before I start bawling and ruin Heidi's moment. "Give me a minute." I squeeze his hand and release it. "Go congratulate your sister. Be nice," I warn him.

Guilt and sadness chase me into the kitchen. Away from the happy announcement. I hate that I feel this way.

Bonnie and Lala are busy cleaning dishes and wrapping up leftovers.

"Hey, Charlotte." Lala beams at me.

"Hey," I mumble and point to the door. "Just going to get some air," I explain without slowing my steps.

The cool evening air slaps me in the face but offers little relief.

Why, why, why couldn't I sit still, smile, and congratulate Heidi like a normal person? Like a good sister would do? It's not about me. She didn't get pregnant to spite me. She doesn't even know...*dammit*. It's been months. Why is this still so hard? Why does it still hurt so much?

I cross my arms over my chest and stare into the woods. An owl hoots in the distance and I narrow my eyes, searching for a glimpse of the nocturnal bird.

"Char?" Murphy's voice breaks the woodland peace. "You all right?"

I wipe my eyes quickly, paste on a bright smile, and turn to face him. "Yes! Congratulations. I'm so happy for you guys. You must be thrilled." I babble out the words at a million miles a minute.

"Hey, come here." He pulls me into his arms, hugging me tight. "Ginger power," he whispers.

I let out a small, miserable laugh against his flannel shirt. Sure, *this* secret Marcel spilled. "Damn it. Marcel told you, didn't he?"

"Don't be too hard on him." Murphy shrugs but keeps his arms around me. "He bared his soul to me when I was in a coma, thinking I couldn't hear him. I used it to my advantage when I woke up."

It so perfectly encapsulates their relationship, I can't even be mad. "Sounds about right." I pull back and peer up at him. "You...kept it to yourself all this time?"

He stares down at me with concern brewing in his eyes. Underneath the brutal biker exterior, Murphy truly is one of the kindest people I've ever known. "He asked me not to say anything."

"I'm sorry." Sniffling, I dab my eyes, and he releases his hold on me. "You know I'm so, so happy for you two, right?"

"Yeah, I know."

"I didn't want to ruin your announcement, so I..."

"It's okay." He motions toward the door. "Everyone has her occupied."

"I just needed a minute."

"I understand." He shrugs. "Heidi was worried about Marcel getting mad. But I was worried about *you*."

His sweet concern breaks the precarious hold I have on my tears.

"Shit, I'm sorry, Charlotte." He pulls me into his arms again.

"It's fine."

"She wanted to tell you guys first, but I thought telling everyone at once would—"

"Give me cover?"

He shrugs. "I guess. Heidi went for it because she figured Marcel wouldn't kill me in front of the whole club."

I dab at my eyes with my fingertips and laugh. "He's more mature than that."

He cocks his head, the corners of his eyes crinkling with laughter. "Is he, though?"

His teasing question pulls laughter from me. "Yes!"

The screen door creaks open.

Marcel's concerned face peers into the darkness. His gaze lands on us and he steps outside. "You okay, Sunshine?"

I must look rattled. He doesn't issue a single threat for Murphy to get his hands off of me.

"Hey, brother." Murphy releases me and throws a hello punch, grazing Marcel's arm.

My body vibrates with the need to get closer to my other half. And as if Marcel knows it, he wraps me in his arms. I rest my cheek against his chest and inhale deeply. The crisp, fresh scent of him fills my nose and calms me.

"I'll see you two inside," Murphy says.

"Thank you," I mumble, without moving.

The door clicks closed and we're alone with nothing but the harsh outdoor lights of the clubhouse in front of us and the dark forest at our backs.

"I'm sorry," Marcel whispers. "I wasn't sure how to—"

"No." I pull back so I can see his face. "I wanted you to stay. I don't want anything to take away from their moment. This is a happy time, and I didn't want to burst into tears and ruin it for them. I needed a second to pull myself together."

He kisses the top of my head and rocks me from side to side in his arms. "Love you, Charlotte. Can't wait to marry you."

"Me too," I whisper.

"We can go home if you want."

"No, I don't want Heidi to think we're mad at her." I sniffle and dab at my eyes with the backs of my hands, praying I'm not smearing mascara all over my cheeks. "She was apparently worried about *your* reaction."

"Why does everyone assume I'm going to lose my shit? They're married, for fuck's sake."

I cock my head at him. He can't be serious.

His lips quiver with amusement. "Hey, can I tell you something?"

"Anything."

He turns his head, giving the immediate area a quick, dramatic search with his eyes. "Promise you won't tell anyone?"

I hold up my hand as if I'm ready to take an oath. "I swear."

He glances over his shoulder one last time, then leans in close to whisper, "I feel a little shitty now that I didn't give Rooster my patch for Shelby."

I doubt he really feels bad about it, but since he's trying to cheer me up by taking my mind off of things, I play along. "Why? You've only met her a few times."

"Yeah, that's what I told Rooster."

"Murphy and Wrath were on the road with her for a while," I add. "It makes sense they'd approve. They had an opportunity to observe her in different situations. Wrath spent time with her at another charter, right?"

"So I heard." His gaze shifts toward the clubhouse. "I guess he was also impressed that in all the interviews she's given, she's never thrown the club's name around."

I'm not sure if her silence stems from her loyalty to the club or self-preservation. Being associated with a motorcycle club might not enhance her sweet, clean country-girl persona. But saying that seems disloyal to my new sister.

"Well, there you go." I run my fingers over his chest. "If you give out your patch to fit in, it'll lose its meaning."

"Rock and Z didn't give theirs either."

"I noticed." I reconsider the patches she received. "Dex makes sense because he was there through the whole tour. Jigsaw because he and Rooster are so tight. He probably knows Shelby the best."

"Absolutely."

"I like her a lot." My gaze strays toward the kitchen door. "She fits in well. Handles the guys with the right amount of sweet and sassy. Heidi adores her."

"Heidi's starstruck," he scoffs.

"Yeah, a little," I agree. "But Trinity isn't easily swayed. Neither is Wrath," I add with a teasing, sour note. "As I well know." I tip my head to the side. "Am I the only ol' lady he's ever voted down?"

Instead of the smirk I expected, he scowls. "I prefer not to answer that."

"I'm kidding. I earned his respect and his patch. That's all that matters."

He runs his thumb along the edge of my cut, stopping to trace the word "Sunshine" embroidered over my heart. "You make me so happy, Charlotte."

"That's all I want." I lean up and kiss his cheek.

He glances toward the clubhouse, the corners of his mouth pulling down. "It'll happen for us," he says with quiet confidence.

I sniffle and nod, praying he's right.

CHAPTER THIRTEEN

Charlotte

THE LAW ISN'T ABOUT THE TRUTH. BEFORE I WENT TO LAW SCHOOL, I thought it was. Now that I've been practicing a few years, I see it through different eyes. Pretty and persuasive words are what it's all about.

Still, I keep at it. I still care. Still want to help kids, even within a system designed to fail.

A pair of tasseled loafers enters my vision as I clear the table of my exhibits, pens, and folders. I don't bother to look up.

"Nice going, Clark." David sounds like he's gargling with lemon juice. We've known each other since law school. I might not have graduated near the top of the class like he did, but out here in the jungle, grades don't really matter.

I continue tucking things into my briefcase. "I had the law *and* the facts on my side." *And your client is a dick.*

"Eh, agree to disagree."

I swing my briefcase over my shoulder and face him. "Well, the judge agreed, and that's all that really matters, right?" I paste on a sweet smile that is fake as fuck.

One corner of his mouth slides up. "Can I buy you lunch? We haven't sat down to catch up in ages."

Before Marcel and I were together, David and I maintained a sort of friendship left over from law school. Lunches weren't uncommon. But I started to see a smug, cruel side of him I didn't like and stopped accepting the invitations. Today doesn't feel like the day to start that up again.

My phone buzzes and I pull it out of my briefcase.

Ol' Man: How'd it go?

Me: I won.

Ol' Man: That's my girl.

The corners of my mouth tug up.

"Charlotte?"

"Huh? Oh, sorry." I tuck my phone away.

"Lunch?"

"I can't—"

"Come on, there's a cafe right next door. You have to be starving after that closing argument."

I *am* starving and the cafe next door was exactly where I planned to go to grab a sandwich before heading back to my office. Change my plans or get this over with?

My stomach growls as if it would like to weigh in on my dilemma.

"Yeah, okay."

"Great." He strides down the aisle leading out of the now empty courtroom, leaving me to follow. He pushes open the wide swinging doors and holds one side open for me.

My heels clack over the marble floor as I hurry to match his long strides. We pass the guarded entrance. One of the officers shouts a greeting to me and I wave.

"They seem to know you well here," David says once we're outside.

"I practice in this courthouse a lot."

"I noticed." He lets out a wry laugh.

Not my fault he didn't ask about the local rules before agreeing to take this case.

There's a line at the cafe but we're eventually directed to a booth in the back.

After we place our orders with the frazzled waitress, David rolls up his sleeves and rests his forearms on the table. "So, is it everything you thought it was going to be when we were in law school?"

I don't have to ask him what *it* is. Lots of lawyers toss this question around. In fact, I think he and I have had this conversation before. "Not at all. You?"

"Nope. Better."

Good for you.

Our waitress deposits our plates on the table. Ravenous, I pull mine closer and snag my sandwich.

"Are you still happy being solo?" he asks.

I pause mid-chew and set my sandwich on the plate. "It's hectic, but I prefer it."

"Really?" His tone drips with disbelief and condescension. "Have you been able to hire an assistant yet?"

I grit my teeth, embarrassed by the answer. "No, it's not easy to find someone. I'm picky about how I like things done." *And I can't afford it.* Picky doesn't sound as pathetic, so I leave it at that.

He chews slowly and takes a sip of water. "Your overhead must be killing you."

I shrug. Marcel keeps offering to take care of the bills but I refuse to have my husband-to-be finance my law practice. "I do okay."

"Your office is so tiny. And cave-like." He shudders as if he needs to emphasize my office is beneath him.

"It suits me."

"Look," he says, a note of exasperation coloring his words, "my firm is looking to hire someone."

I pause, holding my sandwich in the air and raise an eyebrow.

"And I thought of you," he finishes.

I scoff, then realize he's serious. I set my sandwich down again and wipe the laughter off my face. "So I can represent rich assholes like your client? Hard pass."

He chuckles and swipes his napkin over his mouth. "No, the senior partners are looking for someone to do pro bono work. You'd be able to represent all the poor schmucks your little bleeding heart desires. All while having support staff, supplies, and overhead taken care of. No worries. Just concentrate on your beloved riffraff."

God, working at a firm full of smug assholes like David sounds like my worst nightmare. I've never fit in with those kinds of lawyers. But the rest of it sounds like a dream come true. "Why *me*?"

"Uh, you're a good lawyer." He raises his eyebrows like he can't believe he has to explain this. "And I want to look good to the partners so *I* can get a nice, fat bonus this year."

"I'm guessing *I* wouldn't be eligible for a bonus?"

He snorts. "I have no idea. You can discuss that with the hiring partner. The salary alone will be more than you're making now. Without the stress of running your own practice all by yourself."

It's tempting. I'm probably an idiot for not jumping at the opportunity. "Let me think about it."

"What's there to think about?"

"I want to talk it over with my fiancé, for one thing."

"Yeah, yeah, that makes sense." I can't tell if he's agreeing or mocking me. "We have a generous parental leave policy, you know. If that's something you're thinking about." He holds up his hand. "As a friend, I'm sharing information."

At a firm like that, I probably wouldn't be able to come and go as I please like I do now. No long breakfasts with Marcel on the mornings I don't have to be in court. No skipping out early on Friday afternoons to hang with the girls before a clubhouse party either.

"Would I still be allowed to accept assignments from the county?" I ask.

"Sure. You'd probably be *more* likely to be assigned cases because the judge knows you've got the benefit of a firm behind you."

It would be nice to have more resources available so I could focus on my clients.

"If you're interested, I'll have the hiring partner reach out to you. Is it okay if I give him your number?"

"Sure." *Why not?* I doubt I'm the only person they'll consider. Someone's buddy or a son of one of the partners will probably get the job but David's endorsement has further boosted my ego after my court victory. "Thanks for thinking of me."

"You don't look happy for me." I didn't expect Marcel to jump for joy when I told him about my lunch with David. But *some* reaction would be nice.

Marcel sighs and runs his hands through his hair. "I just know how a lot of those old men still behave. And if one of those fucks pats your ass or talks down to you"—he stops and punches his fist into his palm— "I'll have to go in there and crack skulls."

I should've known that was what would run through his mind.

"So sweet and savage." I pat his cheek and he playfully bites my wrist. A ticklish sensation trails up my arm. Giggling, I pull away. "Down, beast."

I might as well wave a red flag. He growls and lunges for me, grabbing my waist and lifting me in the air.

"Mine."

"Always yours." I loop my arms around his neck as he sets me on my feet. "So, that's a no? If they call, should I decline to interview?"

The playfulness vanishes from his face. "Hell, no. If you think it will be better for you, then do it. I'm proud of you no matter what."

"Thank you."

Three quick taps on the glass of the side door draw our attention. The knob twists and Carter slowly peeks inside.

"Geez," he moans, quickly averting his gaze, "are you ever *not* molesting my sister?"

Marcel rolls his eyes. "Come on in, why don't you?"

Carter glances at me. "Well, at least you're dressed."

"Watch it," Marcel growls.

Carter closes the door with a quiet click, turns, and grins at us. "See, that's why I like you, Teller. I can poke fun at *you* all day long, but if you think I'm dissing my sister"—he lifts his fists in the air and pretends to take a swing— "you're all over it."

"You could, oh, I don't know, not poke fun at *either* of us," I suggest.

"Nah, that's no way to live." Carter lifts his chin. A bit of seriousness flattens his lips. "How was your trial?"

Marcel winks and releases me. He roughs his hand over Carter's hair and pulls him into a headlock. "You should've led with that question. Your sister kicked ass today."

Carter struggles to extract himself from Marcel's choke hold. "Ugh, Char, why are you letting him abuse me?" Since he's laughing, I don't think he's as upset as he wants me to believe.

"Let go of me, Neanderthal." Carter swings his arm wildly toward the front of the house. "Your chickens are on a suicide mission. I tried herding them back here, but nooooo. They're biker's chickens, for sure. Yearning for the open road."

Marcel shakes so hard with laughter, he ends up releasing Carter. "The shit that comes out of your mouth, kid."

"Thought you'd appreciate that." Carter raises his eyebrows. "So? Tell me you wiped the floor with David?"

"So much so that he offered me a job at his firm."

Carter's eyes widen. "Seriously? That's not the kind of law you want to do, though. Is it?"

"Actually, he's recommending me to the hiring partner. It's not a firm offer, yet. They're looking for someone to do the firm's pro bono work." I shrug. "It sounded like I'd be doing the same kinds of cases, just with the benefit of a big firm behind me."

Carter's gaze shifts from Marcel to me. "Almost sounds too good to be true, Char."

"It does," I agree. "I'm not getting my hopes up. I'll see if they want to interview me and go from there."

My answer seems to reassure him. He nods and shuffles toward the door.

"You want to run down to Franklin's Butcher with me?" Marcel elbows Carter. "We'll get some steaks to celebrate."

"Sure." Carter screws his face into a frown. "I don't have to ride on the back of your bike, do I?"

Marcel rolls his eyes. "That's Charlotte's spot." He winks at me. "Forever."

Butterflies wake up and swoon inside me. Every damn time. "You know it."

After they leave, I head upstairs to change and tie my hair into a high ponytail. I run over my list of open cases, mentally adding and subtracting things from my ever-expanding to-do list. It would be such a relief to have someone else help me keep track of so many of these details.

Don't get ahead of yourself.

My hand strays to my stomach. Generous parental leave. That's crossed my mind multiple times. I have a plan for all of my clients in case I get pregnant—

You're getting ahead of yourself again.

Pushing those thoughts aside, I finish tugging on a pair of yoga pants, grab my sneakers, and head downstairs.

In the kitchen, I pull a container of blueberries out of the fridge and go outside.

Chickens cluck, squawk, and waddle toward me as I step into the side yard. "Come on," I encourage, tossing a few berries at them. "Backyard. You're *backyard* chickens," I remind them. "No more free-ranging if you're determined to explore the highway."

They cluck in disagreement but follow me to their backyard enclosure, where I toss the rest of the blueberries and lock the gate behind them. "Behave."

A loud buzz from the front of the house pulls me away from the chickens. I turn and cock my head, listening as the sound grows closer. Murphy's bike.

Smiling, I hurry out front to meet him.

"Where's Heidi?" I call out after he turns his bike off.

"A few minutes behind me." He lifts his chin. "Your chucklehead fiancé texted to say we're celebrating your courtroom domination."

Laughing, I duck my head. "He's exaggerating."

"He promised steaks. He better not have been exaggerating about *that.*"

"No." I tip my head back and stare at the darkening sky. "We probably won't be grilling outside much longer. Better enjoy it while we can."

"Pshh." He waves a dismissive hand. "Marcel will be out here grilling until the snow's up to his balls."

I smother my laughter with a hand over my mouth. "You're probably right."

The low rumble of Marcel's truck turns our heads toward the driveway. Behind his truck, I spot Heidi's Hellcat. "Gang's all here."

"You don't mind us coming over last minute?" Murphy asks.

"Never," I answer immediately. "Feels wrong to celebrate without you guys."

He hooks his thumbs in the front pockets of his jeans. "Now that your trial's over, are you ready to work your magic at the adoption?"

I reach up and squeeze his shoulder. "No magic necessary. It's going

119

to be fine." I pause. Never give an absolute yes to a client. It's not a done deal *yet*. "As soon as I can get a date set with the judge."

He nods but still seems troubled.

"It's not because of you. It can take a while to get on the judge's calendar. Totally normal."

"Okay."

Marcel's truck swings into his usual spot.

My brother jumps down from the truck first. "Hope you're hungry, Char. He bought like half a cow."

Marcel grabs two full brown paper bags from the back seat. "He's exaggerating." He leans down to kiss my cheek. "Miss me?"

"Always."

"Barf," Carter murmurs on his way past us.

"Bring these in and set them on the counter," Marcel says, shoving the bags in Carter's arms.

"Yeah, yeah, bossy."

Heidi's car shuts off and Murphy goes to help her out.

"I brought chicken!" Heidi shouts.

"Thicken!" Alexa repeats from her car seat.

"What'd you do that for?" Marcel asks.

"We're always eating your food," Heidi explains. "I thought I'd be polite and bring some for once."

"You didn't have to." I give her a quick hug. "But thanks."

She holds up a small brown paper bag. "I brought hot sauce too."

Murphy groans.

"Fuck." Marcel clutches his stomach. "You remember that time you made us 'barbeque chicken' with—"

"Straight ghost pepper sauce." Heidi hangs her head in shame. "I felt so bad."

"I thought I was going to die," Marcel says.

"I thought my stomach was going to exit my ass," Murphy adds.

Heidi's cheeks redden. "I was trying to do something nice. You guys were working all day. And I was really proud of myself for learning how to cook. I knew you liked chicken wings..."

"She bathed about ten pounds of wings in this death-by-Satan's-tongue pepper sauce," Murphy explains. "We didn't want to hurt her feelings, and we were so hungry that we ate it. Even though we were on fire." He holds out a fist like he's grasping a cup and mimes gulping it down. "We poured milk, water, soda, anything we could get down our throats. Nothing helped."

"Oh my God." Laughter spills out of me until tears leak from the corners of my eyes. "Poor Heidi."

"Poor Heidi?" Marcel raises his eyebrows in indignation. "What about poor *us*? We had to fight over one toilet."

I snort-giggle even harder.

"Took a year before I could even *look* at chicken wings again," Murphy says.

Marcel slaps his gut. "I bet it was sooner than that."

"Whatever." Murphy pushes his hand away.

Marcel approaches his sister with laughter in his eyes. "Let me see what you brought. Just in case you've got instruments of torture in there."

Heidi huffs and pulls a bottle of light green sauce out. "It's *creamy* jalapeño."

Marcel hooks his arm around her neck without looking at the bottle. "I'm just messing with you, lil' sis."

"A decade or so turned it into a funny story." Murphy rubs his stomach. "Sort of."

"Ugh." Heidi shoves the bag in Murphy's hands and turns to unbuckle Alexa from her seat.

"Daddy!" Alexa chirps, reaching for Murphy.

"No hellos for your favorite uncle?" Marcel teases.

Alexa scrunches her face, her gaze bouncing between her father and her uncle. She blows an exasperated noise and turns to Heidi.

Laughing, Heidi lifts her daughter. "Let's go see the chickens."

"They've been naughty, so they're locked in their pen," I warn them.

Marcel and I hang back while everyone else goes to see the chickens. I can't stop thinking of what I will now forever refer to as "Heidi's hot sauce story." The bond the three of them share runs deep. But the longer Marcel holds onto the truth about Rock being his father, the more damage it will cause when Heidi and Murphy finally find out.

I have to help him end this.

I'm a lawyer. I persuade people to agree with my position using just my words all the time.

Still feeling high from my courtroom victory, I curl my arms around his waist and hug him tight. "You know, with them here, maybe tonight's a good night to finally tell them the truth."

He glances down at me with a puzzled expression drawing his eyebrows down.

"Don't pretend you don't know what I'm talking about," I warn.

His gaze returns to Heidi and pain washes over his face. "Not tonight. We're having a good time. I don't want to ruin it."

"Marcel, I understand why you're struggling with this. I do. But there will never be—"

"Rock should really be here, don't you think?" he says quickly.

"So, call him. He's ten minutes away. I'm sure he'd come right now if you told him you were finally going to get this out in the open."

He shakes his head. "Carter's here." His voice hardens as he strengthens his argument. "What am I supposed to do, tell him to go home? That's not cool."

With that excuse, he pulls away from me and jogs over to the chicken coop. He picks Alexa up and growls monster noises, drawing high-pitched giggles out of her.

Damn. My lawyering skills failed me. Marcel's too stubborn.

For the first time in a long time, my persuasive words aren't enough.

CHAPTER FOURTEEN

Teller

THE DARK SKY DOESN'T HINT AT WHAT A GOOD DAY IT IS. GRINDER'S finally getting released from prison.

"Are you sure you don't want me to go with you?"

Irritation rolls off Rock's shoulders. I'm working his last nerve this morning. That's nothing new. Only thing different today is that I'm not taking the usual pleasure in it.

"No, too many people will probably make him twitchy." He lifts his chin. "Let me ease him into life on this side before he gets here and everyone's in his face."

Part of me wants to argue *I'm* the one who should be there to pick Grinder up. *I'm* the one who visited him for years when Rock wasn't able to go. But he's the president. It's his call.

I glance at the clubhouse. "We kept it small-ish. Just family. Trinity's been working on the menu for a week."

He huffs a laugh. "Have a feeling he'll be surprised to see her."

"You worried Grinder won't be pleased about the changes?"

"No." Rock's stare and voice turn distant. "This is what he always wanted the club to be."

"Think he'll be surprised you haven't killed me yet?"

I'm kidding, but Rock's expression turns troubled.

"Don't turn those pity eyes on me, Prez," I warn. "I was only joking."

"Pity eyes, my ass," he grumbles, shouldering past me to head for his SUV.

Big, fat, lazy snowflakes drift toward the ground.

"Watch the roads," I warn. "If you're going the back way, highway departments probably haven't salted them yet."

He stops and turns slightly. "Are you giving *me* driving advice? Who taught *you* how to ride?"

I shrug. "Sucks that it's such a shit day for him to get out."

"I'm sure he doesn't give a fuck about the weather. Freedom's the only thing on his mind today."

"Amen to that." I catch up to him at the SUV. My fingers curl around the edge of the door, stopping Rock from closing it.

He turns his head and raises an eyebrow. "You realize I'm in a hurry, right?"

"Yeah." I lean on the door harder. "Ah, is there any chance...does Grinder know? About us?"

His gaze scans the area over my shoulder before returning to my face. "You make it sound like a secret affair."

I snort. "That might be less complicated."

"Jesus," he mutters. "No, I don't have any reason to think he knows. Unless you told him on one of *your* visits?"

"No fucking way." The corner of his right eye twitches—a sign I've hurt or maybe surprised him? "I mean, I wouldn't bring that up there... or with anyone before I talk to...you know who."

His gaze slides away. Guilt? Something else? Whatever it is, Rock will never admit it. I release the door. "Go get him, Prez. Bring Grinder home. It's been a long time."

"See you soon."

He climbs into his SUV and throws me a quick wave as he drives away. Then I head inside the clubhouse. My gaze scans the room, seeking one person. A pale beam of sunlight filters through the window, landing on Charlotte, illuminating her red hair in its glow. Appropriate.

She turns. Her dark red lips curve into a smile. She raises her hand, giving me a slight wave.

Sparky blocks my path and shoves a blunt in front of my face.

"Emotional Palm Tree. Helps you release all those inner demons," he promises with a doofy smile.

"I've got better ways to release my demons, bro."

"Sex is the only other way." He palms his crotch and mimics an explosion bursting through his fingers. "The union of—"

"Yeah. Got it. Get out of my way." I straighten my arm, pushing him to the side, and continue toward Charlotte. More people move and my sister comes into view, her hands flailing in the air to punctuate their animated conversation. The corners of my mouth slide up. Then guilt creeps along the back of my throat. The regret clinging to me from my brief talk with Rock, or the same guilt that's been following me for almost a year now?

"Hey!" Charlotte bounces off the couch cushion and peers up at me. "I thought maybe you were going with Rock."

"Nah, he doesn't want to overwhelm Grinder."

Her mouth shifts into a sympathetic smile. "I hope all this is okay." She sweeps her arm toward the crowded clubhouse.

"Yeah, although Sparky and his Emotional Pineapples might not thrill Grinder."

"Emotional *Palm Trees*," Heidi corrects.

"You better not go near that stuff," I scold, gesturing toward her barely noticeable baby bump.

She rolls her eyes.

"You realize she's an adult who's already had one healthy baby, right? I think she knows what she's doing," Charlotte lectures me, using her lawyer voice.

"He can't help it, Charlotte." Heidi points to her left ear, then her right. "I'm able to tune him out with precision now."

The two of them snicker at my expense. I smother a smile. Nothing better than the most important women in my life joining together to razz my ass.

Groaning, I wrap my arms around Charlotte's waist and pull her closer. "Is this what I'm in for? Years of the two of you poking fun at me?"

"Decades." She loops her arms around my neck and reaches up on tiptoes to kiss my cheek. "And decades of verbal grenades lobbed your way."

"Can't wait." I lean down and catch her lips in a quick kiss.

"Ugh, my ears may have adjusted, but my eyes can't deal with the horror." Heidi stands and pushes past us. "I'm going to see if Trinity needs anything."

Charlotte pulls away, staring after my sister. "I should go help too—"

"No." I curl my fingers around hers. "Stay with me."

She tilts her head and studies my expression. "Everything okay? Are you nervous about seeing Grinder on the outside?"

Nervous isn't the right word. Guilty doesn't quite capture what I'm feeling either. I was a teenager when Grinder went inside. Not a whole hell of a lot I could've done to prevent it.

"You were just a kid," Charlotte says, as if she'd read my mind. "From the stories I've heard, you've done a lot to turn the club into what Grinder envisioned before he went inside."

I hum a noise of semi-agreement. Maybe that's what's bothering me. It'll be too many changes for Grinder.

Almost an hour and a half later, I catch Wrath slipping out the front door. I crane my neck to look out the window. "I think they're here."

A few minutes go by, and then they enter. I slap Murphy's arm. "Let's go."

Murphy leans into me as we approach. "He sure looks a hell of a lot better than he did last time I visited. Like he aged backward about ten years."

"Freedom will do that to you," I answer. "I'm just glad the parole board stopped jerking him around."

Mindful of what Rock said earlier, I wait until Rock and Z back away to introduce Grinder to Charlotte.

She clutches my hand tighter. "I'm so happy to finally meet you."

I watch in amusement as his eyes widen when they land on Heidi. "Jesus Christ, you've grown up."

Heidi reverts to her five-year-old self, blushing and ducking her head.

"You even remember who I am?" Grinder asks.

"Of course I remember you." She reaches up to give him a hug. "Welcome home, Grinder."

I swear his eyes water from the contact. Uncomfortable as hell to watch a man you've looked up to get emotional.

They introduce him to Alexa. "Well, don't you look just like your momma did."

Heidi beams. "You think so?"

"Absolutely," he answers. I seem to be the only one who notices the grief invading his voice. Going to prison ended his marriage, and he never had children. A bunch of rowdy bikers to discipline doesn't count.

CHAPTER FIFTEEN

Heidi

THE FRONT DOOR CLOSES WITH A SOLID CLICK. A SERIOUS AIR FOLLOWS Blake inside.

"Hey, how was church?"

"Fine." His gaze darts around the kitchen, but he doesn't ask what I'm making. "We need to talk."

"About?" I raise an eyebrow. "You seem tense. What's wrong?"

Blake rubs his hand over his beard for a second before meeting my eyes. "Serena's back… I don't know the details. But she's with Grinder and it sounds like they're serious."

"Wow, that's wild." It doesn't explain why he looks so…*guilty*. "Why are you being all twitchy about it?"

"I'm not *twitchy*." Blake shifts his weight from one foot to the other but holds my gaze. "I wanted to warn you so you're not surprised or upset or anything—that's all."

Is he for real? I slam the towel on the counter with an unsatisfying thwack. "You know, it's bad enough everyone else still acts like I'm the same sixteen-year-old brat who can't deal with complicated grown-up relationship stuff, but for *you* to do it too sucks extra hard."

His deep green eyes transform from concerned to amused. "You're being a *little* bratty right now," he points out, pinching his thumb and index finger together.

I fire a glare at him.

His teasing smile fades. "No one thinks that about you."

"Sure. Then why are you here telling me this like I'll go on a rampage if I run into your ex?"

"I can't help it." He gives me a helpless shrug that makes me want to kick him and hug him at the same time. "I love you and want to protect you from anything and everything."

I flash my ring finger at him—although I kinda want to flash a different finger. "I have the wedding rings." I sweep my arms around me in a wide circle. "The house." I rub my hands over my stomach affectionately. "Your spawn taking up space in my uterus. I'm a hundred percent secure about my place in your life, Blake." A worse thought occurs to me. "Are *you* upset about it?"

"No," he answers without hesitation. "Nothing like that. He seems *really* into her. Like, he tried to choke Steer for saying—"

"Ugh, what the hell did Steer say?" I can only imagine it was something crude and gross. "Why can't he mind his own business?"

"Exactly." Blake chuckles. "The old man's still got it. Practically lifted Steer off the ground with one hand."

A gasp slips past my lips. "Wish I'd seen that." Steer's a boulder of a guy. Then again, so is Grinder.

"Grinder's been through a lot," Blake says. "I want him to be happy."

My annoyance with Blake vanishes. I can never stay mad at him for long. I step into his space, and he curls his arms around me and kisses the top of my head.

"But I can't help it. *Your* happiness is always my priority," he whispers.

Sacrilege, some would say. The club should always come first. Even if Serena hooking up with Grinder bothered me, I'd be expected to keep my mouth shut and not cause the brothers any trouble. I nuzzle my cheek against his soft flannel shirt. "You always make me happy."

We stay that way for a few moments, holding each other. I pull away, my mind running over everything Blake said. "Grinder hasn't even been out of prison that long. How did they even meet? Serena hasn't been around the club for…months." The last time I remember seeing her was when Z took over Downstate.

"No idea." He shrugs. "It didn't seem like the time to ask lots of questions."

My nose wrinkles as I try to do the math. She's only a few years older than me. "He's, like, a *lot* older than her, isn't he?"

"Yeah." He smirks. "Don't say that to him. I think he's a bit sensitive about it."

"I won't." My mouth turns up. "At least *we* won't be the biggest age gap in the club now."

Instead of laughing, he cocks his head. "Does that bother you?"

"Not really." I wave off the question with a flick of my hand. "I'm kidding." Although now that I'm on this path, distant memories surface. "I know you think I'm too young to remember a lot of stuff. But I *do* remember Grinder from when I was little. I remember him telling Mom to knock her shit off and grow the fuck up."

He shifts and glances out the door. "Yeah. Teller trusted him a lot."

"I never understood why he and Rock were sent to prison or any of that stuff. But things went downhill after that, and I missed them." I shrug. "I missed being around the club, period. But you know all that."

He peers down at me and lifts an eyebrow. "And?"

"Fifteen years is a long time. Like, more than half of *my* life. I can't imagine what starting over after losing so much time feels like. How hard it must be."

"Club's been doing everything we can to help him."

"I know." A warm sensation spreads through my chest.

"Well, as much as he'll allow." Blake strokes his hand over his beard. "He's a grumpy son of a—"

"He's got plenty of reasons to be angry." I squint up at him. "Besides, can he really be grumpier than Wrath?"

"Definitely."

Laughter spills out of both of us for a second, then Blake turns serious. "I wasn't trying to upset you, beautiful. And I trust you can handle anything—"

"I know." I squeeze him again. The annoyance of a few minutes ago is replaced with love. It means a lot that Blake wanted to warn me, even if it might have been uncomfortable for him.

"Cookies!" Alexa stomps her little feet against the kitchen tiles. "Aunty T!"

Laughing, I pull away from Blake. "Yup, we're headed there in a minute."

Alexa scowls up at us. A minute isn't good enough. Blake leans over and scoops her into his arms, making her squeal with delight. "Settle down, Cookie Monster. The baked goods aren't going anywhere."

She narrows her eyes but Blake stares right back at her. After a second, she cups his cheeks and pops a loud kiss on his nose.

"Sure, Daddy gets nose kisses. *I* get attitude." I lean in and kiss Alexa's cheek. She grabs my hair in both hands and lands a sloppy kiss on my nose. "Aw, thank you."

"Okay, coat." Blake sets her down. "And boots. Meet me at the front door in five."

Alexa races to find her things and get there first.

"Hey." I grab Blake's hand as he leaves to follow Alexa.

He raises his eyebrows.

"Thank you."

"For?"

"Being you. Giving me a heads-up. Not letting me walk in blind." I take a breath. "All of the above."

"You and me." He holds out his fist and I tap my knuckles against his. "We're a team."

"Team O'Callaghan," I whisper.

"You know it." He presses a quick kiss to my forehead and swats my behind. "Now, let's move out before Cookie Monster has a meltdown."

CHAPTER SIXTEEN

Teller

EXCEPT FOR A FEW BUMPS, GRINDER'S RETURN HAS GONE BETTER THAN any of us expected. Although, due to his parole restrictions and intense relationship with Serena, we don't see him all that often. After church, he's usually quick to hurry away from the clubhouse.

"If I'd been without pussy for fifteen years, I'd be nailing everything with legs," Ravage says one afternoon as Grinder's truck tears down the driveway. "Not settling down with the first hot chick who bounced on my dick."

"You already nail anything that moves," Dex points out. "I think you violated a girl's sweater at the last party."

Rav reaches down to scratch his balls. "It was something scratchy, for sure."

I stand and distance myself from Rav's ball-scratching hands. "This has been…disturbing. But I have my own hot chick waiting for me."

"A miracle." Rav wags a finger at me. "You better get on your knees and thank that woman for putting up with you."

"I plan to."

Dex holds out his fist. "Catch you later."

I tap his knuckles and say my goodbyes.

As I'm trying to escape, I bump into Rock.

"Can we talk for a second?" he asks.

My gaze strays to the ATV I was planning to ride through the woods back to my house. "Yeah, sure."

"Let's get away from the clubhouse." He tips his head in the direction of his cabin.

"All right." I follow him onto the path leading to his place. He's quiet, which isn't so unusual. But the air around him weighs heavy around us.

By the time we're seated at his kitchen table, I'm ready to come out of my skin. "What's up, Rock?"

"Where we at with the DNA testing?" he asks. "Are we going in for a second round or not?"

Fuck. Right. One of my brilliant stalling tactics when we got the news was telling Rock I wanted to take another DNA test before we revealed our relationship to anyone. I thought it'd buy me some time to adjust but instead I've thrown myself into club business and tried to ignore the looming confrontation. I open my mouth to protest my need for more time, but he steamrolls right over me.

"It's been *months*. The club's in a good place. Heidi's done with school. Blake's out of the hospital. Wedding's over. They're not on the road with Rooster and Shelby anymore. What are we waiting for *now?*" His solemn tone is all curiosity and fatherly concern. No hint of the stern presidential lecture I expected.

"Shit, Rock." I run my hands through my hair, unprepared for this discussion. What's a good excuse to give him today?

He stands and goes over to the coffee maker, measuring out enough for a full pot and adding water. "Grinder seems to think we could be brothers instead of father and son." He tosses out the idea like it's a softball instead of a fucking grenade.

Shock rolls down my spine. He shared our connection with Grinder? Without asking me?

"You told him?" I can't examine the second part of what he said yet.

"He'll keep it a secret." He cocks his head. "You realize, at this point, more people know than don't, right? The longer we hide this from Heidi, the more hurt it will cause when we finally tell her." He levels another stern stare at me. "And she'll find out eventually. One way or another. Every secret has an expiration date, and this one is perilously close."

I fucking hate that he's right, even if I won't admit it. "Well, I'm not the one going around telling everyone, now, am I?"

"Wrath figured it out on his own."

I cross my middle and index fingers together in front of my face. "You two are freakishly close."

He shrugs. "He cares in his own way."

"What about Z?" Because if Wrath knows, then Rock probably told Z too.

Rock turns and leans against the counter, crossing his arms over his chest—completely unapologetic. "He *almost* figured it out on his own. I told him because I was trying to help him reconcile his feelings about Lilly keeping Chance from him."

"Yeah, I figured," I grumble. Z's known all this time and hasn't said a word. I can't decide if I appreciate him trying to respect my privacy or if I want to kick his ass. No wonder he didn't choke me to death when I was acting like an ass to Lilly. The fucker knew *exactly* what was setting me off.

"Brothers, huh? Our family tree gets more snarled every time we shake another branch." I cock my head. "What made Grinder suggest that?"

"Some things he remembered about my father." He shakes his head, a hint of disgust clouding his expression. "For what it's worth, *I* don't think that's the case. I respect Grinder, but he's not a fucking scientist. He might've been trying to make me feel better about the situation."

"How would knowing you *and* your dad nailed the same woman be helpful?"

He groans. "Can we cut the shit and get serious for a moment?"

"I *am* serious. Did he like walk in on them or something? Why'd he go *there?*"

Rock ignores my obvious attempts to steer the conversation somewhere—anywhere—else. "Marcel, what's holding you up now? Let's figure out the barrier so we can remove it."

"You need to stop reading Hope's self-help books."

He drills me with a not-fucking-around stare.

"Okay, fine. Heidi's pregnant. I don't want to be responsible for something happening to the baby if I upset her." Given how Hope ended up in the hospital after delivering the news to *us*, Rock should understand where I'm coming from.

He lets out a long, slow, irritated breath. "There will always be an excuse."

Oh, fuck no. "Did you forget what happened to Hope when she told us?"

His jaw flexes, like he's thinking of choking me. "It's not the same."

"The hell it's not."

Rock closes his eyes for a second, probably counting backward from ten. "All right. We've waited this long. But this can't go on forever."

Suspicious of how fast he's letting this go, I stare at him. "That's it?"

"What do you want from me, Marcel? I'm doing the best I can here. You know damn well when this gets out, the fact that we've held onto it so long will hurt people." He squeezes his hands into fists. "I feel like an accessory to a crime, and I don't like it."

"Well, I didn't ask for this either."

Some days, I wish we'd never found out.

CHAPTER SEVENTEEN

Teller

Since Grinder already knows that Rock's my father—or related to me in some way—I catch up with him at the next clubhouse bonfire.

"You seem to be more comfortable hanging around here now," I point out.

"New parole officer isn't up in my business as much." He glances across the clearing at the girls, his gaze landing and staying on Serena. "Damn happy we got Grillo out of the picture."

"Yeah." Grinder's release from prison hasn't been as smooth as we'd all hoped it would be. His first parole officer was a bigger criminal than the criminals he supervised.

He glances at me. "What's weighing you down tonight?"

I lift an eyebrow. "Nothing." *Liar. Just talk to him.* I used to go to Grinder for advice all the time when I was a kid. Why does it feel awkward now? "Remember when you and Lucky taught me how to drive stick?" I ask.

The corners of his mouth curl slightly. "You wanted to restore the club's old beater truck, but your skinny little ass didn't even know how to work a clutch."

"Almost every vehicle's an automatic now," I say, as if it even matters.

He flexes his right hand and rolls his shoulder. "Probably a blessing for me."

I sip my beer and stare into the fire. The pull of the past and my present dilemma leave me with a need to search for answers. I haven't stopped thinking about the possibility Rock and I are brothers instead of father and son since he mentioned it.

Grinder's also staring into the fire. Like the story left him filled with regret instead of fond memories. Now I feel like shit for bringing it up. It's not like me to beat around the bush.

"How'd you stand prison?" The two situations aren't even remotely the same. But going to prison was something out of Grinder's control. And *out of control* is how I've felt every day since I learned Rock was my father. Events that happened before I was even born have somehow gotten a stranglehold on my life.

He shakes himself out of his trance. "What?"

"The whole club knew you had nothing to do with Lucky's death," I explain. He has to know none of us ever blamed him, right? "How'd you stand it? Fifteen years inside for something you didn't do would drive some people insane."

Grinder stares at me with hard eyes. Obviously, he doesn't appreciate the question. I don't look away or apologize. The answer's too important.

"Didn't *get* fifteen years at first," he reminds me.

"Yeah, but you never would've had the extra time added if you hadn't been there in the first place." I wave my hand toward the flames. "If Ruger hadn't asked you to take out those punks."

Another death glare. I'm begging for an ass-kicking if I keep it up. Ex-cons, especially biker ex-cons, are notorious for guarding their prison stories. No brother wants to reminisce about his time inside with someone who hasn't served hard time. My stint in juvie doesn't count.

After a short staring match, he reluctantly opens his mouth. "The first sentence I was able to swallow. Had a lot of guilt over Lucky's death. I survived. He didn't. Besides, I'd done plenty of shit by that point in my life that *could've* gotten me locked up. I deserved to be there. Karma had finally caught up with me."

"Like what?"

Grinder's jaw shifts. His cold eyes bore into mine. "You know better than to ask a brother a question like that."

"We don't lie or hide those kinds of truths from each other."

Especially not about deeds done to protect the club.

"You want details? Fine." He huffs and stares at the sky for so long, I'm about to crack a "how long is the list" joke, when he continues. "The clown your mom was dating back then. The one you asked Lucky and me to scare away?"

"Yeah, what about him?"

"We beat the ever-loving shit out of him to provide the motivation. The kind of beating that could've netted me three-to-five, easily."

That doesn't surprise or bother me. "He fuckin' deserved it."

"We both know that wouldn't have been a defense."

"You still didn't deserve to—"

"Don't talk to me about what I did or didn't deserve." He squeezes his fists tight, then opens his hands and stares at them. "What do you want me to do, Marcel? Live life in reverse? Keep on regretting all the time I lost so I ruin the time I have left?"

"No. Fuck no." A cold drop of doubt extinguishes a few flames of my curiosity. "That's not what I'm trying to do."

"Then what's your end goal here? What's with the questions?"

What *am* I hoping to accomplish? Grinder's been through enough heartache. Why am I trying to poke at his scars? "I want to know how you handled it. How you stopped the regret from eating you alive. How you regained control and made sense of it."

"I just told you, dipshit." He slices his hand through the air in front of him. "Look forward to the future. Leave the past where it belongs." His gaze shifts to the side. "I want to focus on my girl and make a life with her."

My mouth quirks and I quickly glance down. *No fucking kidding he moved fast with Serena.* But I've said enough shitty stuff tonight. So, I manage to bite back the joke threatening to leap off my tongue. He seems at peace around her. That's all that should matter.

"Speaking of," he continues, "you got a beautiful firecracker you're engaged to. I'm looking forward to attending my first post-incarceration Lost Kings' wedding. Why the fuck you dragging your feet?"

I've held back as long as I can. "We can't all sprint to the altar as fast as you're trying to do, Grandpa."

"Altar," he grumbles. "Ain't quite there, yet."

"We all see it coming a mile away."

He rolls his eyes instead of throat-punching me. Considering all the muscle he's put on since he got out, it's a good thing he keeps his fists clenched at his sides instead of launching one at my jaw.

"We were talking about your wedding," Grinder prompts. "Come on. Entertain me."

"I'm not dragging my feet. She's planning things the way she wants them." *Sure. Keep telling yourself that.*

"You're dragging your feet in other areas, though, aren't you?" he asks in a low voice.

I cast a quick glance around.

"No one's listening to us. I might seem like an insensitive asshole, but I get why you're hanging onto this one, Marcel."

"Do you? Because I don't." That's one truth I wasn't able to voice to Rock. "I'm not ashamed, if that's what you're thinking. Well, not of him. My mother, yeah."

"She was a kid too, don't forget."

I glare at him. "Not that much of a kid."

He grunts in disagreement. "What are you so worried about? Club won't care if you're blood related. None of their fuckin' business anyway."

I'm not so sure I agree with that. The club members could start examining each interaction, assignment, or punishment differently once they know I'm the president's son. But that's far down on my list of concerns.

"I don't know what it will do to Heidi and me." I search the shadowy area. Between two pine trees, I make out the shape of Blake and Heidi's tent. They can't hear us from way over there.

"Or you and Blake?" Grinder asks in a low rumble.

"I—yeah, I guess." I keep telling myself he won't care and it won't change anything. But that's a lie.

"The longer you drag it out, the more it's gonna hurt." He follows my gaze. "The greater the risk of losing both of them."

That's one truth I can't escape or mitigate.

"Trust me, son." He claps a large hand over my shoulder, a warm contrast to the cool night air. "There's no prison lonelier than the one you create for yourself."

CHAPTER EIGHTEEN

Charlotte

I CAN BARELY KEEP MY EYES OPEN BY THE TIME HEIDI DROPS ME OFF AT the house. She yawns as she puts the car in park. Even though we followed Hope and Trinity most of the way up the Thruway, the drive felt like it took forever.

"Do you want to come in?" I offer.

She glances at the back seat, where Alexa promptly passed out as soon as we hit the highway. "Better not," she whispers. "Hopefully Blake's already home and can help me get her out of the car."

"He should be."

"Today was fun, right? I think Serena was really surprised."

My lips quirk. Serena's baby shower had been a success. "It was smart to have it at Lilly and Z's place. Serena didn't see it coming."

Heidi glances at the steering wheel, digging her thumbnail into the leather over and over. "I hope it helped her feel…included."

"I think it did." Too tired to examine it further, I pull the door handle. "We'll talk tomorrow."

"Okay. Thanks for riding home with me."

"No problem."

The porch light flickers, drawing our attention to the front door. Marcel stands under the bright glow and lifts his arm in a quick wave.

"Tell him why I want to get home." Heidi squirms in her seat. "Also, I have to pee."

Chuckling, I push my door open. "You want to come inside? I'll wait in the car with Alexa."

"No, go ahead."

"All right." I hop out and slam the door, waiting until she pulls away to head up the stairs.

"She okay?" Marcel asks, meeting me on the porch.

"Baby bladder," I explain.

He follows me into the house and takes my purse from my hands, setting it on the bench in the hallway. "I missed you."

"I missed you too," I admit with more emotion than I expected thinning my voice.

"How was it?" he asks gently, walking me into our living room.

"It sucked." I hate the pout in my voice. But I've been holding it in all day, and Marcel's the only one who will understand.

"Come here." He pulls me into his lap and I curl up against him. He presses a kiss to my forehead. "I shouldn't have let you go."

In his arms, I can finally relax and breathe. "I *had* to be there. I want Serena to feel welcomed. I'm just…prickly. I don't want to feel like this, but I can't help it."

He sighs and reaches over to flick on the lamp. "I wish you'd talk to the girls."

"After all this time? What's the point?"

"Do you want to talk to *someone*?"

"I'm talking to *you*." I pick my head up. "Oh, your sister rammed her whole foot down her throat, saying how easy Hope's pregnancy was. I thought Hope was going to cry for a second."

"Aw, shit. She probably felt awful. You know how much she worships Hope."

"I know. I was about to lose it myself, so I'm afraid I didn't help. I ducked out for a minute. By the time I came back, everyone seemed okay." I chuckle. "Well, except Shelby. Once the girls got to birthing stories, she jetted the fuck out of the room with Trinity."

He rumbles with laughter.

"We basically unloaded a baby store's worth of stuff on them. I don't think Grinder knew what half the things were."

"He's gonna learn," he says with a low chuckle.

"Serena's sweet," I say, remembering the affectionate way she cradled her bump and spoke about the baby. "I hate that I felt so...*jealous*. I mean, they haven't been together that long. I don't even think they were trying to get pregnant and *poof!*"

He stares straight ahead. "She's had a lot of losses too. So, I want to be happy for both of them, but I know what you mean." He squeezes me tighter and looks down at me. "Hey, you know that idea I had for a new club business?"

"Taking over Cedarwood Funeral Home?" I sit straighter, relieved to occupy my mind with something other than self-pity. "Cementing the club's foothold in my hometown?"

He frowns slightly. "Does that bother you?"

"Hell no. I love the delicious irony of the Lost Kings running the Wolf Knights' territory. I wish my uncle was around so you could rub it in his face."

He shakes with laughter. "I'm sure Merlin knows. He went nomad, not into witness protection."

"Good." I laugh. "I hope he's seething about it up and down the East Coast. Or wherever the hell he's riding."

"So vindictive, Sunshine." He kisses my cheek. "I like it."

After we stop laughing, he turns serious again. "I'm going to bring it to the table tomorrow. Rock already knows, obviously. I'll discuss it with him first—"

"Wait, does Murphy know?"

He flinches. "Not yet."

"Hmm."

"What's that *hmm* for?"

"Nothing."

He continues staring at me and I relent. "Shouldn't you talk to him about it too?" I gently suggest. "He's the VP now."

"Yeah, but I'm the treasurer. Money stuff is my area." He shrugs. "He'll find out tomorrow."

"Okay," I answer with uncertainty.

CHAPTER NINETEEN
Teller

"YOU SURE I CAN BRING THIS TO THE TABLE TODAY?" I ASK ROCK OVER A cup of coffee at his dining table the next morning. I glance at Z, who was already here when I arrived. Most of Downstate came with him and I'm not sure I actually want to discuss my plan in front of our Downstate brothers. But Z was our vice president for years so excluding him feels wrong. And with him sitting right here, I can't think of a way to explain my reservations to Rock.

"How solid is your plan?" Rock asks.

"Just an idea so far. I have the place in mind. Guy's mortgaged up to his ears. Business has been in the family for generations. He wants to keep it. Good investment for us." I lift my chin at Z. "If it works, we can look for another one downstate."

Z studies the smooth hardwood table in front of him, slowly tapping his fingers over the surface for a second. "I don't know if I've got the bodies. Excuse the pun." He taps the side of his head. "Or the collective brainpower to run that kind of operation. Rooster's my brightest bulb, and he's spread thin as it is. Jigsaw...I think he'd enjoy the job a little too much."

"Hire someone." I shrug. "You don't need to know dick about the business itself. Find someone desperate for cash and willing to look the other way when we need to utilize the facilities."

Rock sits back and sighs. "It's not like we'll be burning bodies every damn day."

"The need seems to arise more often than I like to think about," Z says.

"All right." Rock slaps the table and stands. "Let's discuss it in church."

The three of us walk through the woods toward the clubhouse. Rock and Z trade barbs. I hang back, barely listening to their banter.

"Why so quiet?" Z asks, stopping a few paces from the clubhouse steps for me to catch up.

"Didn't want to get in the way of you insulting each other."

"Aw." Z slaps my cheek. "It's okay. I got insults for you too, little buddy."

"Get off me." I swat his hand away. "At least you two balance each other out. Grim Reaper." I nod at Rock. "And the clown show." I jerk my thumb toward Z.

Rock snorts.

"Did he just call me a clown?" Z asks with a smirk.

"Indeed," Rock says.

"Disrespectful little shit," Z grumbles. "If Rock's the Grim Reaper, what the fuck does that make Wrath?"

The door to the clubhouse slams.

"The fucking Devil himself," Wrath shouts before launching himself at Z, landing on his back and riding him like a dragon.

"Fucking hell," Z yells. "You trying to cripple me?"

Wrath lands on the ground, gravel crunching under his boots. "Where you been?"

"My place," Rock answers. "I sent you a text."

Wrath slips his phone out and checks the screen. "Missed it."

Rock grunts but doesn't reprimand his SAA. Now, if that were me, I'd get an ass-chewing.

Inside, the clubhouse is quieter than normal.

"They're in the dining room," Wrath says, reading Rock's expression.

"Get 'em down here," Rock orders.

I'm brimming with energy. Under the table, my leg's bouncing up and down. I'm eager to get through the boring parts of church so I can share my new business plan.

Finally, it's my turn.

"All right." Rock nods at me. "Teller's got an investment to discuss."

I sit forward, resting my elbows on the table. "I haven't been able to get confirmation from Whisper, but it looks like Wolf Knights are completely clear of Slater County."

"What about your uncle-in-law?" Wrath asks. "You try reaching out to Merlin?"

"No," I answer with all the slow sarcasm I can muster. "That never occurred to me."

Wrath smirks.

"I've left him a few messages. He's supposed to be at our wedding." As much as I hate Charlotte's uncle, I wouldn't deny him the chance to attend.

"What's the investment?" Sparky asks. "We can't have a grow house way out in Slater. I won't be able to split my time and give the plants enough love—"

Rock holds up his hands, stopping Sparky's freak-out in its tracks. "Easy. This is the only grow op we're running, Sparky."

"Phew. Okay. Thanks, boss."

I raise an eyebrow and scan the other brothers at the table, silently asking if I can continue without any other outbursts. "There's this funeral home in—"

"What the fuck?" Bricks asks with wide, disgusted eyes. "Why would we get involved in *that*?"

"Simmer down and listen," Rock snaps.

"They have a crematorium," I explain. "Grandfathered in, so we don't have to go through the red tape of getting permits and everything."

"Uh…" Ravage raises his hand. "Why do we want a crematorium?"

"Probably to burn the bodies of our enemies." Wrath taps his skull. "Just off the top of my head."

Rock closes his eyes for a second. Inhales a long, slow breath. When I'm sure his head isn't about to explode, I continue.

"It's a good way to wash cash since Crystal Ball is still in decline." I nod to Dex. Apparently, in the past, I've been insensitive about how hard Dex has worked to build our strip club's business. "I know you're doing everything you can there, brother."

Dex shrugs. "Never hurts to diversify. Honestly, this sounds like a great idea. Puts us closer to our support club's territory, too."

"Don't think I've ever heard of an MC owning a funeral home." Stash nods along. "Kinda badass."

"I'm sure we won't be the first to think of it, but yeah, it's not something that will be on the radar of law enforcement," I agree.

Wrath rubs his hands together. "There's so much markup in all that death shit. It's a great idea."

"And on the rare occasion we need to permanently…dispose of someone, it'll be a lot easier to turn 'em to ash instead of worrying about chemicals and burial sites," Z adds.

"Gee, Prez, you're awful morbid under that pretty-boy exterior," Rooster quips.

"Careful, Rooster." Z wags a finger between Rooster and Jigsaw. "I haven't decided which one of you will run our funeral home if we decide to buy one, too, down the road."

Rooster shudders. "Hard pass, Prez."

Jigsaw's scary face folds into an even scarier frown. "Yeah, I realize you think I'd be a good candidate for that job, but I'm gonna pass too."

"You'll do whatever the fuck I ask you to do." Z's expression lacks his usual humor. "But it's a non-issue for now. We'll see how it goes for Upstate first."

"So who's running this place?" Murphy asks.

"The current owner. Nothing will change operations-wise," I explain.

"I'll expect my VP to make an appearance once in a while." Rock nods at Murphy, then to me. "And my treasurer to work the books. But otherwise, we'll be hands off."

"Thank fuck," Bricks mutters.

"You scared of funeral homes, bro?" Wrath asks.

"Not scared." Bricks cocks his head and seems to search for the right explanation. "Just not eager to anger the spirits."

"Damn right, brother." Sparky slaps Bricks on the shoulder. "Healthy respect for the dead."

"This isn't about disrespecting the dead," I assure my two apparently superstitious brothers. "It's business. A place to clean our cash and maybe burn an extra body or two once in a while."

"Gnarly," Stash mumbles.

"We'll be helping out an old family business in our new territory," I add in my most convincing tone.

Next to me, Murphy chuckles. I glance at Rock and he nods.

"That's a plus," Dex says. "Build up some goodwill. Gives us a stake in Slater County."

"Right," I confirm.

"Do we need to take a vote?" Rock asks, sitting forward.

Bricks raises one hand. "Whatever Teller needs to make the deal work."

"Second," Murphy says.

Everyone else voices their yes vote.

I indulge in a mental fist pump. *Fuck yes.* I'm looking forward to a new challenge. Something that will benefit my club and keep my mind occupied.

"All right. Thank you, Teller." Rock slaps the table. "Anyone else?" His gaze moves up and down the table, offering each of us a chance to discuss whatever's on our minds.

Sparky squirms and stares at the door.

"Got somewhere else to be?" Wrath asks.

"I left brownies in the oven," he whines.

"You better not be baking pot brownies in the clubhouse kitchen," Murphy warns. "You promised. Not with the kids around."

"No." Sparky gestures wildly in the direction of the garages and his new building. "Kitchen's done."

"Great, he gets a bakery and immediately burns it down," Z groans.

"Willow's over there," Stash says. "She won't let the brownies burn."

"He just wants to be the first one to *eat* all the brownies," Rav says.

Dex points at Sparky. "Now *that* sounds plausible."

"Brownies aside, does anyone have any other *business* to bring to the table?" Rock asks.

When no one raises their hand, Rock sweeps his arm toward the door, releasing us from church.

ROCK

After church, I normally would've hung around to talk to everyone.

But the constant stress of holding onto this secret leaves me too irritable to waste an afternoon at the clubhouse.

Unfortunately, I'm stopped about a hundred times on my journey from the war room to sweet escape.

"Cool plan," Dex says, nodding at me as I pass the bar. "The funeral home."

Out of all the brothers, Dex is the least likely to annoy me, so I stop. "I think it'll be a good partnership." And I'm damn proud of my son for coming up with the idea and doing all the initial legwork. Of course, I can't say *that* or show him too much favoritism at the table.

Rav ambles up to us and leans on the bar, reaching over it to pull a can of Coke from a bucket full of ice on the counter.

"How do you do it, Prez?" Rav asks, popping the tab on the soda. "Don't you get bored? Restless? Can't do what you want, whenever you want with a family tying you down."

I steal a glance at Dex and he shrugs like he has no idea either.

"Actually, I can," I answer. "When what *I* want is to spend time with them as much as possible."

He stares, the concept obviously not sinking in.

"I wasted enough of my life doing *whatever*." I flick my hand in the air. "This *is* what I want now." I tap my fist against my chest. "They make me happy."

His face pinches, like he's really struggling to understand. It's the only reason I haven't punched him and walked away from this conversation. "It's okay if *you* don't want that, Rav," I say with more patience than I'm feeling. "It's okay if you never want a family. Just be honest about it. With yourself and whoever you're involved with."

His mouth slides sideways.

"And don't judge your brothers who want something different from you," Dex adds.

"That's just it," Rav says, ignoring Dex. "I don't want to be involved with anyone for long. I always get bored."

"Maybe if you stopped *lying* to girls to get in their pants, that wouldn't be an issue," Dex offers. "They'd know you weren't interested in them as actual human beings and avoid you like the plague."

I smother a laugh.

"I don't *lie*," Rav insists. "I'm genuinely interested…until I get in a woman's pants."

Dex shakes his head. "Well, at least you admit it. That's a start."

I've run out of patience for Ravage's internal crisis. I've got plenty of my own to keep me occupied. "You got this, Dex?" I slap his shoulder, tagging him in as relationship counselor for the afternoon.

"Yeah, Prez. Go see your girls," he says, a note of sadness creeping in on the last words.

"You all right, brother?" I ask in a quiet tone.

"I'm good." He jerks his head toward the door. "I'll catch you later."

I thump him once on the back, then slip away.

There's a squeak behind me, and a heavy *thump, thump, thump* down the front steps, a crunch of boots landing in gravel. I ignore whoever it is and keep moving toward the path that will take me home.

"Rock!" Rav catches up to me.

I stop and turn. "What's wrong?"

"I wasn't trying to disrespect Hope or Grace."

"I know you weren't." *Otherwise, I would've knocked you out.*

"Okay. I just wanted to make sure you knew that." His gaze shifts toward the woods. "They coming back with you?"

"Maybe later."

He nods once, then jerks his thumb over his shoulder. "Birch, Hoot, and I are going down to the new clubhouse."

"That's why we built it."

"You haven't picked out a room there, yet."

I cock my head and cross my arms over my chest, confusion about the conversation leaving me searching for something to say. "I thought the whole point was, you guys wanted a place that wasn't *family friendly* as I think you put it."

"Yeah, but you're still our prez." He shrugs and stuffs his hands in his pockets. "Ol' ladies can visit, like during the day and stuff, for family club days or whatever."

I fight back a hundred different sarcastic retorts. "All right. If you mean that, set something up."

He blinks quickly. "Like what?"

"A club family event." I shrug. "What about Halloween? Kids won't be there late, then you can do whatever deviant shit sets your pants on fire."

He smirks, then turns serious again. "How do I do that?"

"You're smart. Figure it out. Get in touch with Hustler, so Upstate and Downstate can plan it together. Have Murphy help you with the family part. Talk to Teller for the funding."

"I can do that." He frowns. "Halloween's a few months away. You're really not going to come by until then?"

I'm not sure why it's so important to him but my brother seems to be wrestling with something. "When do you want me to visit?"

"You're the prez, you can come whenever you want."

I'm aware.

"All right, I'll try to get over there this week," I promise.

"Cool!"

Satisfied I've given Ravage something to occupy his apparently limitless free time, I tilt my head toward the woods. "Can I go now?"

"Yeah, yeah. Sorry."

"It's all right." I put my thumb and pinky up to my ear. "You need something you can always call me."

"Who talks on the phone these days?"

I roll my eyes skyward. *Why do I bother?* "Then text me, send a note by pigeon, or some smoke signals, whatever the fuck works for you."

"Deal." He grins and salutes me.

Shaking my head, I continue my walk home.

The crisp forest air clears my head. By the time I reach home, I'm calmer. Looking forward to an afternoon with my wife and daughter.

I swear to fuck if anyone decides to show up unannounced, I'm going to shoot them.

I step in the front door, toe off my shoes, and drape my cut over the entryway bench. Downstairs is empty and still. Happy chatter from above draws my attention. I jog up the stairs, following the sweet chirps from my daughter and my wife's high-pitched, enthusiastic responses.

A bright glow spills from our bedroom, leading me to the left. All the lamps are lit, and blinds lifted, sunlight pouring in. A good sign.

"What color do you want?" Hope asks. "This one or that one?"

"Dat!" Grace's happy giggles follow.

"Green. Excellent choice. Look at all this hair."

More giggles.

I stop in the bathroom doorway, leaning against the frame to take in the scene. Grace sitting on the bathroom counter, facing the mirror. Hope standing behind her with a green bow clenched between her teeth while she tries to tame Grace's fine curls into a ponytail.

"What do you think?" Hope asks Grace when she's finished.

Grace pats the top of her head and stares in the mirror. My lips quirk at my little girl's serious expression.

"Too tight?" Hope asks.

Grace bobs her head.

"Okay. Let's try a different one."

"Nooooo," Grace wails as Hope unwinds the bow.

Hope reties the bow looser. "Better?"

"Yef."

"Good. Can Mommy get ready now?" Hope picks up a teardrop-shaped sponge and leans closer to the mirror, gently dabbing her face. She gently bops Grace on the nose and cheeks with it, pulling more giggles from my daughter.

"Dada!" Grace shouts, turning my way.

Hope jumps and drops the sponge in the sink, but she's nothing but smiles as I step into the bathroom.

"How long have you been watching us?" she asks, draping her arms over my shoulders and leaning up to kiss my cheek.

"I could watch you two together like this all day long." I press my lips to hers for another quick kiss, then nod to her makeup and stuff scattered all over the counter. "But why don't I give you a break?"

Her lips curve. "She already picked her outfit. It's the floral one on the bed."

"Done." I scoop Grace off the counter, holding her high, then pulling her in for a kiss. Repeating the back-and-forth motion while she squeals with happiness.

I drop her into the middle of our bed and she scampers over to the tiny outfit, lifting both pieces in the air and waving them at me.

I stare at the bright green top scattered with big, orange and yellow flowers and matching shorts. "Bold choice."

She bobs her head and thrusts the outfit into my hands.

"You okay?" I ask Hope after I finish wrestling Grace into the two pieces.

"Yes," Hope murmurs, leaning close to the mirror to stroke mascara over her lashes.

"Who're you getting dolled up for?"

"Myself."

All right then.

"Does Grace need a snack?" I ask.

"Sure. I sliced some pears earlier and there's a tub of ricotta in the fridge."

"Done." I lift Grace into my arms. She laughs and traces her fingers over my cheeks. "All right, giggle machine, snack time."

By the time Hope joins us downstairs, Grace has destroyed three pear slices with cheese. Roughly half ended up in her belly, the other half on her face. Little dots of cheese even made it into her hair.

"Good stuff, huh?" I set her on the counter next to the sink, to take off her bib and clean her face.

"No." She pushes my hands away when I dab at her with a paper towel.

Hope chuckles and leans against the counter, watching us with a smile.

"You want to go around with a dirty face all day?" I ask my daughter.

She scrunches her nose but lets me finish.

I turn and sweep my gaze over Hope's bright pink leggings and black tank top. "You look pretty."

"Thanks." She tugs at the hem of the top. "How was church?"

"Good. Teller brought his idea to the table." I toss the paper towel away and set Grace down. She curls her little arms around my leg. "It went well. Although apparently Bricks is a bit superstitious."

She laughs. "I can understand why it would seem creepy at first."

"Rav tracked me down after to complain that I haven't been to the new clubhouse enough."

"Aw, I thought he didn't want the married folk invading the Den of Sin?"

"That's what I said." I tap my hand against the still-warm coffee pot and pour what's left into my mug. "I tasked him with organizing a family-friendly Halloween party."

She laughs even harder. "So, you punished him by giving him work to do?"

I smile into my coffee cup. "Sure. Why not?"

"You're diabolical, Mr. President."

I set the mug on the counter and fill a water bottle instead. "I think I'll go downstairs and work out. Join me?"

"Which room?" She lifts an eyebrow.

I drop my gaze to Grace who's wide awake and curious about everything. "The gym."

Is that disappointment pulling Hope's mouth down?

I bend over to pick up Grace and hold my hand out to Hope.

Downstairs, I duck into the laundry room in search of a clean pair of gym shorts. When I enter the gym Hope and Grace are sitting on a large, thick blue mat in front of the wall-length mirror. I can't remember the name of the pose, but Hope has the soles of her feet together, legs in a diamond shape and her hands curled around her feet, gently leaning forward. Grace follows her mother's movements for a second or two then rolls to her back, throwing her feet in the air and laughing.

"Giggle monster is right." Hope stretches her fingers and tickles Grace's toes.

This is infinitely better than an awkward afternoon at our new clubhouse.

"Come here." I sweep Grace into my arms and settle onto the weight bench. "You're the perfect size for this."

"Dada!" she giggles and squeals as I lift her up and down.

After a few reps, I sit up and study Hope, standing sideways in front of the mirror, examining herself with a critical eye I don't care for.

I set Grace down and walk up behind Hope, cupping her hips and turning her to face the mirror. "What's with the frown?" I ask.

"Nothing." She runs her hands over her stomach and wrinkles her nose.

I rest my hand over hers, stopping her movement. "Any changes look real fucking good on you."

"I'm not fishing for compliments."

"I'd rather you were," I answer honestly.

"I know it's stupid." She blows out a sad breath. "My mother was always so hyper-critical of me. My father too. But it's her voice I hear, reminding me that I'm too pudgy."

I've known from the day we met that she struggled with those issues, so I figured something like that was going on in her head. "I hate that your parents did that to you," I say gently, pulling her closer. "But *you're* the most important person in Grace's life. I don't want her growing up seeing you doubt yourself, because it will make her question *herself.*"

She stares at me in the mirror and blinks. "Wow."

"Besides, I don't want her thinking her looks and appearance are the only things about her that matter." I snort and shake my head. "Believe me, I'm aware of how fucked up that sounds, given the businesses the club operates."

"You're right." She bites her lip and still seems troubled. "I don't want her to be thirty-eight and still questioning every curve and flaw."

"You don't have any flaws." I wrap my arms around her, hugging her tight. "And I love every single curve." To prove my point, I turn her to face me and slide my hand over her ass. "You fit my hands perfectly."

She pulls away, but I tighten my grip.

"You think she needs to watch us fondling each other?" she asks with a teasing eyebrow raise.

"I'm the only one doing the fondling." I squeeze her ass. "What's wrong with knowing her parents are attracted to each other? It's how she got here."

She releases a loud snort-giggle and leans into me, pressing her face against my chest. Her warm breath and laughter like a soothing balm on my skin. "That's true." She kisses over my heart. "Thank you," she murmurs against me.

"For?"

"Always being *so* patient with me."

"I know no other way." I kiss the top of her head. "When it comes to you," I add.

She laughs again. "Sheesh, you're right. You'd bite the guys' heads off if you had to tell them the same thing over and over." More seriously, she adds. "I know I must be *exhausting.*"

My lips quirk. "Only in the best ways."

CHAPTER TWENTY

Teller

"You're not making me wear a suit for this, are you?" Murphy asks.

"To visit the funeral home?" Rock asks. "No. Wear your cut. He knows who's investing in his place."

"He's okay with his friendly neighborhood MC taking over?"

I flick my gaze at Rock, who answers. "His father knew Ulfric and Whisper back in the day. He doesn't have the usual civilian fears."

Murphy grunts and adjusts his cut, stopping to peer in the mirror over the bar and run his hands over his beard and through his hair.

"Why are you primping?" I ask.

He slowly turns and fixes me with an incredulous stare. "This is a business meeting, no?"

My lips curl into a smirk. "Aw, did you *want* to wear a suit?"

"Fuck off," he growls, stomping out of the clubhouse.

I'm still laughing when Rock slaps my arm. "Not today, knucklehead."

"What? He knows I'm messing with him."

"Let's go." He gestures toward the door. "Unless you want to fuck around some more. This is your deal, right?"

"Fine." I hold up my hands. "I'm going."

Murphy's already in the garage, checking over his bike.

"You don't want to take the cage?" Rock asks. "So we can discuss a plan?"

"We need a plan for this?" Murphy stands and wipes his hands off with a rag. He points to the overcast sky with hints of sun peeking from behind fluffy gray clouds. "We were caged in all winter. It's halfway decent weather today."

"Good point."

"You fix that leak?" I ask Murphy.

"Coolant cap was loose. Should be good to go now."

Rock grunts but holds in his thoughts on the V-Rod. It's not like Murphy doesn't have other rides to choose from. "Why not take your flashy Road Glide?"

"Nah, I'm not sure Slater County deserves to see it yet."

Rock sighs and aims his impatient president face at us. "Can we move along?"

Rooster and Jigsaw's bikes rumble into the parking lot, putting an end to our fucking around. They stop at the far end of the garage. Rock's boots crunch over the gravel as he pivots in their direction.

For fuck's sake, Rock. Who's causing delays now?

Murphy smirks at me as if he's thinking the same thing. But we wander over to join the chat.

"Hey, brother." Rooster pulls me in and slaps my back. "Supposed to meet Z. He here yet?"

Rock tilts his head toward the woods. "At my house with Hope, Lilly, and the kids." He lifts his chin at Jigsaw. "Z looking for you too?"

"Nah, I just tagged along." He slaps Rooster's shoulder. "Don't like my boy riding alone."

Rooster rolls his eyes.

"You mind if I borrow him?" Rock asks Rooster.

"Not at all." Rooster slaps his hand on Jigsaw's back and shoves him forward. "All yours, Prez."

Jigsaw frowns at Rooster, then turns and nods at Rock. "What do you need?"

"Ride with us. We're going out to the funeral home, and I'd like another body with us." The corners of his mouth curl up at the pun.

He can't be serious. "Uh, Rock?" I tap his shoulder.

He throws me a shut-the-fuck-up scowl.

"Yeah." Jiggy throws a look at Rooster who shoots a shit-eating grin and jogs into the woods. "Sure."

"Thanks." Rock turns and walks toward his bike.

I hurry to catch up with him. Behind us, Jiggy's bike starts up again.

"What the fuck, Rock? Why do you want to bring Jigsaw in on this? You heard what Z said. I don't need him trying to collect trophies from the corpses."

He stops and slowly turns my way. "Are you questioning me?"

Behind him, Murphy silently laughs and drags a finger across his throat.

"Yeah, I am." I throw my arm toward the clubhouse. "You just said it. This is *my* deal."

"And?" He raises an eyebrow.

"I don't want him scaring the shit out of old man Cedarwood."

Rock flicks his gaze in Jigsaw's direction. "Rooster wouldn't risk taking him out on Shelby's tours if he couldn't behave himself. I want someone else we trust to have some knowledge about this business venture."

"Then ask Z to come."

"Z's busy."

"What about Dex?"

"Also busy. Crystal Ball needs his attention." He cocks his head. "Jiggy's a brother. He's an officer downstate, not some hangaround. What's your problem?"

"I already told you."

"I'm gettin' offended, Prez." Murphy steps up to Rock and hooks his thumbs in his pockets, rocking back on his heels like a smug jackass. "The three of us aren't enough to scare Marcel's ghoulish pal?"

"He's not my pal." I grit my teeth. Why *am* I so bothered? Since Z took over Downstate, he and Rock have been running the two charters almost as one. But part of me still feels the years-long divide between the two clubs. The desire to shut out Downstate and keep our business a closely held secret is second nature. "You're right," I apologize.

Rock blinks and cups his ear. "Come again? I'm not sure I heard you correctly."

"You heard me," I growl and stalk away.

Murphy and Rock share a word but they're too far behind for me to make out what they're saying. I ease onto my bike and fire it up without further argument. Through a quick set of hand signals, Rock motions for Murphy to ride by his side, and for Jigsaw and me to follow. Makes sense. President and vice president followed by the treasurer and road captain. Not sure why I'm bent about it.

Jiggy rolls up next to me and plants his feet on the ground. "You all right with me tagging along?" he shouts.

Not like I have a choice.

But Jiggy's expression is devoid of his usual mischievous fuckery. He's all business, which makes me feel like an asshole. "Yeah, brother. Thanks for coming."

He nods and slips his visor down, covering his face.

It's a long ride. Pine Hollow sits on the outer edge of Slater County. About forty-five minutes later, we pull into the parking lot behind the large, rambling Victorian house. Rock continues to the edge of the lot, lined in overgrown grass and trees. The house itself is painted what was probably a sunny shade of yellow at one point, with white trim. Large chunks of paint peel away from the siding like open wounds. Carpet that was once meant to mimic green grass covers the wide, wrap-around porch. Now it looks brittle and worn in certain spots. Four different chimneys poke out of the sloped roof.

"This is a nice area," Rock says. "Quiet. Unassuming."

"Until a bunch of bikers roared into the parking lot," Murphy says.

"You wanted to ride," Rock reminds him.

Jigsaw joins our group but hangs slightly back. His gaze lingers on the peeling paint and rickety-looking railing next to the stairs. "Place needs work."

"Yup." I'm already plotting how to wash some cash through the construction costs when we renovate the building.

Rock pulls out his phone, clicks to a map, and studies an aerial view of where we're standing. "What is Pine Hollow? A village? Hamlet?"

"A hamlet. No local government." I rub my hands together, savoring my favorite part of the location. "They rely on the Slater County Sheriff's Department for law enforcement."

"Who are barely competent as it is," Rock says, without looking up from his phone. "Very nice."

I respond with a quick nod, but pride beats in my chest. Club's never done anything like this, and I want it to be a success.

Three cars are parked next to the house. A cheery lemon-yellow mint-condition 1950s-era Ford Thunderbird catches Murphy's eye. "Don't see a lot of those in such good condition."

"Yellow isn't your color," I snark.

"It's a sweet ride," Jiggy says, stopping to study the classic car.

A garage separate from the house has four bays. None are open. "Hearse must be kept in there."

A plaque screwed into the porch railing says *Cedarwood Family Funeral Home and Cremation Company*, spelled out in a fancy—but dated—script. It matches the larger sign at the front of the building.

"That's a mouthful," Murphy says.

"I don't think they'll be open to a name change." I elbow him.

We thunder up the rickety porch steps like a herd of rhinos instead of four bikers. The wide door opens but another screened door creates too many shadows to see who's about to greet us. A latch squeaks. Old hinges scream as I pull the door wide enough for us to enter. Mr. Cedarwood backs up a few inches out of our way.

"Mr. Cedarwood." I hold out my hand to the older man as I cross the threshold.

We're roughly the same height and he looks me directly in the eye. His grip is firm and confident. "Good to see you again."

He wants this deal to work as much as I do.

Rock holds out his hand next. "Rochlan North."

"Ah, father and son." He slides his gaze between Rock and me. "I'll rest easier having a family as partners."

All the air squeezes from my lungs. Fuck. I didn't say anything to Cedarwood about Rock being my father. He just assumed.

Murphy chuckles and mouths, "Mini-me." My gaze darts away.

Rock eases over the awkwardness. "Thank you for meeting with us," he says, without confirming or denying Cedarwood's assumption.

"This is my brother-in-law," I introduce Murphy. "And our friend, Jensen Kilgore."

"Welcome." Cedarwood smiles brightly, seeming not at all intimidated by four bikers in black leather filling up the corridor.

"Do you want a tour?" he offers, graciously sweeping his hand toward the rest of the house.

"Lead the way." Rock follows Cedarwood.

Murphy glances at me. His eyebrows crawl toward each other as if he's asking if the tour's necessary, then he follows Rock.

Jigsaw hangs back, and I slap his arm to get him moving. "I thought you liked dead bodies?"

"Enemies. Bad guys I've carved up," he answers in a harsh whisper. "Not someone's sweet little ol' nana laid out on a slab."

The walls are covered in faded gold wallpaper. Under our feet, the well-worn carpet does little to mask our heavy footsteps.

"Dude really digs yellow," Jiggy whispers to me.

"Someone probably told him it was soothing or uplifting or some shit back in the seventies."

He snickers and keeps walking.

Cedarwood stops in the doorway of what looks like a cross between a morgue and a therapeutic massage room.

A plump, curvy young woman in glasses and protective gear barely turns away from the casket in front of her. From the doorway, we can't see past all the white satin lining, but I'm pretty sure a body rests inside.

"Fuck me, fuck me, fuck me," Jiggy mutters.

"Dad, I'm almost finished with Mrs. O'Leary. I went with a slightly peachier blush. I think she'd like it if—" She glances up, and her voice halts. She pulls down her mask, snaps her gloves off, and steps away from the casket.

"Oh hell," Jiggy whispers.

With her blond hair pulled into a severe knot, thick, black-rimmed glasses, and a lab coat, she looks like she's ready to attend a Halloween party as a "sexy scientist"—you know, if you overlook the playing-with-corpses thing.

"Don't," I warn Jigsaw.

Cedarwood nods at the woman. "This is my daughter, Margot. She's our mortuary cosmetologist." He doesn't bother introducing us one by one.

Jigsaw solves that problem by stepping right up to her and introducing himself. While I share an eye roll with Murphy, I note Jiggy's deliberately positioned himself away from the casket.

"Follow me, gentlemen," Cedarwood says. "Get back to work, Margot."

She scurries away, stopping at a cabinet to grab a fresh pair of gloves.

"Damn," Jiggy whispers, shooting a murderous glare at Cedarwood.

"Easy, killer," I warn.

The five of us file into Cedarwood's office. More worn carpet. Chipped furniture. Wallpaper peeling in spots. But it's large enough to accommodate an entire grieving family. Still, I wonder how much business he loses due to the shabby appearance of the place.

"So," Mr. Cedarwood says, turning his attention to Rock. "Your son says your motorcycle club is interested in investing in my family's legacy."

"We're interested in an arrangement with a business that has roots in the community," Rock says, ignoring the whole legacy thing.

"What kind of arrangement are we talking about? Anything that will get me or my family in trouble?"

Smart question.

"Nothing like that," I say smoothly. "You're the only funeral home in the area. Guaranteed business, right?"

Cedarwood sits straighter, beaming with pride. "We have a good relationship with the local hospitals. Or we used to."

I nod to the shred of wallpaper hanging on by a thread above his desk. "A renovation might inspire more confidence."

He stares at the wallpaper as if he's just noticed its shoddy condition. His gaze pops around the room like he's seeing it for the first time in a long while. "You're probably right," he mumbles.

"Hey, I get it. If you look at the same thing day after day, the flaws disappear." I gesture to Rock, Murphy, Jigsaw, and myself. "We can be your fresh eyes."

"That would be nice. My sons didn't have any interest in helping out."

"What about Margot?" Jigsaw asks.

"Margot's our cosmetologist." Cedarwood flips his hand toward the door in a dismissive gesture. "She can't run the place."

You favor sons over daughters. Got it.

The casual sexism isn't my problem yet. So I continue making my sales pitch.

"What's the catch?" he asks when I'm finished.

"I'll handle the books."

"Our bank has a lot of protocols in place to spot any—"

"I'll handle the banking too." This is non-negotiable. "And occasionally, we might ask to borrow the facilities after hours."

That part he doesn't even question. Just how many off-the-books bodies has Cedarwood burned in his lifetime?

"What did your sons end up doing, if they didn't join the family business?" Murphy asks.

Not a question I'd planned to ask, but I'm actually glad he brought it up. I want to see if Cedarwood's answer matches the information I uncovered.

"One owns A-1 Wine and Spirits in Slater."

"I love that place," Jigsaw says. "They carry all the good stuff."

Cedarwood answers with a pinched face. "Yes, James works very hard to stand out from the rest. Aaron is a dentist."

"He thought fixing teeth was better than playing with dead people?" Jiggy asks.

"We don't *play* with our clients," Cedarwood huffs.

Rock shoots a shut-the-fuck-up face at Jiggy who thankfully sits back and zips his lips for the rest of the meeting.

After our sit-down, Cedarwood finishes our tour of the entire facility, including the family's living quarters on the third floor and the cremation chambers.

Rock works out the details for our lawyers to get together and draw up paperwork. I'll have to sit down with someone at Glassman's firm this week, which will be annoying as fuck, but necessary.

When we're finished, the four of us stand next to our bikes at the back of the parking lot. Every few minutes, a car drives by, but otherwise, the neighborhood is serene.

"Got lots of room for renovations," Rock says, studying the wide, paved area. He glances at each of us. "How's everyone feel about this?"

Murphy shrugs. "Sounds like work for Teller. You're going to be spending a lot of time here."

"Once it's straightened out, it'll be fine."

"You're talking at least a year."

Does he think I don't know this? "Don't worry. I'm not tagging you in for anything other than a visit once in a while."

"Jiggy?" Rock prompts.

Jigsaw presses his palm to his chest. "You want *my* opinion?"

"You're standing here." Rock tilts his head. "I assume there's a functional brain between your ears. Any thoughts?"

He glances at me, then Rock again. "I thought it would be creepier but it's kinda homey. I get that the markups are high, but can the club really make enough bank to justify the hassle?"

"Eventually, yes," I answer, not annoyed by the question. "But having another place—besides a seedy titty bar—to wash cash is the real draw. And access to the crematorium."

"Yeah, that part's cool."

"You tell Charlotte you're going to be doing business in her hometown?" Murphy asks.

"She grew up closer to Slater, but yeah." My lips quirk. "She was bummed Merlin's not around so we could rub it in his face."

Rock snorts.

"Anyone else think his attitude toward the daughter is kinda shitty?" Jiggy gestures toward the funeral home.

"I noticed." I shrug. "Unless it interferes with the business, it's not our problem. We're not here to drag him into the twenty-first century."

"Fair enough."

Murphy doubles over laughing. "You got a thing for blondes, Jiggy? First Shelby's mom…"

"First"—he shoves one finger in Murphy's face— "Shelby's mom was most definitely *not* my first. Blonde or otherwise. And second"—he steps back and adopts a more moderate, almost imperious, tone— "I appreciate females of all shapes, sizes, ages, and colors."

"You know women don't exist to be your dick sweaters, right?" I ask.

"If they were, I'd prefer them warm and tight."

"Enough." Rock squeezes the bridge of his nose. "Yes, the old man's attitude is shitty, but Teller's right. It's not our problem. However, Margot seemed to like you, Jiggy. If it's all right with Z, I'd like you to help Teller with this project."

"Wait, what?" I stop and stare at Rock. "You heard him. He'll be asking her to try his dick on for size."

"How crass." Jiggy shakes his head. "You're the one who came up with dick sweaters, not me."

"He's…available." Rock glances at Jiggy. "Women seem to find him charming."

"They really do," Jiggy agrees.

"Fine. You're right." I glance at the funeral home. "It'll be helpful for Jigsaw to keep her occupied and away from me."

Jigsaw throws his hand up to his forehead in his dickish version of a salute.

Rock slaps my shoulder. "This went well. You feel good about it?"

"Yeah, I do."

"Good. Someone better let Sparky know we're celebrating tonight."

"Fuck yeah!" Jiggy punches his fist in the air and straddles his bike.

Murphy ambles over to me. "Look at us." A smug grin stretches across his face. "Lost Kings moving into Slater."

"About damn time."

CHAPTER TWENTY-ONE

Teller

"Time to celebrate!" I announce as soon as I walk in the house.

"Up here," Charlotte calls.

I jog up the stairs and find her in the bedroom. "You look hot."

She tilts her head, peering at her royal blue sweatshirt and jeans. "Really?"

"You look good in blue." I curl my arms around her waist and slip my hands into her back pockets. "Got two perfect hand warmers if it gets chilly tonight."

"So, tell me how it went." She stares up at me with mischief in her eyes. "Should I call you The Undertaker now?"

"No. It was good. Jiggy's got heart eyes for the girl who puts the makeup on the corpses."

Her nose wrinkles. "Sounds like a match made in hell."

"Your little matchmaking heart never quits."

"No, that's your sister."

I freeze at the mention of Heidi. "The guy, the owner. He assumed Rock was my father. It was…weird."

"The different last names didn't clue him in? What'd you say?"

"Nothing. Rock just went with it. Murphy thought it was funny."

She bites her lip. "You really need to tell them and get it over with."

"Charlotte." Frustration burns through me. I still need time. "Can't you let me have this one thing?"

"Okay, but—"

Shaking my head, I release her. "I don't want to talk about this tonight."

"You need to talk about it sometime. Soon."

"Thanks." I stomp downstairs and outside, running straight into Carter.

"Ease up." He flaps his hands in the air. "Where's the fire?"

"No fire. I'm going to feed the chickens before we head to the clubhouse. You coming with us?"

He frowns and studies me like he's peering through a microscope. "You and Charlotte have a fight?"

"No." I push past him. "You helping me or not?"

He hustles to catch up. "I already fed them and checked for eggs."

"They always want to eat more."

"True."

The hens greet us with happy clucks. They scratch at the seed mix we toss but keep watching us, as if they're waiting for something better. "Nah, that's Charlotte who spoils you with blueberries and shit," I tell them.

Carter snickers and tosses another handful of seed.

"Were you at Bronze's shop today?" I ask.

"Yeah, I got a doozy for you."

Finally something to cheer me up after I acted like a dick to Charlotte. "Don't tell me it was another 'no *regerts*' tattoo."

"Soooo much better than that." He holds his hands high in the air like he's about to paint me a masterpiece. "Big dude. Not as big as Wrath but close."

"This should be gold."

"You have no idea. So, he wants a saying and an arrow. Piece of cake."

"Never." I shake my head. Doesn't he know by now. "It's never a piece of cake."

"You don't know the half of it." He lifts his shirt and traces a line along his lower stomach. "He wants the saying down here and the arrow pointing to his dick."

"Please don't say he wanted 'You must be this tall to ride.'"

"No, that would've been infinitely better." He pauses and takes a breath. "He wants 'Your next tragic mistake' tattooed above the arrow pointing to his dick."

"That's...weird."

"It gets worse. I kept a straight face. No judgment, right? That's what Bronze always says. Can't judge the customers. Everyone has the right to decorate their bodies the way they want."

I can picture Bronze saying that.

"So, he pulls this scroll out of his back pocket and says, 'I want it written out like this,' and I'm like, 'Cool. Let me look at it so I can draw up a stencil and we'll get rockin' on this bad boy.'" Carter mimes someone rolling out an ancient scroll and pretends to peer at it through a monocle. "Uh, sir, this is spelled wrong."

"Let me guess. He got the wrong 'your.'" I've learned this particular error is one of Carter's greatest peeves.

"Yup. It reads, *'You're next tradgec mistake,'*" he says, spelling out the misspelled words.

"Damn. Sounds more like a prediction than a tattoo."

"Right? So anyway he was super pissed. Yelled at me. Called me an elitist asshole. Like, dude, I don't want to ink misspelled words into your skin that you'll be wearing for the rest of your life. Chill."

I'm laughing so hard, it takes a second to respond. "What did Bronze do?"

"Stopped him from killing me. The dude was pissed."

"Are you sure you weren't a little judgmental about it?"

"Maybe a wee bit?" He shrugs. "He was more embarrassed than mad I think."

"Did you end up doing it?"

"Yeah," he sighs. "He had to sit there and stew in his wrongness, but *I* had to pick up his belly flap and get way too close to his junk for my comfort. Bronze gave me a bonus."

I'll have to thank Bronze for looking out for Carter next time I see him.

I glance at his black T-shirt with a drawing of scattered pencils and crayons. "A little bit sketchy" is printed in a flowery font in the middle. "Cute. You design it?"

He tugs on the shirt and stares down at the design as if he'd forgotten what he was wearing. "Yeah. Funny, right?"

"Yup. You going to the party like that?"

He drops the shirt and stares over my shoulder. "You sure you want me to come?"

"Of course I do. Why would you ask that?"

"I know I'm not family." Carter drops his gaze. "Or a brother—"

"Hey." I reach out and squeeze his shoulder. "You're family. You're *my* family and that makes you club family."

"Thanks."

"I mean it."

"I know you do." He blows out a long, slow breath. "You've given me a lot. A place to live. A new career or two." He chuckles.

"You're really talented."

"Charlotte's the only other person who ever thought so." He shifts his gaze to the side. "She claims our dad did, but I don't remember it that way."

The big brother role comes easily to me. Always has. "Well, now a lot of other people know it too." I slap his shoulder. "Bronze has been a friend of the club for years—before my time, even. I wouldn't stick my neck out if I didn't believe in you. And Rock, well, I wouldn't have risked my president's wrath."

"Merlin wouldn't have pissed on me if I were on fire."

"Yeah, but your uncle is a dick. Forget him."

"He's certainly forgotten us." He tucks his hands in his pockets and stares at the ground. "He barely ever texts or calls her."

Good. I promised Merlin a world of hurt if he contacted Charlotte without clearing it with me first.

"Did you tell him to stay away?" Carter asks. "Assert your biker dominion over my sister?"

I choose my words carefully, knowing how much Charlotte wants her little brother kept out of biker business. He's also been lied to enough and deserves at least a piece of the truth. "He hurt your sister. He made things right the best he could, but I don't trust him near her." I hesitate and try to tamp down my anger. "He's still family. If she wants to see him, she can. I just don't want her alone with him ever again."

He nods slowly. "Thank you."

"For what it's worth, I don't want *you* alone with him either."

He kicks his toe against a tuft of grass. "Doubt that'll ever be an issue."

He's right. For his own personal fucked-up reasons, Merlin was always cruel to Carter. "That's probably a good thing."

The corners of Carter's mouth twitch. "True that." He holds out his fist and I tap my knuckles against his.

I lift my chin at the full sleeve of tattoos crawling up his left arm. "You're gonna run out of room soon."

"Nah." He studies the artwork as if he's amazed to find it branded into his skin. "I always wanted to do something like this, but I didn't want Uncle Chuck to think I was trying to be like him or something. Now, I just don't give a fuck."

"It's a beautiful feeling when that last fuck finally flies away." I wave my hand through the air like it's a bird flapping its wings.

His expression loses some of the sadness that had crept over him. "What are we celebrating tonight?"

"Starting a new business venture in Slater County."

"So Wolf Knights are out of Slater. Totally?"

I take a few beats to answer. "Where'd you hear that?"

"Duh." He rolls his eyes. "I may try to blend into the wallpaper, but I still have ears."

"We don't have wallpaper."

He chuckles. "Seriously, so is that Lost King territory now?"

"Looks that way."

"Good."

I raise an eyebrow.

"Like I said, you're more of a family to me than my own was."

"We have a funny way of doing that to people."

"What?" He wiggles his eyebrows and rubs his palms together. "Luring innocents into your freaky bikers-in-the-woods cult?"

A burst of laughter escapes me, even though I know better than to encourage Carter. "Yeah, that."

"Hey," Charlotte calls as she steps out of the side door. "Are we going or not?" She jerks her thumb over her shoulder. "Wrath and Ravage just pulled up out front."

"Why?"

She shrugs and walks over the grass to meet us.

"Hey." I tug on her sweatshirt. "Come here."

Charlotte's too good to me. Never holds a grudge, even when I deserve it. She curls her arms around me and rests her cheek against my chest. I lean down and whisper in her ear, "I'm sorry."

She shakes her head and squeezes me tighter.

"Little dude!" Ravage's voice carries over the grass. His heavy footsteps thunder against the ground. I pull away in time to see Rav tackle Carter from behind, lifting him in the air. "What's good, buddy?"

"Would you stop doing that! Put me down," Carter yelps.

Rav takes one look at my thoroughly unamused expression and sets Carter on his feet. "Hey, I gotta ask you something."

Carter turns his wary eyes on Rav. "What?"

"How are you with the sea creatures?"

Carter's face scrunches into a thoughtful squint. "Be more specific."

Rav spreads his hands out wide. "I want you to paint a giant sea witch on the fuel tank of my bike, so it looks like I'm riding Ursula." He throws in a few hip thrusts in case we can't grasp what he means by "ride."

Charlotte buries her face against my chest and laughs.

"Uh, okay." Carter slides his gaze my way as if he's worried he's being punked. "Are you *allowed* to do that?"

"Yeah. Rock said I could ask you if you had time to do it."

"No. I mean, a sea witch isn't very Lost King-y." Carter wiggles his hands in the air around his head. "Aren't you supposed to stick to crowns and skulls and stuff?"

I duck my head and laugh.

Rav clasps Carter's shoulder. "You raise an excellent point, young lad. But you forget one thing."

"What's that?"

"I do whatever the fuck I want."

"And suffer the consequences," I add.

"Exactly." Rav points to me. "A man takes his punishment like a man."

"You're a fucking expert at that." Wrath slaps Rav on the back, sending him forward a few feet.

"Can I get a sea witch painted on my bike?" Rav asks Wrath with an absolutely straight face.

"Why? You miss your mom?"

Charlotte and I both turn away, laughing even harder.

"Not cool, bro." Rav grins. "But now that you mention it..."

Charlotte

Laughter really is the best medicine. I could kiss my brother for making Marcel smile.

"So, Carter, when are you going to tattoo your own sister?" I tap his arm and run my finger over his colorful sleeve of inked skin. "You've done work for Rock, Heidi, Grinder, Lilly—I'm getting jealous."

He narrows his gaze. "What exactly are you looking for?"

I peer up at Marcel and he winks at me.

"Nope. All the nopes that ever noped in Nopeland." Carter backs away from us, shaking his head vigorously in case all the *nopes* didn't make his answer clear enough.

"But you've gotten *so* good," I insist.

"I'm not branding you with your boyfriend's MC symbol, 'property of' or anything else. Hell to the no." He shoots a glare at Marcel, who chuckles.

"My *husband*," I correct.

"Not yet," Carter mutters. "Ask me to tattoo anything else on you, Char. Anything but *that*."

"Char, it's fine." Marcel finally joins the conversation. "I'll ask Bronze if he'll do it."

"Just make sure it's on my day off," Carter says.

While Ravage and Wrath follow Carter to his loft, I look up at Marcel. "You still want to go, right?"

"Do you?"

I'm not sure how to answer. Every time we've been there lately, it's felt like an emotional crotch-punch. Either someone's announcing they're pregnant, talking about being pregnant, or joking about doubling-up on their birth control. If it's not that, it's tension between Rock and Marcel thick enough to slice with an ax.

"Charlotte?" He seems to sense my inner conflict. "I'll do it. Soon. This week. I'll tell them."

This time he sounds determined and has actually given it a time frame. "I thought you wanted to go get tested again?"

He bites the inside of his cheek and flicks his gaze away. "Come on. We both know I was using that to delay the pain. From everything I've read, there's no other option."

It wasn't unreasonable to want a retest, but I'm not about to hand him an excuse to postpone this again. "Good. Just tell me when. You won't have to do it alone."

"Thanks."

Dread settles in my chest. It won't take long for Heidi and Murphy to realize that I've *also* kept this secret. Suddenly my fear of losing them is bigger than my desire to have Marcel tell the truth.

CHAPTER TWENTY-TWO

Teller

THE SECRETS END TODAY. I MADE A PROMISE TO CHARLOTTE TO SPILL THIS week. Somehow, it's already Friday. I'm running out of time if I want to keep my promise to Charlotte.

Rock and Hope invited us over for breakfast. When we arrive, Heidi and Blake are already there.

Perfect timing.

It's just the six of us and the kids. I'm never going to have a better opportunity to tell Heidi without a larger audience.

After breakfast, we're still sitting at the table, sipping coffee and eating coffee cake.

"This is good, Heidi," Rock says, stabbing his fork into his slice.

She beams, always happy to accept compliments. Especially from Rock. "Thank you."

I catch Rock's eye and nod, slightly tilting my head in Heidi's direction.

Rock frowns and sets down his fork. *Now?* His expression seems to say.

Didn't he lecture me on how this can't go on forever?

"Uh, I wanted to talk to you guys about something," I begin.

Heidi sets her fork down and grins at me, then Charlotte. "Are we wedding planning?" she asks with a hopeful lilt in her voice. "I know you said redheads can't wear pink, but I saw this gorgeous champagne tulle dress with pink butterflies. It would be so perfect on you, Charlotte…" Her voice fades when Charlotte doesn't respond.

Heidi tries again. "Am I going to be an aunty?" she asks with even more excitement.

Charlotte flinches. Under the table, I slide my hand over her leg and curl my fingers around hers. She squeezes my hand twice as if urging me not to lose my nerve.

"Not yet," Charlotte answers.

My gaze lands on Hope, who has her hands braced against the table like she's preparing herself to jump up and comfort Heidi.

Even Alexa and Grace stop to stare at us, although they lose interest quickly.

Heidi's smile fades and her confused eyes dart from Rock, to me, to Charlotte, then Hope. "What's going on?"

"Why you being so twitchy, bro?" Murphy sits back and slings his arm over Heidi's shoulders.

I hate that I'm about to wipe the easy smirk off my best friend's face. After this announcement, things will never be the same between us.

"I'm not trying to be twitchy. There's something I've wanted to discuss…" My voice falters. "News I want to share with you."

Rock clears his throat. "What Marcel wants to—"

"I got it," I cut Rock off. This has to come from me.

Releasing Charlotte's hand, I rest my elbows on the table and lean forward. "Shit, I don't even know how to say it, so I'm just going to spit it out. Rock and I found…Well, this will sound nuts, but it turns out Rock is—Rock's my, uh, father."

Blank. Heidi and Blake's faces. Totally *blank*.

I got the words out, right?

Heidi frowns.

Blake twitches and sits forward. "What do you mean, Rock's your *father?*"

"What are you talking about?" Heidi drops her gaze and absently twirls one finger through her long, brown hair, pulling it in front of her face and studying the ends. "How can Rock be your father?"

"Well, apparently DNA doesn't give a shit what lies your family fed you." The fake amusement I try to inject into my voice grates on my own nerves. Why am I acting like a victim here?

Heidi drops her hair and stares at me. "You're serious? How long have you known?"

I promised myself a long time ago that I wouldn't cause Heidi any more pain. But I can't tell her one more lie.

"For a while now."

"Since *when*, bro?" Murphy asks in a deadly tone that suggests he already knows the answer. Of course he does. Why the fuck else would Rock and I have ever had our DNA tested? "When Inga sued the club?"

"Uh, yeah." I glance at Rock, then Hope, but neither of them moves a muscle. "It came up. That's why we had to get tested again—"

"You've known since *then*?" Heidi explodes. "That was..." Her gaze bounces around the room, stopping at Hope, then Charlotte, as if they'll provide her with a timeframe. "Over a year ago!"

I shoot a glare at Murphy. Heidi shouldn't be so involved in club business.

He scowls back, a fuck-you-I'll-tell-my-wife-what-I-want face that I have no right to question.

Red-faced, Heidi turns on Blake. "Did you know, too?"

"No," he answers, his voice tight with anger. "I didn't."

"I'm sorry." The inadequate apology tastes bitter on my tongue. "You were finishing school. Getting married. I didn't want to...overshadow any of that, Heidi. I wasn't sure how you'd feel."

"I feel *betrayed*." She chokes on a sob, then stabs Rock with an accusing glare. "You knew?" Her hurt eyes land on Hope. "You too?" Her voice breaks. "We were living in your house. Day after day. How could you lie to my face?"

Tears fill Hope's eyes. Her lips part but I cut her off.

"It's not their fault. I asked them not to say anything until *I* was ready to talk about it," I explain.

Heidi's glare softens for a fraction of a second. "Marcel," she whispers.

My sister's always been more compassionate than I deserve. But this time, I might've broken her faith in me completely.

The softness vanishes from her expression. She jumps out of her chair and grips the back of it, shoving it against the table. Murphy stands next to her, the two of them forming a wall of hurt and anger. "Ready to talk about what? That *you* won the Dad lottery? That we're not even—"

"Don't you dare," I warn. "You're one hundred percent my sister. Always will be. No matter what any test says."

"Do you know how many times I wished Rock *was* my father?" A hopeful spark lights her eyes and my stomach spirals. "Wait." She sends a pleading look in Rock's direction. "Is there a chance I'm...?"

I swallow hard, hating to extinguish the thought before it spins out of control. All the things I could say that might let her down gently run through my head. But Rock steps up to shoulder this part of the emotional nightmare.

"No, Heidi." Guilt coats his words, and I feel even worse.

Her eager expression turns bitter as her gaze lands on Charlotte. "You knew too?"

Charlotte's long, deep breath is as good as a *yes*.

Heidi nods slowly but her shaky voice is less than accepting. "So, all that 'you're already like a sister to me' crap you told me was a lie?"

"No, Heidi." Charlotte stands and moves toward Heidi, opening her arms like she can hug the pain away. Heidi dodges the attempted embrace and curls herself around Murphy's arm.

Everyone Heidi loves and respects the most has lied to her face for months and months.

Because of me.

Anger simmers in the air around Murphy. In one arm, he holds my niece; the other, he uses to protect my sister. But the fire in his eyes is aimed at me.

"You *lied* to me. In the hospital." Hurt and hate turn his voice to a deadly rumble. "You threw your old lady under the bus, like that was the only deep, dark secret you had—"

"Blake," I warn.

His gaze shifts to Charlotte, who's frozen in place. No matter how furious he is with me, he won't spill Charlotte's secret.

He swallows hard and shifts gears, his angry eyes burning holes into my skin. "You claimed you were worried I was gonna die. But you still couldn't come clean about this?"

Rock's irritation with how I've handled this must finally reach its boiling point. In a hard voice, he orders, "Blake, sit down and—"

The rolling thunder of Blake's anger picks up steam and spews Rock's way. "I'm supposed to be your VP?" He skewers Rock with a furious scowl. "What was that? Some consolation prize?"

"Fuck no. Not at all. That's got nothing to do with this."

"Blake?" Heidi curls her fingers in his shirt, and he tears his murderous glare away from Rock. She whispers something but I only catch the word "go."

He nods and turns them toward the door.

"Blake, wait." Rock moves fast, skirting the corner of the table to reach for Blake's shoulder.

"Don't fucking touch me." Blake jerks away.

"Stop. Let's talk this out." I'm practically begging, but I don't make a move toward them.

"*Now* you want to talk?" Blake roars. "Fuck you, Marcel."

"Daddeee!" Alexa wails, throwing her arms around his neck. "Nooo."

"Shhh." He releases Heidi to rub Alexa's back and whisper something reassuring to her all while striding toward the exit. He and Heidi move together like a team that's practiced running from heartbreak their entire lives. Heidi scoops up her purse and Alexa's bag, then reaches for the doorknob.

"Heidi, please don't leave like this," Hope pleads.

Heidi chokes on a sob and shakes her head. Refuses to even look at Hope.

Chasing them down will only make it worse.

So I sit there and do what I do best.

Nothing.

CHAPTER TWENTY-THREE

Murphy

Move.

Get out.

Run.

My heart pounds with fury as Heidi and I hustle through the woods to the garage.

"Do you want to stop at the house?" I ask Heidi.

"Nope."

Glad we're on the same page. We'd be like sitting ducks there. Waiting for Rock and Marcel to show up and demand forgiveness.

Fuck both of them.

The old truck that I loaned to Grinder is in the clubhouse parking lot. He's nowhere in sight though.

Good.

No one needs to witness our family meltdown.

Our family *betrayal*.

Hell, maybe Grinder knows too. Everyone in the fuckin' world seems to know except us.

Our truck's unlocked. Heidi flings the back door open and quickly buckles Alexa into her car seat.

"Momma!" Alexa's ear-piercing wails tear at my heart and push my anger even higher.

"Murphy!" Rock snaps. Behind me, leaves crunch and twigs crack under the weight of his quick steps and heavy boots.

Fuck this. I need to get out of here. *Now.* Before I do something that will feel good in the moment but bring misery later.

"Get in," I say to Heidi in a low voice.

A sob catches in her throat. I hold open her door. As she climbs in the cab, her eyes briefly meet mine. "Please, let's get out of here," she whispers.

Her anguished voice and tear-streaked cheeks further ignite my fury. "Don't worry. We're going," I promise her.

Once she's tucked inside, I slam the door shut and hurry to the driver's side.

Rock catches up to me, grabbing my arm. He attempts to yank me around to face him, but I center my weight and hold firm like a mountain.

A mountain of pure rage.

"Murphy, stop!" he orders. Rock's presidential voice. He expects me to obey. Any other time I would.

Not today.

"Don't," I seethe.

"Let's go inside and talk." He gestures toward the clubhouse.

"No."

"Murphy, I'm—"

"I don't want to hear it!" I roar, ripping my arm out of his grasp. "Don't pull your president bullshit on me, either. This"—I wag my finger in the space between us and the truck— "isn't club business. This is family business. My family. You don't get to order me around. You've been lying to my fucking face for *months.*"

His jaw twitches. Rock's not used to people raising their voices at him. Maybe later I'll regret it, but I'm too pissed right now. I jump in the truck but Rock blocks me from shutting the door.

His mouth twists in an anxious frown as he peers at Heidi. "Heidi, please. I'm sorry. Come back to the house and talk to us."

"Pop-pop!" Alexa wails, reaching her little hands toward us.

Ignoring Rock, Heidi turns in her seat and tries to soothe Alexa.

"Blake," Rock pleads, still hanging onto my door as if that will stop me from getting the hell out of here. "You can't drive when you're this upset. Not with them. Please, stop."

The rational part of my brain understands—and probably agrees with —him, but the rest of me is so pissed off, his words are a match to dynamite. "You don't get to tell me what to do, Rock. You're not *my* father."

With those parting word bullets, I yank the door out of his grasp and slam the door shut.

He slaps his hand against the glass.

Ignoring him, I fire up the truck. I tug my seat belt on and turn to Heidi. "Buckled up?"

"Please get us out of here," she whispers.

"You got it."

As much as I'd love to stomp on the accelerator and tear out of there in some over-the-top dramatic fashion, I don't want to scare Alexa or accidentally hit Rock—no matter how pissed I am with him right now.

He steps back and doesn't pull any emotional grenades out of his back pocket—like flinging himself on the hood.

Both of our phones vibrate to life, buzzing incessantly until Heidi yanks hers out of her purse and shuts it off. She grabs mine from the console, powers it down and tosses it in the glove compartment.

I rocket down the driveway faster than normal, creating a bit of a bouncy ride.

"Wee!" Alexa shouts.

I glance at her in the mirror. Her little red cheeks are still damp, but she thrusts her fists in the air and yells, "Wee!" again as the truck bounces.

I blow out a relieved breath. Thank fuck, she's not too traumatized by all that bullshit.

I wish I could say the same for Heidi.

And myself.

When we reach the turn for the county road, I stop and check in with my wife. "Which direction?"

Normally, we'd go right and follow the road into Empire. Left takes you deeper into Empire County—cow country. I glance in the rearview, worried Rock or Teller might be following.

"Right," Heidi whispers.

I turn the wheel.

Heidi raises her middle finger as we pass the big rooster-shaped mailbox at the end of her brother's driveway, and I let out a bitter laugh. Grassy fields, a house or farm every couple miles, eventually lead to a village where many of the houses have stood for over a century. I have to slow the truck to navigate the tighter roads.

The sign for Ward's Market comes into view. I pull into their small lot and park the truck on the side of the small brick building out of view from the main road. I leave the truck running and turn to Heidi. "Where do you want to go?"

"I need to...think. I need to be away from them for a while." She lifts her gaze, her watery brown eyes pleading with me. "Please."

"Anywhere you want, beautiful."

She bites her lip and stares out the windshield. "The Adirondacks?" She blushes and drops her gaze. "Maybe that place we went to our first...time together?"

Everything about *that* feels right. Even if everything about today is all wrong.

"It's like three hours away though. Is that okay?" she asks. "We don't have to go that far—"

"It's perfect. Let's do it." I shift the truck into drive and pull out of the parking lot.

She's quiet as I follow the back roads to the Northway. I reach over and rest my hand on her leg. "Are you okay?"

"No."

"I mean, physically. The baby?"

"Oh," she whispers, resting her hand on her stomach. "My heart's racing, and I feel like I'm going to puke. I can't believe he—"

"Don't. Not right now." I don't like that she's not feeling well. "Let's take a few breaths and calm down. We'll talk about it when we get there."

"Okay." She slides her hand over mine. "We'll call this our babymoon getaway, then."

"I had a different place in mind for our babymoon."

"You did?" she gasps. "You were planning a vacation for us?"

Yes, please. Let's talk about that instead. Anything to get her mind off what just happened. "Yup."

"You always take good care of me."

"You're not going to ask where I wanted to take you?"

"Nope. I trust you." Her voice falters again. "You're the only person I can trust."

"Same." The weight of that word drags me to hell. I've trusted Marcel with my life, with everything, for so long.

With a few words, Marcel managed to expose his giant lie *and* alter the bond we've shared for more than twenty years.

CHAPTER TWENTY-FOUR

Rock

EVERYTHING IN ME IS SCREAMING TO GO AFTER MURPHY. THE FEAR THAT he might not come back gnaws at me. Even after a quick chat with Grinder, my unease remains.

I also *really* want to strangle my son.

All the ways Marcel and I could've handled this differently scroll through my head on an annoying loop as I stalk through the woods back to my house.

Months ago. I should've forced him to do this months ago. In a planned, controlled, more compassionate way. Not just blurting it out over fucking coffee cake.

Heaviness pulls at me as I step onto the porch. "I'm too old for this shit," I grumble.

I catch Charlotte's upbeat tone as I open the front door but can't make out her words.

Hope's anxious eyes land on me first. *"Are they okay?"* she mouths.

I shake my head.

"Well, that could've gone better," Marcel smirks as I walk into the house.

It takes a few seconds for his words to sink in.

Don't punch him. "Gee, ya think?"

My gaze lands on his anguished eyes. His smirk disappears. The ass chewing I planned to hand him evaporates.

"Is Heidi okay?" he asks.

Heidi's eager voice asking if I was also *her* father haunts me. Crushing that seed of hope before it took root hurt like a bitch. "Don't know. They left."

He frowns and pushes his chair away from the dining table. "Why'd you let them leave?"

"Are you shittin' me?" I approach fast and Hope hurries to place herself between the two of us.

"Rock." Her tone's firm, like she's trying to tame an attack dog. Any other time, her voice *would* soothe my irritation. Not today. Not after that scene.

Charlotte stands behind Marcel, resting her hands on his shoulders. Whether she's trying to offer him support or keep his ass in the chair, I can't tell.

"Did they say where they were going?" she asks.

"No." Why didn't I see this coming? *Heidi* taking it hard was a given. Murphy? I knew he'd be pissed at Teller for upsetting Heidi. Maybe offended that we waited so long to tell them. But that's not all I deciphered from our heated exchange.

You don't get to tell me what to do, Rock. You're not my *father.*

"Heidi's not the only reason you've wanted to keep this under wraps for so damn long, is she?" I ask, taking Hope's hand and approaching the table with a cooler head.

"No, not really. I don't know." Marcel shakes his head, misery falling around him like a cloak.

I tap his phone, sitting on the table. "You call them?"

"About a hundred times. Keeps going to voicemail."

No surprise there. "What about you?" I ask Charlotte.

Her eyes widen. She glances at Marcel, then Hope. "I can try…"

"She's not answering my calls either," Hope says.

"Where do you think they went?" Marcel asks me.

"How the fuck would I know?" I snap.

"You didn't ask?" Marcel's snide tone rubs my last nerve.

"He wasn't in the mood to hand me his itinerary." I blow out an annoyed breath. *Don't strangle him.* "They're together. He won't do anything stupid while Heidi and Alexa are with him. They have each other. They'll be okay." Who am I trying to reassure?

"They just need some time," Hope says.

"It's okay," Charlotte adds. "It's done. It's out in the open. That's what's important. We'll repair things when they get back. Everything will be okay." Seems like Charlotte's trying to reassure herself as well.

This is it. The worst happened. The truth is finally out. But I don't feel any relief.

"Everything will be okay," Charlotte says again.

Now there's nothing left to do except lie to ourselves some more.

CHAPTER TWENTY-FIVE

Murphy

THE STUFFY RESORT WE STAYED AT LAST TIME WE WERE HERE DOESN'T have any rooms available. I stalk out to the parking lot to give Heidi the bad news.

"That's okay," she assures me as I climb into the truck. "We weren't totally comfortable here anyway. And I bet they're not kid-friendly."

I don't know how she can stay so upbeat when our whole world's been turned upside down.

"Let me find someplace." She pulls out her phone and holds it up. "The signal sucks up here."

"Let's get out of this place. If you get more bars, tell me and I'll pull over."

We're at the bottom of a hill when she yelps, "Got it!"

"Really? Here?" The road's surrounded by trees and rocky hillside. I pull off onto a half-circle of dirt meant for travelers to stretch their legs and enjoy the view.

"Yup. Still good." Heidi leans over her phone, tapping on the screen. "Not a lot of options on Expedia," she murmurs.

"I'm not surprised." Rural New York is full of places untouched by technology *or* time. "Find something nice. Doesn't matter how much."

"Oh! Here's something…" Her excitement fades from her voice. "You might not like it, though."

"What is it?"

"The Tall Pines Lodge and Waterpark has a suite available. I always wanted to go there when I was a kid, but it's probably—"

"Let's do it." I shift the truck into drive, flip my blinker on, and pull onto the road.

"Are you sure? It's probably crowded and full of annoying families and kids."

"We're with *our* kid," I point out.

"Yeah, but she's not annoying. Other people's kids are."

When I stop laughing, I glance over at my beautiful, now-smiling wife. "Book it. Alexa will be thrilled."

"We don't have bathing suits…or anything. Shoot. I don't even have a toothbrush with me."

"There's a huge shopping center right near there. We'll get what we need."

"Are you sure?"

"Yup." I glance over again. Her fingers are still hovering over the screen. "Hurry up and book the room. My wallet's in the console." I bump my elbow against the middle section of the seat.

"Okay." She lifts the lid and pulls out my wallet, plucking out a black credit card. While she reads through the terms and conditions of booking the room for two days, I navigate our way back to the Northway and head south.

"Sorry we came all the way up here just to drive two hours back." She opens the console lid again and tosses my wallet inside.

"I don't mind driving. I'm with you. That's all that matters." If anything, the long ride has helped calm me down. Hard to be pissed when I'm focused on the road and keeping my girls safe.

"We can check in any time after five."

"Perfect." I reach over and curl my hand around hers. "Gives us time to do some shopping and get what we need."

HEIDI

As Blake predicted, Alexa's enchanted with the water park. She fussed when we woke her up to go shopping. But a glittery white bathing suit, new sandals, a unicorn beach towel, and water toys cheered her up.

If only my own happiness could be bought so easily.

Blake said to forget about it for now. We'll talk about it after Alexa falls asleep. But the news from this morning hovers over me like a storm cloud. Every time I'm distracted by my daughter's laughter and Blake's smile, a lightning bolt reaches out to zap me with the truth.

Marcel's only my half-brother.

What does that mean for our relationship?

Oh my God. That means little Grace is his *sister.* Why'd it take me so long to figure that out?

My temples throb.

"Heidi!" Blake calls out.

I find him grinning and pointing at Alexa, happily paddling in the water in front of him.

Fighting off my anxiety about my pregnant body in this too-small swimsuit, I wade through the cool waist-high water. I dodge playful, splashing children, a woman swimming laps, and finally reach Blake's side.

"Looks like all the swim lessons at Z and Lilly's paid off."

"Water memory," he says. "I kinda wish we'd built a pool at the house now."

"Wouldn't that be difficult?"

He shrugs. "Anything can be done with money."

"Hmm." At least he's smiling now, although the tightness in his shoulders suggests he hasn't forgotten the ugly scene from this morning.

He slides a glance at me and one corner of his mouth curls up. "You look hot, by the way."

I reach to adjust the slightly too-small bra top. "I feel like I'm popping out all over the place."

"You are. And I like it." He hooks an arm around my waist and yanks me closer, water sloshing all around us.

"Hey!" Alexa yells. "Momma, watch meeeee!"

Keeping me tight to his front, Blake turns me in his arms so I can see Alexa. "Don't move," he breathes against my ear.

The water's warm but my body shivers. "Why?"

"Because what's going on in my shorts isn't family-friendly."

Laughing, I bend over, bumping into him.

"Ow," he growls. "Well, that helped."

Laughing even harder, I swim away from him, taking Alexa's hands and spinning her in a circle.

He crouches in the water, humming the *Jaws* theme, and approaches us slowly.

"Daddeee!" Alexa frowns, watching his stealthy movements. She flicks her concerned eyes my way. "Momma?"

"Daddy's playing shark."

She scowls, then mermaid flaps her feet, splashing water in Blake's direction. He captures one ankle and drags her closer, careful to keep her above the water.

"Nooo!" she shrieks and laughs.

While they play, I skirt around them and lean against the edge of the pool, hooking my elbows over the side and lazily kicking my feet in the water.

On the opposite edge of the pool, a boy maybe nine- or ten-years old shoves a little girl in the water. She screams and thrashes around. I push off the edge of the pool but before I get far, a man scoops her out of the pool. "Why'd you do that to your sister?" he yells at the boy.

The boy gives him a smug smirk and runs away. A shrill whistle and a shout of "No running!" pierce the air.

Marcel never played those kinds of cruel big brother pranks on me when I was little. I felt safe whenever I was with him. Was he a natural-born protector? Or did he feel responsible for my safety because our parents were so lax? I touch my stomach, hoping Alexa will look out for her siblings and not resent them.

A hand tickles my hip under the water. Blake's big body rises next to me, with Alexa on his shoulders.

"Yeeee!" She lifts both arms in the air like she's finally living out all her mermaid fantasies.

Dripping water over my shoulders, Blake leans in and brushes his lips against my neck. "You all right?"

"Did you see that?" I lift my chin toward the dad and the drenched little girl who's still crying.

"Yeah." He lifts Alexa off his shoulders and dips her toes in and out of the water. "That dipstick dad should've been paying attention to his kids instead of trying to eye-fuck the teenage lifeguard."

"Ewww." I glance at the lifeguard station, but it's empty now. No sign of the little boy.

Alexa's quiet, swirling her fingers through the water while Blake holds onto her, keeping her afloat. "Are you hungry?" I ask my daughter.

"No."

Blake and I share a look. Intuition says she's not far from a meltdown. It's been a long day with a lot of excitement.

I let out a loud yawn. "The chlorine's making *me* sleepy."

Alexa yawns with me and nods.

"Let's dry off, change, and find some dinner," I say in my most enthusiastic voice, even though I wasn't lying. I'm suddenly exhausted.

"Yeah!"

Blake carries Alexa out of the pool, and I stop at our chairs to wrap her in a towel.

We head to our room, dripping and making squishy noises in our new flip-flops. After a quick rinse, I help Alexa into one of the outfits we bought and fix her hair. It's gotten darker, closer to my color than Axel's now. I've grown to love my hair color, but oh, how I used to wish it was lighter. Like Marcel's.

No wonder he and I don't look that much alike. It's not unusual for siblings to have different hair or eye colors, but for some reason, it's always bothered me that Marcel and I have such different features. I chalked it up to a desperate need to fit in somewhere, a longing to maintain family ties even though my parents abandoned me.

But maybe part of me always knew the truth?

CHAPTER TWENTY-SIX

Murphy

AFTER DINNER, ALEXA PASSED OUT AND I HAD TO CARRY HER UPSTAIRS. Exhaustion tugs at me. Even though we turned today into something good, the ugliness of everything we left behind still hangs between us, waiting to be dissected.

We're in the center of the king-sized bed, watching some comedy, but neither of us are really paying attention to what's on the big-screen television.

Heidi glances at her phone. I peer over her shoulder and note all the missed calls and texts from her brother, Rock, Hope, and even Charlotte.

Marcel's face as he spat out the secret he'd been hiding for so long haunts me every time I close my eyes.

Asshole.

Shit, I'm even angry with *Charlotte*, which jacks up my fury at Marcel even higher.

"Ugh. I can't deal with any of their texts. I'm *so* mad," Heidi whispers. "They've *all* been lying for months."

The hurt in her voice rouses the savage beast in me again. I curl my arm over her shoulders. "I know."

She clears the messages on her screen and pulls up Trinity's number.

Heidi: *Can you let everyone know Blake and I are fine?*

Trinity: What's wrong???

I'm proud of Heidi. The immature asshole in me wanted to let them all stew and worry about us for a few days. Thankfully, my wife is more of an adult than I am.

Heidi: Family vacation. We'll be away for a few days.

She shuts off her phone and sets it on the nightstand. "There."

My phone buzzes.

Wrath.

"Fucking great," I mutter. Not in the mood for his bullshit, I decline the call and shut my phone off again. Everyone I need is right here in this room.

"Now can we talk about it?" Heidi asks.

"What's there to say?" I have so many questions. Technically, the answers ain't my business, but I can't help wondering how the fuck this even happened. "I still can't believe it."

"Me either."

She snuggles closer to me, careful not to disturb Alexa. "I don't know what I'd do without you." She strokes her hand over my chest. "Thank you for getting us out of there."

"Let's leave," I whisper, running my hand over Alexa's hair.

"Uh…" Heidi lifts her head and gestures to the spacious hotel suite around us. "We did."

"No, I mean let's leave *New York*." The words come out slowly as a plan falls into place. "Let's move."

She blinks. "And go where?"

"I don't know. Tennessee? The Deadbranch charter is always open to me." The Virginia charter would welcome us too, but it doesn't feel far enough away.

Her nose wrinkles. "We're not close to anyone there."

I'm not sure if I should mention this but I'm done keeping secrets from Heidi. "When Priest visited, I got the feeling Steer might be sent down there soon."

"Really? Well, at least we'd know someone." She tilts her head. "If anyone was moving to Tennessee, I assumed it would be Rooster."

"You're probably right. I doubt Rooster will stay in New York much longer. It's not convenient for Shelby to be all the way up here. And apparently Priest strongly hinted he'd like Rooster either in Tennessee or heading up the Nomads."

"Oh shit," she breathes, eyes going wide. "If Rooster goes, then Jigsaw goes."

"Right."

"Z worked so hard to fix Downstate. That would suck, to lose so many of his officers."

Pride swells in my chest. My club has no idea how lucky they are to have Heidi as an old lady. "It would. And I'm not sure who he could count on to step up."

"You could help Z. You did it before."

I shake my head. If I'm moving, I want to put more distance between us and New York. "It's not far enough away." *From your brother.*

Her gaze shifts toward the window. "You'd really give up being vice president?"

Anger burns at the back of my throat. All the second-guessing and ball-busting Rock's been doing to me lately take on a new meaning. "Rock hasn't let me be much of a VP." The truth slaps me in the face. "He's been lying to me since I accepted the patch."

The hard expression on her face softens, and she cups my cheek. "That was personal, though. It had nothing to do with your ability to be his VP."

Rock tried that excuse too, but it doesn't fit the facts. "Doesn't matter. Result's the same. He doesn't trust me. And I sure as fuck don't trust him now. *Or* your brother." His betrayal stings so much sharper than Rock's.

"Move away from Marcel?" she whispers. "I never thought I'd do that again."

Fuck, I forgot about her time living in Alaska with fuckhead Axel. "It wouldn't be like when you moved to Alaska. You wouldn't be alone and isolated," I assure her without mentioning Axel's name.

"You're right. It'd be nothing like that. I actually *like* Tennessee. Being close to Nashville could be a lot of fun. We'd get to know our Deadbranch family." She glances at Alexa. "I could see us living there." Her thoughtful expression shifts to a disappointed one. "But we just built our dream home."

"I'll build you another one. Cost of living's cheaper down there, for sure." I raise an eyebrow. "We could have a swimming pool in the backyard."

"We could do it." She wraps her arms around me and squeezes. "You, Alexa, and baby"—she pats her stomach— "are all the family I need."

"Same here, beautiful."

Away and fully out from under Marcel's shadow? The idea feels like a tangled knot of betrayal and excitement inside my chest.

"Why did they wait so long to tell us? That's what hurts the most," Heidi whispers. "He said it was because of school, then our wedding, you being in the hospital…"

"Your brother's a master at coming up with excuses." More anger than I'd intended vibrates through my words.

"Wait, what did he tell you about Charlotte?"

Shit, here I am whining about people lying, and I never told Heidi this. But it was Charlotte's pain to share—not mine. "He told me Charlotte had a miscarriage shortly before Grace was born."

She sucks in a deep breath, and tears fill her eyes. "Oh, no," she breathes out. "Oh my God, and I keep bugging them about having a baby." She slaps her hand over her mouth. "Why didn't she say anything?"

"I guess she didn't want to talk about it or want Hope to know." I shrug. "I didn't probe too much. Your brother was kind of torn up about it himself but wanted to respect her wishes. You know, until he blabbed it to me to cover up his own secret," I finish with a bitter laugh.

"Ugh. He really never said anything to you about Rock?" Heidi squints at me.

"Nothing."

"You two are so close. I thought you talked about everything?"

"So did I."

"I just don't understand."

"This is going to sound pathetic." I pause and think of how to put my feelings into the right words. "Even though he's a piece of shit who abandoned you guys, Teller had a dad for ten years." My voice falters, but I push out a rough rasp to finish the thought before I lose the nerve. "I *never* knew mine. And—"

"Rock's been like a father to you in a lot of ways," Heidi finishes for me in a quiet voice.

I knew she'd understand. "I guess."

She bites her bottom lip and squeezes her eyes shut. "Do you think *that's* one of the reasons my brother didn't want to tell us? I know he said he was worried about *my* reaction. But do you think he was worried *you'd* feel left out or something?"

The question hits me like a hot poker to the chest. Is Marcel sensitive enough to think of that?

Fuck. Yeah, he probably is. As pissed as I am, I know it's true.

"Shit." I tip my head back and stare at the ceiling.

"No wonder Hope's been so awkward." Heidi's eyes widen. "They've been making *her* keep this secret too."

Knowing Hope and how much she cares for Heidi, that probably killed her.

The whole story starts to take a different shape in my mind. "Now I'm pissed with your brother for forcing Hope *and* Charlotte to lie about this for so long."

Her jaw sets in a firm line, and she crosses her arms over her chest. "Me too."

Our eyes meet and after a few seconds, we burst out laughing.

"You want to go home, beautiful?" I ask.

She glances around the room. "Not yet." Her warm fingers curl around my hand. "I like being away from everyone...alone time for us. For *our* family." She drops her gaze. "We might not have had the best beginnings or good parents, but we won't repeat any of those mistakes with our kids."

My throat tightens. "No, we won't." I rest one hand over her stomach and the other on Alexa's back. Our daughter sighs and wiggles in her sleep. "I'll always be here to take care of my girls. Always."

Heidi curls into my body, a soft, gentle weight against my chest. "And I'll always support you no matter what. If you think Tennessee's the best place for our family, I'm calling shotgun."

I swallow hard. Talking this out with Heidi moved me closer to forgiving Marcel. But the idea I'd tossed out in anger—moving a few states away—still holds a forbidden appeal.

Could Heidi and I leave everything we've ever known behind?

A few days ago, I would've said no.

Now, it's a possibility.

CHAPTER TWENTY-SEVEN

Teller

By Monday morning, I'm out of my mind with worry.

No one, except Trinity, has heard from Heidi or Blake.

Blake's even dodging Wrath—his business partner—something I thought he'd never do. I managed to fuck up every aspect of my best friend's life.

"Now you know why I didn't want to do this." I stab an accusatory stare at Rock, who showed up on my doorstep right after sunrise.

He glares right back. "Waiting so damn long sure as fuck didn't help." He pushes away from the kitchen door where he's either been staring out the window or lecturing me since he got here.

Charlotte eyes both of us carefully from her spot by the coffee maker. "Do you want me to stay home?"

"No." She might be worried we'll kill each other if she leaves us alone. "We'll be fine," I assure her.

"Call me if you hear from them." She finishes filling her travel mug and grabs her briefcase.

"I will." I stand and walk her to the front door.

"I'm sure they're fine." She squeezes my hand. "Try not to worry."

"I'll try."

"And stop blaming Rock," she says in a lower voice. "This wasn't easy for him either. Try to work together instead of butting heads."

"I don't think we know another way."

She cups my cheek. "You're smart. Figure it out." She leans up on tiptoes. "I love you."

"Love you too."

Outside, she tosses her briefcase on the passenger side and climbs into her truck. As I'm about to close the front door, the big grill of Wrath's GMC pickup comes into view.

"Motherfucker," I grumble.

Leaving the front door ajar, I return to the kitchen and start another pot of coffee. "Your enforcer's here," I say over my shoulder. "Word of warning—I'm not in the mood for his bullshit today."

"Well, I'm never in the mood for yours, yet you keep throwing it at me." Rock pulls out a chair at the dining table and sets his coffee mug down with a thud.

"Where you at, welterweight?" Wrath's voice booms from the hallway.

"The house ain't that big, bro," I shout back. "Figure it out."

He appears in the doorway between the kitchen and the hall a few seconds later. "I see you woke up annoying today."

"Having him on my doorstep at the ass crack of dawn will do that to you." I jerk my thumb toward Rock.

Wrath raises his eyebrows and shoots Rock a "what the fuck" look.

"Why are you here?" I shove a mug of coffee in Wrath's hands and sit at the table across from Rock.

"What the fuck's going on with Murphy? Heidi sent Trin a text about a family vacation. He missed his shifts yesterday. That's not like him."

I glare at Rock.

Wrath drags a chair to the side of the table, sort of placing himself between Rock and me. "You finally do it?" he asks Rock.

"God dammit," I snarl. "Is there *anything* you don't know?"

"He didn't tell me, if that eases your hurt little feelings." Wrath cocks his head. "It almost feels like it's been obvious since the night we met your little thieving ass. But because of the age...I never...but, brother, after those tests and Rock was so...beaten down, almost...it just clicked." In an almost kinder tone, he adds, "I didn't say a word to anyone. Not even Trinity."

That has to be the most serious speech Wrath's ever given. I let his words sink in without responding. I doubt there are a lot of things he doesn't share with Trinity. "You really didn't share such a juicy story with your wife?" I ask.

Across the table, Rock sighs.

"It wasn't my story to share," Wrath says, ignoring the dickishness in my question. He shrugs. "I assume you told Z?" He nods at Rock. "After that mess with Chance."

"Christ." I rub my hand over my neck. "I was such a dick to Lilly when she first came back."

"I mean…" Wrath grins. "To be fair, you're always a dick. I doubt anyone noticed."

"Thanks, asshole."

"Happy to help." He slaps the table. "Give me the short version."

I lift my gaze to Rock. He can field this question.

"My knucklehead of a son thought after breakfast the other morning would be the *perfect* time to finally share the news," Rock explains, "without giving me any warning."

"What'd you need a warning for?" I sneer. "You've been bitching at me to do it for months. So, I did it."

"Easy, fuckers." Wrath holds out his hands like he's talking to two sparring fighters. "What happened?"

"Heidi didn't take it well."

"Understandable," Wrath says.

"Murphy blew up outside the clubhouse," Rock says, staring into his coffee cup like he's worried I laced it with rat poison or something. "Surprised Grinder didn't tell you about it."

The usual devilishness is absent from Wrath's face. "Murphy didn't take it well either, huh?" he asks.

"No," Rock sighs.

"I warned you not to daddy them too much when we found them," Wrath says.

"Christ, you're an asshole." Rock stands and grabs his cup, then walks to the counter for a coffee refill.

"Sorry," Wrath mutters.

I jerk my body and fall out of my chair, twitching on the floor. "Did you actually apologize for something?"

Wrath toes me with his boot. "Yeah, just not to you. Get up, dipshit."

I pull myself off the floor and slide into my chair again.

"All right." Wrath slaps the table. "As far as we know, they're okay. A bit rattled. But okay?"

"According to Trinny," Rock says. "They won't answer anyone else's texts."

"Not even Hope?" Wrath raises an eyebrow. "Shit."

"Heidi didn't give Trinity a hint where they were?" I ask.

"Nothing." Wrath shakes his head. "She sent a screenshot to Charlotte."

"Yeah, saw it." Disappointed, I wave my hand in the air.

"Is anything else going on I should know about?" Wrath asks.

"Like what?" Rock snaps.

"You've been a bit of a dick to Murphy lately."

Rock slams his mug on the counter. "Why does everyone keep saying that?"

"So someone else noticed?"

"Grinder mentioned it." Rock lifts his chin at me as he returns to his seat. "Have I been harder on him than usual?"

"He's your VP now." I shrug. "Harder role than road captain."

Wrath nods slowly, like he's about to drop a truth bomb we won't like. "You should've told him about this when you made him VP." He pierces Rock with a disapproving stare. "All you did was undermine him and make him think you don't trust him."

Rock traces his finger in a line down the table. "They're two separate things. Club." He slaps his hand on one side of the line, then the other. "Family."

"Fucked-up family," I add.

"That's bullshit and you know it." Wrath crosses his index and middle fingers together. "The club *is* our family. Your blood relationship doesn't change that. I shouldn't have to explain this very basic concept to you, brother."

"He's right," I say, dropping my gaze to the floor. "I'm sorry, Rock. It's my fault. You wanted to tell them months ago."

A heavy hand lands on my shoulder. I glance up, expecting to find Rock, but it's Wrath. "There's no way to prepare to have your whole history rearranged," he says with more sympathy than I'd expect from Wrath. "Club still needs to come first."

I nod.

"Apologize to Murphy. And mean it." He squeezes my shoulder to emphasize his point. "Stop treating him like your little bro. He's your VP now."

"Shit." I huff out a laugh. "Who would've seen that coming?"

"Right?" Wrath lifts his brow. "I always assumed he'd take over for me if I dropped dead."

"You *do* beg for death on a regular basis," Rock says.

"Don't blame me because the truth is hard to swallow. You need to apologize to him too." Wrath pierces Rock with an intense stare. "Your ability to own your mistakes and do what needs to be done to fix them is what makes you a good leader. All the brothers—well, except me—fear you. But we *respect* you more."

Rock chuckles. "Thanks, brother."

Wrath slaps the table and stands. "Heidi sent another text this morning. Said they'll be back by noon."

"What the fuck?" I sputter, reaching to check my phone. "Why didn't you say that when you got here?"

"I wanted to assess the situation first," Wrath says without a hint of apology.

"Thanks," Rock says in his least thankful tone.

"Anytime." He lifts his hand on his way out.

After Hurricane Wrath departs, Rock and I stare at each other.

"What do you want to do?" I ask. "Think they'll stop by here?"

"I'll stick around—

My phone buzzes, cutting off Rock's answer.

Heidi: Are you at your house?

Me: Yeah.

"It's Heidi," I explain without looking away from the screen. Another message pops up.

Heidi: Can I come over?

Me: Just you?

It seems like an eternity before she responds.

Heidi: All three of us.

I let out a slow breath and close my eyes.

Me: I'll be here.

CHAPTER TWENTY-EIGHT
Teller

"Pop-pop!" Alexa runs over the uneven grass toward Rock.

Murphy glares at him, like he'd rather chew on glass than say hello.

Rock leans over and swings Alexa into his arms. "There's our little mermaid girl."

Murphy's jaw twitches as he watches them. He shakes his head and turns toward Heidi still lingering by the tailgate of Murphy's black truck.

"Hey." I approach them slowly. "You all right?"

Heidi curls her hand around Blake's. "We're good."

"Can we talk?" I gesture toward the house.

"I'd like to." Heidi clings to Blake's hand, making it clear all *three* of us are having this conversation. Fair enough.

At the porch steps, Blake hesitates and tugs Heidi toward him. "You two should talk first," he says in a low voice.

"Are you sure?" Heidi asks.

"Go on." He lifts her hand to his lips and kisses her knuckles. "I'm not going anywhere."

I hold open the door and nod to Blake after Heidi steps inside.

She stands in the hallway, awkwardly twitching as if it's the first time she's ever been in my house.

"You want something to drink?" I ask.

"Sure." She follows me into the kitchen.

I pull out a pitcher of lemonade Charlotte made and pour two glasses.

"Where's Charlotte?" Heidi asks, taking a seat at one end of the kitchen table.

"At the office." I take the chair Wrath used earlier, so I'm closer to Heidi. She shifts away, the chair scratching over the floor, as if she needs more space.

"I'm sorry," I begin.

She raises an eyebrow. "For?" She lifts the glass to her lips, taking a sip and puckering her mouth as the tart sweetness registers.

"I should've told you sooner. Instead of being a coward, I probably should've told you one-on-one."

"You're a lot of things, Marcel. A coward isn't one of them."

"An emotional coward then."

She tilts her head as if she's considering that suggestion. "So, this is why you've been so weird with me lately?"

I sit back in my chair with a thump. "Have I been weird?"

"I don't know." She traces the tip of her finger over her glass. "Once you got over being mad at me for marrying Axel, and Charlotte soothed your inner demons, we were kinda close." One corner of her mouth curves, like she's latched onto a fond memory. "Remember the house we shared down in Florida. We all had fun together, right?"

"We did."

"Then, I don't know, you seemed to change. I thought maybe you were still mad about Blake and me getting married—"

"I was never mad about you two being together."

She slants an incredulous look at me but doesn't call me out. "I thought it was maybe tension from helping Z out downstate or something."

"Yeah, that was rough."

"Then, you were there for me every day when Blake was in the hospital. After, I don't know..."

"You took off on the road with Rooster and Shelby for a bit, don't forget."

She pierces me with stern eyes. "Maybe that didn't come out right. *Physically*, you've been there. Helping me with Alexa on the days I have to work and so we could go out on the road. But lately when we're all hanging out, you've been...I don't know...distant?"

"I didn't mean to be."

"Then I thought it was maybe something else. In one of my psychology classes we talked about how it's normal for siblings to sort of separate and go their own ways in young adulthood while they each go out and create their own families—"

"*Nothing* about our family psychology is normal."

"Jeez," she snorts. "You're not kidding. Club life isn't normal, either."

I'm not sure what to make of her earlier statement. "I'm sorry if I've been distant. This has been a lot to absorb."

"I can't imagine." The corners of Heidi's mouth turn down. "It had to be a weird thing to discover at your age."

"At my age... Are you calling me *old*?"

She blinks as if she's not sure if I'm teasing her. Then playfulness replaces the confusion in her brown eyes. "Well, now that you mention it..."

I slide my hand over hers and squeeze. "You'll always be my sister."

"Yeah, you can't get rid of me that easy."

I release her. "Be honest. Is Blake all right?"

Her eyes turn wary, shrewd. Her immediate instinct is to protect her husband, not satisfy my curiosity. As it should be. "He's fine. It was a... shock. But once we talked through it..." she shrugs. "I think now he's more mad at you for forcing Charlotte and Hope to keep this a secret for so long." Her gaze drops as if that's something still bothering her. How much damage have I done to their sisterhood?

"I didn't know what else to do," I explain as honestly as I can. "I hated asking them not to say anything, but I needed time. Then it was just this *thing* hanging over me that I didn't want to deal with."

"Me?"

"No, not you. Never you, Heidi." I tap the table, so she'll look at me again. "So, where'd you guys go?"

"It's a secret." She runs her fingers over her lips like she's zipping them shut.

225

"Okay." I can't exactly argue she's not entitled to her own secrets.

We sit in silence for a few seconds. Heidi stares at her lemonade and traces her thumb over a bead of condensation sliding down the glass. "Rock must've been...young. Mom...was his babysitter, right? That's kind of fucked up."

Unease crawls over my skin. "Now it makes me wonder if that's why our...your dad left. Maybe he realized I wasn't his, got pissed, and ditched us." I can't believe I just admitted that to my little sister.

"Yeah," she scoffs. "The *or something* being he was a shitty person."

"That too."

"I don't have any memories of him."

Guilt slips under my skin. One more thing I took away from her. "I do." I shrug and glance away. "They're not bad ones. Not all of them, anyway. But now..."

"Have you thought about finding Mom and asking her about it?"

I had considered finding her, then immediately discarded the idea. "What's the point? What can she possibly say? 'Oops, sorry I never mentioned when I was a teenager, one of the kids I babysat knocked me up?'" I pull a disgusted face. "Not a conversation I want to have with her."

Heidi shudders and wraps her hands around her lemonade glass. "I never, ever want her around my kids."

"Damn right."

"What the heck happened?" She wrinkles her nose. "Did they date?"

"He remembers her but not a whole lot more than a few bits and pieces." I gag. "I don't think it was what you'd consider *dating*."

"What's this mean for you...and for the club?"

"Don't know, yet."

"It shouldn't matter. Lots of clubs are legacy clubs," Heidi says as if she's ready to go to battle for me. "That one we met in Texas, Savage Dragons? Remember Blaise? He took over the club for his father."

"Didn't think you were paying that much attention." My lips curve. My sister may pretend to be a carefree ol' lady when we're around other clubs, but she's always observing and taking in information. "The Demons too. Chaser took over for his dad. I have no intention of running the club, though."

She grins at me. "That's because Alexa and Grace are going to run it one day."

Thinking about the sheer volume of dirtbags in club life brings an immediate no to my lips. "Then I'd have to kill a whole lot of bikers. And I sure as shit don't want them hooking up with one."

Her smile slips. "Easy on the overprotective vibes."

"You're dreaming if you think I and every single one of my brothers won't look out for the girls."

"Looking out is great." She drops her gaze to her feet, studying her boots. "It's the whole no-dating-until-she's-thirty vibe that's tired."

"Heidi—"

"No," she says firmly. "All that overprotective talk teaches girls that it's okay to be controlled by the men in their lives. As long as it's done out of 'concern' or 'for their own good.'"

Without thinking through what she's saying, I blurt, "That's bullshit—"

"Can you really not see the difference?" she interrupts in a firm but calm voice. Obviously, she's thought about this a lot. "Can you close your mouth and actually listen to what I'm saying?"

It rubs my ass but she has a point. I snap my mouth shut.

"It's not 'cute.' I don't want to teach my daughter to not think for herself."

While it rubs against thirty or so years of personal beliefs, feelings, and experience, what she's saying starts to sink in. "It's not because I think you can't take care of yourself or that the girls won't be able to when they're older. It's because I love you and them. I worry all the time. I know what it's like out there. A lot of men are fucking scum, and I want to protect all of you from the bad ones."

"Then teach them about the *good* ones," she insists. "Help them develop and listen to their gut instincts." She presses her hand to her stomach. "Not to rely on a big strong uncle all the time."

"I can do that." I rest my hand on her shoulder and draw her closer. The corner of my mouth twitches. "But I'm still gonna fucking murder anyone who hurts my family."

Finally, she laughs. "Fair enough, big brother. Just give us a chance to do it first."

My sister *has* cracked a few skulls on her own. Saved our asses more than once. "Alexa already has a pretty badass mom."

"It took a while to get there," she says with the limited scope of youth.

ROCK

Relief spread through me as soon as Murphy and Heidi showed up at Marcel's house.

They're safe. They both seem calmer. Heidi's willing to talk to Marcel.

I glance at Murphy. Hunched shoulders, tight posture. Leaning against the side of his truck, like he might bolt any minute.

He's *not* ready to talk.

"Thickens, Pop-pop!" Alexa yells in my ear. I set her on the ground and she runs toward the hens, making them squawk and flap their wings.

"Easy," Murphy calls out. "Don't scare them."

"I not!" she shouts back.

"Let's talk." I say to Murphy. Doesn't seem like he's going to say anything to me otherwise.

His hard stare doesn't offer an ounce of forgiveness. "Do I have a choice?"

I grit my teeth and resist the urge to throttle him for the disrespect. "You always have a choice."

He scowls, and for a second, I think he's going to tell me to fuck off. "Did you even want me for your VP?" he asks. "Or did Z force that on you?"

Let's get right into it, why don't we?

Stunned by the question, I rock back on my heels and stare at him. "Of course I wanted you as VP. Z made the nomination, but he didn't have the last word."

"Then why didn't you trust me enough to tell me?"

"I *do* trust you." I stare at the sky, searching for the right words. "The club should've come first. But this threw me. I never saw it coming."

"Yeah," he rasps. "I can imagine."

"This…" I gesture toward the house. "It doesn't change anything."

228

"Why lie to ourselves? It changes a lot of things."

"You're family. The club is our family."

"Sure," he says, but he doesn't sound convinced.

"Other clubs make it work."

He snorts. "Uh-huh. The son's usually the VP. You want me to swap places with Teller? You know I'm shit with numbers."

The question throws me. Is that what he thinks? "Not at all. I need you right where you are."

He shifts his jaw from side to side.

I lift my hands and wave my fingers between us in a give-it-to-me-straight gesture. "Get it out. Let's have the conversation you wanted to have the other day."

"You're not ready for that conversation."

"Yes I am. We both are."

He jams his hands in his pockets and stares at the ground. Like something's percolating behind his angry facade but he's not ready to say it out loud.

"Forget our roles as president/vice president, club protocol, bylaws, or any other bullshit. Say what you need to say," I encourage.

"You two have been having little secret meetings for months."

"That's not true."

He rubs his knuckles over his chest. "I know *get lost* vibes when I feel 'em."

Some of that was probably me trying to get Marcel to come clean but the instinct to protect my son keeps that thought in my head. "It wasn't intentional." At least *that's* the truth.

"Okay, setting this family tree issue aside." He waves his hands toward Teller's house. "I can't seem to do anything right in your eyes lately. And the personal stuff isn't the only thing you kept from me."

"Give me an example."

"The fucking funeral home. Isn't that something we should've discussed before you sprung it on me at the table? Z knew before I did. And he's not even your VP anymore."

His words hit me like the high beams of a car racing along a dark, country road. And I'm the dumbass standing in the middle of the highway squinting into the glare. "You're right. I'm sorry."

The apology seems to take the wind from his anger. "Huh. Didn't expect you to actually apologize."

"I don't do it often."

"No shit," he mutters.

"What else?" We're making progress. I think.

"I don't know." He drops his gaze. "You've always been hard on us. But it's just been different. I thought it was the new role I took on...but now..."

"That's probably part of it. Don't forget, it took Z and me a long time to work out a balance."

He seems to consider that. "You're sure you trust me?"

"To represent the club? To have my back? Yes, without question." I run my hand over the back of my neck. "It's not *your* abilities I'm questioning."

"Whose are you questioning?" He snorts. "Yours?"

"Well, I fucked *this* up."

"Now I see it," he says slowly.

"What's that?"

He waves his hands at me. "That martyr bullshit Wrath's always saying you pull. I get it now."

"You realize I'm responsible for all of you? If I don't question myself from time to time, I've got no business at the head of that table."

"I know," he says quietly. After a few beats of silence, he squints at me. "Was it weird?"

"What?"

"Well, you've caught him in some...embarrassing positions and vice versa over the years. Finding out he's your son after the shit you've seen..." He lets out a long, low whistle.

I snort, then full-on laugh. "Yeah, fucker. It shed a whole new light on the last few decades. Your buddy also accused me of child abuse for all those times I choked his disrespectful ass."

He bursts out laughing. "What a baby."

"Besides the weirdness, I felt guilty I didn't know." I clasp my hands behind my neck and stare at the sky for a moment. "I wasn't there for him the way a father should have been. All the stupid shit and fucking around I did, seems so ridiculous when I had a son who needed me."

"Weren't you a kid yourself?" He frowns. "Besides, you *were* there for him...for both of us."

"Not out of the kindness of my heart," I admit, tired of them acting like I had altruistic reasons for looking after them when they were kids. "You realize that, don't you? I knew you'd be good for the club and wanted to eventually recruit you."

He shrugs. "So? I had a crackhead for a mother, Rock. You imposed some order in my otherwise chaotic life. Made me finish school. Helped me earn money to support myself. Stop trying to turn your good deeds into something ugly."

Fuck me. "You spend too much time around Wrath."

One corner of his mouth lifts. "Who knew we'd end up so tight? Always thought he hated my ass."

"Nah, it takes him a few decades to warm up to people." We stare at each other for a few beats. "Are we good?"

"You tell me." Caution colors his words.

"It's been a rough year."

"Yeah." He scoffs. "You became a new dad two times over."

What an absurd truth. "I guess so."

"You lost Z to Downstate. Grinder finally got out of prison."

"You almost died on me," I remind him.

He rubs his hand over his scalp. "Shit, yeah."

"Seems like we crammed in ten years of drama." I stare at him for a minute. "You know I'm proud of you, right?"

"You've mentioned it." He flashes a tight half-smile.

"First time I met you—"

"I was a scared little boy, worried you were gonna kill my best friend."

I nod to acknowledge his memory, then share my version of the story. "You put yourself in front of Heidi. Trying to protect her from me."

"Kinda pointless."

"Yeah, but brave." I press my fist against my chest. "Things were rough at home for you. But you rose above it and turned into a good man."

He lets out a humorless laugh. "Did I?"

"Yes," I answer without hesitation. "I know I've asked you to do things for the club that civilians wouldn't consider 'good.' Morally gray to some, maybe. But not to us and the code we live by. You've always done what needed to be done to protect your brothers. Without question. Not everyone has the strength to do that."

My words seem to ease some of the tension from his body. "It's all I know."

"We still have some adjusting to do, but we'll get through it."

In the end, all this pain will leave us stronger than before.

CHAPTER TWENTY-NINE

Hope

After Rock sends me a text saying things are calmer at Teller's house, I pack Grace's things and head for my car.

When I arrive a few minutes later, Murphy's truck is in the driveway, facing the road, as if he wanted to be prepared to make another quick getaway.

My heart hurts for all the pain we've caused.

I catch sight of Murphy and Rock in the backyard. While Alexa's happily watching the chickens, the guys seem deeply involved in their conversation. Deciding to leave them to work out their issues, I gather Grace and tap on the front door.

Teller opens it a few seconds later. "Hey."

"Can I talk to Heidi?"

"Yeah, of course." He opens the door wider.

The house is quiet. The emotional fireworks must've fizzled.

My guilt isn't as simple to snuff out.

"Hey, Gracie." Teller holds out his arms for his little sister. "Here, let me take her?"

"Sure."

Grace lights up as Teller pulls her into his arms. "She's in the living room."

"Okay." As much as I've dreaded this moment, in a way, I'm relieved it's finally here.

Heidi's on the couch, staring at her phone. She leans forward and sets it on the coffee table. "Hey, Hope."

Good grief, how can I not know what to say? I've had plenty of time to prepare. "How are you?" I ask carefully.

"Fine." Her answer's clipped. Unlike Heidi.

I force my feet to move across the carpet and sit next to her.

"Did you lie to protect me?" she eventually asks.

"Yes, and because I knew he needed time."

She blows out a long breath and finally looks at me. "Why?"

"Why what?"

"Did you want to protect me?"

Isn't the answer obvious? "Because I love you, Heidi."

She sniffles and nods. "So, not a club thing?"

"No." It sounds cowardly, but I say it anyway. "It wasn't my information to share, or I would have told you."

She stares straight ahead, seeming to consider my words. "Wow, yeah. I think it would've been a lot weirder coming from you instead of him."

The tightness in my chest eases. This can be repaired.

The corners of her mouth lift. "Is guilt why you bought me those expensive boots for my wedding?"

The question throws me. "What? No. I've watched you work so hard the last few years. I wanted you to have something nice to celebrate your accomplishments."

She kicks out her feet so I can see she's wearing one of the pairs I bought her. Purple with a tapestry panel and row of buckles. Then she tucks them against the couch.

"I'm jealous," she whispers.

She doesn't need to explain. I felt it when she tried to ask Rock if he was her father too. I slide closer and slip my arm around her shoulders. Her body's stiff, and she ignores my attempt to comfort her, but I don't back away. "I understand."

"That's pathetic, isn't it?"

"Not at all."

Finally, she relaxes and leans against me, resting her head on my shoulder. "When do we finally outgrow all the trauma our parents inflicted on us?"

I sigh. "When I find out, I'll let you know."

Murphy

Things seem stable now that the air has been cleared.

I pop into Marcel's living room to find Heidi and Hope.

"Hey, Murphy." Hope stands and holds out her arms, then drops them to her sides as if she's worried I'm mad at her.

"Come here, first lady." I pull her into a tight hug. Couldn't stay mad at her if I wanted to.

"Are you all right?" she whispers.

"Yeah, I'm fine." I pull back, holding her at arm's length. "I don't blame you." Shit, I don't even blame Rock. My issue's with Marcel. "This must've sucked for you."

She nods, then shakes her head, dismissing my concern. "I love both of you." She reaches down and squeezes Heidi's shoulder.

"We know." Heidi smiles up at her.

I'm relieved they've talked it out. She and Heidi seem to be solid. That makes what I have to tell Heidi easier. I jerk my head to the side, motioning for her to follow me into the hallway.

"What's wrong?" she asks.

"Nothing. I gotta run down to Furious. Will you be okay here or do you want me to bring you home first?"

"I'll ride up with Hope and Rock later." Her mouth quirks. "My SUV's still here in Marcel's garage if I need to make a quicker getaway."

My expression stays the same.

"I'll be fine," she assures me. "Go. Before Wrath dreams up some creative punishment for your absence." She leans up and kisses my cheek. "Thank you for this weekend."

I capture her in my arms, lifting her just a bit. "We needed it."

"We did," she whispers.

"You and me." I press a kiss to her lips. "We'll always be okay."

The corners of her mouth lift. "Team O'Callaghan for life."

"Yeah, beautiful." I set her down but keep my hands on her waist.

"Are your hands ever not all over each other?" Marcel groans.

I turn and he's standing in the hallway, hands on his hips and a flicker of uncertainty in his eyes.

"Can we talk for a sec?" he asks.

A wave of trepidation propels me toward the door. "I can't. I need to run down to Furious."

He drops his gaze and firms his jaw. My body tightens in anticipation of a fight. Part of me wants to give in and ease his conscience. The other part of me wants to let him stew for a while. My childish instinct wins as I open the door and he doesn't stop me from leaving.

Heidi squeezes my hand.

"I gotta go," I tell her.

She bites her lip but nods. She'd rather I stay and hash all this out with her brother but won't ask me to do it.

Marcel looks so fucking miserable, I throw him a bone. "We'll talk later."

"Okay."

I hustle out of there before I change my mind.

Why I thought Furious would be a better location for my brooding ass, I don't know. Wrath's ready and willing to abuse me the second I walk into the gym.

"Enjoy your little getaway, bro?" he asks from the doorway of his office.

"Thanks for covering for me." I don't offer any excuses or explanations.

"You all right?" Wrath's considerate curiosity sets off my bullshit meter. I can count on one hand how many times he's shown genuine concern for my feelings about anything.

"I'm fine." I brush past him but he stops me with a hand on my chest, pushing me back a few steps. "The fuck? Get off me."

"You want to talk?"

"Jesus Christ. You know too?" How many other people did Rock and Marcel tell before they finally came clean with Heidi and me?

"Rock and I go way back. I can read him pretty well," Wrath explains. "It didn't take a lot to figure it out. You know I've always busted Teller's ass for acting like Rock's mini-me."

"Yeah, acting like it, not actually—wait, did *you* know all along?"

"Fuck no. How could I?" He slaps his abdomen. "My intuition is smarter than my brain, I guess."

That actually pulls a chuckle from me. Wrath rarely pokes fun at himself.

"So where'd you go?" he asks.

I tell him and he shudders with revulsion. "Better you than me, bro. Way too many kids at a joint like that."

"Fuckin' A," I agree.

"How's Heidi?"

A few years ago, I'm not sure Wrath would've given a shit about Heidi's feelings on any subject. "Better. I left her at Marcel's. Rock and Hope were there too."

"You didn't have to come in."

"Yeah, I did." My body tightens with annoyance. "Orders aren't going to sort themselves."

"You can't avoid him forever," he says with annoying accuracy. Of course he knows exactly why I'm here.

"Not trying to," I lie.

He cocks his head but doesn't call me out. "There's a stack of invoices waiting on your desk for you."

"Perfect." I finally manage to move past him.

Once I'm at my desk, I send Heidi a quick text to make sure she's okay. She answers with thumbs up and heart emojis, which puts me at ease.

I work through the stack of papers, pushing all other thoughts away. I'm halfway through when Jake knocks on my open door.

"Nice of you to show up." He smirks and saunters into the room, plopping into one of the chairs in front of my desk.

I study him carefully. He and Wrath have been business partners and friends for a long damn time. Would Wrath have shared the reason I took off with Jake? Ultimately, I doubt it. It falls too close to club business for Wrath to discuss with outsiders.

Over the years, Jake's become my friend too. I still don't feel like talking about it. What would I even say? "Had some things to take care of."

"Is Heidi all right?" he asks. "The baby? Everything okay there?"

"Yeah, brother. Thanks for asking. She's good."

"Okay." He slaps the edge of my desk and stands. "If you need something, let me know."

"Thanks, Jake."

The rest of the afternoon goes by quickly. Wrath dips out early, leaving me to close the gym.

I lock the doors and step into the back parking lot. A bike I'd recognize anywhere is parked next to my truck. Marcel's leaning on it, staring at the night sky.

"I should've known you wouldn't leave me alone," I say as I walk up to him.

He drops his gaze to the blacktop.

"You couldn't talk about this for fucking months," I grumble, throwing my bag onto the passenger side. "Now, all of a sudden, you gotta hunt me down at work?"

Teller

Maybe ambushing Blake at work isn't fair. At least I waited until the gym was closed.

"What can I do to fix this?" I ask, fighting all my natural instincts to respond with something snarky.

"What's there to fix, Marcel?"

He may be trying to hide it, but I sense the hurt and distrust in his question. Wrath's words return to me. But no matter what he said, this rift goes deeper than the club and our roles in it.

"You're my best friend. My brother in every way that matters. I should've told you when I found out. But I didn't know how to say it. I wasn't sure how to tell Heidi. And I didn't want to make things awkward for you two."

"Well, at least you finally respect our relationship. So, I guess that's something." His words hang heavy.

"Give me some credit. I'm not as obnoxious as I used to be."

"I guess," he grumbles.

"Are you mad because I kept the truth from Heidi or from you?"

"Does it matter? I'm pissed I was on death's doorstep in the hospital, and you lied to my face."

"I didn't *lie*. I just told you a different secret."

"Yeah, way to throw Charlotte under the bus, you dick."

I love that he's so protective of Charlotte. Even if it means he calls me a dick on a regular basis.

"It was the more painful secret," I say quietly.

"Fuck," he mutters.

"I'm sorry. I hated hiding it from you. We've never kept secrets from each other."

"How was it easier to tell that undertaker dude but not me? That's really fucked up."

"What?" My face contorts in confusion. Then I realize he means Cedarwood. "I didn't tell him. He assumed. Shocked me too." I shrug.

He frowns as if he doesn't quite believe me.

"Why would I lie about it now?" I throw my hand in the space between us. "You even made a mini-me joke."

One corner of his mouth twitches. "I guess so."

"Everything I thought I knew about myself—my family, my history, my damn identity, was flipped upside down, Blake." I frantically think of the best way to explain it. "*Thinking* of Rock as a father figure then having him actually *be* my father was a real fucked-up pill to swallow." *There's* the reason I needed to have this reckoning with Blake away from Rock.

"Yeah," he says with slow sarcasm. "You're a regular Luke Skywalker."

I scratch the side of my head and frown at him. "Are you comparing Rock to Darth Vader?"

Finally, he cracks a smile. "No."

We stare at each other.

I got nothing left to say. No more explanations to give.

"I wish…" He jams his hands in his pockets and looks away. "I hate that you went through that alone."

I open my mouth to protest. Rock, Hope, and Charlotte all knew.

"Yeah, yeah, Rock and Hope knew. Your girl knew," he says, as if he's read my mind. "But I know you couldn't be honest with them the way you can be with me." He shrugs. "I hate that you dealt with that on your own."

My throat tightens. "If you make me cry, motherfucker…"

"What?" He throws his arms out wide. "You gonna punch me?"

"Maybe." He's asking for it with his arms wide open, so I grab him and yank him in for a hug.

For a second, he freezes. Then he returns the hug. "I'm sorry I didn't take it well at first," he says against my shoulder.

I release him and shrug. "Hey, I hightailed it to Canada when I found out."

He dips his chin. "That was when, huh?"

"Yeah." Shit, I don't want him doing the math again. "Thank you for doing what Heidi needed. Being there for her. It tore me up, thinking about how to tell her."

He releases a long, slow breath, his gaze falling somewhere over my shoulder. "She loves you. I think she's happy for you but a little sad for herself. It is what it is though."

One of my least-favorite phrases. But he's right. "Are you okay if we tell the club, now?"

Blake takes longer to answer than I expected. "Yeah, it's your news to share. Not mine."

"I know. I don't want to spring anything on you again."

"Jesus, Marcel, you don't have to run everything by me now."

I slap his shoulder. "Yeah, I kinda do. You're my VP."

He scowls and shakes his head. "I gotta get home."

"All right. I'll follow you."

I breathe a sigh of relief as I straddle my bike. Things aren't back to normal yet, but this is progress.

CHAPTER THIRTY

Rock

"Before we leave the table, I'd like everyone's attention." I bow my head, considering all the ways to say this. Not that I haven't thought about it endlessly for months.

I turn and catch Teller's eye. He sits forward and nods. He's ready to get this out in the open too.

"Teller and I have some news we wanted to share with the club."

Jesus Christ, I can't believe I'm airing my business like this. Even if it is to my brothers.

I have everyone's attention. Every head at the table, turned my way. Everyone waiting for whatever I'm about to say. "Ah, a couple of months ago, I found out…" I glance at Teller again. *Spit it out.* "That Teller's my son."

"What?" Bricks shouts. "How is that possible?"

"That's what I said," Teller mutters.

"Boss?" Sparky slowly raises his hand. I grit my teeth, knowing nothing serious will come out of our favorite stoner.

"Yes?"

He tilts his head and pouts, adding sad puppy eyes to the expression. "Are you *my* daddy too?"

Stash howls with laughter, then shoves Sparky. "Not cool, bro."

To my left, Marcel has his head down and his fist covering his mouth. His shoulders shake. The fucker's laughing.

Murphy rolls his eyes and stares at the ceiling, looking like he'd rather be anywhere but here. *You and me both.*

"I don't know why I bothered," I grumble.

Dex blinks. "I think we're all just a little shocked."

Not all. Steer, Hustler, and the rest of Z's crew are wearing various versions of bored and confused faces.

"Wait," Rav says, "is this really new information? I already thought you two were father and son." He swivels his head, searching for another brother at the table to agree with him. "Didn't we already know that?"

Wrath snickers into his hand. Under the table, I launch my foot, landing a solid kick to Wrath's shin. He wipes the smirk off his face. "No, this is brand-new information," he says with every bit of sarcasm he's capable of.

Asshole.

"Prez." Dex's gaze swings between Murphy and Teller. "This seems like an, um…sensitive family matter. You didn't have to share it with everyone if you needed some time."

"We've waited long enough," Marcel says. "I took some time to adjust." He tips his head my way. "So did he, I guess."

"Is Murphy your kid too?" Rav asks. "Because that would make a lot more sense."

"No," Murphy growls.

Sparky's busy tracing his finger over the table, like he's trying to solve a puzzle. "No, that wouldn't be right. Then Heidi'd be like his half—"

"Enough, Sparky," Z says. "Let it go."

I let out a short whistle to grab their attention. "That's it. That's the announcement. Feel free to go on about your lives now."

Dex raises his hand slightly. "Prez, is this something you want us to keep to ourselves?"

"How the fuck exactly is it going to come up in conversation?" Wrath asks.

Ignoring Wrath, I nod at Dex. "I thought it was important for my brothers to know. I don't care if people outside the club find out, but I'm not planning to make any other announcements." I glance at Teller. "Unless you want to."

"I guess they'll find out at the wedding." Marcel shrugs. "New name and all."

Stash squints at us. "You're taking Charlotte's last name?"

"No, dipshit." Marcel jerks his thumb at me. "His."

"You're marrying Rock?" Rav asks.

"Did you all inhale Sparky's stash of edibles before sitting at the table today?" Wrath asks.

Grinder turns to me, an amused smirk twitching somewhere under his full beard. "You should probably put it in the bylaws that brothers can't come to the table high."

"Why are you here again, Grandpa?" I sneer.

"I wouldn't have missed *this* for the world."

Stash wags a finger between Grinder and me. "Wait, is Grinder your dad, too?"

"No," I growl.

"All right." Z claps his hands and stands. "That's enough *genetics for bikers* for today."

"Wait." Dex presses his palms toward the table, motioning for everyone to stay put. "Rock, are you worried this changes how we feel about you at the head of the table? Because I'll tell you right now, it doesn't."

"Yeah, boss," Bricks adds. "We've always known Teller and Murphy were your favorites—"

"Hey," Wrath interrupts.

"But I think I can confidently speak for everyone when I say..." Bricks stops to glance at each of his brothers. "That we trust you. Trust you with our lives, Prez. No matter who's related to you."

I swallow hard and take a second to respond. "Thank you."

Birch raises his hand. "I'm with Rav on this one. I assumed you were Teller's dad all along."

"Same, honestly," Hoot says.

I can't help it. Laughter explodes from me. *Fucking hell.* "That's great."

"Oh, fuck! Your first time—the babysitter story!" Rav snaps his fingers together. "That was Teller's *mom*?"

"Jesus Christ," Z mutters. "Are you that fucking slow?"

"If you think about it, it's kinda cool," Rav says. "If Rock ever leaves us, we'll have a spare."

"That's…" I don't even know how to respond. "Heartwarming. Thanks."

Sparky wiggles his hand in the air in a swimming-fish motion. "You must've had some super-swimmer sperm awfully young."

Why didn't I dismiss everyone when I had the chance?

Z snorts and rolls his eyes at Sparky. "You're just jealous because yours swim in circles."

Ignoring Z, Sparky lobs another question. "Does Hope know?"

I nod once. "She had the pleasure of telling us."

"Aw, man. And she never seemed stressed about it either. And she still tolerates Teller's annoying face up in your biz all the time. So that's good." Sparky shakes his head. "Wait, does that mean…" He stops like he's rubbing his last two brain cells together really hard. "You guys found out back when we took that test to find out if we were the baby daddy of Inga's kid?"

"Boy, you don't miss a thing," Wrath deadpans.

"Yeah, that's how we found out," I answer.

"Cool." Sparky grins. "At least something good came out of that gross situation."

"The *something good* was none of us fathering that bitch's brat," Stash says.

"Well, that too."

"All right." I drum my knuckles against the table. "Any other questions?"

"Are we celebrating?" Sparky asks. "This seems like a cause to celebrate."

Stash side-eyes his buddy. "When *don't* you want to celebrate?"

Grinder and his wise-old smirk stick around after I dismiss everyone. "More brilliant commentary to share?" I ask as he approaches. "Don't you have a pregnant fiancée to hover over?"

"Nah, I'm proud of you." He glances at Murphy, then Teller, still sitting in their spots. "Guessing you all got things sorted?"

"More or less," Murphy answers. "I'm staying put for now."

I stop and stare at Murphy.

Had he considered *leaving* over this?

One of the doors flies open, smashing into the wall, and the question I wanted to ask is forgotten. Sparky's eager face appears.

"Easy, Sparky," I warn.

"Oops, sorry." He glances at the door. "Are you coming? It's party time. No more ruminating over the past."

"Ruminating, huh?" Teller smirks. "Willow leave out her dictionary for you?"

"I'm going to ignore your hostility." Sparky lifts his chin. "This is worthy of celebration."

Marcel glances at me, relief tugging at the corners of his mouth. "Yeah, it is."

For the first time since we found out, it actually seems true.

CHAPTER THIRTY-ONE
Teller

I never got to go home after church. One person or another stopped to talk to me. Word about Rock and me spread. Eventually, a smaller group of us move into the dining room where Trinity's fixing a table full of drinks and snacks for everyone.

"That's some news," Trinity says, handing me a cup of punch.

I accept the punch and take a sip. The too-sweet tang of something fruity mixed with the sharp burn of alcohol sears the back of my throat. I cough and set the cup on the table. "Wrath really didn't tell you?"

"It wasn't his secret to share," she says without a hint of annoyance at her husband. At least that means one woman in Heidi's life hasn't betrayed her trust. "Do you feel better that it's out in the open now?"

I roll my shoulders, noticing how much lighter I feel. "I do. It sucked. But I shouldn't have put it off for so long."

"You did it when you were ready." Her voice rises above the chaotic chatter filling the room. "No one else can tell you how to feel about something so cataclysmic."

"Your husband had a slightly different opinion."

Her gaze shifts to somewhere in the crowded dining room behind me, probably landing on Wrath. "I'm sure he did."

"Thanks, Trinity."

She focuses on me again, her lips curling into a teasing smile. "Does this mean we can begin planning your wedding for real now?"

"That's not what was holding up our wedding…" The protest dies in my throat. Is this why Charlotte and I have taken so long to set a date? Or was it our grief over our miscarriage causing the delay? "Maybe it was. I don't know."

"I just want an excuse to pull out my pink binder. Lilly and Z skunked me by getting hitched in California." Her mouth turns down. "Then things got so messed up with Heidi and—"

"It's been a rough year."

"Right. But you two deserve to have the wedding you want." She rubs her hands together. "I think Charlotte's the first of us to want a white wedding dress."

"She does?" We haven't even talked about it.

"She's going to be a beautiful bride."

"That she is." I grab my cup of punch off the table but don't want to toss it in the trash in front of Trinity. I search the room for Charlotte but find Sparky sitting on top of the bar huffing on a giant water bong. He tosses a bleary-eyed wave my way.

"I think she's in the kitchen," Trinity says, pointing me in that direction. "Tell her not to go far." She pats my shoulder and darts down the hallway. Off to get her pink binder probably.

Good. Trin's right. It's about time Charlotte and I tie the knot.

CHARLOTTE

Trinity doesn't mention Rock and Marcel's newly revealed relationship when she catches up to me outside of the ladies' room. Nope, she's on a mission to get us married a.s.a.p.

Music throbs through the crowded clubhouse. But Trinity herds me through the crowd, pulling Hope, Lilly, and Heidi along with us. We traipse up the stairs into what used to be Hope and Rock's suite at the clubhouse.

"We haven't been here in a while," Hope says, picking up books and placing them on the shelves. She dusts off a windowsill and smooths wrinkles out of the bedspread.

"Well, no one will bug us up here." Trinity climbs into the middle of the bed and opens her pink binder, resting it on her lap. "All right. Guest list." Trinity studies a sheet of paper with columns of names on it. "Between Upstate, Downstate, Virginia, the guys out west." She vaguely waves her hand in that direction. "That's about fifty-five people. You probably need to invite some Devil Demons. Chaser and Mallory just had us at their big anniversary party," she murmurs.

I'm impressed. And a little embarrassed that including a lot of these names didn't occur to me.

"No one's heard from Sway or Tawny since the raid Downstate, so we can cross them off the list." Trinity swipes her marker so thoroughly over their names, they're completely blacked out. "Too bad, so sad."

I snort with laughter. "Do we even know what happened?"

"Nope," Trinity answers without looking up. "Don't know. Don't care."

Hope chuckles.

Lilly squeezes her eyes shut and clasps her hands together like she's praying to every deity she can think of. "And may they never find their way back home."

"Carter and Mercy," I remind Trinity.

She flicks her amber eyes up. "Got them." Her tone's somewhere near *this isn't my first rodeo*. "Will Carter bring Bianca?"

"Uh, I'm not sure. Add her just in case."

"Got it." Trinity flips a page. "That covers Teller's family."

"Oh my God, does this make me stepmother-of-the-groom or something?" Hope asks.

"It does," I tease. "I promise I won't ask you to wear anything matronly." I raise one hand as if I'm ready to swear on a stack of Bibles.

"Thank you," Hope says with a prim nod.

It feels so good to be able to finally talk about this out in the open.

Trinity taps her pen against the page she's working on. "What about your uncle, Charlotte?"

"I don't know where Chuck is these days. I've gotten maybe one or two random texts from him and that's it."

"So, we'll mark him down as a maybe." She scribbles some more notes. "Your mom—oh, shit." Trinity lifts her head, staring at me with wide, apologetic eyes. "I'm sorry. I forgot."

"It's okay." I shrug, relieved at how little it bothers me.

"Geez." Hope taps her finger against her bottom lip. "Now that I think about it, *none* of us have had our mothers at our weddings."

"With good reason," Heidi mutters. I wrap my arm around her shoulders and squeeze, and she hugs me back.

"That's why *this*..." Trinity spins her finger in a circle, indicating each of us. "Our chosen family, our *sisterhood*, is so important."

"Blood doesn't guarantee love or acceptance," Lilly adds.

"Thank you," I whisper. "You don't know how much it means to me that you understand. Other people say crap like, 'Oh you have to forgive her, she's your mother.' As if just because she's dead, I'm supposed to forget she betrayed me in the most evil ways."

"Fuck 'em," Trinity says. "If they haven't lived it, they can shut the fuck up. Just because you're related by blood doesn't mean you owe them forgiveness."

"Can we have that stitched on a pillow?" Lilly asks.

"I got your pillow right here." Trinity whips one of the pillows out from behind her and smacks Lilly in the chest with it.

Lilly snatches it away and bops Trinity over the head.

"All right, girls." Hope reaches over and grabs the pillow from Lilly's hands. "That's enough."

"See? We don't need a mom. We have Hope," Heidi says, grinning.

"Amen." Trinity raises her palms toward the ceiling. "Now, where do you want to get married?"

"Honestly, right in our own backyard," I answer. I've given the location a lot of thought. "We certainly have the space."

"And it's close to the clubhouse," Heidi points out. "So the, um, rowdier guests won't stay all night."

I chuckle and shake my head, refusing to admit I'd considered the same thing.

"Perfect." Trinity claps her hands. "Backyard weddings are my specialty."

"Are you going to open a wedding planning business next?" Hope asks.

"No, smarty-pants." Trinity gives her a teasing shove. "I like to take care of my sisters. I don't want you to have any stress on your special day."

Hope's mouth twists down. "Well, now I feel bad you did all the planning stuff for your own wedding."

"But it was fun for *me*." Trinity slides her gaze my way. "If you want to do it, I'll step back."

"No, no, no." I shoot a quick look at Hope. "Pipe down."

"Okay." Trinity glances up and looks each of us in the eye. "How formal are we going to be? Matching rows of bridesmaids and grooms—"

"No." I bite my lip. "If you guys don't mind...we talked about keeping it small. Mercy and I have been friends for a long, long time. And Marcel wanted to include my brother...So we were going to ask Mercy, Heidi, Murphy, and Carter to maybe stand up for us."

"Thank God," Lilly mutters.

Hope blows out a similar relieved breath but doesn't say anything.

"Is that okay?" I ask. "You're sure you're not—"

"The wedding is to celebrate you and Teller," Hope says. "If you want to keep things simple, you should."

"Thank you. Oh! We did want Grace and Alexa as flower girls. And Chance for ring bearer, if you think he'd be okay with it?" I ask Lilly.

"I think he'd love it. Thank you, Charlotte."

"We want the little guys included," I explain. "No need to find babysitters or anything like that."

"I don't know," Lilly says in a teasing voice. "When there's a toddler meltdown in the middle of the ceremony, it might make you think twice about having your own."

She's kidding but for some reason, her words hit me like a punch in the stomach.

Hope pins her with a look. "Whose toddler do you expect to melt down?"

"Ooo," Trinity sings. "Retreat, Lilly. Retreat."

"Charlotte?" Hope's alarmed tone seems like it's a million miles away. "Are you okay?"

Heidi touches my shoulder.

"What?" I swipe at my eyes, surprised to find dampness on my cheeks.

"Charlotte, what's wrong?" Lilly sits next to me. "I'm sorry. I was only kidding."

My throat's too tight to get any words out. Heidi slides her hand over mine and squeezes. I glance up and she tilts her head, sympathy shining in her deep brown eyes. *She knows.*

"Murphy told you?" I whisper.

She nods. "Not until, you know, everything blew up." She bites her lip. "I've been wanting to tell you I'm sorry for all the *when will I be an aunt* jokes but didn't want to bring it up if you didn't want to talk about it."

At least I don't have to actually say the words. The girls all seem to understand.

Hope runs her hand over my back. "When was it, Charlotte?"

I shake my head and blow out a breath. "Right around the time Rock and Teller got their news."

"Oh, Charlotte." Hope pulls me into her arms. "I wish you'd said something sooner. I'm sorry."

Trinity reaches over and rests her hand on my leg, a gentle offer of support.

"I'm having trouble getting pregnant now," Lilly says quietly.

I lift my eyes to hers, grateful to have the focus off of me.

She shrugs one shoulder in a nervous or embarrassed way. "One broken condom gave us Chance but now we're raw-dogging it all over the place and nothing."

I burst into much-needed laughter.

Hope blinks several times. "Thanks for the visual, Lilly."

"Besides all the...*raw dogging*," Trinity says, "did you see your doctor?"

"No. I'm afraid of what they might tell me," Lilly admits.

"Mine was kind of a jackass," I say.

"You should go see my doctor," Hope offers. "She's very kind."

Although she's still sitting right next to me, Heidi's gotten awfully quiet. I squeeze her hand. "I am *very* excited to meet my new niece," I assure her.

Lilly reaches across my lap to touch Heidi's leg. "Me too."

"I know," Heidi says.

"Should we head downstairs before the guys get themselves into trouble?" I suggest.

Heidi rolls her eyes. "Ten dollars says Blake and my brother are already in some sort of trouble."

"I'm not taking that bet." I look at each of their faces and can't understand why I waited so long to tell them this. "Thank you. I feel a lot better. Just having it out there."

"You don't have to go through anything alone." Trinity looks at me, then Lilly. "Ever. No matter what."

We all agree.

"Hey," Heidi says. "Don't tell her I told you, but I think Shelby's writing a song for you guys. For your wedding." Heidi sighs and rests her hand on her chest. "I'm totally not jealous at all."

"Really? That's so sweet."

"All right." Trinity slams her binder shut. "Speaking of Shelby, she and Serena should be here soon." She lifts her chin at Hope. "Will you run home with me for a sec?"

"Of course."

We file out of the bedroom and Hope locks the door behind us.

In our absence, the party's gotten louder and rowdier. Brothers and their bunnies for the night have moved to the upstairs hallway, but some haven't bothered to take their activities into a bedroom. A girl with her shirt pulled down to expose her enormous tits has her mouth wide open, about to swallow Hoot's dick. I accidentally kick the heel of one of her shoes, almost face-planting. She shoots a glare at me.

"Sorry," I mutter, shielding my eyes and hurrying past them.

"I didn't need to know Hoot's dick was pierced," I whisper to Lilly.

She giggles and bumps into me while she turns, craning her neck to see. Moans and slobbering noises propel us faster toward the stairs.

At least downstairs, there's more conversation than fornication going on.

"Perfect timing." I spot Shelby wandering around the party and wave to her.

"There y'all are!" She races over, hugging each of us. "Hoo boy. Rooster got called into the principal's office." She jerks her thumb toward the war room. "Jiggy's searching for a bedmate. And Serena ain't here yet. I thought I was on my own."

"Nope. Trinity wanted to do some wedding planning."

"Aw," she pouts, "what'd I miss?"

"I'll fill you in," Trinity promises. "Hope?" The two of them wind their way through the crowd and out the front door.

Lilly hugs me again. "Call me whenever you want to talk," she says against my ear.

"I will."

Heidi yawns and rubs her stomach. "I need a nap." She squeezes my arm. "If you see Murphy, tell him I went to the house."

"Do you want us to walk you home?" I ask.

"No." She waves off the offer. "Shelby just got here."

"Did they all just ditch us?" Shelby squints at the front door.

"I don't think it was intentional."

"Oh, well." She flashes a quick grin and loops her arm through mine.

Jiggy waves to us from one of the couches in the corner. Shelby tugs me across the room. For such a tiny woman, she's awfully strong.

"Hey, there, songbird," Jiggy tips his head back and flashes a warm smile at Shelby, then me. "And ray of sunshine."

I chuckle. "Hey."

"Hey, Jiggy." Shelby cocks her head. "Ya find what ya needed?"

He squeezes his arm around the tanned blonde practically sitting in his lap. "This is Amy. Amy, this is Shelby." He nods to me. "And Charlotte."

"Hiya." Shelby wiggles her fingers.

"Sit, join us." Jiggy nods to the space next to him.

Amy doesn't seem as welcoming. Either she's missed that we're already patched and therefore not interested in stealing Jigsaw away or she's seen our patches and assumes we'll be mean to her.

Ignoring her, I reach for the filmy material of Shelby's dress. It's made up of layers and layers of gauzy lilac fabric with vibrant butterflies scattered over it. "I love this, by the way."

"Yeah?" She plays with the frills covering her chest. "I thought it might be a little too baby girl, ya know? Rooster and I don't play that game."

Jigsaw rubs his hand over the side of his head. "As long as you don't put your hair in pigtails and call him *Daddy*, I think you're fine."

Ignoring Jigsaw's advice, I nod to Shelby's silver cowboy boots. "Damn, if we were the same size, I would *so* steal those boots."

She beams at me and sticks her foot out to show them off. "Rooster bought 'em for me."

"My boy has a foot fetish," Jiggy announces.

"Hush your mouth." Shelby leans over and gives him a playful shove.

Amy's dizzy gaze narrows into something catty as she stares at Shelby. She points one long orange fingernail at Shelby's waist, almost poking her in the stomach. "Aren't you a little chubby for that kind of dress?"

Shock wipes the sweet smile off of Shelby's face. She blinks, then seems to find her cool. "I dunno, aren't you a lil' bitchy to be flappin' those lips in my ol' man's clubhouse?"

The girl pushes against the couch as if she's about to launch herself at Shelby. Jigsaw wraps his hand around her chicken-wing arm, holding her in place. "Don't you fucking dare," he warns. He releases her and she wobbles out of his lap. "Get the fuck outta here."

"What?"

Jigsaw ignores her and snaps his fingers at one of the prospects. The movement also catches Steer's eye, and he follows the prospect over.

"Jiggy, come on," the girl whines. When he still won't look at her, she stands and stomps her feet. "Fine." She casts her conniving gaze around the room.

"No." Jiggy stands and blocks her path. "Get the fuck out of our clubhouse."

"Jigsaw," Shelby starts.

Jiggy ignores her. When the prospect arrives, he shoves the girl into his arms. "This one needs to go."

"What's going on, brother?" Steer asks.

"Amy needs to learn some respect." Jiggy stares down at the quivering prospect. "Do *not* let her back inside that door or you'll clean every toilet in this clubhouse with your motherfuckin' tongue."

"Y-yeah. You got it, Jiggy." He grabs the girl by the arm and marches her toward the front door.

Steer snorts as he watches them leave.

"The fuck you laughing about, bro?" Jigsaw drops into his seat again. "He's doing *your* fucking job."

"You didn't have to do that on my account, Jiggy," Shelby drawls.

"Eh." He waves off her concern with a flick of his hand.

"Jiggy's trying to impress you, Shelby," Steer taunts. "He's hoping you'll take pity on his poor, lonely willy one day."

I roll my eyes. One way or another, this won't end well for Steer.

"You got a death wish, Steer?" Shelby asks. "Rooster hears you talking that trash, he's—"

"Fuck that," Jigsaw snaps. "My willy's allergic to anyone who disrespects my brothers' girls. That's all."

"That's sweet, Jiggy." Shelby covers her ears with her hands. "Now, I don't wanna hear nothin' about any of y'alls' willies ever again. Okay?"

"Yeah, and keep 'em in your pants." I point to the ceiling. "I've been traumatized enough tonight by what I saw upstairs."

"Good luck." Sparky pops up from behind the couch and drapes his arms over the back of it.

"Damn!" Shelby clutches her chest. "You almost gave me a dang heart attack. What're you doing hiding back there?"

He just gives us a goofy grin, then climbs over the back of the couch and drops onto one of the cushions. "Talking about where to park their willies is their favorite topic."

"Jigsaw," I say. "That was commendable, and we all appreciate you sticking up for us."

He nods and winks at me. "I'm able to rise above my baser instincts to protect my family."

"Dream on, Charlotte." Steer wags a finger at me. "Jigsaw doesn't want Shelby telling her momma about all the pussy he pulls."

Shelby heaves out a long, dramatic sigh. "Not this again," she mutters.

"At least you admit I get more ass than you," Jigsaw says with a shit-eating grin.

"It's just 'cause you look all broody and scary." Steer slashes a line across his face. "They see your scarred mug and wanna heal you."

Jigsaw grits his teeth, the first sign I've ever seen from him that the guys' joking around has gone too far.

"That's not cool, Steer," I say, even though I know damn well I shouldn't get involved.

"No, no," Jiggy argues with exaggerated sarcasm. "Bullshit Bob is right. When I was a kid, I thought to myself, 'Gee what will make the ladies drop their panties when I'm older? I know, I'll slice up my face.'"

The sadistic smile slides off of Steer's lips. "Sorry, bro. Charlotte's right. That wasn't cool."

Jiggy stares at him for a second, as if he's trying to decide if Steer's apology is sincere. "All right, brother."

Shelby leans against me. "Sheesh, what'd I do to that girl, anyway?" She nervously tugs at the bodice of her dress.

"Stop." I rest my hand over hers. "You look adorable."

"Damn her," she says in a lower voice. "I packed on a couple pounds since being off tour. Now I'm gonna be all self-conscious about it."

"Don't you dare give her another second of thought," I say in my sternest big sister tone. "You're gorgeous, and she was just jealous all the attention wasn't on her."

"Yeah, you look a lot better with a few extra pounds on you," Steer adds. He lifts his chin at me next. "You too, Charlotte."

"Shut the fuck up," Jigsaw snaps. "No one asked you."

I blink and tug on my vest. *Is it snugger than usual?*

"Never fear, songbird." Jiggy leans in close to us. "When I finally claim an ol' lady, she'll fit into the sisterhood. I don't like catty ones."

"I only like 'em if they're using those claws to dig into my back," Steer adds.

"Great, so glad you're still here," Shelby grumbles.

I wrap an arm around her and hug her closer, then squint at Jigsaw. "I seem to remember you moaning about Upstate infecting your charter with monogamy not that long ago."

Jiggy's face transforms into a wide, unashamed grin. "It's possible I may have made such a statement in the past. But you can't hold me to everything I've ever said."

"No one has time to keep track of the shit that comes out of your mouth," Steer says.

"What's wrong, Shelby?" Serena asks, joining our group. "You look a little miffed."

I move down to make room for her.

"One of the bunnies implied Shelby's fat, and Jiggy kicked her ass to the curb," Steer says.

"Thanks. Tell everyone," Shelby mutters, tugging at her dress again.

Jigsaw slowly pulls a knife from a sheath at his side. He digs the tip against his index finger and spins it slowly. "If you're tired of your guts being on the inside, just say so, brother."

That finally encourages Steer to lift his big frame off the couch and melt into the crowd.

"Sorry I missed the fireworks." Serena rests her hand on her stomach. "I would've aimed my puke stream at her."

"Ewww." Shelby giggles and tugs on Serena's hand, encouraging her to sit with us. "Come here, little momma. How're you feeling?"

"Like I just had my head in the toilet bowl for fifteen minutes." Her gaze searches the room. "Have you seen Grayson?"

Jiggy jerks his thumb toward the war room. "He's in there. You all right?"

"Better now."

"Steer, Jiggy, get your asses in here," Z thunders from the war room.

Jiggy snaps to attention and hauls ass to obey his president. Steer follows at a more leisurely place.

"His head's halfway to Tennessee," Shelby mutters as Steer closes the war room door behind him.

"You and Rooster thinking you might follow one day?" Serena asks.

Shelby's wide eyes and dropped jaw suggest she and Rooster *have* discussed moving. Damn. That would really make things difficult for Z. Would Marcel have to move down there and help out again?

Shelby recovers quickly and waves off the suggestion. "Nah, I like it up here so far."

Serena and I share a look. That wasn't exactly a firm no. A bit of melancholy settles over me. In the short time I've gotten to know her, I really like Shelby. I'd hate to see her leave.

CHAPTER THIRTY-TWO

Teller

THE PARTY HAD GONE WELL INTO THE NIGHT. CHARLOTTE'S UP BEFORE ME the next morning. As I stumble into the kitchen, she greets me with a sunny smile.

"Whoa." I stop and stare. "What are you wearing?"

She runs her hand over the sheer dress covering a tiny two-piece swimsuit. "A bathing suit."

"We don't have a pool. Where are you planning to swim?"

"You don't like it? I got it for our honeymoon but thought I'd try it out now." She gestures toward the kitchen window. Sunlight streams in, bathing the room in a warm morning glow. "I was just going to sit outside for a few minutes and get a little sun."

"Sun? Sunshine, you burn like a marshmallow."

"I know. But last night when we moved the party out to the bonfire, we were talking and Trinity said she read this article about women who don't get enough vitamin D can have fertility problems and…" Her voice trails off and her bright smile fades.

"Hey." I curl my hands over her hips and pull her close. "You worried about that?"

"Well, I'm in my cave-like office all day." She flicks her wrist toward the clubhouse. "All the parties are at night. I don't know."

I curl my fingers around her wrist and shift her hand to my cock. "You need vitamin D, all you gotta do is ask, Sunshine."

Sweet laughter explodes out of her, and I recite a quick prayer of thanks that my corny horndog jokes still crack her up. "That's better."

She leans into me, pressing her palms against my chest, and stares up. "Want to sunbathe with me? I know you work outside all the time but—"

"I'd love nothing more." I slide my hand down her back and squeeze her ass. "Especially if you're in this." I take her hand and run my thumb over her engagement ring. Can't wait to add a wedding band. Already bought it. "Trin said you're thinking of a white wedding dress?"

Her eyebrows pinch together. "Too traditional? It's stupid, right? It'll get dirty, and—"

"Stop. Wear whatever you want. You'll be beautiful." I pull back and run my gaze over her. "You look hot in white."

Her smile returns. I rest a finger under her chin and tip her head up. "I like seeing my girl happy."

"I'm happy." She slides her arms around my waist and squeezes. "You make me very happy."

"Are you relieved everything's out in the open and we don't have to censor ourselves anymore?"

"Honestly, yes."

"I'm sorry I made you do that."

Her mouth slips into a serious line. "I'd do anything for you, Marcel."

I pat her butt again. "I'm going upstairs to change. Meet you outside?"

"Deal."

Upstairs, I find a pair of swim trunks I haven't used since our visit to National. Damn shame it's been that long since I've seen Charlotte prance around in a bathing suit.

I find her on a lounge chair underneath the pergola Murphy helped me install. She has the netting on all four sides open, but the thing still has a roof. "How is that getting you any vitamin D?" I ask.

She shields her eyes and glances up at me. "The sun. It burns."

Shaking with laughter, I drop onto her chair next to her. It's sturdy. Meant for two people. We've put it to the test plenty of times.

Farther back in the yard, the chickens cluck and warble. Wind rustles through the forest, swaying the branches of a pine tree that's closer to us than I prefer. I should go get my chainsaw and take that fucker down.

Not today.

I lay back and stretch my arm out, encouraging Charlotte to snuggle closer. Normally, I'd feel like a lazy son of a bitch, sitting around doing nothing during the day. But spending time with Charlotte—actual moments where we can talk, connect, and just be together—is rare, so I soak up every second. "Sunbathing in New York isn't quite the same as Mississippi."

"No. My God. I thought that was the thirteenth circle of hell, it was so hot."

"You're not going to like where I'm going to suggest we honeymoon, then."

"Let me guess," she says in a dry tone. "Somewhere with lax banking laws in the southern hemisphere."

I grin and hug her tighter. "This is why we're so perfect together."

"Rock and Hope got to go to Hawaii." She pouts. "Wrath and Trinity went to Belize."

"Belize might work." I tease my fingers over the tops of her breasts, ready to burst out of the skimpy suit top. "I'll need to hire a very private villa or something. Can't have anyone else seeing you in this."

She tips her head down. "Steer implied I was getting fat last night."

Rage drowns out all the other noises around us for a second. "He did *what?*"

She relays the story and I wonder if Rooster and Shelby are having a similar conversation this morning.

"Then Jiggy threatened to spill his guts on the floor and Steer left."

"What a jackass." I rest my hand over her belly button. "I'm sorry."

"We were thinking he must already have his head in Tennessee since he's moving there soon."

"Yeah, well, pissing off all his brothers up here isn't the smartest move. Deadbranch will probably be the first charter Priest sends Rooster to investigate when he's on the road this summer."

"Have *you* ever thought about moving to one of the other charters?"

"What? No. My whole family...everything is *here.*"

"I know." She tips her head down. "I was just wondering."

I slide my hand lower. "You know what I was wondering?"

Her hips shift as if her body knows the answer to my question. "No, what?"

"If I can make you come just by rubbing your little clit through your swimsuit." I lean in and press a kiss to her cheek. "What do you think?"

"No," she whispers. "I don't want to traumatize Carter again. He just recovered from the last time he caught us out here."

"Try again, Sunshine. He's not home. I checked."

"But—"

"He's booked up at Bronze's all day. Then headed to Bianca's."

A light breeze rustles through the tall pine trees, emphasizing how peaceful it is outside.

I leave my hand resting against her stomach, the tips of my fingers millimeters from the edge of her bikini bottoms. "May I?"

Her chest rises and falls faster. "May you what?"

I stroke my middle finger lightly against her soft skin, showing her exactly what I want to do. Her nipples press into hard little points against the thin white fabric. I drop my head and wrap my lips around one, sucking through the material.

She gasps. "Marcel."

I release her nipple. "What's it going to be, Charlotte? Under or over?" I tease my fingers along the elastic waistband and her legs fall open. "Not good enough. Say it."

"Say what?" The corners of her mouth twitch.

I slide my hand up over her belly to cup her breast and flick my thumb over her nipple.

"Oh," she moans.

"You want more?"

"Yes."

I reverse direction, teasing just underneath her bottoms now.

She releases a shaky breath. "Please make me come."

I shift my body closer, sliding my arm under her shoulders and kiss her forehead. "See? Was that so hard?"

"You're insufferable." She turns on her side and cups my cheek, leaning up to press her lips to mine.

I hum an encouraging noise and she parts her lips, letting me stroke my tongue against hers. My hand is trapped between her thighs now. I wriggle it free and stroke my middle finger over her mound. "Open," I order against her lips.

She shifts, planting her foot against the cushion and lifts her knee, giving me access. I still take my time, lazily sliding one finger over her bottoms, tracing her slit through the material.

Her kisses deepen. The little noises coming from her throat increase. It takes so much to unravel Charlotte but once I finally do, it's always so beautiful.

"Over or under?" I ask, dipping my finger under the elastic.

"God, I don't care. Just don't stop touching me."

For a few lazy minutes, I slowly stroke up and down. Each time my finger slides up, I graze her clit, applying more and more pressure. At the next touch, she gasps.

"Now you're ready."

"Uh-huh." She nods and strokes her fingers over my cheek.

I slide my fingers under her bikini bottoms. My hand's bigger than the damn thing and stretches the material tight, but I don't want to stop touching her, and somehow, it's hotter this way. She's all smooth, soft skin underneath. No familiar landing strip of hair.

"Fuck," I groan.

"I had to, or I looked like I had a clown trapped between my legs."

"What the fuck?" Hard laughter shakes my body to the side.

Her lips curl into a playful smile.

"No clown talk." I wrap my other arm around her neck, covering her mouth with my hand.

Her eyes widen, heat flaring in them. She parts her thighs again.

"That's better. Good girl," I praise.

Her slick tongue darts against my palm.

"I'll give you something to lick in a minute, Sunshine," I assure her, keeping my hand right where it is. Shaking the clown image from my head, I return to my exploration. My finger slides through her wetness and I groan. "You're going to feel so good wrapped around my cock in a few minutes."

She nods frantically and licks my palm again.

"Not yet. Be a good girl for me." I slide my finger over her clit and slowly circle until she moans and squeezes her eyes shut. "That's it," I whisper.

She stretches, arching her back. A full-body shudder works over her, and she spreads her legs to give me better access.

"What a good girl." I reward her by moving my hand from her mouth and slip two fingers inside her, heading straight for the spot that makes her toes curl every time.

"Ah." She lets out a sharp sound, then squinches her face tight, as if she's concentrating on every touch.

"Relax. Stop thinking so much." I nuzzle against her neck, kissing and sucking while still stroking in and out of her. "Let go."

She bucks her hips and moans even louder. "That's good. Right there."

She's trembling right on the edge, and as much as I enjoy taking her there and back, today I want to push her right over. Hard and fast. I'm so hard for her, I'm actually in pain.

Her body jerks, arching against my hand. She sobs, uncontrollable little sounds.

When the sharpest part of her orgasm ebbs, she looks up at me with hazy, unfocused eyes. I'm addicted to that look. I didn't know what it meant to feel like a king until I unlocked this woman.

I slide my hand out of her bottoms. "Need more than that, Sunshine."

She reaches for me, tugging at my shorts. "Oh, my." She turns on her side so she's facing me, and kisses along my jaw. "Your cock's so fucking hard, I don't know if I can get these off."

Lightning crackles over my skin, scorching heat shooting straight to my dick. "I don't care if you cut them off. I need you on top of me, now."

She kneels next to me and works on freeing me with deliberate speed.

When I'm finally naked, she curls her fingers around my cock and strokes. "This looks painful," she teases.

"You have no idea."

"Would this help?" She leans closer and kisses the crown of my cock. "Or this?" She opens wider and slides her hot, wet mouth over me.

"Fuck." I thrust my hips up, chasing more of her sweet mouth. She settles between my legs, taking as much of me as she can then withdrawing, swirling her tongue in lazy circles around the head. Pressure builds. "Char."

She looks up.

"One more time. All the way." I rest my hand at the back of her head, slowly pushing her down.

She moans around my cock.

"Ah, fuck." I tug her hair. "Come here."

She sits up and hooks her thumbs in her bikini bottoms.

"No, leave them on." I grip her by the waist and guide her over my cock. "That's it." I reach down and shove the white strip of fabric aside. "Come to me."

She curls her hand around my cock and guides me to her. We groan at the same time as I slide deep inside her. I squeeze my eyes shut.

Her movements start slow, quickly building to a fast, frantic bucking. The bathing suit top isn't enough to contain her breasts. I yank the cups down, pinching her hard nipples. The rush of adrenaline she sends coursing through my body should be enough to kill me.

"Oh!" Her body moves faster. Pussy clenching around my cock. Short frantic breaths. A sweet sobbing sound as she comes again.

That pushes me off my own cliff of pleasure and shatters me into a million pieces—every one of them belonging to Charlotte.

CHAPTER THIRTY-THREE

Charlotte

MARCEL AND I DOZE, TALK, AND PLAY WITH EACH OTHER FOR MOST OF THE day. We grill outside together. Part of me feels guilty that I'm enjoying our alone time so much.

"Do you ever wish we lived up at the property with everyone else?" he asks me as I'm slicing cucumbers for our salad.

"No. Actually, I was thinking how nice this was—just the two of us." I slide a guilty look at my brother's loft.

"I promised Carter he'd always have a home," he says, making my heart melt.

"No, no, I'd never ask him to move. Unless he wanted to. He might not want to still live with us if he gets married or whatever." I consider his question. "Why? Do you wish we lived up there?"

"Not really. You're right. Everyone would be in our faces more than they already are. I didn't know if you wanted a newer house or something…bigger?" He drops his gaze to the off-the-shoulder sweater I threw on over my bathing suit. "A pool?"

"I wouldn't mind that." I gesture toward the back of the property with the knife in my hand. "We have the room if you want to build."

"Maybe," he says absently, turning to flip our steaks.

"I'm going to run inside and grab some salad dressing."

"Can you bring me a platter, too?"

"Sure thing, handsome." On impulse, I lean up and kiss his cheek. "Thanks for all the sunny orgasms today. They really hit the spot."

He bursts into laughter. "My pleasure."

I hurry into the house, humming as I search through the refrigerator for the dressing. I set that on the counter and bend down to look for a grilling platter.

"I bet it's in the dishwasher," I mutter. Sure enough, that's where I find the one I want.

I pass the nook where I keep my phone plugged in. A notification blinks on the otherwise black screen. I pick it up and carry it outside with everything else.

"I thought we said no work today?" Marcel nods to the phone in my hands.

"There's a message." I hand him the platter and set the dressing on the table. "I don't want to ignore it if it's a client. Or if Carter needs something."

"I'll allow it." He winks at me.

I swipe my thumb over the screen and stare at the long list of missed calls. "Oh my God."

"What?" Marcel's spatula clinks against the platter. "Everything okay?"

"I don't know. I have like a dozen missed calls from Bianca." My voicemail is jammed full. All Bianca. I hit call instead of listening to them.

"Charlotte!" she screams into the phone. "Oh my God, I've been trying to call you."

A lead balloon of fear settles in my stomach. "What's going on? Is Carter okay?"

"No," she sobs. "Someone grabbed him."

Marcel moves closer, motioning for me to turn the speaker on.

"What do you mean someone grabbed him?" I shout. "Who? Where?"

"I don't know. Some guys." Her voice lowers. "The cops are here."

Marcel grabs the phone from my hand. "Bianca, what happened?"

"We were outside my apartment. Just talking next to his car." She sobs and hiccups through each word. "He was parked at the curb in front of my brownstone, like he always does."

Marcel lets out a frustrated growl.

"This…this sketchy black van pulled up right next to us. Two guys in black hoodies jumped out. Grabbed him. Carter punched one. I jumped on the back of the other guy, but he elbowed me in the face. They wrestled Carter into the van and sped away. I got a few numbers off the plate." Anguished sobs choke off any more words she may have been trying to say.

Marcel paces away a few steps, barking out orders to Bianca for more information.

My vision swims.

Fear and horror singe my blood. My baby brother's in trouble. Why didn't I know? Sense it somehow?

"Miss, who are you talking to?" a deep voice asks in the background.

"Carter's sister."

"Miss Clark?" The deep voice becomes even louder. "This is Officer O'Flannery. We need you to come to the station so we can get some information—"

"What are you doing to find my brother?" I shout.

"Everything we can. We have several witnesses. His girlfriend says your uncle is a leader of a local motorcycle gang? Is that right?"

"For fuck's sake," Marcel mutters.

"Where can I meet you?" I ask.

He gives me the address of the station. Not sure I have any intention of actually going, I quickly jot it down and hang up.

TELLER

Charlotte's terrified eyes and frantic movements rip out my insides.

"Jesus Christ." I run my hands through my hair, settling them at the base of my skull. *What the fuck is happening?* "We're going to find him, Charlotte."

"Is it club-related?"

This isn't the time to fuck around and try to protect the club. Charlotte and I are way past that. She's too smart to swallow any bullshit. "I honestly don't know. We don't have an issue with anyone that I know of right now."

"Marcel," she whispers. "If something happens to him… If he… I can't live with that. Do you understand?"

"I hear you."

"I know he's not a brother—"

"No. He's *my* brother. He's club family. I swore I'd protect him, Charlotte." And boy, did I fuck *that* up, apparently. Someone had the balls to abduct him in broad daylight. In my club's territory.

My mind's racing. Who could possibly have an issue with us? Why involve Carter?

What if it has nothing to do with us?

"How much do you know about Bianca? What's she into?"

Charlotte snorts. "I don't know. They've been friends for years."

I'm already tapping out a text to Rock, Wrath, Murphy, and Dex. They'll spread the word. I add Z, Rooster, Jigsaw, and Grinder in too. They have a longer ride to get here.

"Will they try to contact us? A ransom?" Charlotte asks.

"I don't know," I mumble, not looking up from my phone.

Rock answers right away.

Rock: Be at your house in ten.

"Thank fuck."

Charlotte's phone dings.

"It's Merlin!" she yells.

I reach her in two steps, my hand out. "Give it to me."

She nods and slides the phone into my hand.

"Hello?"

"Figured you'd answer her phone," he answers.

"What's going on?" This better not be a fucking social call.

"You tell me," he says slowly. Highway noises muddy up the background.

"I'm not in the mood to fuck around with you."

He coughs a few times. "You missing anyone important?"

"Yes," I grind out through my teeth.

"Thought so. I got a call. Not sure why they think I give a shit."

"Are you fucking serious?" I stalk into the house, slamming the kitchen door. "Charlotte's beside herself."

"Yeah? And what about you?"

"I'm getting him back with or without your help. But I'd rather have you tell me what I'm dealing with. Where are you?"

"Close by."

"How close?"

"Near Empire. Ain't exactly like I know your address."

I give him the information, and he says he'll be here in an hour.

"What'd that asshole say?" Charlotte asks.

"A whole lot of nothing."

A tear leaks from the corner of her eye. "We have to find my brother."

"I will, Sunshine. I promise."

Someone throws a fist against the front door, then opens it before we answer. Rock's heavy footsteps thud over the floorboards, and into the kitchen. "What do we know?"

"Nothing. I just heard from Merlin. He's on his way here." I squeeze Charlotte's shoulder. "I think he knows more than he wanted to say over the phone."

"You're also inclined to not trust him," he points out.

"True."

"The cops want me to come in and answer questions." Charlotte glances from me to Rock. "I don't see the point though."

Rock nods. "Now that we know Merlin's involved somehow, it's probably better if you don't go."

We're interrupted by Murphy and Wrath showing up. Wrath demands an immediate briefing on all the information I have.

Heidi and Trinity must have come too. I hear their gentler voices offering assurances to Charlotte that everything will be okay.

Will it, though? We don't even know what we're dealing with.

Why Carter?

He's mouthy, no doubt. Did he piss someone off at the tattoo shop? Not everyone finds his sarcastic jabs as amusing as I do. If it's another MC, it's a pussy fucking thing to do. You got beef with me, come at me. Or come at the club. But not my family.

Carter's innocent and goofy face flashes in my head. I promised I'd look out for him. He was in my club's territory. He should've been safe.

"Teller." Rock snaps his fingers in front of my face. "Stay focused. Now isn't the time to spiral into blaming yourself."

How'd he know that's where my mind went?

"Who would take Carter?" Murphy asks, concern bleeding into his voice. As much as he loves ragging on Carter, I know he thinks of him as a little brother same as I do.

"I don't know. Bianca didn't have a lot of details. She's stuck talking to Empire PD."

"This is bad." Wrath runs his hands over his hair. His gaze slips to Rock. "We can't get bogged down dealing with cops. We gotta find him *fast*."

Z walks into the kitchen, lifts his chin at me, but doesn't say anything.

"Can't be Wolf Knights. They're gone from Slater," Murphy says. "And they sure as fuck wouldn't go after family. Asshole or not, Merlin's still a patched brother."

"Just because it's not a Wolf Knight doesn't mean it's not connected to them," Rock points out. "Merlin was dealing with all sorts of shady folk."

"That's done," I say. "Or it should be."

Murphy runs his hand over the scar on his scalp. "I'm not so sure we got every fucker involved in what happened to me. And that was the same club Merlin was dealing with."

"Remy said they haven't had issues at the racetrack since that went down," Z says.

"Chaser's brother wanted to start moving cargo through our territory," Murphy reminds us. "Maybe Quill didn't like the limitations we slapped on his business."

Rock shakes his head. "He took responsibility for the member of his crew that went after Serena. He made it right."

"He *executed* him right in front of us." Z points a finger-gun at the floor and pulls the trigger. "Besides, why come after Carter, of all people, now?"

Murphy holds up his hands. "I'm trying to think of all possible scenarios."

"No, you're right," Rock says. "We need to list every possible threat so we can rule them out one by one."

"We don't have time for that," I growl. We need to do something *now*.

A tap at the side door draws our attention. Through the glass, I make out Dex's tall frame and shout for him to come in.

"What's going on?" He pants as if he ran here instead of rode his bike. "I got here as fast as I could. Malik's watching Crystal Ball but said he'll close up early if we want him to."

"No, better he stay there and keep an eye on the girls," Rock says.

My gaze drops to a small box in Dex's hands. "What's that?"

He holds out the white cardboard box. It's no bigger than something you'd stick a fancy coffee mug in to give as a gift to someone. "Charlotte Clark" is written on top in bold, black letters.

My stomach drops.

Dex bites the inside of his cheek as if he doesn't want to say where the box came from. "It was sitting on my bike when I left Crystal Ball."

"Why the fuck would anyone leave something for Charlotte there?" Murphy explodes.

"How would they even know that's a way to get something to her?" Wrath asks.

This is bad. This is so, so bad.

I take the box from Dex's hand.

"Don't let her open that," Murphy says. "You don't know what it is."

"I don't know what *what* is?" Charlotte asks, standing in the hallway. Trinity and Heidi stand behind her. "I heard my name."

Charlotte's gaze drops to the box in my hands. Her body trembles. "What is that?"

"We don't know yet."

"Someone left it at Crystal Ball?" She steps closer. "My name is on it." She snatches it from me and runs her nail over the tape holding the top closed.

"Charlotte, don't," Rock warns.

She ignores him and flips open the top. It's not like any of us are going to tackle her.

"What is that…" She gulps and her eyes bug. "Is that a…*toe?* Oh my God!" Charlotte screams. The package goes flying across the room. "Carter," she whispers. "Oh my God. Did they do *that* to Carter?"

"What the fuck?" Wrath shouts.

"Shit," Murphy whispers.

Rock returns with the box. A note's scribbled on the underside of the top flap.

Tell Merlin to answer his phone.
Each missed call, he loses another part.

Wrath steps up next to Rock and gingerly takes the box out of his hands. "Well, that narrows down our list. Got something to do with Merlin's misdeeds, not ours."

I meet his grim stare, then Rock's, then Murphy's. "Time to make *them* bleed."

CHAPTER THIRTY-FOUR

Teller

RAGE IS ONLY HELPFUL IF IT DOESN'T CLOUD MY ABILITY TO FORM A PLAN of attack. I take a breath, forcing air into my lungs. Clear head. Singular purpose.

Save Carter.

Punish anyone who hurt him.

There's a hesitant knock on the front door. I count the brothers in front of me. Rooster, Grinder, and Jigsaw have all slipped into the house at some point.

That only leaves one person who should be at the front door.

Merlin.

Wrath leaves the kitchen to let him in.

The second Merlin's rusty voice hits my ears, I'm on the move.

My boots rapidly clunk over the hardwood as I storm down the hallway.

It's been a couple of years, but I'd recognize this gnarled jerk anywhere.

He opens his mouth to greet me.

In two smooth movements, I whip my forearm against his neck, pressing him backward until he hits the wall. He lets out a surprised gasp for air.

I slip my hunting knife out of the sheath by my hip and press the tip under his chin, cocking his head at an awkward angle.

"You piece of shit," I snarl. "This is on *you*."

He holds his hands up in surrender. "Hello to you too, Teller."

"Don't get fucking cute with me." I dig the tip of the knife deeper into his flesh, not yet drawing blood, but close. "Give me one good reason I shouldn't slit your throat."

He doesn't flinch. "I got none."

"Easy, Marcel." Not even Rock's deep, presidential tone calms me. "Put the knife away."

The war inside me rages. Obey my president? Or tell my father to fuck off? I hate both options for different reasons.

"You here to help or get in the way?" Wrath asks Merlin, stepping up next to me, not even attempting to take the knife out of my hand.

At my back, I sense the rest of my brothers forming a wall between this scene and the girls.

"Marcel," Rock says, still calm but firm. "Put the knife away. *Now*. We'll talk this out at the table."

No matter how badly I want to separate Merlin's useless head from his shoulders, I can't continue to disrespect Rock like this in front of everyone.

Merlin also might be the only one with any answers.

Without taking my eyes off him, I lower the knife and tuck it into its sheath.

"That's it," Grinder says in a low voice.

Rock's hand lands on my shoulder and yanks me backward. My arm drops from Merlin's throat. He bends over, coughing and choking on the sudden intake of air.

"Thanks, Rock," he gasps.

"Don't thank me yet," Rock seethes. "You piss me off, I'll blow a hole in your skull myself."

"Great." He rests his hands on his knees and continues coughing. "So glad I hurried out to the middle of nowhere for this abuse."

"That's nothing compared to what those sick fucks are probably doing to your nephew right now," I rage.

That seems to remind Merlin that he's not here for a social call. He straightens. "Noted."

Behind us, there's a scuffle and low, angry voices.

"Let go of me!" Charlotte snaps.

"Char," Murphy pleads but it's too late.

She throws the box at her uncle's feet. "What have you done?" she screams.

"Calm down, girl." He bends over and picks up the bloody box. He reads the note, then scowls. "What was in it?"

"A toe!" Charlotte sobs. "Carter's fucking toe."

"Oh, Jesus Christ," Merlin breathes. "Where is it?"

"On ice in the fridge!" Jigsaw shouts from somewhere behind us. "Gotta keep it cold."

Charlotte breaks down into sobs that tear at my heart. She collapses against me. I hold onto her, stroking her back but not saying a word.

I lift my gaze and Rock jerks his head in the direction of the clubhouse. "We need to sit down with everyone." He shifts his angry gaze to Merlin. "That includes *you*."

"All right."

My brothers stop and either squeeze Charlotte's shoulder, pat her back, or offer some words of comfort on their way out. Merlin doesn't even look at Charlotte and me as he follows them out of the house.

"Let's go up to the clubhouse," I whisper to her when only Rock and Murphy remain. "I want you there where it's safe."

Charlotte sniffles and lifts her head. "Okay."

Trinity helps her collect a few things, and they meet us in the kitchen. Tension and fear pull Charlotte's mouth down, but she doesn't shed another tear. She's eerily calm and stoic as we lock the house and file outside.

A sob escapes her as we pass Carter's place.

"It's okay, Sunshine."

"We're going to find him," Rock says.

Not whole, though.

I push that thought away. Carter's stronger than anyone gives him credit for. He's going to be okay.

Tension rules the clubhouse when we arrive. Hope and Lilly hurry to take Charlotte from me. Lilly leads her over to the living room couch, but Hope curls her fingers around my forearm, stopping me from going directly into the war room. "How bad is this?"

"Bad, Hope. Someone grabbed Carter."

"No," she whispers.

My gaze lands on Merlin standing by the bar with Wrath. Not a friendly conversation. More like Wrath's guarding Merlin to make sure none of us kill him.

"Charlotte's uncle has the answers." *I hope.*

"We'll take care of Charlotte." The intense stare Hope drills into my skull hints at her bloodthirsty, protect-the-family-at-all-costs side. "Bring him home."

"I intend to."

She releases me, stops to talk to Rock, then sits next to Charlotte, curling an arm around her shoulders.

Rock motions for us to move toward the war room. Wrath, Merlin, and I enter last. Brothers scowl as we enter with Merlin. Rarely—if ever—do we have members of other clubs at our table. Even though we were always on good terms with the Wolf Knights MC, that was because of their old president, Ulfric. My brothers are all aware how shitty Merlin's treated Charlotte in the past and don't seem in a forgiving mood tonight.

Dex stands. "Does he need to be here?"

Rock throws him a sit-down-and-shut-up glare. "Merlin's got information we need."

"Let's hurry the fuck up." Ravage pounds his fist against his palm. "Little dude isn't built for this kinda shit. It ain't right."

"Easy, bro," Wrath warns. "We all want Carter back, but we need to know what we're dealing with."

Merlin stares at Wrath with wide eyes. Shocked, I guess, that Wrath, of all bikers, is concerned about his nephew. The kid Merlin likes to imply is gay because he didn't want to join his MC.

Wrath seems to sense Merlin's disbelief and focuses his scary eyes on him. "Carter's club family. *We* protect our own."

Wrath's meaning couldn't be clearer. *Unlike you.*

If I thought Merlin was capable of feeling shame, I'd say that was what was turning the fucker's cheeks red.

No one wants to give up their seat to Merlin. He ends up wedged in a chair between Grinder and Wrath, the two enforcers.

Merlin does a double take, shifting his body in the large wooden chair. "When'd you get out, brother?" he asks Grinder.

"While ago." Grinder waves off the attention. "We can catch up when we get Carter back."

"All right." Rock paces behind his chair at the head of the table. "Here's what we know. Carter was at his friend's apartment downtown. He was standing next to his car, talking to her. A van pulled up. Two men dressed in black grabbed Carter and wrestled him into the back of the van."

"He fought back?" Merlin's incredulous tone stokes my rage.

"That's what the girl said." Rock's clipped answer suggests he expects no interruptions. "Carter's friend says there were at least two more guys in the van—one behind the wheel and one who threw the doors open."

"Bianca called the cops." I pick up where Rock left off. "She got stuck giving them statements but called Charlotte. She got a partial plate number."

"I ran it," Z says, "But it'll take days to track down every vehicle on the list."

"Vermont or New York plates?" Merlin asks.

"New York."

"Finally…" I raise my voice. "Dex left Crystal Ball and found a package waiting on his bike, addressed to Charlotte. That was the box you saw at the house. The message inside was for *you*."

Murphy leans forward, staring Merlin dead in the eye, and presses his index finger against the table. "Start. Talking."

Merlin hangs his head and seems to gather his thoughts. Or he's trying to decide how free he wants to be with information that might get him killed.

"Who's been trying to reach you?" Rock asks. "Let's start there."

"What's left of Sons of Satan MC."

"Motherfucker," Z growls. "Those assholes, again?"

"It's not quite like that." Merlin runs his hand over his head. "I think I know why they went after my family."

"Enlighten us," Rock says.

"I've been out on the road." He meets my eyes. "You know that."

I acknowledge it with a chin lift.

"Well, I've been picking up some extra cash moving product for some of their other charters in the south."

"Where in the south?" Rooster asks slowly.

"Nowhere near your Deadbranch charter or your National headquarters."

"Jesus, Merlin, you serious?" Rock shakes his head. "Wolf Knights always stayed away from hard drugs."

"Yeah, well, it ain't like Ulfric set us up with a retirement plan, either. A man's gotta make a living."

"You're a fucking nomad. How many expenses you got?" Wrath sneers.

"Enough."

"All right." Rock circles his hand in the air in a get-to-the-point gesture. "How did we get here?"

There Merlin goes, scrubbing his hand over his head again. "You got lice or something, Merlin?" I ask. "Stop stalling."

He shoots a glare at me. "I knocked up the president's daughter last time I was in town. He ain't real thrilled about it."

You gotta be fucking kidding me. Charlotte and I can't get pregnant but this ancient motherfucker's knocking up some meth head MC princess?

The room's silent as we all stare at him, waiting for more information.

"And?" Rock prompts.

"I'm out on the road. Wasn't planning on a kid."

"So, you ditched your responsibilities?" Grinder snarls.

"It ain't like that. I'm sending her money. Covering her doctor's bills and whatnot. I just ain't got time for that shit. I barely know her, and we don't have a whole lot in common."

"How old is she?" Z asks.

"She's legal," Merlin snaps, shifting his gaze away from the table.

Sure she is.

I catch Grinder's eye, and he frowns at me. I respond with a quick shake of my head. No, I'm not comparing his situation to Merlin's. Not even a little.

Merlin's explanation doesn't ring true.

"So, they risked kidnapping Carter and mutilated him just to get you

288

to call your baby mama?" I raise my eyebrows to punctuate how stupid that sounds. "That doesn't make sense."

"Eh, the president and his son Sticks have it in their heads that a few shipments I delivered were light." He presses an imaginary pipe to his lips and fake inhales. "They're using too much of their own product."

"Are they?" Rock raises an eyebrow. "Or did you think you could pull a fast one on some tweakers?"

Merlin covers up his annoyance with a smirk. "They ain't the brightest."

Neither are you.

"What do they want?" Rock asks.

"Money." Merlin shrugs. "Shotgun wedding. Ain't got the former and ain't doing the latter, so I've been avoiding their calls."

Jiggy sits forward. "Did you get fucked in the ear with a stupid stick while you've been out on the road?"

Z presses his fist to his mouth and coughs.

"What happened to you, bro?" Bricks asks in a slow, shocked way that makes it clear how far Merlin's fallen in his eyes.

Merlin's blank expression says he's got no answers, but he's saved from digging for some by his phone ringing.

He jerks an old cell out of his pocket and flips it open. "What?" he snaps.

We watch as he gives clipped answers to whoever's on the other end. Merlin's gaze flicks to me. "No, don't do that. I can get what you need. Although, I should take off some since you cut up my nephew."

This fucking asshole. I jump out of my chair and am about to leap over the fucking table. Murphy tackles me, leaving me clawing for Merlin like a kid being dragged out of a candy store.

"Yeah, yeah, I got it. You're sure that's all you want?" He wiggles his fingers at Wrath for a pen. Wrath quietly slides a pen and notepad over. Merlin scribbles a few things down, then turns the pad toward me.

$100K. 7 P.M.

He lifts an eyebrow.

"Yes," I hiss. *What's there to talk about?* "Tell them *yes.*"

"Yeah. Yeah," Merlin says into his phone. "Yeah, I'll see June too." He rolls his eyes. "I'll see if we can make that work."

He takes down a few more notes, then hangs up.

"You could've asked to speak to Carter," Wrath points out.

"Gee, sorry. I'm not up on kidnapping protocol." Merlin meets my eyes. "You really got that kind of cash, Teller?"

"Not your business."

"You sure Carter's worth it?"

"Yes," Rock snaps. "He's club family."

"He ain't related to you." Merlin's gaze slides to Wrath. "Or you."

"He *works* for me," Rock says. "And he's going to be my son's brother-in-law."

Merlin frowns but doesn't ask any obvious follow-up questions.

"He's working for a friend of the club, too," Z adds.

"What the fuck work is he doing for your club that's so damn important?" Merlin snaps.

Grinder rolls up one of his sleeves, showing off the newest Carter original inked into his forearm. An owl with the chain of a pocket watch wrapped around its feet. Carter had been really excited when he came up with the design. Looking at it now tightens my chest. We *have* to find him.

"My nephew did that?" Merlin asks, as if his influence is somehow responsible for Carter's talent. "Damn."

"He's doing custom paint for us at Rock's shop too," Bricks adds. "Real talented artist."

"Well, shit. All those faggy drawings he was always wasting his time on had a purpose after all." Merlin smiles.

Rock stands. "Use that word in my clubhouse again or say that shit to Carter and I'll scatter your parts from here to Mississippi." He spits the threat out like a hail of bullets. "No one will ever find your body. You feel me?"

"Geez, when'd you all get so sensitive?" Merlin searches the table for someone who agrees but gets nothing.

"Enough bullshit." I stand. "Where are we meeting them?"

"They have a camp on the Vermont side of the border." Merlin lifts his chin at me. "Not far from where we took our little nighttime excursion."

If he thinks he's going to rattle me by alluding to his Wolf Knight brother that we killed and buried in Vermont, he's mistaken. I told Rock about it the night it happened. My conscience is clear as far as my club's concerned.

"Camp for what?" Jigsaw asks. "Hunting? Roasting marshmallows? Singing songs by the fire?"

"Cooking meth," Merlin answers.

"Why the fuck were you involved with these jokers, again?" Rock snaps.

Merlin bristles. "It's irrelevant at this point, Rock. I stepped down. Left my club, my home—"

"I don't got a violin tiny enough for this shit," Rooster says.

"I lost everything," Merlin protests.

"Spare us the fucking sob story." Rock leans in. "Those are all consequences of *your* actions."

Wrath taps his finger against his jaw, a sure sign he's about to say something obnoxious. "If I recall, your options were go nomad or go to *ground*."

Merlin likes to act like he'd given up the gavel willingly because it was the right thing to do after his fuckups. Guess Wrath just blew that illusion to shit.

"I wouldn't put it that way." Merlin lifts his chin. "We ain't sittin' here to discuss ancient history, though, are we?" He nods at Ravage. "We're here to get my nephew back."

Murphy clenches his fists on the table but keeps his thoughts to himself. The tension rolling off him says he's having a hard time not jumping over the table and punching Merlin's jaw just like I want to do.

"Can we focus, please?" I ask with as much calm as I can muster under the circumstances. "How do we find this place?"

"It's way out in the woods. They'll hear us coming from a mile away," he warns.

"Do you know how to find it or not?" Wrath asks.

"I can locate it." He shrugs. "But they want to make the trade at a park outside Ironworks."

Wrath catches my eye. "I don't like it. That's leaving Carter with these psychos for way too long." Wrath turns to Merlin, seeking some sort of response, but Merlin's a statue.

"These guys are dumb and unpredictable," Rooster says. "They already cut off the kid's toe."

"They fucked with the wrong MC," Dex adds. "They need to be taught a lesson."

"Look, I know trust isn't at its zenith right now," Merlin says.

"That's putting it mildly," I grumble.

"But I'm here to see this through and get him back."

"Good." Probably be the first decent act he's done all year.

Wrath sits forward, glances at Rock, then Z, then sits back. Something's bothering him that he doesn't seem to want to share.

Rock appears to pick up on his enforcer's unease. He nods at Bricks. "Can you take Merlin down to the dining room and map out the location?"

"You got it, boss." Bricks stands and pushes in his chair.

Rock nods to Stash, Hoot, and Birch. "Help him out."

"Yup." Stash is the first to jump out of his chair.

Merlin narrows his eyes at Rock but isn't in a position to complain. It's a perfectly reasonable request. And if he balks, four of my brothers will be happy to motivate him.

As soon as they've left, Rock focuses on Wrath. "What's bothering you?"

"I overheard some of the conversation." He jerks his thumb toward the chair Merlin just vacated. "They only asked for fifty thousand."

"Motherfuckin' piece of shit!" I shout.

"Simmer down," Rock warns.

"He fuckin' lied to our faces."

"Let Wrath finish."

"And," Wrath continues, ignoring my outburst, "they expect him to marry that girl. Tomorrow."

"Doesn't sound like he has any intention of doing that," Rooster comments.

Wrath taps two fingers on the table in front of him. "They want *both* things before they release Carter. The money *and* the wedding."

"So, what was he planning to do?" I ask. "Take off with the extra money and leave Carter to be chopped into pieces?"

"Maybe," Wrath says slowly. "Or he figures the extra money will bail him out of the wedding."

"Uh, sounds like the wedding is more important than the cash to these clowns," Dex points out.

"Exactly."

"But if they don't bring Carter to the exchange, we're going to notice," Jiggy says. "What was his plan for that?"

"Invite us to the wedding?" Z shrugs. "Merlin isn't the brightest bulb."

"He's scared," Grinder says slowly. "He didn't expect all of us to be this concerned." He lifts his gaze to me. "Probably thought you two would work it out with them alone."

"Yeah, and so what if it gets Carter killed?" Murphy snaps. "This is bullshit. Let's get directions to the camp, gut Merlin and drop him in a ditch on the way to rescue Carter."

"Easy." Rock holds his hand up in front of Murphy's face. "Let's call that plan C."

Wrath's our enforcer for a reason. "What do you think we should do?" I ask him.

"I think we should take two teams. One can go to the meet with Merlin and the cash. The other goes to the camp. Once we see them leave for the meeting, we go in and find Carter."

"They'll leave someone there to guard him," I point out.

"You got a problem taking them out?"

Would I hesitate to pull the trigger to save Carter?

"Nope."

CHAPTER THIRTY-FIVE

Charlotte

THE LOUD BUZZING IN MY EARS DOESN'T ALLOW MANY OTHER SOUNDS TO penetrate. Around me, Hope, Heidi, Lilly, and Trinity try to engage me in conversation. Alexa and Chance play on the floor but become more and more agitated the later it gets. Grace wails. The kids can sense something's wrong, even if no one's told them what's going on. Normally, I'd do anything to try and ease their fears, but I'm frozen with my own.

After a while, I realize it's just Lilly and me in the living room of the clubhouse. Her voice seems to come through a pool of water. Slow and muffled. "I'm sorry, Charlotte."

I'm numb. All I can do is nod.

"Carter's such a sweetheart." She holds out her arm to show me a piece of the tattoo sleeve he's designed. It gives me something to focus on and some of the fuzziness in my head clears. "He's so funny and smart. We have the best conversations when he's working on me."

I sniffle and stare at the ink. I'd recognize my brother's style anywhere.

"He told me you're the one who always encouraged him to continue with his artwork." Lilly squeezes my hand and scowls at the closed war room door. "That your uncle always made fun of him for drawing. And you were the only one who supported his passion until Teller came along and talked him into trying out tattooing."

I laugh and wipe at my damp eyes. "Marcel's persistent."

But would my brother even *be* in this mess if it wasn't for my relationship with the MC?

Trinity rests her hand on my leg and squats down in front of me. Her grim expression sends splinters of fear spiraling through my stomach.

"What? Did they find something out?" I ask.

"Just checking if you're okay." She hands me a bottle of water. "Drink something."

I accept the bottle but set it on the couch next to me. "Thanks."

"Hope and Heidi brought the kids over to Heidi's place."

"That's good."

"You want us to go over there with you?" Trinity asks. "Or you can come to our place if you want a little quiet."

My gaze strays to the war room again. Why haven't they come out yet? We're wasting so much time. "Ah, not yet. I want to talk to Marcel when they're done."

"Okay." Trinity takes the seat next to me.

The war room door opens and my uncle strides out, flanked by Bricks and Birch. Hoot and Stash bring up the rear. Almost as if he's a prisoner they're guarding.

My body coils tight, ready to kick and claw until Uncle Chuck gives me some answers. But I'm wedged in between Lilly and Trinity.

And maybe part of me fears the answers.

They move quickly down the hallway toward the dining room. Uncle Chuck stares straight ahead, avoiding eye contact with me.

I try to return my attention to what Trinity's saying, but I can't.

The thought of my brother hurt, bleeding, alone or caged in with some psychopath stokes a burning rage inside me.

By the time my uncle returns, I'm a hurricane of anger. I explode off the couch, racing across the room to land in his path. I slam my palms against his chest, knocking him back a few steps.

Bricks stares at me, stunned.

My uncle's jaw drops.

I hadn't taken a good look at him back at the house.

If I thought he'd aged twenty years when he finally told me the truth about my mother's dark betrayal, he looks like he's aged another twenty since then. Life on the road hasn't been kind to him.

Good. My hardened heart doesn't want to show him any mercy. He's never had any for my brother.

"Where is he? What did you do?" I demand.

"Char, relax." Uncle Chuck holds out his hands in a "whoa lil' lady" gesture. "We've got this handled."

Behind me, someone whistles.

"Maybe it's time to stab him again," Trinity says.

Chuck frowns at her.

"Don't look at her." I poke him in the chest. "Answer me."

He shackles his hands around my wrists, driving me backward.

"Get your fuckin' hands off of her, Merlin." Bricks shoves Chuck enough to loosen his grip.

"I'm fine, Bricks," I say. "Give us a minute. Please."

Bricks shifts his gaze to the war room, as if he wants to call all the brothers for help.

"Please?" I repeat.

Bricks nods but moves closer to the war room. If Chuck touches me again, Bricks will get Marcel and the rest of the club out here. I desperately buckle a leash around my temper. I want answers more than I want to see Chuck get his ass kicked.

Chuck's helpless blue eyes meet mine. "I never thought they'd come after my family. I swear it."

"Especially since you don't give a shit about Carter or me."

He shakes his head but holds my gaze. "I'm here, ain't I?"

I open my mouth to argue, then stop. He's right. He's been on the road for a couple of years now. We haven't exactly kept in touch. No one would've known where to find him. He could've easily ignored my phone calls.

"You know my reasons." He lifts his eyebrow, as if I need the reminder that Carter's only my half-brother and that Chuck's always hated him for something out of Carter's control. "I can't change the shitty way I behaved in the past. But I'll get him back to you."

I burst into tears and curse myself for showing any weakness in front of him.

"Aw, shit, Charlotte." He wraps me in a slow, awkward hug. "I shoulda done better by you," he whispers. "Don't have it in me, though."

What an understatement. "I know you don't."

He releases me. "I need to talk to your man again. We're going to fix this."

I nod. "Okay."

I've never hated him more.

CHAPTER THIRTY-SIX

Teller

"THAT'S OUR PLAN, THEN." ROCK RUNS HIS GAZE OVER THE BROTHERS sitting at the table. "I don't want to tip Merlin off too early, so we won't split until we're already out there. Ravage and Bricks will go with Merlin." He nods at me. "Teller, Wrath, Dex, and Murphy, you're with me." He glances at Z.

"I'm with you." Z nods at Rooster. "Stick with Merlin."

"You got it."

Z nods at Grinder and Jigsaw. "You two come with me."

Jigsaw glances at Rooster, then Z. "Okay."

"They left the package for me," Dex says. "You think I should be at the meet with Merlin?"

Rock doesn't usually appreciate having his orders questioned, but he seems to consider Dex's observation. "You're right. Just in case. Let's do that."

Dex nods.

"Also, before we leave, give Remy a call and see if they've had any issues with those guys out there lately."

Dex pulls out his phone and stands. "I'll do it right now."

There's a knock on the door and Bricks peers inside. "We got it, boss."

Merlin brushes past Bricks and reclaims his seat next to Wrath.

Something must've rattled him. His shifty gaze won't settle on any of us. Instead, it bounces around—

the window, his hands, the table.

"Look, I, uh…" He glances at Wrath, then Grinder, maybe deciding sitting between our two enforcers isn't the safest place to be. Especially since the last time he was in a room alone with Wrath, he got the shit beaten out of him. "I should come clean before we head out there."

Wrath catches my eye and smirks.

"What'd you lie about now?" I ask.

"I didn't *lie*." He glares at me. "They only asked for fifty K."

"What were you planning? Steal the rest and run?" I sneer.

He rubs his hand over the back of his neck. "Buy my way out of this thing with the president's daughter and make sure Carter's safe."

"What's wrong?" Wrath flashes a dickish smile. "Don't feel like getting prodded down the aisle with a shotgun tomorrow?"

Merlin's weathered face tightens with surprise. "You heard my call?"

"The highlights," Wrath confirms.

He side-eyes Wrath. "I ain't taking another beating from you."

"I'll decide that," Rock says.

"You're not my prez," Merlin shoots back.

"Whoa." I hold my hands in a "time out" gesture. "Whip out your dicks some other time." I wait until I have Merlin's attention. "On top of the chaos you've already caused, you fuckin' lied to us. Why come clean right before we leave?"

He jerks his thumb over his shoulder. "My niece had a few choice words for me."

Shit, I should've asked Hope to get Charlotte out of the clubhouse. Although, knowing how stubborn my woman can be, she wouldn't want to be far from us.

I cock my head. "So you dug deep, found your conscience, and dusted it off?"

"Fuck off, Teller," he snarls. "You're still a self-righteous little prick."

"Enough." Rock slams his fist into the table to get our attention. "We're going in two teams. You'll meet with your new in-laws. Rest of us will go to the camp for Carter."

"Appreciate that, Rock." Merlin dips his chin as if he's about to make a noble offer. "But I should make things right and get Carter myself."

Rock pinches the bridge of his nose. My father has patience for a lot of things. Stupidity isn't one of them. "They're expecting you to be at the meet," he reminds Merlin in slow, deliberate words.

"Oh, right."

"You been smoking their product?" Wrath asks.

"No. I don't touch that shit." His outrage seems to deflate when he realizes Wrath's fucking with him. "I ain't one of your bros."

"Oh, I'm aware."

Ignoring Wrath, Merlin focuses on me again. "You need time to get the money together?"

For an amount that large, I either need to hit the safe at my house, the one in the basement here at the clubhouse, or the one at Crystal Ball. Merlin doesn't need to know we keep that kind of cash so close to home though. "Yeah, I'll need a few. Why don't I meet up with everyone down at Ward's?"

"You need a vest," Rock reminds me. "I'm not having you get shot again."

"Now he's definitely going to get shot, Prez," Murphy says. "Why'd you have to say that?"

"Thanks, jackass," I mutter. "I'll stop and get one."

"I'll bring the hardware," Wrath says. "Place is in the middle of nowhere. We don't have to worry about being quiet."

"Fuck yeah." Z punches his fist in the air.

"Uh…" Merlin rubs his knuckles over his chest. "Can you look out for June? She's tiny." He holds his hand a few inches above the table. "Black hair. Pregnant."

"That's her name?" Rock asks. "June?"

"Yeah."

"She gonna shoot at us first?" Jigsaw asks.

"I don't think so."

"Great," Wrath mutters.

"I don't know for sure she'll be there." Merlin shrugs. "But just in case."

"We got it," I say.

"Let's get ready." Rock claps his hands. "Meet out front in ten. Teller, see you at Ward's."

Everyone agrees to their assignments and stands to leave.

On my way out, I stop in front of Z. "Thanks, brother. You don't have to do this."

"The fuck I don't." He gives me a quick shove. "My son calls him Uncle. Lilly loves him." The corners of his mouth lift. "She can't stop talking about all the artwork they're planning together. He's family, Teller. We got this."

"Thank you."

He slaps my cheek. "Get your head on straight and let's get these motherfuckers."

I dip into the living room. Charlotte's waiting where I left her. She lifts her head and our eyes lock. Taking her hand, I kneel in front of her and kiss her damp cheeks. "I'm going to get him back, Sunshine. I promise," I whisper.

"Promise me something else."

I search her face, waiting for her request.

"Kill them. Whoever took my brother and...*hurt* him. Kill. Them."

"I promise." I press her face between my palms and kiss her hard on the lips. "I'll kill 'em all."

CHAPTER THIRTY-SEVEN

Teller

"Teller!" Swan races down the front steps of the clubhouse.

I stop and wait for her, keenly aware I need to stop by my house for the money, body armor, weapons, and get my ass on the road.

She skids to a stop and grabs my arm. "Are you going to find Carter?"

"Yeah." I can't tell her much more. She's been around the club long enough to know that.

"Please, please, bring him back safe," she pleads.

Any other time, I might tease her about whatever relationship she and Carter have going. Tonight, I don't have it in me. "We will."

And I'm going to gut every motherfucker who hurt my family while I'm at it.

"What can I do to help?" she asks.

"Stay put. Don't leave the property. See if the girls need anything."

"Of course."

I rush to my truck and jump in. A few minutes later, I pull up to the front steps of my house, leap out, thunder up the porch steps and barge inside.

Clear head.

Standing in the entryway, I stop and run through a list of what I need. The safe upstairs has cash. I head there first. Kneeling on the floor of the closet, I punch in the code for the safe and start stuffing roughly the right amount into a backpack. I ain't a fucking bank and can't waste time counting every dollar.

While I'm standing in the closet, I strip down and jump into a pair of black camouflage, waterproof, tactical cargo pants. The material's sturdy and shouldn't snag on anything and the pants have loads of easy-to-access pockets and pouches. The Kevlar vest will add enough bulk, so I slide into a long-sleeved black compression shirt.

Next, I hit the nightstand by my side of the bed for a handgun. I press my palm to the screen and the biometric safe that takes up the entire bottom drawer clicks open.

No wimpy .22 pistol tonight. I wrap my fingers around the textured grip of my 10mm Kodiak. It's practically a damn cannon, but I had it at the range recently and feel comfortable using it.

I sling the pack over my shoulder, holster the gun at my side, and pound downstairs. The vest I need is in another safe along with an assortment of long guns.

Merlin said the place was a camp. So we'll either be outside or searching small tents and buildings? My fingers briefly brush against my hunting rifle. But then I choose my KSG bullpup shotgun, instead. Its small size will make it easier to use in tight spaces and the dual tubes will allow me to have more rounds available if the situation gets dicey. I grab my bulletproof vest, a knit cap, and rush out of the house. A few minutes later, I'm in my truck headed to meet my brothers.

Everyone's waiting in the side parking lot at Ward's grocery store.

Rock leaves his bike and climbs into my truck.

"You're going to sit in the passenger seat?" I ask, unable to keep the shock out of my voice.

"Guess I finally trust you." He motions to the windshield like he's ready to go right now. "Stop fucking around."

Rooster pulls up next to me in his truck. The big diesel shakes everything in the immediate area. Merlin's in the passenger side, wearing a sour expression. I leave my truck running, grab the backpack of cash, and jump out.

"Here's the cash."

Merlin opens the door and I toss the pack in his lap.

"How do I know this big, bearded fucker isn't going to gut me and leave me by the side of the road?" He jerks his thumb toward Rooster.

"You don't!" Rooster shouts. "That's what makes it so exciting."

I snort-laugh, flip a thumbs-up at Rooster, and slide behind the wheel again.

Murphy climbs into the back seat and slams the door with a harsh thump. "Let's go."

Grinder, Jigsaw, and Dex take off ahead of us on their bikes. Wrath and Z follow in Wrath's truck. Rooster goes next and I pull out of the parking lot last.

"We should've brought his toe," Murphy says. "Coulda brought him to Ironworks Emergency Room on the way home."

"I think a toe is the least of Carter's concerns right now," Rock says.

That kills the conversation for a while.

It's a long fucking ride to Vermont.

CHAPTER THIRTY-EIGHT

Teller

"WHAT THE FUCK IS THIS?" ROCK MUTTERS. "LOOKS LIKE AN ABANDONED garbage dump."

"Smells like one too," Z says, pinching his nose.

I step out of the shadows of the grove of ancient maple trees giving us cover and scan the vast area. "A backwoods meth-making camp."

"This is why making meth is bad, m'kay, kids," Wrath says in his best Mr. Mackey voice.

"Jesus." I step up onto a large, flat bolder and lift my binoculars, searching for any sign of Carter. Nothing but old, rusted campers and trailers dotting an open field of overgrown weeds and hilly slopes. Piles of trash and empty cans tangle in long blades of grass. Circles of dirt and fried grass mar the land like mangy spots on a dog. Piles of burned logs and rings of stones indicate they risk using some areas of their campground for bonfires. Glass from shattered bottles glitters in the dusky light.

Twigs and dried brush crackle under my feet as I jump off the rock and return to the safety of the trees. "One spark and this whole camp will go up in flames."

Wrath pulls a lighter out of his pocket. "Let's save that for later."

"You see anything?" Murphy asks me.

"Nothing useful. There have to be ten or fifteen trailers set up. No way to tell which one Carter might be in. Or where they store the pregnant chicks."

"Shit," Rock mutters, turning toward the circle of dirty and broken blacktop where we'd parked our vehicles.

"Pretty much," Z says.

Rock snarls at him.

"Easy." Z holds up his hands. "I want him back too, Rock."

"I didn't see any movement," I continue. "I gotta imagine they left at least one person guarding Carter."

Rock glances at the seven of us. "Let's split up into two teams. We'll do a sweep and clear each trailer. See if we find anyone we can pry Carter's location out of." He pulls a hunting knife from my glove compartment and flips it in the air, catching it neatly by the handle. "Using any means necessary."

"I'm down with that," Murphy agrees.

"What do you want to do if we find the girl?" Z asks.

"If she's hostile, leave her ass here," Rock says. "Carter's my main concern. If we find her, and she wants out, we'll take her."

Wrath's gaze strays to the open field again. "She shoots at me, I'm shooting back."

"Let's try not to shoot unless we know what we're shooting at. I don't want Carter catching a bullet." Rock glances toward the camp again. "And we don't want to strike anything that might light this place up."

Wrath nods.

We're all aware of how flammable the chemicals used to make meth can be. And how unstable the people making the shit are after having their brains rotted out on the fumes.

Rock taps my shoulder, then points to Murphy. "We'll go right. Wrath, you stay here and cover us."

Wrath scowls.

"You're the most accurate under these conditions." Rock sweeps his hand in a circle, then nods to the rifle in Wrath's hands.

They stare at each other for a few tense seconds, then Wrath responds with a tight nod.

Z points at Jigsaw and Grinder. "We'll take the left side. Meet you in the back."

I return to my truck and fill my pockets with ammunition. The shotgun gets strapped to my side in a single-point sling.

The first structure we encounter looks like an old RV from the seventies. At one time it was probably brown with orange pinstripes. Now, it's some version of a faded tan with white lines breaking up patches of rust and dirt. Over time, the wheels seem to have rotted into the ground.

The thick stench of shit and piss assaults my nose as we creep closer.

Rock pulls his T-shirt up over his nose and motions for me to keep moving.

"This smells like their outhouse," I grumble.

"Yeah." He glances around. "Watch where you step."

"Fucking great."

Behind me, Murphy gags. "Give me diaper duty over this, any day."

Rock chuckles, then coughs.

The smell intensifies. My eyes water and beg for mercy.

The door has a board screwed to it to keep it closed. Rock and I flank each side. I reach out and flip the board up. The door screeches open. Heat and stench roll over us in waves.

"Stay there." Careful not to touch the door, Rock steps over the rusted metal pieces that probably used to be a short staircase and lifts himself into the RV. "Carter?"

Yellow glow from Rock's flashlight briefly sweeps the interior, revealing the stuff of nightmares.

Murphy slaps my shoulder. "This makes that shitty poor kid camp we went to that one summer seem like a four-star resort."

I snort at the vague memory. "Yeah, you pissed in the lake every day 'cause you were scared of the latrines."

"Fuckin' A, I was. Those asshole counselors kept telling us stories about the toilet monster eating a fat ginger camper every summer." He shakes his head. "I wasn't risking it."

A louder snort of laughter bursts out of me.

Rock jumps out of the RV and slams the door shut. The board falls into place with a quiet thump. "Fuck, that's disgusting. No one's in there."

"Puts 'filthy biker' into a whole new perspective," Murphy says.

"Got that." Rock sweeps his hand in front of us. "Let's move to the next one."

A tall metal container stands in front of us. About the size of a short school bus. It doesn't have any windows. Just a door with a secure latch at one end.

"Looks like a fuckin' death trap," Murphy grumbles. He quietly twists the handle and the door falls open with a rusty sigh. We stand to the sides of the door. When no bullets come flying, Murphy pokes his head inside and shines his flashlight. The light briefly illuminates what looks like a cozy living room. Cozy for a shipping container.

"It's all one room." Murphy steps inside. "There's a bed all the way in the back."

"Carter?" I call out.

Nothing.

Murphy creeps to the other end and drops to his knees, shining his light under the bed. "Not even a dust bunny."

"Must be the president's palace," Rock mutters, staring at the side of the container. He steps around the corner and I follow. A crudely painted version of the flaming devil the Sons of Satan MC members wear in their center patch fills up the entire space. Orange, red, and black letters spell out S.O.S.

"At least we're in the right spot," I say.

Rock shrugs.

Across the field, I make out three shadowy figures checking out a similar shipping crate. "Doesn't look like Z's having better luck."

"No." Rock's gaze searches the field. "Let's hurry. Who knows how long Merlin can keep them."

Under the cover of the building, I pull out my phone and check for any texts from Merlin. Nothing.

We check out another old RV. At least this one isn't being used as the camp's outhouse.

"You surprised we haven't run into anyone at all?" Murphy asks.

"Kinda." I run my hand over my pants, the leather from my gloves rasping over the rough, tactical material.

We clear another structure. Two motorcycles in various states of assembly litter the front. My boot catches on a piece of wire and I stumble. The wire twangs and clinks. Murphy wraps his hand around my arm, righting me before I make even more noise.

"Walk much?" he whispers.

"Thanks." I'm too tense to respond to the teasing.

Something squeaks ahead. An animal large enough to move the tall grass as it scurries away from us.

"Probably a fucking rat," Rock mutters.

"Surprised there aren't more critters around this dump," Murphy says.

Under my body armor and compression shirt, sweat slides down my back. This is taking too damn long. What if Carter's not even here?

Still wary this could be an ambush, I peek into the next camper. It's so small, I have to squeeze through the hole that serves as a door. Nothing inside but piles of blankets. I toe each one with my boot. "Carter?"

Nothing.

I jump out of the camper, landing in the brittle grass with a muted thud. "Clear."

A breeze picks up, intensifying the foul odor that permeates the place. To my right, something creaks in the wind. A short hill blocks my view. Only what looks like the top of a crude rectangle appears.

"What the fuck is that?" I mutter, marching up the side of the hill.

"Stay low," Murphy urges, pressing his hand to my back. "Jesus, you're a walking target up here."

My body responds to his words and crouches lower, but my mind's racing as the structure comes into view.

We stop and stare.

Two tall, thick wooden posts have been driven into the ground. A large crossbeam connects the two posts, forming a crude gallows.

"An MC who takes punishment seriously," Murphy mutters. "Jesus Christ."

Another creak. My gaze narrows on the middle of the structure. A rope dangles from a metal loop. At the end of the rope, a human figure hangs from the neck, swaying in the breeze.

Bile burns the back of my throat.

Carter's playful, goofy smile fills my mind.

I can't tell Charlotte this.

No. Please. No.

CHAPTER THIRTY-NINE

Charlotte

"CHARLOTTE?" A HUSHED WOMAN'S VOICE WHISPERS IN MY EAR. "Charlotte, it's okay."

I pry my eyes open, staring into darkness. Nothing seems familiar. Dark, shadowy shapes. A bedroom?

My head throbs.

Behind me, someone shifts. An arm slung over my waist moves to my back. "It's okay."

Heidi. A relieved breath rushes from my lungs. "Where are we?" I croak.

"My bedroom."

I sit up and wince as pebbles bounce around inside my skull. All the crying left me raw and limp. "Any word?"

"No. But they won't until…" Heidi sucks in a deep breath. "There's something to tell us."

"Are you mad you didn't go with them, little hammer?" My attempted joke saws through the silence at an awkward angle.

"I'm scared for Carter."

"Me too," I admit. "And I really want to kill my uncle."

"I don't blame you." She stares at the closed bedroom door. "I wouldn't be surprised if they come back without him."

A phone buzzes against the nightstand.

"That's yours," Heidi says. She rolls over and flips on a light, then hands me my phone.

"It's Bianca. She's here. Well, she's at my house."

"Marcel didn't want you to leave the property." Heidi's worried eyes dart to the door, as if she's calculating how fast she'll need to sprint to cut off my escape. "What if she brought the cops?"

"I'm not going." I hesitate, reading Bianca's text again. "But she can come up here, right? She's been to parties on the property before."

"Yeah. Let's see if Sparky or Stash will run down and pick her up."

"Stay here. I'll be all right."

She follows me into the hallway, stopping to peek into Alexa's room.

"What's up? Did you hear anything?" Lilly rasps from the doorway of one of the bedrooms.

"Bianca's at our house. I'm going to ask one of the guys if they'll go pick her up."

Lilly glances over her shoulder. "Do you want me to go with you?"

"No." I force a quick smile. "I'll be fine."

Downstairs is illuminated by soft night lights. I find my shoes and slip them on.

Outside, I stare up at the dark sky, then check my phone. Still nothing from Marcel. Anxiety twists my stomach into a knot. As quietly as possible, I move down the long row of steps and onto the path away from Murphy and Heidi's house. I reach a wider path and take a left, following the row of solar lights that will lead me past Trinity and Wrath's place, Hope and Rock's home, and eventually to the clubhouse.

The entire downstairs of Hope and Rock's house is lit up. Maybe Rock sent Hope some information? I jog up their front steps and tap on the door, praying I don't wake Grace.

It takes a few seconds for the door to open. Trinity flashes a quick, grim smile. "Anything?" she asks.

"No." I step inside and Trinity closes the door behind me.

Hope joins us, phone clutched tightly in her hand.

"I was heading to the clubhouse to see if one of the guys can go pick Bianca up and saw your lights on," I explain. "I thought maybe you'd heard…"

"Nothing yet," Hope says. "Service is bad out there and they won't want to take chances—"

"I know."

"You want me to go to the clubhouse with you?" Trinity asks.

"No, it's okay."

Outside, an owl hoots and a quick gust of air swirls leaves in a funnel. "That's not ominous or anything," I mutter, quickening my steps.

The harsh glow of the floodlights around the clubhouse is a relief. I hurry to the front door. Sparky, Stash, and Swan are hanging out in the living room. A heavy cloud of smoke billows around Sparky.

"Sunshine, do you bring us good news?" Sparky calls out with a bleary smile.

Well, I guess he's not driving anywhere.

"Carter's friend is at our house, and I was looking for someone to go pick her up," I explain as I walk closer. "I don't have a vehicle up here and—"

"Teller didn't want you going anywhere," Stash reminds me. "You're on lockdown."

"I can go." Swan raises her hand even though she's only a few feet away from me. "I've met Bianca before."

I hate asking her to do something that's really my responsibility. "Are you sure you don't mind?"

She tips her head toward Sparky and Stash. "I think I'm your only option."

"Thanks."

"I'll ride shotgun." Stash slaps her leg and stands, holding out his hand to pull her off the couch.

"Great." Swan barely holds back an eye roll. "We'll be right back, Charlotte."

Feeling a bit awkward now that it's just Sparky and me, I stand next to the couch, absently staring at the television but not registering what's on the screen.

"Pull up a cushion, Sunshine." Sparky pats the couch. "I'm harmless."

"I know that." Fear of Sparky wasn't stopping me. I force a quick smile. "I'm tired and worried and—"

"Out of sorts?"

"Yes." I drop onto the couch and sink into the cushion. Tears prickle my eyelids. "I'm so scared. I should've done something more to protect him."

He blows out a slow stream of smoke, then neatly stubs his blunt into an ashtray. "Char, we all know you take good care of your brother. He's a grown-ass man, though."

"He's still my little brother."

He squeezes his eyes shut. "You and Teller really are a cosmic match. I'm so thankful the universe brought you two together."

I can't help chuckling. "Me too."

"Rock won't stop 'til he gets Carter back." He curves his arms over his head like a giant umbrella. "He's the glue that keeps us whole. The shelter that protects us."

"That's an awfully heavy burden to place on one man."

Sparky cocks his head like he never considered that. "But it's his calling. And now he has his peace to recharge him when we drain his batteries."

"Hope?"

He nods solemnly. "Mother of Kings."

Harsh laughter bursts out of me and I slap my hand over my mouth to contain it. "Does she know that's her new purpose in life?"

"Of course she does," he answers like it's obvious.

"What's your role, then?"

He surveys the clubhouse with narrowed eyes as if the answer might be found in the fireplace, behind the bar, or up the stairs. "The trickster of healing."

"There's more depth to you than just a trickster."

"I didn't go with them because I wouldn't be helpful," he says, ignoring my comment. "Just so you know. It wasn't because I don't care about Carter."

My throat tightens. It seems really important to him that I understand this point.

"I'd get in the way and probably make things worse." His bloodshot eyes slip to the side.

I reach over and squeeze his hand. "I'm glad you're here."

"I'll help medicate Carter when he gets here too."

My nose stings but I force the tears away. "I'm sure he'll appreciate that."

I can't force any hint of humor into my words. I'm too damn scared Carter might not come home.

CHAPTER FORTY

Teller

"What is it?" Rock's harsh, angry whisper breaks through my trance.

I don't have an answer for him, though.

He reaches my side and stares at the body twisting in the breeze. "Christ."

My heart kicks a painful thump. Not giving a fuck who might be lying in wait to shoot me, I take off, jogging down the hill toward the hanging body.

"Marcel. Fuck." Rock's heavy footsteps pound behind me. "Wait."

My steps slow as I get closer. Something about the body isn't right. It's too puffy, the limbs bobbing in the wind instead of hanging limp.

Relief pumps through my veins. It's not Carter.

"Is it a…" Murphy steps forward, craning his neck. "A blow-up sex doll?"

"Fucking psychos." I don't dare take out my flashlight and shine it. I can make out enough details without turning us into an easy target.

A crude mustache and beard have been scribbled onto the face of the doll, in an effort to give it a masculine appearance. *Goober* is spelled across the doll's forehead in thick block letters that remind me of the box that had been addressed to Charlotte. Whether it's meant to be an insult or someone's actual road name, I'm not sure.

Rock's face locks into a grim scowl as he studies the doll. "It's wearing an S.O.S. cut."

My gaze slips lower. More black marker had been used to draw a replica of the Sons of Satan MC colors. "Traitor" is scrawled in red across the chest of the doll.

"A threat? A warning to other members?" Murphy asks.

"Who fucking knows." Rock kicks at an empty beer can on the ground. The area's littered with cans, broken bottles, cigarette butts and other trash.

"Must've been the highlight of their weekend," Murphy says. He squints, studying the tree line behind the gallows.

"They could've hosted an elaborate 'out bad' ceremony." Rock shrugs.

Our MC has never been into theatrics. You fuck over the club, you die a quick, painful death and we bury you in places no one will ever find your pieces. End of story. Taking the time to doodle on dolls seems silly.

"We haven't come across any human bodies. Maybe this was a message?" Murphy suggests.

"The stench of this place is so bad, there *could* be a corpse somewhere and we'd never know the difference." I turn to head back the way we came. "This isn't our mystery to solve."

Z, Jigsaw, and Grinder stand on the top of the hill. Z jogs down to meet us halfway.

"Is that…?" He lifts his chin toward the gallows.

"Blow-up doll," I explain.

He lifts an eyebrow. "Okaaay."

"What we got here?" Jiggy asks, meeting up with us. "A little Salem Biker Trials cosplay?"

"Something like that." Rock smirks and pats Jiggy's shoulder.

We reach the top of the hill and Grinder gives us a frustrated hand wave. "Come on," he urges. "Don't have time for this."

The last structure waits for us to the right of the hill. A large, rusted-out rectangle that looks like it came directly from Satan's trailer park. The largest of all the other structures we've seen—practically a palace in this place. At one time, someone tried to give it a homey touch with flower boxes dotted around the perimeter. The flowers must've withered under the relentless stench. Nothing but dry dirt fills the cracked boxes now.

We split up into two teams again. Z, Grinder, and Jigsaw circle around the back of the trailer before coming around to the front.

Thump.

I cock my head toward the trailer, waiting for the sound to come again.

The three of us crouch under the windows, putting our backs against the rippled metal siding. On the other side of the front steps, Z, Grinder, and Jigsaw adopt a similar stance. Z points at the trailer in an exaggerated sweep of his arm, then cups his ear. Rock raises his fist to signal he heard it too.

"Carter has to be here," I whisper. "They probably have someone guarding him."

Rock nods. "Nice and slow." He turns toward Murphy. "Stay here."

Murphy opens his mouth as if he's about to protest, then closes it.

A fresh dump of adrenaline surges into my blood stream. Tension knots my stomach. The weight of the gun in my hands offers some reassurance.

Rock and I creep onto the rickety boards that constitute the front "porch" of the ramshackle structure. We flank the sides of the door to avoid standing dead center, turning sideways to keep our bodies as thin a target as possible.

Murphy, Z, Grinder, and Jigsaw crouch below the stairs, out of sight.

Rock reaches out and strikes his knuckles against the flimsy door twice.

No answer.

I close my eyes, straining to hear what's happening on the other side. A shuffling sound. My eyes pop open and I stare at Rock. He cocks his head toward the door.

The click-clack of a shotgun.

Fuck.

A blast punches through the trailer door, sending pellets and splinters exploding outward.

Searing fire slashes across my hip.

"Not again."

Haven't I taken enough fucking bullets in my lifetime?

CHAPTER FORTY-ONE

Teller

THE SHOTGUN BLAST RIPPING THROUGH THE FRONT DOOR PROPELS ROCK and me backward, missing the steps entirely.

I land in the dirt with a punishing thump to my ass that rips the air from my lungs, jars my spine, and numbs my legs.

For a few terrifying seconds, my mind returns to the accident. The afternoon Mariella died. A hard bump against my back tire. Laying down my bike. Mariella's terrified screams. *So much pain.* Blood spreading across pavement. Waking up in the hospital and not feeling a fucking thing below my waist.

"T, you whole?" Rock's question whispers through my fog, pulling me out of the flashback.

I'm finally able to draw in a great, big, greedy gulp of air.

Beads of sweat roll down the sides of my face. The sting in my side doesn't increase. I take a few more slow breaths. Wiggle my toes and bend my bad leg. The burning in my side feels more annoying than life-threatening. I've had enough injuries over the years to recognize the difference.

"I think so," I finally answer. "You?"

"Yeah."

I groan as I sit up. My fingers stray to the dagger of fire in my side and come away wet. Not enough blood to indicate anything vital has been hit. I shake my bum leg. Hitting the ground seems to have rocked my system more than whatever pierced my flesh. My probing fingers graze something sharp stuck right above the waistband of my pants and underneath the edge of my Kevlar vest. I yank, wincing at the increased burn as I slowly pull out whatever embedded itself in my flesh.

I stare at the long, thick, bloody splinter. A chunk of door. *That's it?* I breathe a sigh of relief. Not a bullet.

Rock crouches next to me, placing his back toward the trailer, protecting me like a human shield. "Are you bleeding?" he asks a shade louder than necessary given our situation.

"Just a chunk of their cheap-ass door." The pain is annoying but tolerable and seems to be subsiding after the extraction.

A strong hand wraps around my upper arm and yanks. "Get out of the way in case they come outside," Murphy hisses in my ear.

Right. Someone shot at us.

Did I hit my head in the fall?

Shaking off the thousand thoughts racing through my mind, I roll to my feet and crab-walk to the side of the trailer, pressing my back against the metal frame.

"You all right?" Murphy asks, probing my bloody side.

"I think I'll live." I brush his hands off me. "You just *had* to make that crack about me getting shot."

His eyes widen like I slammed my fist into his gut.

"I'm kidding. Relax." I bump him with my elbow.

"Want some more of that, motherfuckers?" a man screams from inside.

Grinder answers by firing a few shots into the air.

Whoever's inside steps into the doorway. Just enough to see the tip of the shotgun, not the person holding it.

Click-clack.

Boom!

Pellets hit the dirt, spraying bits and pieces in a cloud.

In the distance—*pop!*

A bullet whizzes through the air.

There's a wet *thwack* and the hard, unmistakable thud of a body hitting the floor.

The corners of Rock's mouth twitch. "Figured Wrath could make that shot."

There's no way to know how many people are inside. The six of us stay put, straining to catch any more sounds.

Creak.

Thump-shuffle-thump. Someone banging against a wall? The floor? I can't quite place the sound.

Muffled talking?

A word that sounds like someone mumbling my name through a mouthful of socks.

I tap Rock's arm and he nods.

"Carter?" I say just above a whisper.

More muffled noises. Frantic now.

On the other side of the porch, Z wildly waves his arm, then points to the trailer. I nod and stand, wincing at the pain flaring to life in my side.

"Easy," Rock warns but he doesn't try to stop me.

Moving a whole lot slower than I'd like, Z and I creep toward the porch. Grinder and Rock stay close to our backs. Z steps inside first. Gun tight to his chest but ready to fire, he sweeps through the trailer. I pull my shotgun in front of me, pointed toward the floor, but fingers at the ready.

"Carter!" I yell.

A muffled yelp responds.

Hope and relief twist together in my chest. *Please let that be Carter.*

Z and I move toward the sound.

The trailer shakes and groans with our combined weight pounding through it.

I stop at a narrow doorway. My gaze sweeps over the cramped bathroom and lands on Carter. Duct-taped to the drainpipe connecting the sink to the wall, but alive.

Relief floods my system. He's alive. We found him.

The stupid drainpipe has to be the only sturdy thing in here. Carter's twisted the tape into a long, thin knot from trying to break free.

Crouching on the filthy tile, I pull out my knife and slice through the tape securing him to the metal.

"You came for me," Carter rasps as he rips the tape off his mouth.

Dried blood lines his temple. Anger quickens my pulse. Cutting off his toe wasn't enough, they beat him too.

"Of course I did." I hold out my hand. "Come on. We gotta go."

His face twists with anguish. "What about Bianca? Is she okay?" He squeezes his eyes shut. "She tried to help. One of them hit her. I was scared they ran her over."

"She's okay as far as I know. She called Charlotte and told us what happened."

He blows out a relieved breath. "Good. I felt so bad—"

"We can talk about it later. Let's get out of here," I urge.

He bites back a groan and stumbles as I pull him off the floor. "What's left of my foot is asleep."

A tornado of rage stings my skin. "How many toes did they take?"

"Just the little toe." Carter hops on his uninjured foot and struggles to put weight on the other. "It's okay. It got in my way most of the time, anyway."

Bitter laughter sears my throat. "Come here." I wrap my arm around his waist and encourage him to put his arm over my shoulder and lean on me.

"They sawed it off almost as soon as they got me into their death van." Carter shudders. "Wanted me to know they meant business."

"Fuckers."

He flexes his hand. "I'm just glad it wasn't a finger. I need those." He pretends to hold a paintbrush in the air.

"You all right, kid?" Rock asks from the hallway.

Carter's eyes widen and he stumbles again, fully leaning against me. "Rock? You're here too?"

"Took a knock to the head, huh?" Rock's low grumble makes it clear what he thinks of Carter's surprise. "Whole club's worried about you. Half of 'em are outside." He reaches for Carter's arm to steady him. "Teller's not kidding, we gotta go. Can you walk?"

"Yeah." Carter lifts his left leg. "Bleeding stopped a while ago. Still stings and throbs like a bitch, though."

He limps and hops next to me but doesn't complain as we navigate through the messy trailer. Cool air beckons from the wide-open front door. Carter hops faster toward freedom.

"Get me the fuck outta here," he mumbles, scrambling ahead of me.

The dead body sprawled in front of the door stops us. I hadn't bothered to look at him when we came inside. Now, I stop and study the owner of the shotgun. Black hole in his forehead says he's beyond CPR. His vacant eyes stare at the ceiling and whatever's beyond.

"Don't think you're headed in that direction," Carter spits out.

"He the one who cut off your toe?" Rock asks.

"No, but he was a real asshole." Carter taps his cheek where a red spot darkens his skin. "Thumbs. That's the guy who cut my toe off. They called him Thumbs. I was scared shitless he was going to take *my* thumbs as a fucking trophy." He croaks out the last few words.

Rock pats his back.

"June!" Carter's eyes widen and he whips his head around, eyes wildly searching the trailer. "We have to find her."

"Shit," Rock mutters.

"No, she tried to take care of me," Carter insists. "We can't leave her here."

"She's the reason they *took* you," Murphy says.

Carter's voice drops. "They're not nice to her, either."

"Let's get you out of here, first." I slap Murphy's shoulder. "Help me."

With our assistance, Carter hops and limps down the steps.

Outside, he stops and faces me, grabbing onto my vest to keep himself upright. "You're not making me ride on the back of your bike, are you?"

I lift an eyebrow. Glad to see they didn't beat his twisted sense of inappropriately timed humor out of him. "If I say yes, are you planning to stay?"

He glances at the trailer. "Hell no."

Wrath jogs up to us, still carrying his rifle.

"You all in one piece, Scribbles?" Wrath's quick gaze slides over Carter.

I lift my chin. "Nice shot."

"Thank Grinder for drawing him into the open doorway," he says.

"Wait, I get a road name, now?" Carter asks.

"Wrath's gotta name everyone," Murphy mutters.

Wrath's mouth slides into a half-smirk. "I name you, it means I most likely won't kill you." He hooks an arm around Murphy's neck and drags him into a choke hold. "Even if you piss me off."

"Peachy." Carter grins. "I can live with Scribbles."

"It covers all the bases of your talents." Wrath releases Murphy and slaps Carter's shoulder. He frowns when Carter wobbles to the side. "You all right?"

Carter holds his foot out. "I'm missing my *toe*."

Wrath meets my eyes. Scary fuck or not, Wrath's code is the same as mine—club business doesn't involve cutting body parts off of guys like Carter.

"It's okay." Nerves push Carter's voice higher. "I don't need it. I'd rather get the fuck out of here."

"We're going," I assure him.

"Rock!" Grinder shouts from deeper inside the trailer.

"Stay here," I warn Carter.

Z, Rock, and I follow Grinder's voice to a bedroom at the back of the trailer. A small, dark-haired woman dressed in black pants and a black T-shirt is tied spread-eagle to the bed, tears leaking from her frightened eyes.

Grinder kneels at the foot of the bed, slicing through one of the ropes. "Help me," he growls.

As Rock, Z, and I crowd into the room, her eyes widen and she screams into the cloth stuffed in her mouth. She coughs and chokes, frantically thrashing her head from side to side.

"It's okay, June!" Carter yells from outside. "They won't hurt you."

"If we wanted to hurt ya, we'd leave ya tied up," Z says in a bored tone, neatly slicing through one of the ropes binding the girl's wrists.

"Stop moving," I snap, tugging on the bandanna tied around her face. "I don't want to accidentally slice your cheek."

She goes stone still.

I carefully cut the material away from her face. She spits out the gag, wiggles her jaw, and sobs.

Once her limbs are free, the girl backs up to the wall and wraps her arms around her knees. She doesn't say a word, but eyes us warily.

"Yeah, I don't trust you either, sweetheart," I sneer, quickly scanning the room for signs of any other weapons. A peek inside the nightstand yields a pistol, bottles of lube, and other stuff I don't want to think about. I tuck the gun in a side pocket of my pants. Need to toss it later—

fuck knows how many bodies can be traced to it—but for now, I want it out of June's reach.

Jigsaw's big frame fills up the tiny doorway. He lifts his chin at the girl and rubs his gloved hands together. "What's this? Consolation prize for our toy box?"

"No," Grinder grumbles. He slaps Jiggy's chest. "Stop staring at her like you want to hang her over a barbecue pit."

Jiggy sniffs the air Hannibal Lector-style. "But she looks like she'd be tasty with a ribeye and a rich, imperial stout."

The girl whimpers and hugs herself tighter.

Chuckling, Z pushes Jigsaw away from the room. "Cut it out."

Rock stands at the foot of the bed, hands on his hips, and stares at the girl. "What are we doing with her?" he asks me.

If this really is the daughter of South of Satan MC's president, I get why he's not eager to take responsibility for her.

I'm not exactly thrilled about it myself.

I kick the side of the bed to get her attention. "You really try to take care of my brother?"

Face all red, blotchy, and bruised, she turns and lifts her chin with defiance and sticks out her tongue.

"Careful." Z casually flicks open a knife. "We can put that tongue to use, sweetheart."

She glares at him.

"We don't have time for this shit," I grumble.

"Yes. I tried to help Carter," she croaks.

"Do you want to stay here?" Rock asks.

She slowly shakes her head.

"You gonna behave?" I ask her.

She throws a hard scowl at me.

"Yeah, I got a little sister." I let out a dark laugh. "Those pissy faces don't work on me."

She scoots off the bed and reaches for a black, hooded sweatshirt on the floor. I slide my gaze over her. Thin and flat as a board—malnourished, almost. If she's pregnant, she must be in the early stages.

Not my problem.

"We're meeting up with Merlin," Rock says to her.

She freezes.

Rock sighs. "No one's gonna hurt you."

We follow her out of the trailer at a respectable distance. She doesn't try to grab anything. Doesn't even blink at the body she has to step over to reach freedom.

"Who is he?" Grinder asks, toeing the dead guy.

"My uncle," she says over her shoulder.

"So much for family loyalty," I mutter to Rock.

"Can you blame her?"

Outside, the weight of the night seems to press down on me. Fatigue tugs at my eyelids and I'd love nothing more than to crawl into bed and sleep for days.

Too bad we still have a long night ahead.

CHAPTER FORTY-TWO

Teller

Rock and I stand outside and stare at the trailer.

"Should we take the body?" I ask.

"Fuck," he mutters.

Wrath flicks the lighter in his hands. "I have an idea."

"June," Rock calls out, ignoring Mr. Firestarter.

She steps away from her huddle with Carter.

"Anyone else here?" Rock sweeps his hand in a circle. "Maybe hiding? Or tied up like you were?"

June flicks her gaze around the camp.

"Any women or children?" Grinder clarifies.

"Or animals," Z adds.

She shakes her head. "Women aren't allowed up here."

"That explains a lot," Murphy grumbles.

"Why were *you* here, then?" Wrath asks.

She cocks her head, like it's a stupid question. Quick, sharp laughter explodes past my lips. This chick throwing attitude at Wrath warms my soul.

Wrath snarls, looking awfully similar to a mastiff guarding a junkyard.

"We searched all the buildings," I say to Rock. "Didn't find anyone else."

He grunts a noise of agreement.

"They were hiding her from Merlin," Carter says.

"Why? Thought they wanted him to marry you tomorrow?" Wrath asks June.

"Ewww," Carter whines. "She's younger than me, for fuck's sake."

June shudders.

Rock stares at the sky, like he's searching for patience among the stars. "You got somewhere we can take you? Family? A mother?" he asks.

"My father killed her a long time ago." June's raspy voice carries years of sadness.

Well, fuck.

Rock stares me in the eye, a look that says he still doesn't trust her brewing in his gray depths.

I don't trust her either, but I shrug. "We'll figure it out. Let's get the fuck away from here."

"Now might be a good time to visit your undertaker," Murphy suggests, nodding at the body.

"I'll go with you," Jiggy volunteers.

"Let's get your truck," Rock says to me, jerking his thumb at the dead guy. "I'm not dragging his carcass out of here."

I take in the uneven fields. "I don't want to blow a tire."

"For fuck's sake," Wrath bellows. "Time to put your monster truck to work instead of treating it like a show pony."

"Fine, all right."

Impatient to leave, Wrath shoves his rifle into Grinder's hands and encourages Carter to get on his back for a piggyback ride.

"Uh." Carter wraps his hands around Wrath's neck and stares at the ground. "I don't know about this."

"You're fine." Wrath takes off, sprinting across the field with Carter bouncing and bobbing on his back.

I stop and place my hands on my knees, laughing until I wheeze.

"You all right?" Rock rests his hand on my back. "Is your side worse?"

"No." I fling my hand out toward Wrath. "It's the mountain man carrying Carter like he's King fucking Kong that's killing me."

Rock chuckles.

Next to me, Murphy's silently shaking with his own laughter.

"Good Christ," Grinder grumbles, stomping ahead of us. "Move your fucking asses."

"You heard Grandpa." Z slaps Rock's shoulder. "Get moving."

We make it to the grove of trees and our vehicles.

Wrath carefully sets Carter down. "Can you hop your ass into Teller's big rig?"

Carter side-eyes him like he doesn't want to risk another ride on Wrath's back. "I think so."

Now that we're all together, Rock stops to check his phone. "I need to let them know we have Carter." He meets my eyes. "No need to hand over your money, if we don't have to."

Jigsaw stares at Carter's bloody sock. "Damn," he breathes out, "I hoped they were fucking around and the toe wasn't yours, or something."

"Did they really send you my toe?" Carter's eyebrows crawl up his forehead. "Did you put it on ice, maybe? Charlotte didn't see it, did she?"

"It's on ice," Jiggy confirms, then finishes with the bad news. "Back at Teller's house."

Carter's mouth turns down. "Eh, I guess I don't need a Frankentoe."

"Get in the truck." Rock places his hand firmly between Carter's shoulders and gently shoves him toward the back door.

"Are we done with this cousin-fucking MC, yet?" Z asks.

Rock pierces June with a stare that nails her in place. "Your father's the president?"

She bites her lip and nods.

"Trip?"

"No." She shakes her head. "Trip was sent to prison a few months ago. A lot of the brothers were. My...my father challenged him right before that went down. And won," she adds as if that part matters.

"Who's your father?" Rock asks.

"Whitey."

Rock glances at me and I shrug. Name doesn't ring a bell. "Sticks is your brother, right?" I ask June.

Her nose wrinkles but she nods quickly. "Some of the brothers think he's the one who ratted them out to the Feds."

Wrath and I share a look. We'd run into Sticks before. Young patch holder. He was loose-lipped when *we* prodded him with a few questions. Ratting to the Feds wouldn't surprise me one bit.

"Did he?" Rock asks.

Her gaze drops to the ground, like she suddenly finds the broken pavement fascinating. "I don't know."

Rock sends an eye roll my way. "Sounds like a *yes*."

"I'm just a girl. They don't tell me club stuff." She crosses her arms over her chest like that's the end of our discussion.

I study her carefully. They probably *don't* tell her anything too important. That doesn't mean she doesn't *know* things.

Rock turns away. "Watch her. Dex hasn't answered. I'm going to call him."

I briefly consider calling Charlotte, but we're not exactly out of danger yet. "Who's Goober?"

"Uh...another patch holder." She shifts on her feet and slides her gaze toward the woods behind us. "A friend of my brother's. Why?"

"You know where he is?"

"No."

"I'm not getting an answer from them," Rock says, tucking his phone away and tugging on his gloves. "Let's get the body and get out of here."

The distant roar of motorcycle engines replaces the quiet chirping of crickets.

Too late now.

"Any chance that's Merlin and the others?" Grinder asks.

Wrath shakes his head. "Doubt it."

June slides toward my truck, her sneakers scraping through the sandy gravel, leaving a trail behind her.

Carter opens his door and beckons her closer with a wave of his hand.

"Guess she's riding with us." I lift my chin. "How many of 'em went to meet Merlin, June?"

"At least three," she answers without hesitation. "They left Con here to watch me and Carter. My father, his enforcer, and my brother all left to meet Merlin. All patch holders." She lifts her chin as if that's something to be proud of.

"Being a patched brother ain't exactly a threat with this MC," Jigsaw snickers. "They're fucking clowns."

"Clowns who cut off Carter's toe," I remind him.

"Yeah, they're definitely on the Pennywise end of the clown spectrum," Jiggy agrees.

"Can we play rate-a-clown some other time?" Rock nudges me toward my truck. "We have a body to collect."

"And some bodies to drop," Grinder reminds us, jerking his head toward the approaching engines.

"You're still on parole," Z reminds him. "Why don't you and—"

"Like fuck am I leaving you here, dipshit." Grinder cracks a faint smile. "I mean, Prez."

"The motherfucking disrespect from this one," Z grumbles. A grin plays over his face. He clearly doesn't give a shit about Grinder's refusal to leave.

The engines grow even louder.

Rock slaps my shoulder, then Murphy's. "Go get the body." He glances at the bed of my truck. "Hope you got room in there, we'll have more than one by the time we leave."

"We'll be right back." I open my door and climb in.

Murphy hauls himself into the passenger side and slaps the dashboard. "Let's see what this pretty thang can do!" he shouts, like we're about to recreate a scene from *The Dukes of Hazzard*.

"Knock it off."

I fire up the engine, back out of my spot, careful not to hit any of my brothers who don't bother to move the fuck out of my way, then put it in drive and jump the short mound of dirt in front of us. We land with a bounce in the open field and I hit the gas.

"Woo!" Murphy hits the dash again. "I knew she had it in her."

I flick my gaze to the rearview. "Hang on, Carter."

He and June are buckled down and hanging onto each other. He nods at me. "I just want to get gone."

Driving seems a hell of a lot quicker than our stealthy walk through the property had been. I plow over the rough terrain, jerking the wheel to the left or right to avoid debris that seems to be scattered everywhere.

"Jesus, fuck," Murphy breathes.

"Aw, what's wrong? Not having any fun?" The insanity of the night coaxes my inner asshole out of hibernation and I give the steering wheel another quick twist.

"Keep being a dick and you're gonna flip this thing," he warns.

The trailer comes into view and I hit the brakes, skidding into a neat circle that sends a flowerbox flying through the air and ends with my tailgate a few feet away from the front steps and clouds of dust billowing around us.

"Show-off," Murphy says, throwing open his door and leaping out of the truck.

I'm a little slower sliding out. My side burns in protest. I press my hand over the wound and ease out of the truck.

"You all right?" Murphy shouts.

"Fine." I drop the tailgate and roll back the truck bed's cover. "Hey, fun story, when we took you to the hospital, I wanted to load you back here but Heidi and Charlotte wouldn't let me."

Murphy gives me a sarcastic *really, fucker?* head tilt. "I'll grab his legs. Just push if you're too weak to lift him."

"I can lift him, asshole."

That might have been a bit too optimistic. A new pain rips into the skin where I'm still bleeding. "Shit. Let's roll him onto a sheet, first."

I run-hobble to the room where we found June and rip the filthy quilt off the mattress. We spread it out next to the body and roll the guy into a neat corpse burrito.

I give the body a quick test shove. "Better." Together, we ease it out onto the front step.

"Almost there." Murphy's not even a little out of breath.

We push and slide the big floppy body, then lift and toss him into the truck. I roll the cover into place and slam the tailgate shut. "Now, let's hope we don't get pulled over."

"Wouldn't that just be a fucking perfect end to this shitastic night." Murphy taps his fist against mine.

Gunfire explodes in the direction of where we left everyone.

"Shit." We haul ass into the truck.

In the back seat, June whimpers. "Please, please don't give me back to them."

My indifference toward her cracks. "Stay down and out of sight back there with Carter."

"Okay." The seat belt unclicks and there's a rustling sound as she slides onto the floor.

I didn't mean right *now*, but whatever. Something presses into my back. She must've wedged herself between Carter's feet.

I press the accelerator to the floor, not as worried about the obstacles this time. My brothers—and my *father*—are under attack. They need our help.

"You ready?" I ask Murphy, concentrating on the grassy field in front of us.

Murphy twists and snags his bag from the back seat. "Yup." He tugs a Glock out of one of the side pockets, then a few extra loaded magazines, stashing them inside his vest. "Go right."

"What? Why?"

He leans forward and points the muzzle of his gun toward the tire tracks I left on our earlier romp into the grass. "'Cause that ditch is gonna hit a lot different coming at it from this way."

I turn right and head for a narrow opening between a cluster of trees. Branches screech against the metal as we roar through. My headlights sweep over the scene in front of us, too fast to make out any details.

We hit a mound of dirt hard. The truck bounces and flies a few feet in the air. We land with a jarring thump, the engine screaming. The knobby tires dig into the broken pavement, spraying bits of rock and dirt everywhere.

I screech to a stop, dust billowing around us. The scent of burning rubber fills the air.

In the glow of my headlights, four Lost Kings MC patches stare back at us. By the height and shapes it has to be Grinder, Z, Rock, and Wrath.

Rock turns, shielding his eyes with a hand. Even though I doubt he can see me, I feel the weight of his stare telling me to hurry up and get my ass over there.

I flick the lights off. "Stay here, Carter. No matter what."

"Trust me, I'm not moving a muscle." He groans. "You're lucky I didn't puke all over your upholstery."

"June, you all right?" I ask.

"Yes," she squeaks.

Murphy and I jump out, boots grating against the gravel. He

swaggers around the front of the truck, snorting like a bull. "Let's end these motherfuckers once and for all."

It better be the end.

And not the beginning of something worse.

CHAPTER FORTY-THREE

Teller

Rock turns as we approach. "Got what we need?"

"Yup."

The corners of his mouth curl up. "Good. Look who showed up." He steps aside. Three men lined up and facedown on the ground. I recognize the South of Satan MC patches. Farther away lay three Harleys, wheels still spinning.

"Couldn't even let 'em dismount properly?"

"They came in hot," Wrath says. "Shootin' like we're in the Wild fucking West."

"Nice work." I pull out my hunting knife and run my gaze over the trio at my feet. Heidi gave me the knife one Christmas. I should've brought a different one with me for tonight's wetwork. "Which one of you is Thumbs?"

The guy facedown to my left kicks his foot out. "Him."

"Shut up, you stupid fuck," the one in the middle says.

I grab him by his belt and turn him over.

His eyes widen at the knife in my hand.

Mine widen with recognition. "Fuck." I glance over my shoulder at Rock. "We've dealt with this asshole before."

Rock moves closer and stares down at him. "Slow learner, huh?"

"Fuck you. You and your bullshit club ain't got the right to take over

Ironworks *and* Slater. Don't matter what Whisper wanted. Wolf Knights are out. They don't get a say. We coulda run that area."

Rock does a slow, sarcastic look around. "Sure. Absolutely. You seem equipped to handle the job."

"We should've killed him when we had the chance." Guilt settles in my stomach. Carter wouldn't have been hurt if we'd taken this punk out last time.

Wrath stares down at Thumbs. "The beating should've been enough for him to learn some respect." He kicks the guy next to Thumbs. "Seems Prez, here, doesn't have control over his crew."

"Fuck you, asshole."

More vehicles draw closer, drowning out everything else. I recognize the Harleys and breathe a sigh of relief. Our guys are whole.

Rooster's truck pulls up in the rear with Merlin still inside.

Dex jumps off his ride and stalks straight toward Whitey, slamming his boot into the president's ribs.

"I take it the meeting went well?" Rock raises an eyebrow at Dex.

"We need to get Rooster to a doctor," Dex answers without taking his eyes off Whitey.

"Why? What happened?" Jiggy shouts.

Rooster's door creaks open and he slides out of the truck, landing heavy on the gravel. "I'm fine."

"Fucking pussy," Whitey mumbles.

"Yeah?" Rooster's deadly voice rumbles as he picks up speed, boots slapping against the ground. "That right?" He cocks his gun, aims at Whitey's thigh, and shoots. Blood explodes over the dirty denim covering the man's leg.

Whitey screams and digs his nails into the ground, trying to drag himself away.

Wrath stops his attempted escape with a boot on Whitey's back. "We'll get you a Bandaid in a minute. Sit tight."

"That's for the knife in my side, fucker." Rooster tucks his gun away and nods to Rock. "Sorry for the interruption. Please continue."

Merlin ambles up behind Rooster. A smug grin twists his mouth. I hate even the appearance that my club's aligned with him. His shitty decisions led to this entire mess. And somehow, he managed to use my club to extract himself from the problem he created.

"You find Carter?" Merlin asks, as if he actually cares.

"Yes," I answer.

"June?"

"Yup."

He nods and hooks his thumb in his belt. "What're we doing?"

Rock slaps his hand against Merlin's chest, pushing him back a few steps, where Z intercepts him with a hand between his shoulder blades.

"Give me a reason not to burn you with them," Rock seethes.

Merlin glances down at Rock's hand. "I'm club family?" He lifts a shoulder. "Your son's marrying my niece."

"Loyalty makes you family. Not blood," Rock sneers. "Try again."

Still wedged between our two presidents, Merlin slides the backpack off his shoulder and carefully tosses it at my feet. "I didn't run with your boy's money."

Rooster's gaze shifts from Z to Merlin to Rock, like he's caught between having something to add to the conversation, but not wanting to stick up for Merlin.

"Spit it out, Rooster," Z says.

"Merlin stopped this scumbag from stabbing me in the chest." Rooster slams his boot into Whitey's leg, right above the bullet hole.

Whitey howls. His body rocks back and forth, like he's trying to turn himself over.

Dex is also slow to come to Merlin's defense. "Things got chaotic. He could've bailed, but he stood with us."

"Aww, so touching," Thumbs snickers.

Murphy kicks his arm. "Shut your mouth. My brother hasn't decided how hard you're gonna die tonight."

I wave the knife at Thumbs and he snaps his mouth shut.

"I've been trying to do the right thing," Merlin says.

"Right thing woulda been marrying my daughter," Whitey shouts. "Fuckin' scumbag."

"Or not fucking her at all," the other guy, who I now recognize is Sticks, adds.

Merlin rubs a spot between his eyes, like the whole night is giving him a headache.

You and me both.

"We don't have time for a big production." I nudge Rock's shoulder. "We killing them here or at the funeral home?"

"Here will be easier. Less chance of them getting loose." Rock shoots one final warning glare at Merlin and releases him. Z steps closer to Rock, whispering something in his ear.

I nod to Merlin. "Whitey's all yours." I refuse to be the only one killing men tonight.

Merlin nods and pulls out a revolver.

"Get him up." I motion to Thumbs with my gun.

Murphy pulls Thumbs to his feet.

His wild eyes search our faces as my brothers and I close in on him. "I don't want to die."

As if he has a choice. "You should've thought about that before you went after my family."

"We didn't have a choice!" Whitey yells. "Merlin couldn't be reached any other way."

"You always have a choice," Rock says. "You chose the cowardly one."

"Don't kill me." Thumbs squeezes his eyes shut. "Please, don't kill me."

"Did Carter beg you not to hurt him?" I ask in a calm voice.

Despite the situation or maybe because he's trying to get me to kill him quicker, Thumbs smirks. "He cried like a little pussy."

"Yeah?" I dig the tip of my gun into his chin. "Did that make you feel like a big man?"

"No...no," he stammers.

To my right, there's movement. We're all so focused on Whitey and Thumbs that Sticks has managed to belly crawl a few feet away. He lurches to his feet and takes off running for the woods.

"Get him," Rock growls.

"He ain't going anywhere." Z throws his arms wide. "We're in the middle of nowhere."

"The road's not that far away." Dex starts running after the guy.

"Good point." Z sprints after Dex.

Rooster presses his hand to his side. Blood oozes between his fingers. The corner of his lip curls as if he's fighting off a wave of pain. "I got tarps in the back of my truck. Some ratchet straps," he offers. "We'll roll 'em up like carpets."

Jiggy cackles and rubs his hands together. "I'll get 'em." He slaps Rooster on the back. "Stay put."

Rooster nods and closes his eyes briefly, swaying on his feet.

"Bro, you don't need to stick around for this." I tap Rooster's shoulder. "You've done enough tonight." More than I have a right to ask him to do. I jerk my head toward my truck. "Watch Carter and June for me? I don't want them seeing this."

"You got it." Rooster slaps my arm and heads for his truck, stopping to talk to Jigsaw for a minute. Rooster ends up pulling his truck next to mine, blocking off Carter and June's line of sight.

"Carter should see the risks you're taking to cover his ass," Merlin says.

"No," I answer in a flat tone. "He shouldn't."

"It's not his ass we're covering, is it?" Rock asks in a deadly tone.

"I'm just saying, the boy needs to man up," Merlin insists.

I blow out a quick, annoyed breath. "Takes all kinds of men to make the world spin, Merlin. Carter's fine how he is." Carter's the kind of man who spent months painstakingly painting murals of unicorns and mermaids all over my niece's bedroom walls. Something that brings her joy every day. Right about now, it seems a hell of a lot more "manly" than anything Merlin's accomplished in his whole pathetic life. And more useful than executing people in a desolate field in the middle of the night.

Merlin grunts but keeps his mouth mercifully shut.

Z and Dex drag Sticks back to our party by the arms. Whatever methods they used to subdue him, he's now quiet.

"Wait." Jigsaw steps in front of Sticks. "*Did* you rat out your club?"

"He did what needed to be done for our club," Whitey says. "Ain't your business."

Merlin kicks Whitey in the chin, the crack of his teeth banging together loud enough to make *my* teeth ache. "No one's talkin' to you."

"You couldn't take over the club by honest means?" Rock asks. "Or handle it internally? You thought handing over half your club to the Feds was the best way to protect your club?"

"Fuck you."

Nothing worse than a fucking rat. The whole point of *outlaw* life is living *outside* the law. Running to law enforcement to solve your internal club matters is as low as it gets.

I meet Rock's eyes.

A long time ago, we'd buried our own club's president for the good of the whole club. We could've easily offered Ruger up to the Feds. Instead, one day he just *disappeared*. Rock set the president's ring on the table, silently letting everyone know Ruger wouldn't be returning. We voted him in as our president. The ones who didn't like it, left. Sway's method of protest was to form the Downstate New York charter. And as much friction as the two charters had over the years, we didn't go to the cops to sort it out.

Rock nods once, as if he's also thinking of our past deeds.

People outside our brotherhood who don't follow our code would never understand. But we don't need them to.

We are our brother's keeper.

And no one else's.

"Look." Whitey holds up his hands but with the bullet in his leg, can't quite sit up. "You still need to make things right with my daughter," he says to Merlin. Then he glances at Rock. "We'll stick to our side of the border. We won't say a word. You won't have to worry about us again."

"You think you're in a position to bargain?" Rock asks, disbelief dripping from his words. "The time to stay out of New York was two years ago."

Whitey ignores him and focuses on Merlin again. Not sure why, Merlin isn't in a forgiving mood either. "We're gonna be—"

Merlin raises his gun and without another word, shoots Whitey in the head. Bone, blood, and lumps of brain explode onto the ground. Whitey slumps over.

Thumbs screams and stares at his dead president.

Sticks doesn't look at his father. He squirms and tries to break free again.

Next.

I approach Thumbs.

"Don't kill me," he pleads. "I'm sorry. I'm sorry."

"Unfortunately for you, my ol' lady made me promise to kill whoever took her brother. And cut off his toe. Not a smart move sending her that package."

"Here." Z tosses a tarp at me. "Let's at least try to minimize the DNA splatter."

I drape the material over the guy's head, making him look like a kid dressed up for the darkest Halloween of his life.

"No!" he shouts, fighting to pull off the sheet.

But it's too late for him.

"I always keep my promises."

I squeeze the trigger.

CHAPTER FORTY-FOUR

Teller

MARGOT'S WAITING FOR US IN THE PARKING LOT OF THE FUNERAL HOME. I'm not sure what her father told her about my phone call. But she's dressed in all black, even has her hair tucked up under a black knit cap —like she's planning to rob a bank with us.

"She's fucking adorable," Jiggy mutters.

"A little murder get your libido up?" Dex asks.

"It's always up." Jiggy grins.

"For fuck's sake," Rock mutters. "We're not done yet. Focus."

I stop Z from opening the tailgate of my truck. "The less she sees the better."

Rock, Jigsaw, Murphy, and I meet Margot in the center of the parking lot. Her anxious gaze sweeps over us, stopping at the bloody spots on my side. "Are you hurt?" she asks.

A strangled noise hums in Jigsaw's throat but I ignore him.

"I'll be all right." I jerk my head toward the crematorium. "I'm not sure what information your father gave you…"

"He said to give you whatever you need." Her gaze skips over us again, like maybe she shouldn't have been so quick to do what her father asked.

"Show us how it works." I nod to the low brick building. "That's all we need."

"Oh. All right. I can do that."

Jigsaw and Z follow us into the building, to what looks like an oversized cinderblock furnace with metal plating around the outside. She walks us through the process of burning the bodies. It's slower than I realized. And it seems like a cleaner way to leave this Earth than what these guys deserve. It'll certainly be less messy than how we disposed of Grinder's old parole officer a few months ago in the basement of Loco's diner.

We sure have seen a lot of death this year.

Some of it caused by us.

Others, we stood by and allowed, because it's what our outlaw code demanded.

Does all this death make us men or monsters?

After we've shoved the first body into the fire, I pose that question to Rock.

He stares at the flames for a few beats. "It's either us or them. That's the life we've chosen." He glances over. "I'd rather be on this side, standing next to my son, than burning."

"Me too." After a few more seconds of silence, I ask, "Should we have let Sticks go?"

Whitey and Thumbs had to die, no doubt. Sticks had been a bit of a question mark. At least until he made a run for it.

"If he ratted out his brothers, what do you think he would've done to us?" Wrath asks. "Not worth the chance."

"Just another loose end to tie up later," Z agrees.

My cheeks heat, either from the flames in front of us or because Wrath and Z overheard our conversation, but I keep my expression blank. "What about June?"

"Ain't gonna be any evidence left." Wrath nods to the flames. "Even if she goes to the cops, what exactly is she going to tell them?"

"Next contestant!" Jigsaw shouts and elbows us out of the way.

Z makes a shooing motion with his hand at me. "Go have your existential crisis conversation somewhere else, Teller. I'd actually like to get home to my wife before the sun comes up."

"Can't go any faster," Dex warns, helping Jiggy move the corpse. "You heard what Margot said."

"Mr. Whitey's gonna have to wait his turn," Z says.

"He should've gone first," I grumble, staring at what's left of Whitey. "Fucking pig. Beating his own daughter. Leaving her tied up like that. Planet is better off."

"God will judge him." Dex clasps my shoulder. "We just set up the meeting."

"Praise Buddha," Rock mutters.

Jiggy toes the guy with his boot. "I think the magical sky daddy's gonna pass on this one and send him straight to the demon's dinner table."

The tension of this never-ending night breaks and I laugh for a solid minute. "You have a gift for words, Jigsaw."

He grins and rests his hand against his chest. "I do, don't I?"

Behind us, the heavy steel door creaks opens and all of us turn. Even if it's Margot, it doesn't matter. She's smart enough to know we're not here in the middle of the night to dispose of our household garbage.

But it's Grinder with Carter and June standing behind him.

"Kids asked if they could watch." Grinder lifts an eyebrow, silently asking if we have a problem with it.

Rock waves them inside. I had a different response in mind.

"You should wait outside." I slap Carter's back and nudge him toward the door.

"You kidding? I ain't missing this." He kicks one of the blanket-wrapped bodies at our feet. "This asshole cut off my toe. He smashed Bianca's nose with his elbow. I watched him beat June." His eyes fill with shame and he ducks his head. "I couldn't do anything to stop it. The whole time I was thinking, 'I can't wait for Teller to get here and kill this asshole.'"

My chest tightens. "Is that right?" *My brother-in-law sees me as a killer? Great.*

He meets my stare, concern wrinkling his forehead. "Well, yeah. I mean, if losing my toe wasn't a big enough crime, I figured him beatin' on a pregnant chick would be a death sentence." He puffs up his chest. "I woulda pulled the trigger myself if you'd let me."

"You don't want that responsibility." My voice takes on a sterner edge than I intended. "And I don't want it for you."

He seems to chew on that for a moment. Then he lifts his chin, determination brewing in his eyes. "If he'd gotten loose...and threatened you." His gaze strays to my brothers. "Any of you. I would've shot him."

Who knew when I met this mouthy kid he would've managed to get under my skin so thoroughly? I swallow the lump in my throat. "Good to know."

He shrugs. "I mean, I probably would've missed, but I wouldn't have run away. The instinct to hurt someone threatening you is there." He taps his chest. "It has to count for something, right?"

Much needed laughter rumbles out of me. "Yeah, it counts. Thanks, Carter."

Wrath steps behind us and wraps his arm around Carter's neck, holding him in a looser choke hold than he'd use on Murphy or me. "You want to learn to shoot, Scribbles? I can take you to the range." He squeezes and Carter's eyes bug. "As long as you listen to everything I say."

"Yeah." Carter coughs and curls his fingers around Wrath's forearm, trying to pry it off his throat. "I'd like that. I also enjoy breathing, if you don't mind."

"Oops." Wrath releases him.

Murphy punches Wrath's arm. "If your biceps get any bigger, you ain't gonna be able to wash your own damn face."

That's just an invitation for Wrath to flex his arms and show off.

Merlin tugs at one of the bodies, moving it closer to the fire. "You guys always fuck around this much when you've got serious shit to deal with?"

"Yes," Rock answers in a weary tone. Then he slides his gaze my way and throws me a smirk.

Merlin glances at June. Something resembling concern creases his face. "She shouldn't be here. Fumes ain't good for her."

"I'm not pregnant," June whispers. Her gaze latches onto mine and she won't even glance in Merlin's direction. "My father blackmailed him. I never wanted that. But I didn't have a choice. We never even..." Her cheeks redden and she shrugs a shoulder toward Merlin. "No offense, but you're older than my father was."

Merlin's eyebrows shoot up. "What?"

"My father caught me with one of the brothers," she says in a voice barely above a whisper. "Well, Sticks caught us and tattled to our father.

To stop them from beating me, I told them I was pregnant." She squeezes her eyes shut. "I knew they'd kill Goober if they thought it was his. I was supposed to be off-limits to any of the brothers. You don't touch the president's daughter, right? Not that it ever stopped them from—anyway, I told them you and me hooked up last time you visited. You got really wasted at that party. I figured you wouldn't remember what happened that night."

Merlin just stares at her.

The conversation I had with Heidi about reining in my overprotective side and teaching the girls to trust their gut tickles at the back of my mind.

"Awful big risk, lying like that," Rock says.

"It saved me from a beating." Remorse fills her dark eyes. "I'm sorry, though. I didn't know they were going to get so crazy over it. Goober and I were planning to run away." Her bottom lip quivers. "But they found out and…"

"What'd they do to him?" I ask.

"I don't know," she whispers. "They said they had something special to show him. I never saw him again after that."

Rock glances at me. His eyes seem to be saying what I'm thinking. Goober's dead somewhere on that property. The doll we found hanging had probably been a stunt to fuck with the guy before they killed him.

Her gaze lands on Carter. "I'm so sorry. Merlin did everything they asked. I never, ever thought they'd attack a civilian."

Merlin stares at the closed door, probably wishing he could escape. "That's, uh, not the only reason they went after Carter. Your Dad figured out that I skimmed some money." He shrugs. "Your lie about me being the father of your kid mighta actually saved my life."

Guess all the secrets end here in this chamber of death.

Sometimes the truth is only a few lies away.

CHAPTER FORTY-FIVE

Teller

We step outside and the cool night air washes over me. Standing in the dark, quiet parking lot of the funeral home, I'm overwhelmed with the need to unlace my boots and touch my toes to the grass.

Later. When I'm home.

I feel nothing for the men we killed tonight. They brought it upon themselves. If they'd left Carter alone and stayed away from my club's territory, they'd still be living their lives.

Every action has a reaction. A consequence.

They broke the simple outlaw code and paid the price.

I tip my head back. The bright stars pinpoint the inky black night sky. Not far from here, Charlotte can see the same stars.

I can't wait to get home to her.

I'm thankful I *will* be going home to her.

Tonight's events could've gone differently.

I glance over my shoulder at the funeral home and mentally examine each step of the night. We took plenty of precautions. I flex my fingers, my leather gloves irritating my skin. I'll toss them in the fire with the last body. No fingerprints should've been left behind. Since we're the closest MC to South of Satan's territory, if someone complains about their disappearance, eventually law enforcement *might* ask us questions. But I doubt anyone will care enough to bother.

A heavy hand lands on my shoulder. I don't have to glance over to know it's Rock but I do. He tilts his head back and inhales a deep, cleansing breath. "You can head home, if you want." He side-eyes me. "You need to take care of that hole in your side."

"I'm still standing. I'll be fine. This was my mission. I'll see it through."

He nods once. "Few more hours and they'll be nothing but ash."

"And we'll scatter them in the dirt where they belong," I agree.

Charlotte

A loud, vibrating buzz pulls me awake.

I unglue my cheek from the sticky couch cushion.

Buzz. Buzz. Buzz.

Where's that coming from?

Pocket.

I reach for my phone and stare at the screen.

Ol' Man

Thank God. "Marcel! Are you okay?" I answer.

"I am now," he rasps. "Hearing your voice cured what's ailing me."

Love for him squeezes the air from my lungs. I'm almost scared to ask my next question. "Did you find Carter? Is he okay?"

"He's surprisingly cheery, considering the night we've had."

I burst into laughter and tears at the same time.

"Talk to your sister. She's worried about your ass." Marcel's voice moves farther away. There's a strange roar in the background. My heart lurches. *Carter's okay.*

"Char?" Carter says. "It's me. I'm alive."

"Carter! Oh my God," I sob. "Are you all right?"

"Uh, I've been better."

Marcel grumbles something in the background.

"I'm okay, Charlotte," he says with more confidence. "Wrath gave me a road name."

"What?" Laughter cuts through my tears. Who worries about road names during a rescue mission?

"Yup. Scribbles. I like it."

"I like it too," I whisper. It's perfect, actually. "When are you coming home?" I need to see him and make sure he's really okay.

"Uh, you know your ol' man's not fond of me asking questions." He lowers his voice. "And, uh, Rock's MC president face is much more terrifying than his boss face."

I'd seen a small glimmer of that side of Rock when we were in Mississippi. "Well, keep that to yourself."

"Believe me, I will." He's quiet for a second. "Uncle Chuck actually came too."

"He did." I strain to hear what's going on in the background. "Is my ginger twinny okay?"

Carter chuckles. "Yeah, he's on the phone with Heidi, I think. Oh, your man wants you again."

"Charlotte?" Marcel's low rumble comes over the line.

"Do you need me to come help with anything?"

"No, we'll be a little longer. Where you at?"

"Uh." I blink and take in my surroundings. All my laughing and sobbing seems to have woken Bianca and Swan. They both stare at me with wide, expectant eyes. I nod quickly to indicate Carter's okay. "Clubhouse downstairs," I answer. "Swan and Stash brought Bianca up and we crashed in the living room."

"Good. Stay there."

"I will," I promise.

ROCK

"Good news." Z tucks his phone in his pocket and joins us. "Doc said he'll come up and treat our injured soldiers." He slaps Teller on the shoulder. "Bad news, he's going to charge us triple."

I stare Z down. I've known him for far too long. There's something else he's not telling us.

"*Really* bad news." Z takes a careful step away. "Carla's coming with him."

"Jesus Christ. This night keeps getting better and better." I stab my fingers through my hair.

Teller snorts. "Who gives a shit? Getting her out of your life was the best thing that ever happened to you."

"While that's true," I answer, "I don't want her bothering Hope."

Murphy steps up. "I'll make sure that doesn't happen."

"See," Teller jerks his thumb at Murphy. "Hope's ginger-headed personal superhero won't let anything ruffle Mom's feathers."

I pinch the bridge of my nose. It's too late for this. "A lot of punchable words in that sentence."

My son has the nerve to wag a finger in my face. "What'd I say about child abuse?"

"In your case, it should be swift and often?" Murphy guesses, throwing a fake punch at Teller's gut.

I take a deep breath. The irritation in my chest slowly turning to affection for these two knuckleheads. Thankfully they seem to have repaired their relationship and things have returned to normal. A little murder always speeds up the healing process between brothers.

"God help you," Z mutters, squeezing my shoulder.

Grinder lifts his chin. "The same Carla I'm thinking of?"

"Unfortunately," I answer.

He rubs his palms together. "Been itching to give that bitch some choice words for years."

"Do it after her husband stitches everyone up," I warn him.

"She found some other poor sucker to irritate to death?"

I sigh, both bored and annoyed with the subject of my ex-wife. "Yes. If we're done rehashing ancient history, I'd like to head back to the clubhouse for a shower." Last thing I want to do is take the filth of the night into the home I share with Hope and Grace.

CHAPTER FORTY-SIX

Teller

MY TRUCK'S THE FIRST ONE TO PULL INTO THE CLUBHOUSE PARKING LOT. Rooster slides his truck into a spot near me.

The rest of the guys roar in one by one.

Rock had returned in Wrath's truck. Whatever they wanted to discuss, I'm sure I'll hear about later.

Murphy's in my passenger seat. Carter and June are sound asleep in the back.

Murphy twists around and watches them for a minute. "I almost hate to wake them up."

"You're such a dad."

"Speaking of, what are the odds Wrath and Rock didn't kill each other on the way back?" Murphy asks.

"Nah, Z was with them to mediate. They'll be fine."

Murphy jerks his head toward the back seat. "They're kinda cute together."

"Please don't."

I open my door and Swan jumps back. "Is he okay?"

"Yeah. Exhausted but he'll be okay."

Inside the truck, I hear Murphy attempting to wake up Carter and June.

"Hey," I say to Swan. "We brought a girl back with us. She's had a rough time. Think you could get her settled in a room, some clean clothes, or whatever?" A long time ago, Trinity would've taken charge in a situation like this. Swan needs a bit more persuading to tend to the new girl.

"Sure." She hesitates and wrings her hands again. "I can do that. What's her name?"

"June." I walk Swan to the other side of the truck, where Murphy's helping June out and introduce them. "Swan's going to find you a place to stay."

June nods quickly. "Thank you."

Once they disappear inside, Murphy slaps my arm. "Your little bro's hard to wake up."

"Blake!" Heidi runs down the front steps and launches herself at him.

"Geez, he's fine," I grumble.

"Teller?" Carter calls from inside the truck.

I return to the other side and open his door. "Hey, sleeping beauty."

He smirks and turns, dangling his feet over the edge. "It's really starting to hurt now," he says quietly.

"Sorry. The doc should be here soon."

"Cool." He reaches for me, curling his fingers to motion me closer. "I meant what I said before. Thank you for giving a shit and finding me." He swallows hard and shifts his gaze away. "I know I give you a hard time but—"

"Kinda comes with the territory."

"Yeah, I know you and Murphy are always busting on each other but…guys like you don't usually look out for guys like me."

I cock my head, picking up on some pain under those words. "What does that mean?"

"You know." He waves his arm up and down. "You're all ultra-alpha and stuff."

"Ultra-alpha?" I squint at him. "That sounds like the name of a deodorant."

"You could snap me like a crayon if you wanted to." He flicks his finger against my arm.

"Believe me, there've been days…"

"I don't know why I'm bothering." He smirks. "The blood loss must be making me loopy."

"Hey, I think I understand what you're saying." I pat his leg. "I'll always look out for you."

"What's up, Scribbles?" Wrath knocks me out of his way. "You need a lift inside?"

Carter chuckles. "And *he* could snap *you* like a twig. So at least there's balance in the universe."

I laugh with him, because it's not a lie. "What's higher than ultra?"

He shrugs. "Mega?"

Wrath's gaze shifts between the two of us. "Sparky sneak out here with some of his special brownies for you two, or something?"

"Carter!" Charlotte races down the front steps. "Marcel, where is he?"

I push the door open wider. "Waking up from his nap," I say.

She reaches my side and throws her arms around me. "Thank you."

I wrap my arms around her. "Easy," I groan.

She steps back, eyes widening as they skate over the blood caked into my shirt and pants. "Well, I guess we should start a bonfire."

Wrath nods as if Charlotte's his star student. "Sunshine knows the drill."

"Most of it is *my* blood," I explain.

"What happened?" She starts pulling at my shirt. "Ugh." She turns toward Carter. "Are *you* okay?"

"Not gonna lie, sis. I've been better." He holds out his foot, showing off his bloody sock. "It hurts."

"I'm so sorry." Anguish twists through her apology.

The need to punch Merlin for causing all this suffering singes my knuckles. I scan the parking lot, searching for him. *There.* He backed his bike against the tall wooden fence that marks off the woods from the clubhouse's parking area at the top of the driveway.

Must be concerned about making a quick getaway.

He should be.

But I can't muster any annoyance with him. He stepped up tonight. Handled Whitey's execution without question. Didn't even flinch when June explained he'd been played for a fool in front of all of us.

Bianca steps next to Charlotte.

"B, are you all right?" Carter slides out of the truck and the two of them wrap their arms around each other. After a few whispered words, she helps him hobble into the clubhouse.

Charlotte slams the truck doors shut.

Slow boot steps grind over the parking lot. I glance up. Merlin approaches, eyes on Charlotte. The urge to stand between them burns down to my soul but I force myself to stay still. She can handle him. And I'm right here if he steps out of line.

"You gonna let me talk to my niece?" Merlin stops in front of us.

Charlotte squeezes my hand. "I'm standing right here, Uncle Chuck. Talk to me."

I keep my expression blank.

Merlin blows out a breath. "Suppose it can't get any worse." He fixes his eyes on Charlotte's face. "I kept my promise."

"You did." She gives him a tight nod. "Thank you."

"Would you hate it if I said I'm thinking of sticking around? And that I'd like to see you *and* Carter more often?"

"Why?" She tilts her head, studying him. "Another MC sees value in Carter, and you need to figure out why?"

Ouch. Pride flows through me. My woman's shrewd and not afraid to speak her mind.

Merlin blinks as if he hadn't even realized that was the reason until Charlotte said it. "No. I've had a lot of time to think out on the road."

Bullshit. I hadn't bothered to tell Charlotte the shitty way Merlin had talked about Carter when he sat at the table with us. Don't need to. She knows who her uncle is. Whatever epiphany he claims he had while he was out on the road is pure fabrication.

"I'd like to be closer to family." His gaze shifts to me. "Your club going to let me settle down in Slater?"

Sure, make *me* look like a controlling asshole trying to keep him away from his niece. "Depends."

"I'll still be a nomad as far as my club's concerned but that'll be my home base. Nothing more."

I shrug, not willing to commit until I've talked to my club.

Wrath slaps Merlin's shoulder. "We'll find you a room if you want to stay here tonight. We have a new clubhouse down in Empire but it's a long ride after the night we've had."

Merlin glances at the clubhouse. "Yeah, I'd appreciate that."

"Good." Wrath steers him away from us. "I'll go over the rules of the house with you."

Charlotte bites her lip as Wrath leads her uncle away. "Oh, Chuck's going to love *that*," she whispers.

"You think he was sincere?" I ask.

"Too soon to tell." She shrugs. "He's acted remorseful before. I'm sure right now he believes what he's saying, but Chuck will always look out for Chuck first."

"Smartest woman I know." I curl my arm around her shoulders and try not to lean on her too hard. "Let's see what's happening inside."

"Tell me whoever did this to you is in worse shape?" she asks, steering us toward the front door.

"Last I saw, he had a bullet between his eyes, so yeah."

I swear she mutters *good* under her breath.

The front steps send a fresh wave of pain rolling from armpit to ankle. Charlotte turns her head. "Should we go in through the kitchen? Fewer steps."

"No. We're almost there. I'm fine."

She holds the front door open and I hobble inside without further pain. Trinity stops us by the bar.

"Carter's down in the champagne room with the doctor." The corner of her mouth twitches. "Bianca's with him. I helped Swan find a place for June. I'll keep an eye on her."

Trinity might as well be nominated SAA of the old ladies. Nothing gets by her when it comes to the club's safety. "Thanks."

She squints at me. "You all right?"

"I'll live."

She squeezes my shoulder quickly, then hugs Charlotte before hurrying down the hallway.

ROCK

As soon as I open the front door to our house, Hope rushes toward me. Doesn't even question my wet hair or change of clothes.

She wraps her arms around my waist. No words need to be spoken.

Instant peace settles over me.

"Bad night?" she finally asks.

"One of the worst."

She pulls away and stares up at me. Concern shines in her green eyes. "Is everyone okay?" The hint of fear in her voice stabs straight through me.

"A few small injuries. Doc's coming up to take care of them." I peer down at her. "Carla will be joining him, so don't bother going to the clubhouse for now."

She shrugs off my warning with a scowl. "She's the least of my concerns. Is Carter okay?"

I give her a brief rundown of everyone's injuries. "I have to go back to the clubhouse and keep an eye on things."

"All right. I'll see if Heidi will watch Grace and be over to check in on everyone."

"You don't have to do that." I curve my arm around her waist and pull her close, pressing my lips to her forehead. "But I think having our first lady make an appearance wouldn't be a bad thing," I say, reversing my earlier warning.

"I appreciate you warning me about Carla," Hope says, judging my mood shift correctly. "But the club's more important than any run-in with your ex. I can handle her."

"I know you can, baby doll." I squeeze her tighter. "Still want to protect you from everything I can."

"Are you hurt at all?"

I release her and hold up my right hand. "A few scrapes and bruises from a *conversation* with a reluctant party."

She rolls her eyes, but takes my hand, carefully inspecting the cleanup I'd done and brushing her lips over my knuckles. "You need ice on this," she murmurs against my skin.

"Your kisses are more healing than any ice."

"You need your hands to twist the throttle, Mr. President."

"Don't I know it." My lower back throbs, reminding me of other mishaps. "Got a sore ass from jumping off a porch and landing on the ground."

Her lips pinch but she holds back the scolding I know she's dying to give. "What about Teller? I know he doesn't want to hear it but he still needs to be careful and not aggravate his back injury."

Guilt prickles through my chest. "He was walking when I left him."

The corner of her mouth twitches with dissatisfaction at my answer. "We made use of the funeral home."

She lifts an eyebrow. "How'd that go? Did the owner have questions?"

"No, he sent his daughter to do the dirty work of dealing with us."

She flicks her gaze away. "Can she be trusted?"

"I think so. We brought Merlin's girl home with us." I give Hope the brief version of that fucked-up story.

"Trinity will assess her," Hope says, shifting into shrewd lawyer mode. "I'll talk to her too, get a feel for where her head is at."

"Like Wrath said, not a whole lot she can do without any bodies."

She slants an annoyed look at me. "Cases have been made on circumstantial evidence before. Plus, you guys brought her right to the funeral home."

It's Hope's nature to examine every detail and find the weaknesses. She may not be working as a lawyer right now, but her clever mind never stops figuring out ways to protect the club.

"What did you do with their bikes?" she asks.

"Moved them into the woods and covered them."

"Electronics?"

"Same."

She stares ahead for a few beats, her mind in overdrive. "I want to look up who owns the property, so we can anticipate who might ask questions in the future. I don't want us to be caught off guard one day."

"I assume it's the South of Satan's property—"

She slants a no-kidding look at me. "I doubt they're as savvy about putting their businesses and property into shell companies."

My lips twitch. "No, probably not. I'll have Z get you the information."

She pops a kiss on my cheek. "Thank you."

"Let me go up and see Grace for a minute, then I'm heading back."

"Okay, I'll text Heidi or Trin and meet you over there."

Hell help me, but somewhere in the very distant future, I better die first.

Without Hope, life wouldn't be worth living.

CHAPTER FORTY-SEVEN
Teller

EVERYONE'S STILL TOO KEYED UP FROM THE EVENTS TO RELAX OR UNWIND. Plus, outsiders are in the clubhouse. Not exactly the time to rehash what happened. Brothers have either gone to their rooms or are down in the dining room stuffing their faces. I'm still leaning on Charlotte harder than I want to think about.

My gaze lands on a familiar figure sitting on the couch by herself.

"Steer me that way," I say to Charlotte.

"Who's that? The doctor's wife?"

"Rock's ex-wife." I can't remember if I ever told Charlotte that before. It's not like we see Carla all that often or that she's relevant today.

She might hold pieces of my past, though.

"Give me a minute," I whisper to Charlotte.

"I'll get you some Advil." She pats my chest and walks away.

"I see you stuck around." Carla flashes a brittle smile as I fall onto a couch cushion not too far from her.

My mother might be the only other woman I hate in this world more than Carla.

"Longer than you did," I quip.

"What'd you get into this time? Oh, don't tell me." She touches three fingers to her lips in a mocking way. "Club business."

"Tell me something, Carla," I lean in closer to her. "Why'd it bother you so damn much that Rock looked after us? Blake and I were just kids. My sister was a baby." I can't shake the feeling that she somehow knew who Rock was to me but I don't want to ask her directly.

Her gaze turns distant. "The three of you were like a hungry pack of stray dogs." She spits out the last word, then meets my eyes. "I wanted us to have our *own* family, not adopt riffraff whose parents didn't want to take care of them."

Twenty years ago that might have hurt my feelings. Now, all I feel is relief. "You leaving was the best thing that ever happened to him." I stare her down until she looks away. "He finally has the family he deserves. With a *good* woman."

Carla snorts. "Did that poor thing stick around?"

"She understands what loyalty means." The *unlike you* is implied.

As if she'd been summoned, Hope steps in the front door. Her gaze roams around the clubhouse. Searching for Rock, no doubt. But her eyes land on me and she hurries over.

I don't know if someone told Hope that Carla was here and she took extra care fixing her long auburn hair into smooth waves, picking out jeans and a pale blue sweater that hug all her curves, or she just rolled out of bed and shuffled over to the clubhouse looking so effortlessly beautiful, but the contrast between Hope and Carla couldn't be more stark. It gives me immense satisfaction. Carla had been extremely vain and superficial when she was married to Rock.

Carla squirms and runs her hands over her short, ragged ponytail, pulling it even tighter.

"Hello, Carla," Hope says in a soft, but not exactly welcoming, tone.

"I don't envy you," she sneers at Hope, instead of offering a normal hello. "You must have fun wondering every night where he is. And *who* he's with." Carla tilts her head. "Is he still working at the strip club, bedding all the dancers?"

Ignoring the taunt, Hope does the most perfectly Hope thing. She turns to face me, giving Carla her back. She cups my chin and tips my head up, staring me in the eye. "Rock and I want you and Charlotte to stay at our house tonight so we can look after you." She squeezes my chin gently. "Non-negotiable."

My lips quirk. "Yes, Mom."

376

She bops my nose. "What'd I tell you about that?"

"Who's with Grace?" I ask, more to rub it in Carla's nose that Rock and Hope have a daughter, than out of worry for my little sister.

"Heidi's watching her."

Carla lets out a *told-you-so* snort.

"I want to check on Carter," Hope adds, still pretending Carla doesn't even exist.

"He's with the doc." I lift my chin toward the hallway. "Trin said they turned your yoga studio into a hospital ward."

Charlotte returns and hands me a glass of water and four Advil. Worry and exhaustion have left her pale. I pull her down next to me and curl a protective arm around her. "You should go home with Hope and get some rest. Carter's okay. I'll be fine."

She shakes her head.

"Get used to this," Carla says to Charlotte. "It never ends."

Charlotte's not in the mood to be fucked with tonight. Her face smooths into her lawyerly mask. "Aren't you married to the doc who's patching everyone up? You hardly seem to be in a position to judge anyone."

Carla sniffs and stands. She spots Lilly by the bar and joins her. Poor Lilly.

"Z asked us to behave." I slap my hand over my mouth. "Damn."

Hope chuckles and sits next to Charlotte. "Surely there must be another crooked doctor between here and Union looking to make some extra cash?"

"It's not like we can put an ad on LinkedIn." Charlotte bumps Hope's shoulder. "How would that read? *Outlaw MC seeks unethical but competent doctor to stitch bullet wounds and other assorted injuries?*"

"Excellent pay but no benefits," Hope snickers.

Exhaustion and tension from the night seem to send them into a fit of giggles. After everything I've seen and done tonight, their laughter is the best medicine in the world.

Rock joins us and rests his hand on Hope's shoulder. "Something funny, baby doll?"

"I think they're just tired," I answer. "Everyone responds to stress different. Laughing is their coping mechanism." The corners of my mouth twitch. "Yours is threatening to punch me."

"That's *not* a stress response," Rock growls. His expression softens as he runs his hand through Hope's hair. "Are you all right? Did she say something to you?"

"Who?" Hope blinks up at him.

Fatigue overwhelms me. I should've done what Rock did and run upstairs to take a shower. Rinse the filth that followed me home down the drain.

I curl my hand around Charlotte's and push myself to the edge of the couch. "I'll get an infection waiting around for the doctor." I stand, tugging Charlotte up with me. "I'm going upstairs. Doc should see Rooster before he sees me, anyway."

Rock nods and holds my gaze. "That's a good idea."

Medical concerns are the last thing chasing me up the stairs.

I desperately need Charlotte's sunshine to wash away the darkness of the night.

To burn all my sins away.

CHAPTER FORTY-EIGHT

Charlotte

WHATEVER HAPPENED TONIGHT WEIGHS HEAVILY ON MARCEL. I FOLLOW him upstairs, holding his hand tight.

In all of my relief and joy to have my brother back, I didn't stop to consider what Marcel might have *done* to get Carter back.

I'd asked him to kill. And he came home bloody.

At the door to his old room he hisses in a sharp breath. I rest my hand on his back. "Are you okay?"

"Yeah." He pushes open the door and we step inside. I reach for the overhead switch but he stops me. "Don't."

"I need to look at you."

He tilts his head toward the bathroom. "I'll clean up in the shower."

"All right." I reach up, gingerly slipping his cut off his shoulders. "Let me take care of this." I turn and search the open closet for an empty hanger, draping the leather over it and dropping it over the metal bar. My eyes quickly scan the rest of the closet's contents. A few T-shirts. A flannel. A pair of jeans. Boots. At least neither of us needs to run home to grab any clothes.

When I turn around, he's still rooted in the same spot. Watching me.

"Come on." I hold out my hand and he takes it.

In the bathroom, he drops onto the closed toilet lid and starts unlacing his boots. I slide the shower door open and flip on the hot water. When I return to Marcel's side, he's only managed to take his shoes and socks off.

"Where are the gloves you wore?" I ask.

He blinks up at me. "Incinerated."

"Good." I glance at his long-sleeved shirt and cargo pants, wishing he'd been able to burn those too. Although, driving home naked probably would've gotten him pulled over rather fast. "Kevlar?"

"In the truck."

"I'll grab it later. We'll detail your truck tomorrow." I lift my fingers, gesturing for him to put his arms up. "Hope you're not attached to this shirt." I grip the hem and tug it over his stomach. He lifts his arms, allowing me to draw it over his head.

"No." He curls his hands around my hips, drawing me closer and rests his forehead against my stomach. I run my fingers through his hair, waiting for a sign he's ready to continue. After a few heartbeats, I shift my hands lower, kneading his tight muscles.

"Let me see." I push his shoulders.

He flicks his gaze to mine. Regret or pain flashes in his teal eyes.

"Do you want to talk about it?" I ask.

"Not really. It was rather straightforward. Not the worst—" He snaps his mouth shut.

I rest my finger under his chin. "You don't have to hide any part of yourself from me. Nothing will ever change how I feel about you."

"I'd rather not make you an accomplice after the fact," he says in his usual blunt tone.

"Don't forget our attorney-client privilege." I wink at him. Then more seriously, I ask, "Is South of Satan going to be a future problem?"

"Not the Bennington, Vermont chapter." He runs his hands through his hair. "Well, depends on what happens when their old president and his crew get out of prison."

"*If* they get out of prison. Trip got a hefty sentence."

"Right." He flashes a quick smile. "Forgot what a good researcher you are."

"How much of a loose end is June?"

"Don't know." He stares at the closed bathroom door. "They were pretty awful to her. Carter said she tried to take care of him and took a beating for it. We found her gagged and tied to a bed hidden in the back of a trailer." He shakes his head like he wants to knock that image loose.

"Stand up," I encourage and he complies. "Damn," I hiss when I get a better look at his side. "This is a mess."

He twists, trying to see the wound. "I pulled a big chunk of wood out of it."

"Yeesh." I work on unbuttoning his pants and he lifts an eyebrow. "Don't get cocky," I warn.

"I'm always cocky."

"Don't I know it." I work his zipper and wince as I push his pants down. "I'm not into blood play. I just need your clothes out of my way."

"Whatever you say, Sunshine."

The inappropriate jokes are better than his dark silence and listless answers. They give me hope he'll be okay. I reach up and press a quick kiss to his lips. "Let me clean this and then you can be as cocky as you want."

"Mmm." He lets out an interested growl and tugs at the collar of my T-shirt. "Take this off."

"This isn't one of the club's naughty nurse pornos, buddy."

He barks out a laugh, then winces, glancing at his side. "Has Downstate made a nurse porno?"

"How would I know? Probably," I mutter, searching through the medicine cabinet. I finally find what I want and twist the taps, scrubbing my hands clean. "What did this?" I gesture to his torn flesh.

He twists again, the movement drawing attention to his inked skin rippling over firm muscles.

Not the time.

"A chunk of door." He rubs his fingertips together. "Like one of those cheap particle board doors. Maybe a pellet from a shotgun. I pulled a piece about this big out." He holds his thumb and index finger about three inches apart.

"Great. Who knows how filthy it was or if there are little splinters in there. It just had to find that small, unprotected section between your vest and pants." I dry my hands and lay out each item I plan to use— gauze, peroxide, a bottle of liquid that says "wound care wash" and tweezers. "Let's clean you in the shower first."

He lifts an eyebrow and hooks his thumbs in the waistband of his boxer briefs, teasingly lowering and raising the material.

"Yes, yes, you're incredibly sexy and I can't wait to jump you." I twirl two fingers in the air. "Now, hurry up."

He points to my chest. "Seeing your tits would really speed up the healing process."

I smother my smile—shouldn't encourage his behavior—and strip off my T-shirt. "Better?"

He stares at my bra like he's trying to burn it off my body with the power of his mind. "No."

"Get in the shower." I wave an exasperated hand in the air and bite my lip to hold in my laughter.

He steps in but leaves the door open. "I need your help."

I strip off the rest of my clothes, grab one of the bottles from the sink, and join him. "Better?"

He cups my breasts. "Much."

"Jesus." I flick open the cap of the small bottle. "Stand under the spray for a minute."

We switch places. He hisses through clenched teeth as the hot water slices over his skin. "Fuuuuck, that stings."

"This probably won't feel much better. Want a washcloth to bite on?" I ask, handing him a square of terrycloth.

"No, smart-ass." He tips his head back, staring at the ceiling. "Just do it."

Wincing, because I can't stand causing him a second of pain even if it's to help him, I squirt some of the wound wash liquid on the torn skin. He's silent. Doesn't move a muscle as I take the washcloth and start rubbing at all the dirt and caked blood.

Finally, I can see the extent of his angry red, damaged flesh. "It's so jagged, I don't know if stitches will help. But we'll let the doctor figure that one out." I probe the area and my finger brushes against something sharp. "Hold on."

I lean out of the shower and swipe the tweezers off the sink.

He braces himself against the shower wall as I kneel to get closer to the wound. "Deep breath." I grab the sliver with the tweezers and pull. "Just particle board, huh?" I hold back vomit as a long, thin metal shaving appears.

"Fuck. No wonder it hurt so fucking much." He plucks it from my fingertips and studies the thin gray strip, then lets the water wash it away.

"Better?" I ask, dabbing with the washcloth again.

"Since you're down there…"

I glance up and meet his cocky stare. "Yes, I noticed your giant erection trying to poke out my eyeball." I curl my hand around his cock and squeeze. "I didn't know pain turned you on."

"It's not the pain." He closes his eyes. "It's you naked on your knees taking care of me."

"Uh-huh." I stroke him gently, just lazily sliding my hand over his flesh, enjoying the way my touch seems to uncoil the tension from his body. Admiring the rivulets of water running and glistening against his muscles. His eyelids drop and I lean forward, wrapping my lips around his cock.

"Charlotte," he sighs, threading his fingers through my hair.

I hum and suck him deeper, slide back, then take him again. His legs shake and he braces his palms against the tile. I open my mouth, releasing him and using my hand, then gently lick the tip, stopping to wiggle my tongue against the underside.

His hands drop from the wall and gather my hair into a tight knot. I moan from the sweet tugging sensation prickling over my scalp and suck deep, taking him to the back of my throat.

"Char." His voice holds a note of warning. "I can't be gentle right now."

I hum and nod to encourage him, and relax my jaw. He grips my hair tighter and moves his other hand to the back of my head, pressing tight. He lied, though. No matter how rough he is, there's always an edge of gentle protection to his movements. He cradles my head, careful not to ram me into the shower wall with each hard thrust.

"Fuck, I love the way you swallow my cock," he whispers in a harsh rush of words. "You love it too."

Good God, his teasing raspy voice ignites a throbbing between my legs.

I flick my gaze up, staring at him. Just a hint of the devil lurking behind his eyes peeks out. His lips quirk. "Too full of cock to give me a smart-ass answer, huh?" He thrusts again and I moan around him.

I shift my legs apart and slide one of my hands down.

He tugs on my hair in warning. "Don't you dare."

A shudder of excitement flutters over me. I tighten my lips and suck harder.

"Fuck," he gasps.

Even though I know each telltale sign that he's close, the first spurt takes me by surprise. He presses me closer, coming down my throat. I swallow and hum, accepting everything.

Breathing hard, he releases me, and presses his hands to the wall again. "Give me a second, Sunshine." But as he says it, he reaches down and offers his hand, helping me off the slippery floor. He hugs me close, our wet bodies slipping against each other. He cups the side of my face, his thumb brushing my cheek. "Thank you." He crushes his mouth against mine.

Careful not to touch his injury, I curl my arms around him, leaning into the kiss.

TELLER

Showering with Charlotte dissolved the filth of the night into steam that drifted away, leaving me restored.

My knees are still weak from coming but I'm not finished. We quickly dry off in the bathroom and by the time we step into the bedroom, I can't wait another second.

"I need to taste you." I push her on the bed and unhook the towel tucked over her breasts.

"What? No, I'm fine. You need to have the doctor look at that cut."

"Doc can wait. I need to make you come." I kneel in front of her and curl my fingers behind her knees, pushing them apart. "Need to shove my face between your thighs. Best medicine for me."

She falls back on her elbows, keeping herself lifted so she can watch everything I do to her. I rub my cheek against her inner thigh, nuzzling her soft, pliant flesh. Still damp from our shower, she smells like sweet rain. "You were going to touch yourself in the shower, weren't you?" I tease, running my tongue along the crease between her leg and hip.

"That tickles." She laughs softly and twines her fingers in my hair.

"Not trying to tickle you. Trust me." I run my middle finger through her slickness, slow and teasing. A hint of what I want to do to her. I stop and trace circles around her clit. Once. Twice. Two trips are all she needs to buck her hips and beg for more.

I push one finger inside her, groaning at how wet she is. My cock jerks, already eager to be surrounded by her. Sliding my palms against her thighs, I open her wider.

I do exactly what I promised and press my face against her pussy, inhaling her scent, then trace my tongue through her slit, stopping to swirl around her clit.

"Oh." Her thighs quiver and her hands grip my hair tighter.

I pull back and lightly flick the tip of my tongue against her. "Like that?"

"God, yes."

I circle her clit with my tongue again. Her hips rock forward to meet me. A thousand dirty words I want to whisper come to mind but I can't take my mouth off of her for a second.

Desperate noises bubble past her lips. Her hands grasp at my hair, my head, anything to get closer. I bear down on her thighs, pinning her like a butterfly. Now that she's so close, I attack her clit with pure focus. Breathing hard, tearing at my hair, she breaks apart. So wet against my mouth. I'm absolutely drowning in her love, she's both the current dragging me under and the air in my lungs.

Panting and boneless, she flops against the mattress. Her fingers loosen their grip, but she leaves them resting on my head. I run my hands down her legs, squeezing and kneading, stopping to kiss a few ticklish spots. I ease my sore body next to her, careful with my bad side. Every inch hurts, but I almost take comfort in the aches. It's pain I've earned. For the next few days it'll be a constant reminder of the crimes I committed tonight. Even when the pain fades, I'll have another scar. A silent sign of what I'm capable of doing to protect the ones I love.

My throbbing cock is a different matter. I roll myself, hovering and caging her in with my body. She wraps her hands around my biceps, sliding and squeezing.

"Already?" She lifts an eyebrow.

I stare into her eyes. "I need your pretty pink pussy squeezing my cock."

Her lips part.

"Hmm?" I shift my hips, sliding the tip of my cock through her slickness. "Think you can do that for your man?"

"I'll do anything for you." She tilts her hips and spreads her legs wider, making room for me to push inside. I let out a satisfied groan as she gasps. "God, you feel amazing," she whispers. Her forehead creases. "Are you sure you're okay?"

I jerk my hips forward, filling her to the hilt.

She squeaks in surprise.

"You tell me." I lace my fingers over the top of her head to hold her in place while I drive into her.

"Ergh." She moans an unintelligible noise and plants her heels in the mattress, arching to meet each hard thrust.

Her mouth falls open and her body locks in pleasure. Her pussy clamps hard around my cock. I keep going, riding right through her climax and pushing her into another. I drop my forehead against her shoulder, falling into the pleasure and pain, losing myself in her body. I come inside her in a rush that races down my spine, burying my face against her neck, licking salt from her skin.

Breathing hard I roll to the side. She shifts, snuggling closer, and I curl my arm around her waist. She tilts her head so she can see my face. I use one finger to brush sweaty strands of hair from her cheek.

"I love you," she whispers, curling her hand around my wrist and bringing it to her lips. "Are you okay?" she asks without shifting her gaze.

She's not asking about my external injuries.

"I don't like putting myself in this role of vigilante justice warrior," I say. "I feel like an asshole even saying it like that but I'm not sure how else to word it."

She props herself up on one elbow and stares down at me but her gaze is almost distant. "What do you think would've happened if we'd just let the cops handle it?"

I frown, unsure of how to answer that question.

"Let's say Empire PD is actually full of competent individuals." She slants a look that says she doesn't believe that's the case at all. "And they took my brother's abduction seriously. How long do you think it would've taken them to find Carter based on the information Bianca gave them?"

"I don't know. Merlin never would've gone to the cops. And he had the missing pieces of the puzzle."

"Exactly." She traces one finger against my stomach. "That hole in your side is from someone shooting at you. Their president beat his own daughter?"

"Yeah."

"If you hadn't killed them, do you think they would've just gone quietly away? Or would they have kidnapped *me* next? Or Heidi?"

My jaw tightens.

"Just because you and your club would never go after a daughter, or sister, or nephew, to get to them, doesn't mean other MCs play by the same rules." She rests her hand over my heart. "You have honor." She closes her eyes briefly. "I don't care what 'the law' says. Sometimes, killing your enemies is the only way. I will defend your actions with my last breath, Marcel."

My breath stutters. She truly sees and understands every part of me —even the sinister ones—and loves me anyway.

CHAPTER FORTY-NINE

Teller

I SIT UP AND SLIDE OUT OF BED.

"Where are you going?" Charlotte asks. "You need to rest."

"Can't. If I fall asleep now, I won't get up for at least a day. Rock will want all of us at the table. And I still need to see the doctor." I lean over and kiss her cheek. "You can stay here, though."

"Like hell." She sits up and wrinkles her nose, glancing down. "Boy, you better have put a baby in me that time."

I laugh so hard, I swear I rip my wound open wider. "*That's* what you're thinking about?"

Her smile fades. "I can't help it."

A sigh escapes me. I'm too exhausted to talk about this now.

Someone bangs on our bedroom door and Charlotte scoots off the bed, rushing to hide in the bathroom.

"Give me a minute," I yell. Where the fuck are some pants? I find jeans in the closet and slip them on, then open the door.

Blake's leaning against the frame. "Rock wants us downstairs." His gaze drops to my side. "You see the doc yet?"

"No, Charlotte cleaned me up."

He cranes his neck, searching the small bedroom. "Where is she?"

"Bathroom." I jerk my thumb over my shoulder.

"She okay?" he asks in a low voice.

"Yeah."

His smirk returns. "Swan and Bianca are, uh, taking turns helping Carter through the healing process."

Charlotte pops out of the bathroom, running a brush through her long, damp hair. "I hope that's not a euphemism for my brother's having a three-way downstairs."

"Definitely not," Blake says. "Purely medical for the moment. Just saying, it might be headed in that direction, though."

"Looks like that offer to stay at Rock and Hope's will come in handy," Charlotte says. "I don't need to know about my brother's intimate matters."

I grab a shirt and my cut, then we follow Blake downstairs.

The clubhouse is a bit livelier now. Carla's sour puss is nowhere to be seen.

"Is the doc even still here?" I ask Blake.

"Yeah. Carla's helping him stitch Rooster, then it's your turn."

"Fucking great. I don't want that bitch anywhere near me."

"Heard she got mouthy with Hope." Blake flashes an evil smile. "That's why she's sticking close to the doc now."

Rock's waiting near the war room doors. For the first time in a long time, he actually looks weary.

I stop next to him. "Do you need me to do anything?"

"Nah, this is going to be quick."

Thank fuck.

I ease into my chair and nod to each of my brothers as they enter the room. When everyone's in place, Rock takes his seat. I catch his eye. "Can I say something, first?"

He regards me carefully, then nods once.

I stand so I can see everyone. "I want to say thank you. Tonight was rough." I knock my knuckles against the table, suddenly unable to find the right words. "I couldn't have gotten Carter home safely so fast if it wasn't for your help. It wasn't club business, yet you all had my back. Charlotte and I both...thank you." Feeling like a naked asshole, I drop into my seat.

Blake pats my back.

"We got you, brother," Dex says.

"You'd do the same for any one of us," Bricks adds.

"I'm sorry I didn't do more," Sparky says in a low voice.

I look up and meet his bloodshot eyes. "You did, though. Charlotte said you helped keep her mind off things. Appreciate you looking out for her, brother."

He straightens in his chair. "We did have an enlightening conversation. She's brilliant."

"Yeah." I smile wide. "She is."

I meet Rooster's bleary eyes across the table. Whatever the doc gave him must be hitting him hard. "I'm sorry you got hurt too, brother. Anything you need, just let me know. Anything."

He lifts his chin.

"Okay," Rav interrupts. "Now that Carter's home safe, can we please talk about the fact that he has *two* hot chicks fussing over him?"

How'd I know Rav would be the one to ruin the moment? "No," I growl.

"I always assumed our little dude was gay," Rav adds as if I hadn't voiced my objection.

"Stop assuming stuff. It makes you look like a bigger asshole than normal," Jigsaw says.

"Don't get offended." Rav shoots a smug smile at Jigsaw. "I didn't say there's anything *wrong* with being gay, I just said—"

"We heard you," Rock interrupts. "Now, knock it off."

"He's got a point." Stash holds his hands out in front of his chest like he's carrying two watermelons. "Bianca has a fantastic set of tits. Every time I've seen her she's been in one of those corset things, showing 'em off. So fucking hot."

"Shut up." Sparky shoves his buddy. "Not cool." Whether he's defending Bianca's honor or worried about something else, I can't tell, and don't care.

"Then Swan. *Swan!*" Rav continues. "Who knew she went for little artsy dudes?"

"Jesus Christ." I pinch the bridge of my nose and stare at my lap. "Can we not discuss my brother-in-law's love life? I already know way more than I want to know about everyone at this table. I'd rather not expand that knowledge."

"Agreed," Rock says, taking over the meeting. "It's been a long night. I want to go over a few things, then let everyone get some rest." His gaze shifts to Rooster, then to me.

Z glances around the table. "We might need to go over this again in the morning."

"It's already morning," Wrath says.

"First," Rock's tone captures our attention, "Merlin's an overnight guest."

"I explained house rules to him," Wrath says. "But everyone keep an eye on the girls around him. That includes June."

"That the skinny black-haired chick Swan brought in?" Sparky asks.

"Yes." Rock rubs his forehead. "Keep an eye on June too. I don't completely trust her."

"You thinking we should give her some cash and send her on her way?" Z asks. "Maybe some airfare to the other side of the country?"

"Maybe."

"Trinity's going to suss her out, get a feel for where her head's at," Wrath says.

"Trin has a knack for that." Murphy nods. "Good idea."

"She's basically our enforcer for the ol' ladies," Dex adds.

Rock ducks his head, shoulders shaking for a second. When he faces us again, he's completely serious. "Yes."

"So, is this shit with South of Satan done?" Bricks asks.

"For now, yes." Rock drums his fingers against the table. "Their old prez and half that charter's in prison. Doubt the prez will give a shit about the ones who disappeared tonight. Whitey's the one who ousted the old president. Sticks is the one who ratted out his club to the Feds…" Rock shrugs.

"We did them a favor," Jigsaw says.

"I don't know if they'll see it quite that way," Grinder says. "Best to keep tonight's events to ourselves."

"Merlin sure as fuck ain't gonna tell anyone," Z says.

"Holy shit." Jigsaw squeezes his eyes shut and rocks sideways in his chair. "Mind fucking *blown* when June said she never even fucked him."

"Yeah…the look on his face." Dex shakes his head. "Almost felt bad for him."

"I didn't," I grumble. "She looks like she's barely out of high school."

"How much you think Whitey shook him down for?" Murphy asks.

"Who gives a fuck?" Wrath dismisses the question with a wave of his hand. "He deserves it for being stupid."

"Amen to that," I mutter.

CHAPTER FIFTY

Charlotte

THINGS MOSTLY GO BACK TO NORMAL AFTER THE NIGHT CARTER WAS abducted. He stays close to our property or spends time at the clubhouse. Bronze told him to come back to the tattoo shop whenever he's ready.

I finally got Murphy's adoption on the calendar and this morning we went to court. Marcel, Rock, and Hope joined us to watch Murphy formally adopt Alexa.

I couldn't stop throwing up before court. Not from nerves. I knew our case would go smoothly.

"Well, you were right." I step out of the bathroom staring at the stick in my hands, afraid if I look away the result will change.

"I told you," Marcel says, but there's nothing smug about the intensity on his face. "It would happen when we were ready."

He grasps my free hand and pulls me closer. "Are you happy?"

"I'm scared," I whisper.

"Understandable."

The corners of my mouth quirk up. That's my man. Blunt and to the point.

"Do you want to tell everyone tonight?" he asks.

"No, tonight's about celebrating the O'Callaghan clan." Murphy is such a proud dad, he deserves a night to celebrate the commitment he's made to his girls. "Your sister already suspects, but I'd still like to wait until I'm farther along to make any announcements."

"Can we move the wedding date up, though?" he asks.

"Yes, absolutely." I curl my hand over the back of his neck. "I can't wait to marry my handsome king."

His expression softens and he runs his fingers through my hair. "Are you sure you still want to do it in the backyard?"

"This is our home, I can't think of a better place to pledge our lives to each other."

His gaze shifts. *Was pledge our lives too formal?*

"Do you think the name change will be finalized soon?" he asks.

Shoot, I should've realized that's what he's concerned about. "Don't be mad, but I asked Mara if she could help me speed it up."

"You did?" His teal-blue eyes widen and he cocks his head. "Why would I be mad?"

"I wasn't sure you wanted me to spread your personal business around to my colleagues."

"I don't care. I like Mara and she would've found out at the wedding anyway."

"Good." My stomach rumbles and I press my hand over it to muffle the obnoxious sound.

"Are you sick?" Concern darkens Marcel's eyes.

"No. Hungry."

He releases a relieved breath. "*That*, I can fix." He curls his warm hand around mine and we head downstairs to the kitchen.

I sit at the kitchen table and Marcel sets a glass of water in front of me. "Thanks."

"What do you feel like?" he asks, peering into the refrigerator.

"I don't know."

My phone vibrates from its stand and I cross the kitchen to see what it is.

Uncle C: Who's walking you down the aisle?

Not you. My thumb hovers over the send button, then quickly hits backspace until the letters disappear. I resist further temptation to respond by setting my phone on the counter facedown.

Ugh, I don't need this today. I only want to celebrate good things for our family, not dwell on the bad.

I scowl at Marcel. "My uncle seems to think he has an invitation to our wedding."

Guilt darkens his features for a second.

"You didn't." I rest my hands on my hips.

"He—"

"Don't you dare say 'he's family' or 'it's business.' Neither excuse is acceptable."

"Charlotte," he pleads.

"Don't even try to use that 'please be reasonable' tone with me."

"Charlotte," he tries again, sterner this time.

"Fine, but he's absolutely *not* walking me down the aisle."

"Good." He holds up his hands. "That's all you."

"I'm perfectly capable of doing the job myself."

"Yes, you are."

"Actually." I bite my lip, not sure how he'll feel about this. "I wanted to ask Rock if he'd consider walking me down the aisle."

He steps closer, resting his hands at my waist. I lean into him. "Do you think that'd be okay?"

"I think it would be perfect."

Carter taps on the kitchen door. I reach over to unlock it and let him in.

"Are we going up to the clubhouse?" he asks as he walks in.

"In a bit," Marcel answers. "I'm making something for your sister. You hungry?"

Carter shrugs. "I could eat."

I chuckle. Carter can always eat. I return to the table, taking a long sip of water.

Carter's gaze narrows on me. "You seem off. Did everything go all right in court?"

My little brother is almost too perceptive sometimes. "Flawless." I tap my phone. "I'm annoyed that Chuck asked who's walking me down the aisle."

"Definitely don't let Chuck do it," Carter says, limping toward the table.

I bite back the cry bubbling in my throat. He's still limping and in pain, even if he won't admit to the pain part.

"I'm fine. Stop looking at me like my goldfish died," Carter grumbles.

"We're moving the wedding date up," Marcel says to smooth over the moment. "You're still my number two, right?"

"You sure you want me up there, Teller?" Carter asks. "Won't it look weird that I'm the only one not wearing one of your bad boy vests?"

Marcel hesitates for a second. "Don't you finally want your shot with Mercy? You'll walk her down the aisle."

A sly grin spreads across Carter's face. "I have more than I can handle, bro, but I appreciate the thought."

"Don't encourage him," I say to Marcel.

A few minutes later he sets a perfectly golden grilled cheese in front of me.

"Oh my God." I bite into the crispy, buttery, cheesy bit of heaven and close my eyes.

"You all right, Charlotte?" Carter asks. "Never seen you get so worked up over grilled cheese before."

Marcel shoves a plate in front of Carter.

Carter tips his head back. "You're such a good dad already."

I freeze, mid-bite.

Marcel has a smooth answer prepared. "Took care of Heidi when she was little. So, I have experience."

"I've heard. She talks about you like you're freakin' Thor." He flicks his hand at Marcel. "Without the thunder and pesky sibling rivalry."

Marcel slants a look my way and I shrug.

"Oh man," Carter moans with a mouthful of grilled cheese. "This *is* good. I'm sorry I doubted."

"The secret is the garlic seasoning on the bread." Marcel sets a bowl of pickles and olives on the table with a soft clink. He sets a smaller bowl of baby dill pickles next to my plate.

I tip my head back and meet his amused eyes.

"You got any apples?" Carter slides out of his chair. "Char, you want apple slices?"

"Sure."

Marcel directs him toward a bowl of fruit on the counter and hands him a knife.

Two of my favorite men, side by side in the kitchen. Uncle Chuck would roll his eyes so hard they'd fall out of his head. The thought makes me snicker as I bite into a crisp, tangy pickle.

"What's funny, Sunshine?" Marcel asks, setting his own plate across from me and sitting. His eyes crinkle at the corners when he smiles at me. Like, he's bursting to share our news right now.

I could be wrong, but I don't think we'll keep this secret for long.

At least this time, we'll be hanging onto something joyful instead of painful.

CHAPTER FIFTY-ONE

Teller

BLAKE'S BUSY GRILLING A FEAST ON THE BACK DECK OF THE JUMBO HOUSE he built for my sister when we arrive.

I set down the two bags of wood chips I'd brought up, leaning them against the railing next to his Cadillac-sized combination grill and smoker. "Got my workout for the day, carrying those all the way out here."

"Why didn't you use one of the ATVs?" His gaze strays to Charlotte, talking to Heidi and Alexa in the yard below us. "I think Charlotte likes you. You don't have to keep showing off to impress her."

"Nah." I grin and slap his shoulder. "A little tip for you, it's always good to keep the magic alive."

He chuckles and adjusts one of the knobs on the smoker.

"I feel shitty I didn't bring you a present." I stare at my empty hands and back to Blake's face.

"You brought the wood chips I needed." His eyebrows knit together. "You're here. What else do I need?"

"I'm..." I hesitate and run my hand over the back of my neck. We're past this, aren't we? Blake doesn't need my approval or my gratitude. Every action shows how much he loves my sister. "I'm proud of you. Not many men would step into the role of fathering someone else's kid so selflessly and so completely." Shit, Heidi's own father couldn't do it.

The realization hits me hard, wiping my mind clean of anything else I had planned to say. "Thank you."

His face pinches, hands clench and release at his sides. Several emotions seem to flow over him. Maybe I said too much. Overstepped, yet again.

"You know I don't ever want to lie to her." He stops and seems to search for the right words. "But I don't want her to grow up feeling different." He gestures toward Heidi. "Especially since we're having another girl."

My fucking eyes sting. Must be the smoke coming off the grill.

"I love Alexa like she's my own," he continues. "I hope that adopting her the second I was able to will make sure she never doubts herself. Or how I feel about her."

No words. What can an uncle say to that?

"Holy shit, are you speechless?" he asks.

"Don't ruin it," I warn.

"Seriously, though. Don't thank me for doing the only thing I know how to do. I hope over time people forget and don't constantly bring it up around her, you know?"

"Yeah, I hear what you're saying." He wants to protect her from even the smallest emotional scars. "Love you, brother." I reach for him, giving him a quick, tight hug.

"You're awfully huggy lately," he says, pulling away and slapping my shoulder.

"Only with family."

One heavy hand slaps down on my shoulder, and another on Blake's. "You two want to step aside and let me handle this?" Wrath asks.

"No." Blake shrugs him off. "My grill, my way."

"What's welterweight doing? Supervising?" Wrath squeezes my shoulder.

The corners of Blake's mouth twitch, like he's considering telling Wrath I've been over here getting all emotional with him. Then his smile fades. He points his grill tongs at the bags of wood chips. "Talking about all the different kinds of wood chips. Pecan, Apple, Hickory, Plum—"

"I got it." Wrath nods quickly, then slaps Blake's shoulder again. "Congratulations. You're a lucky man."

Blake's shoulders tense, waiting for whatever obnoxiousness is about to come out of Wrath's mouth. "How's that?"

Wrath lifts his chin in Alexa's direction. "You've officially got a cool-as-shit daughter."

Blake's expression relaxes. "Yeah, I do."

We spend time bullshitting about grilling, and a run Wrath wants to take to visit our Virginia and Tennessee charters. "This time, we need Rock to come. You too, Teller." Wrath elbows Blake. "Deadbranch needs to see how a real president behaves."

Blake chuckles, "Yeah, go tell him that."

"Call me when the steaks are done." Wrath grabs two cans of seltzer from the cooler and joins Trinity on the outdoor couch.

Charlotte jogs up the steps and rushes past us into the house.

"You all right?" I call after her.

"Yup!"

Blake's mouth twists. "Got news to share?"

I sigh and jam my hands in my pockets. "She doesn't want to say anything yet."

"Heidi already told me Charlotte was puking before court." His smile grows wider. "She's *very* excited. But I understand if you want to keep it to yourselves for now."

"Thanks."

Heidi joins us, rubbing her back and staring after Charlotte. "She okay?"

"Are *you*?" I ask.

Murphy steps behind her and starts kneading a spot on her back that makes her close her eyes for a second.

"Thank you," she says, smiling up at Blake. She sniffs and stares at the grill. "And I'm starving."

I lift the grill lid to show her the steaks.

"That's great." Heidi slides her gaze between the two of us and grins. "But what are you guys eating?"

CHAPTER FIFTY-TWO

Teller

"THIS ISN'T WHAT I HAD IN MIND FOR A BACHELOR PARTY," I GRUMBLE. In two weeks Charlotte and I are *finally* getting married. Wasting an entire night at Crystal Ball is the last thing I need.

"And *you* know I wouldn't ask unless we really needed you there," Rock says in his quit-your-bitching tone.

And yet, *he's* not going. "Fine."

"Bro, things are finally turning around," Dex explains. "We've got Loco's girls starting the early shift. Then amateur night at nine. Place will be packed. Blue and Butcher are out. I really need the help."

"I already said fine." I cross my arms over my chest, not giving a fuck if I'm acting like a petulant asshole. "I've got a ton of shit to do before the wedding, though."

"Monday, I'm all yours," Dex promises. "I'll help you with whatever you need."

I blow out a quick breath. "Thanks."

"We're not mind readers, knucklehead. If you need help, just ask," Rock says in a slightly less annoyed voice.

"I'll cover the champagne rooms," Ravage offers, as if it's a completely selfless act. "Tonight, I mean." He glances at me. "Unless you're setting up a champagne room at your wedding?"

I shoot a glare that wipes the smile off his face.

"Yeah, that's a hard no, Rav." Dex shakes his head. "I need *you* on the floor. Wrath, will you take the champagne rooms?"

Heh. At least Wrath got roped into this too. He hates hanging out at Crystal Ball more than I do.

"You sure about that?" Wrath lifts his eyebrows. "'Cause I'm in a mood tonight. A customer gives me lip, I might shove him through a wall."

Dex shuts his eyes and slowly inhales through his nose and exhales slowly through his mouth. Must've borrowed one of Rock's breathing tricks to stop himself from murdering us when we piss him off. "Yes. Your terrifying face should make anyone think twice about breaking the rules."

Wrath, naturally, takes that as a compliment. "You owe me," he says to Rock. Then he lifts his chin at me. "I can help you in the mornings this week too."

"Thanks." I glance at Rock, still feeling annoyed about this. "Z's only two hours away, why not tag him in? He knows CB in and out."

"He's got his own club to run." Rock tilts his head. "Do you need an ass kicking? Because we can go outside and I'll beat that disrespectful attitude out of you and *then* send you to work at Crystal Ball for the night. *Or* you can just do what I fucking asked you to do and quit running your mouth."

"Fuck! I already said yes."

Wrath points at me, then Rock. "You two need a little daddy-son bonding time? Wanna go out back and toss around a football or something?"

"I'm gonna toss something around in a minute," Rock growls, glaring at me.

"All right. Relax." Murphy holds out his hands, one in Rock's direction and one in mine. "I get why you don't want to be there, bro. But that's what the club needs tonight. Birch and Hoot are downstate, so we're short on bodies."

Ignoring the deft way Murphy's trying to mediate between Rock and me, I nod to Dex. "It's been a while. I might be rusty."

"Just stand there and look scary. You see anyone put hands on the girls, *discourage* them once. Second time, throw them out."

I hope a motherfucker gives me a reason tonight. Like Wrath, I'm in a mood.

"Remy promised to come help out this weekend," Dex says. "I gotta train him and show him around the place a few times before I'll trust him on his own, though."

"About time they start putting the *support* in support club," Wrath says.

Murphy sits forward. "They've helped us out a lot. Christ, Grinder's had them landscaping Serena's friend's yard for fuck's sake. What more do you want?"

Wrath rolls his eyes, as if landscaping isn't in the support club description.

"We've been leaning on them a lot. And they've come through every time," I add, agreeing with Murphy. "That's a long ride for Remy. He got anyone coming with him?" I ask Dex.

"Griff will do it." Dex's lips quirk. "Eraser and Vapor, not so much."

"Pussy whipped." Ravage grins. "But I get it. Ella and Juliet are cute as hell."

"Juliet's like my niece, you clown," Dex seethes. "Watch yourself."

"I said she's *cute*, not that I wanted to—"

"Don't finish that sentence," Dex warns.

Rav wisely shuts his mouth.

"All right." Rock slaps the table. "We good?"

Everyone says yes and Rock lets us go.

Except me.

"Stop right there." Rock stands, blocking my path.

Murphy's halfway to the door but he stops and reverses direction.

"Not you," Rock says.

"Nah, Prez." Murphy crosses his arms over his chest. "I think your VP should stick around for this conversation."

I don't dare laugh.

"What's with you?" Rock asks me.

"Nothing. I just fucking hate spending time there, that's all."

"Club. First." Rock enunciates each word slowly. "Or did you forget that?"

It's not even a business the club needs any more. I bite my tongue to stop myself from expressing that opinion. As I get older, I like to think I've learned when to share my thoughts and when to keep my mouth shut. Unfortunately, I fail at it more often than I want to admit.

"Is Crystal Ball still good for the club?" There, that's more diplomatic.

Rock stares at me.

Shit, did I actually leave him speechless?

Murphy lets out a long, shrill whistle. "He's got a point."

"Does he?" Rock asks.

Murphy runs his hand over the back of his neck. "Yeah."

Rock turns to me. "Do we or do we not still wash the cash from selling Sparky's crops through CB?"

"Yeah," I admit. "We do. We also wash it through Furious."

"On paper, we sell enough protein powder to leave a herd of elephants constipated," Murphy confirms.

Rock stares at him for a long moment. "Thanks for the visual."

I try again. "Once the funeral home's set up, we can use that—"

"Marcel," he says slowly. "We've never shared our investment windfall with National. How's it going to look when Priest visits and we're all fucking around? There aren't enough dead bodies in Slater to account for that kind of money."

"Market continues on its downturn, we won't have to worry about it," I mumble.

"That got you worried?" Rock asks.

I shrug. "Not really. I pulled enough cash out. I keep us diversified. Smartest move is to stay the course. Historically, things always bounce back. Just might take a while." I pause for a second. "I know you think I yank my dick and play farmer at my house all day long but I *do* actually manage the club's investments."

"Never said otherwise." Rock tilts his head, studying me for a second. "Charlotte got a problem with you being at CB?"

"She's working late, I haven't had a chance to tell her—"

"I mean in general."

"What woman likes her man hanging around a strip club?" I ask. "You might believe Hope when she says it doesn't bother her—"

"Leave my wife out of this."

I hit a nerve with that one, so I retreat.

Murphy catches my eye and cocks his head. His expression says *tell him.* "How come you're not sending Murphy?" I ask instead.

Murphy glares at me.

Rock doesn't answer.

"You don't want to risk upsetting Heidi when she's so close to her due date?" I guess.

Rock sighs. "Wrath claims his presence at Furious is vital."

"More vital than *Wrath's?*" I raise both eyebrows.

"I know you think I'm at the gym yanking my dick and lifting weights all day, but I *do* actually work." Murphy mimics my earlier comment.

Did I sound like that much of a jackass?

"Charlotte's pregnant," I blurt out. "She's working late trying to wrap up some of her cases to hand over to Mara and another friend of hers."

Rock's harsh expression softens. "Why didn't you tell us?"

"It's early. We're trying to be cautious." I swallow hard, not wanting to share so much. But Blake already knows and Charlotte finally talked about it with the girls. "She had a miscarriage last year, so she wants to wait to tell everyone. Make sure everything's okay."

"Aw, fuck, Marcel. I'm sorry. I wish you'd said something."

I shrug. "What's there to say? She had a tough time moving past it. Didn't want to tell anyone." I run my hands through my hair. "Looking back, I probably should've made her talk to someone sooner."

"I don't think 'making' Charlotte do anything will end well for you, bro," Murphy says, lightening things up a little.

Rock huffs out a short laugh then turns serious again. "I'm sorry, Marcel."

"Thanks." Now I really feel like a jerk. "I'm sorry I gave you a hard time. I just..." I wave my hands in the air. "The club's supposed to be about freedom and not doing shit we don't want to do. I really hate being ordered to work at Crystal Ball like I'm a fucking prospect all over again."

Rock's mouth twists, like he's trying not to laugh. "I'm proud of you for correctly identifying your feelings."

"It's only taken him thirty-two years," Murphy mutters.

Ignoring him, Rock adds, "And I accept the apology."

"I won't give Dex any more shit tonight," I promise.

"Thank you." He pauses. "I hear what you're saying. That's always been the paradox of the club. The goal is not to conform. To live outside of society's rules. And we do—to a certain extent. But we have lots of rules and laws defining our world. They're *our* rules, though. You see the difference?"

"Yeah, I do."

His mouth quirks. "There're fine lines separating antisocial outlaws who keep to themselves, outright anarchy, and spending your life in and out of prison."

"I'll choose option A."

"I thought so." He holds out one arm, motioning me closer. "According to Dex, things are working out well with Loco's girls coming in. And the amateur night is new. That's why he wants extra help. Make sure Loco's girls are looked after, okay?"

"I will."

Murphy claps his hands together. "Everyone feel better?"

Rock hugs each of us to his sides. He squeezes me harder than necessary and leans closer to my ear. "You get mouthy with me like that at the table again, I'm going to take you out back and clean your clock. You feel me?"

"*Clean my clock.*" I smirk. "Who still says that?"

"I do." Rock pushes us away. "Get out of here."

We step out of the clubhouse and find Wrath, Dex, and Ravage waiting for us outside the garage. Wrath's even more irritable than he was at the table, glaring at us as we cross the gravel lot.

"The fuck took so long?" He runs his shrewd enforcer gaze over me. "Shame you're in one piece. I hoped Rock was kicking your ass."

"Just a therapy session," Murphy says.

"I wanna *gooooooo!*" Rav shouts at the sky. "There are chicks getting naked right this very second and we're standing here in the parking lot talking about our *feeeeelings*. What a bunch of *bullshit!*"

Wrath checks his phone. "If it'll calm your tantrum, no one's getting naked yet."

Dex nods. "Loco's girls won't be there for another hour."

"Oh, thank fuck. Can we go?" Ravage whines. "It'll take almost a fucking hour to get there. I want to be early."

Wrath and Dex fire up their bikes, drowning out Rav's yowling.

"RC," Wrath shouts at Dex. "Take the lead."

Dex nods.

"You seem to need some extra supervision tonight, Teller," Wrath shouts. "You ride next to me." He pats his leg like he's calling one of Z's dogs to his side.

I glance at Murphy who shrugs. "Whatever."

It's still daylight when we arrive. Murphy waves to us as he continues on to Furious.

Crystal Ball isn't much during the day. A nondescript gray and white box in a sea of cracked pavement. Hardly the dazzling fantasy experience we advertise. At night, when the neon buzzes to life, it'll look livelier, if not still dated. At least the new clubhouse we built next door has a clean, modern exterior.

We line our bikes in a row up against the back of the building. I toe my kickstand down and ease off, setting my helmet on my seat.

"Blacktop looks like shit," I say to Dex.

Wrath smacks me upside the head.

"I'm so glad you're here," Dex says, shooting a sarcastic smile at me.

"No, seriously. When we're getting the work done at Cedarwood, I want to divert some of it here. Maybe freshen it up. Just because it's the only strip club in the area doesn't mean it has to look like a dystopian bomb shelter."

"Yeah, okay." Dex glances down and kicks a chunk of blacktop. "I guess you're right. It's looking rough. I don't spend a lot of time outside."

"Who *cares*?" Rav yells. "The good shit is *inside*. You know that, right?"

"Yes, Captain Perv." I gesture toward the large metal door that Dex is busy propping open. "If the place looks nicer on the *outside*," I say in a slow, deliberate voice, "maybe we'll get more customers. More customers will mean new, pretty girls will want to get naked here. Does that dumb it down enough?"

"Whatever," Rav scoffs.

"You should've been at Deadbranch with us," Wrath says to me. "Their club is something else."

Dex snorts. "It looks like a cokehead's version of a whorehouse."

"It's got a gothic, bordello theme going," Wrath agrees.

I side-eye him. "That sounds like something Trinity would say."

"No shit." Wrath shakes his head. "But as soon as she said it," he snaps his fingers, "it clicked."

"Their security is shit, though," I say. "Isn't that where someone took pictures of Shelby and splashed them all over the internet?"

"They suck, for sure," Wrath says. "But I think with Steer down there things will improve."

"If you're done critiquing our place, can we get to work?" Dex asks.

Another bike pulls into the lot and stops at the end of our row.

"That better be Remy parking next to us." Wrath squints at the rider.

"It's Remy." Dex shoos us inside. "I'll talk to him."

If Dex wants responsibility for our support club, I'm not arguing.

"The inside is definitely better," I say to Wrath. "Z did good with the remodel."

Wrath slides his gaze over the larger stage with three poles instead of the one it used to have. "You're right. The exterior should reflect what's inside."

The next hour is a slow build to chaos. Willow arrives first and preps the bar. Then Malik pulls into the back parking lot with a mini-van full of strippers. *A mini-van.*

"This is weird," I say to Wrath in a low voice. "We sure they're all here willingly?"

He studies the girls as they get out of the van clown-car style, one after the other. They're talking and laughing with each other. None of the cattiness our regular girls usually display.

"Malik's a straight shooter," Wrath says, narrowing his eyes. "Protective over the girls. Doesn't tolerate anyone messing with them. I can't see him trafficking strippers. Even at Loco's direction."

"All right." I nod and move away from the dressing room. That's the last place I want to be once the girls pile in. Listening to them fight over lockers, vanity tables, makeup, stage time, shoes, and mirrors gets ridiculous. They're almost worse than bikers when it comes to fighting over territory.

For a while, I stay out of the way by helping Willow behind the bar. Girls come out and do some practice twirls on the poles. The DJ tests a few tracks that make my temples throb.

Rav leans over the bar, his gaze landing on Willow's ass.

I slap his arm to break the spell. "Knock it off."

"What?"

Malik trudges toward us, stopping next to Rav.

"What's good, brother?" Malik slaps Rav's open palm, then reaches over the bar to tap mine.

"Not bad." For one of our prospects, we see very little of Malik. Guy is always working here, Loco's place, or at his pawn shop in downtown Ironworks. "You ever get to take a day off, Malik?"

He holds out his hands. "And do what?" He glances over his shoulder. "Got access to as much free pussy as a man needs. A roof over my head. Hit up the diner when I need to eat. Life is good, money man."

Talk about no bullshit. "I guess when you put it that way."

"I'll be working the door." Malik lifts his chin. "Night's about to get started."

A few hours later I'm reconsidering all my life choices that landed me in this poorly lit nightmare with the horrible soundtrack.

Rav has mostly been behaving himself. He and I are standing in the back corner of the club where we have a good view of the floor.

"Who's that?" Rav nudges Malik's shoulder.

Christ, what now?

I follow his line of sight to a pretty Black girl with long braids, spinning around the pole. Flashes of blue and green from her costume catch the light with every rotation.

Rav's practically drooling on himself.

For fuck's sake. "Don't you dare harass the dancers," I warn.

Malik smirks at me as if that's a lost cause where Rav's concerned. "She's one of Loco's girls. Off-limits."

"Christ, Malik, you might as well have laid down a challenge," I mutter.

"That's Desna." Malik casts a smirk at Rav. "She'll chew your skinny white ass up."

I reach out and slap Rav's cheek. "Close your mouth."

"Look at that ass…those thighs," Rav mumbles. "I wanna wear 'em like a scarf."

"That's…weird." I flick my gaze to Malik, but he's now focused on one of the customers sitting at a table next to the stage.

"Excuse me," he says without throwing us a glance. He storms over to the guy, wrapping one big meaty hand around the man's wrist. With the pulsing music, I can't make out the conversation.

"We're supposed to be here to control the crowd," I say to Rav. "Stop eye-fucking the dancers."

He jerks his head toward the stage. "She can't even see me all the way back here."

"Thank fuck for small favors." I shift my gaze to Malik, confirming he has his situation handled. Should I go back him up? Or will he be insulted?

"Stand here and look scary" isn't always the most helpful job description.

While Malik twists the guy's arm behind his back and frog-marches him to the exit, I catch another customer grabbing a girl's ass cheek as she walks by him.

"Motherfucker," I grumble, pushing toward the handsy asshole.

"Let's fuck him up," Rav shouts behind me.

The music drowns out most of what he said but a few customers scramble to get out of our way.

I catch up to the girl. Even in her stripper heels, she barely reaches my chest. "You all right?"

She nods quickly then scowls. "He almost knocked me on my ass."

"Go on. I'll take care of him."

"Thanks." She saunters to the next table. The suited man eyes me before acknowledging her presence with a polite nod.

Good. *Keep your fuckin' hands to yourself.*

Now to deliver that message to the groper.

Guy must be dense as fuck or just not paying attention. He reaches for another girl. His stubby little fingers graze her thigh as she passes.

I shackle my hand around his wrist, snapping his arm up in the air, lifting him out of his chair.

"What part of *no touching* is confusing?" I shout in his face.

"Huh?" His blank expression take a few seconds to catch up to what's happening. Crystal Ball can't legally serve alcohol but that doesn't stop patrons from getting wasted before they come into the club. If they're obviously intoxicated, whoever's manning the door should turn them away, but some slip through.

I squeeze his wrist harder.

"Okay, okay. Sorry."

I throw his ass back into his chair. "The only thing I want to see that hand doing is waving dollar bills."

He pulls a wad of cash out of his pocket. "Okay. Okay, I got money. See?" He shoves the stack of ones toward my face.

"Good." I lean down so we're almost nose to nose. He rears away, but runs into Ravage, who's leaning over the back of the chair. "I will break whatever part of you I see touch another girl, are we clear?"

He swallows hard. A bead of sweat rolls down the side of his face. His gaze drops to my cut, quickly scanning my flash. People like him pretend outlaw bikers are a cute fairy tale—until they actually cross paths with one.

"I hear you, bro." He nods to my cut. "I ride too."

I bend his wrist to an awkward, painful angle. "I ain't your bro." I release him so fast, he rocks sideways.

Ravage squeezes the guy's shoulder—hard. "You don't want to go home to your wife and explain how your fingers got broken, right?"

"R-right."

"Good." Rav pats his shoulder.

Now that he's been sufficiently warned, the girls working the floor feel safe enough to swarm over to him.

Rav and I step back, leaning against the wall that runs to the hallway backstage. Someone propped open the exit door and a crowd of nervous young women are milling around, while Lexi talks to each one, marking down information on her clipboard.

"Amateur night is the *best*." Rav cackles with evil glee. "Girls are like timid deer. And someone always wears something without Velcro and gets stuck in their clothes on stage."

"You're a psycho."

"What? It's cute."

"Bullshit," I snort. "Half the time we don't even get amateurs. It's pros from other clubs trying to scope us out." At least that's how it was ten or twelve years ago.

"Bro, there *are* no other clubs around. We're the last one standing for like a hundred miles."

"Whatever." My strip club days are so far behind me, I couldn't care less.

I sweep my gaze over the customers again. Handsy seems to be taking our threats seriously.

Loud chatter from the hallway draws my eyes that way again. Just more wannabe strippers crowding inside.

There's something familiar about one short, extra-curvy girl with long black hair so dark it has to be dyed. Chunks of hair dyed pink and red match her pink panties and red lace dress.

"Oh," Rav groans. "Now those are some *amazing* pillow thighs."

"Pillow what?" I mutter, studying the girl.

Hell the fuck no. I push through the crowd, frowning at the girl. Praying it's not who I think it is.

I touch her shoulder and she turns. Her mouth drops open in surprise.

"Bianca, what the fuck are you doing here?" Carter's little friend doesn't belong anywhere near this place.

"What are *you* doing here?" she sasses back.

"Working."

"You *work* here?"

"None of your fucking business. Now why are *you* here?" Why do I even care? She's Carter's friend. She's close to his age, so more than legal. Not my responsibility.

She gestures toward the stage. "I want to try out."

"Welcome, Bianca." Ravage slides next to me, oozing sleaze. Of course he remembers her name. "Girls line up in there." He points to the dressing room. "Did you give Lexi all your info? DJ will announce you one by one."

Suddenly Rav's a professional.

Bianca ignores him and fixes her inquisitive eyes on me. As if I'll dash her dreams of stripper-stardom with one word.

I shrug. "You don't need my permission."

She turns but I tap her shoulder, stopping her. "Does Carter know you're here?"

She jerks away from me. "Carter's busy."

That doesn't answer my question. But it's not my problem, so I shrug and let her go.

Ravage rubs his hands together like a pervy little bridge troll. "Line up. Get a number. Take your turn on the pole, darlin'," he encourages.

She flashes a quick smile. "Thanks, Ravage."

"She remembers my name," Rav says.

"You're hard to forget. And not for good reasons."

"You gonna tell Charlotte?" Rav asks, lifting his chin toward the dressing room.

"I'm sure it'll come up at some point."

Rav's predictions about amateur night come true. A girl gets stuck in her see-through dress thirty seconds into her first song and runs off the stage crying.

A fight breaks out in the dressing room between one of our regular dancers and one of the amateurs.

I need to get things up and running at the funeral home so I have a good excuse to *never* come here again. The thought makes me snort with laughter.

"What's so funny?" Rav asks.

"Nothing."

CHAPTER FIFTY-THREE

Charlotte

OUR BEAUTIFUL FARMHOUSE HAS BEEN TURNED INTO A BUSY WEDDING venue. No matter how simple we said we wanted our wedding to be, the decorations and guest list spiraled out of control.

This morning, Trinity, Serena, and Mercy turned our bedroom into my bridal suit. Marcel was sent packing to Carter's loft to get ready.

Serena has me perched on a bench in the nook of our bay window where she said she had perfect natural lighting to work with. I can't help my gaze from straying to all the activity going on outside.

"Look up, Charlotte," Serena reminds me.

She dabs and pats something cool but sticky all around my eyes. There's a soft clickety-clack and she snaps open a plastic box full of tiny colorful rhinestones.

"What are you doing to me?"

"Trust the process, Charlotte," she murmurs, carefully selecting a stone and placing it on the tip of some metal poke-y-looking device.

I close my eyes and let her have her way with my face. I've never seen her makeup looking anything less than flawless so hopefully she can recreate the same magic for me.

"Thank you so much, Serena. I know the timing is, uh, precarious." I nod to her still-dainty baby bump. The woman's due to give birth soon and somehow managed to maintain her cute, earth mother pregnant silhouette, while I already feel like a circus bear.

"Not yet." She presses her hand to her stomach. "He's still got some baking to do. And Gray hasn't finished the nursery."

"Yikes. We haven't even gotten started on a nursery yet." I glance at our bedroom door. Twins mean we're going to need more room.

"I hope my brother appreciates all the effort," Heidi says from the couch where she's nursing the newest member of the family. "All he's doing is showering, maybe running a comb through his hair, and getting dressed."

Mercy bites her lip and closes her eyes. "And he'll look damn fine doing it."

"That he will," I agree.

"There. Perfect." Serena stands back and studies my face.

"Wow," Mercy breathes out, the two of them studying me like I'm a butterfly pinned to velvet. Makes sense. My stomach won't stop fluttering like a thousand butterflies turned loose. "Now that's a glam wedding look," Mercy pronounces.

Serena finally lets me turn and look in the lighted mirror.

"Oh my God." Gone are the circles under my eyes. Serena managed to give me an almost ethereal glow. Above a set of fluffy false lashes glued to my eyelids, a row of tiny clear rhinestones line my lashes, sweeping into a glittering but elegant wing. "It's beautiful. Thank you."

"*You're* beautiful," she says softly. "Congratulations, Charlotte."

"Thank you."

"Let's get started on your hair," Swan says, hefting a big black kit onto the window seat.

Someone knocks on the bedroom door.

"Who is it?" Mercy yells.

"Just me." Shelby quickly opens the door a crack. "Are ya decent?"

"More or less." I wave her inside with a flick of my wrist.

"Your brother's downstairs, fixin' to give ya something," she says.

"Give me something?"

Shelby shrugs. "I didn't ask."

"I'll text him and tell him to come up when I'm done with your hair," Swan promises. She pulls out her phone and quickly taps out a message, then shoves it in her pocket. "What do you think about sweeping some of your hair back, so we can show off your pretty eyes, but leaving the rest long, loose, and curly?"

"Perfect."

When Swan's close to finishing, Heidi steps out with the baby and returns a few minutes later with Carter.

"Hey, girls," Heidi says, grabbing everyone's attention. She jerks her head toward the door.

"I'm still in my bathrobe," I remind Heidi.

"Hope's coming up to help you with your dress," Carter says.

"What's up?" I ask Carter when we're alone.

"You look pretty," he says in a thick voice.

"Don't you dare cry." I move from the window to the bed, patting the space next to me. "How's Marcel?"

"Antsy." He fidgets and runs his fingers over a slick black portfolio in his hands. "Murphy challenged him to an ax-throwing contest."

"He what?"

He shrugs. "Yeah, they're lumberjacking it up in your backyard."

Nothing those two do surprises me anymore. "What's that?" I nod to the portfolio he's clutching.

He finally sits next to me and slowly passes the folder into my hands. "I made this for you."

"Something from my favorite artist on my wedding day?" Excitement pushes my voice up a few octaves. "Gimmie."

"It's a multi-part gift."

Eager but worried I'll wrinkle it, I carefully pull the thick paper from the sleeve. Vibrant colors immediately grab my attention, then the details come into focus. A skull with coins over its eyes wearing a crown of flowers. Rays of sunshine illuminate the background. Majestic. Hopeful.

"Carter," I breathe out. "It's beautiful."

"I can *not* tattoo 'property of Teller' on you, Charlotte. I can't." He sticks out his tongue in an extra-yuck face. "But—if you like this, I'll ink it for you."

"Really?" I squeal. "I love it. It's perfect. It incorporates Marcel's patch, his role in the club, and his name for me all into one brilliantly beautiful piece of art." I sit forward and hug him. "I can't believe you did this for me."

"I felt bad that I gave you a blanket *no* when you asked if I'd do a piece for you." He lifts his hand and roughs it over his already tousled hair. "I know gifts shouldn't come with conditions. But this one does."

"I can't get it inked on my lower back?" I guess.

"Well, that too."

"Okay, what?"

"Teller has to get one too."

"Matching tattoos, huh? I'm not sure if he has any free skin available."

He scrunches his face into a yuck-frown. "He has a spot and I gotta tell you, inspecting your husband's body was really low on my list of life priorities."

I burst into laughter, squeezing my eyes shut so tight, one of my fake lashes sticks to my lower lash line. "Oh, crap." I gently pry it loose. "I don't want to ask Serena to fix that."

"Sorry."

"So, he was okay with you dictating his next tattoo, huh?"

He snort-laughs. "Yeah. He wants your name and anniversary too."

"Wait, so he can get *my* name tattooed on him, but I can't get his?"

He raises his hands in a helpless shrug. "I don't make the rules, Sis."

"So, is Rock throwing axes too?" I ask.

"No, he was supervising." He hesitates. "I think asking him to walk you down the aisle means a lot to him. All things considered."

My smile freezes in place. "All things considered?"

"Heidi and I talked. You know, about Rock and Teller's *relationship*." He shrugs and slowly lifts his gaze to mine. "We have things in common, in…certain areas. So I thought I could help her."

My mind runs at a hundred miles an hour, thinking of all the things he might be referring to.

"Char, look at me," he pleads.

He's quiet while I work out in my head what the hell to say.

"I know, Charlotte. About Dad. You know, *not* being my dad."

"Chuck's such an asshole," I mutter, reaching for his hand and squeezing.

He returns the affectionate gesture. "Chuck didn't tell me. Well, not directly. I overheard him and mom arguing about it a long time ago."

"You did?" *Oh my God.* What an ugly argument that must've been for Carter to hear. "How come you never told me?"

"I already lost Dad." He shoots a grin at me that's more pained than silly. "Mom seemed iffy about me most days. Chuck hated me. I couldn't lose you too."

"Carter," I cry and fling my arms around him, yanking him closer for an awkward hug. "You'd never lose me."

"Ugh, no crying on your wedding day." He hands me a tissue. "Have you always known?" he asks quietly.

"No. Chuck told me...after Mom died."

"When he had his meltdown and you had to stab him?"

He may seem goofy at times, but Carter's ability to piece information together has always been uncanny. "Yes," I answer carefully.

"Is that what you fought about?" His forehead wrinkles. "I thought he'd *love* to let the truth about me see the light of day."

"No, that's not what our argument was about."

He squeezes my hand, neither encouraging nor discouraging me from continuing.

"Does Teller know too?" he asks in a small voice.

My jaw tightens. I don't want Carter to get the wrong impression. "He was there when Chuck told *me*. I needed his help to get Chuck to admit...other things."

He closes his eyes briefly. "Please say Teller beat whatever information you needed out of him?"

"Not quite."

"Bummer." He opens his eyes. "Did it have anything to do with what happened to you in law school?"

I suck in a shocked breath. "What...what are you talking about?"

"Char," he says gently. "You changed. So much. I traced the timeline back to your winter break. I'd been sick with the flu, I didn't remember much. You took care of me. Then *you* ended up sick. Later I realized you didn't catch the flu, it was something else."

Shit, shit, shit.

How much does Carter really need to know?

He sits back slowly, a terrified light entering his eyes. "Did Chuck do something to you?"

No, Mom did.

Can I sully the memory of the mother he loved? It almost broke *me*, and I already had plenty of grievances against my mother. Carter tolerated all her hateful antics and continued taking care of her up until the day she died.

But now I see it differently.

He *knew* the truth for years. All the shit he swallowed from her takes on a new tone. He was silently begging her to love him, despite the violent way he was conceived.

As flawed as Uncle Chuck is, he tried to make things right with me in his fucked-up biker way. I can't allow Carter to think Chuck is the kind of monster who would violate his own niece.

"No, not Chuck." I squeeze my eyes shut. The corset I'm wearing under my bathrobe digs into my flesh, reminding me that my future is waiting and the past should stay in the past. "Please don't make me talk about this on my wedding day."

"Charlotte, look at me," he pleads.

When I finally open my eyes, he's staring at me with a mixture of love and frustration. "You don't have to tell me anything you don't want to. Or you can purge it all out of your system now. So you don't have to worry about another hidden truth sneaking up on you later. Go into your marriage unburdened by the past." He hesitates. "Sorry, that sounds dumb."

"No it doesn't." In a way, he's right. I'll always be worried about slipping up and him finding out some other way. And the worst, ugliest truth buried deep down is that I'm still ashamed of what happened. That my own mother hated me so much, she arranged for her drug dealer to rape me so she could skip away from a debt. Marcel's burned almost every trace of that shame away with his love and affection. But hiding it from Carter...even if I think I'm doing it for his own good, irritates my soul like lingering dirt I can't scrub away.

Is it better for him to know the truth? Or would I be doing it for selfish reasons? A way for me to ruin the last bit of his love for our dead mother?

I just don't know.

Damn, I wish Marcel was here to give me the answer. Encourage me one way or another. But just like I let him figure out when he was ready to tell Heidi the truth about his relationship to Rock, he'd want me to decide how much to tell my brother on my own.

"Why didn't Teller want me to know the truth about who my real father was?" Carter asks.

I blink, startled at the shift in topic. "He thought it would hurt you more than help you." I shrug. "Mom was gone. There was no one around who could give you any good answers."

"I would've liked to talk to Dad about it. How he could stand looking at me day after day." His hands curl into fists.

"He loved you."

"I don't know about that." His pain-filled eyes meet mine. "I felt the distance between us, sometimes. Like he was forcing himself to love me. I'd catch him watching me with," he flicks his fingers around his face, "this hatred burning in his eyes. I never understood what I did wrong."

Jesus, I never realized that. My breath catches and I wrap my arms around him, yanking him into a fierce hug. "You didn't do *anything* wrong."

"And Mom, sometimes she loved me. I was her 'baby boy' that she'd shower all this attention on. Then, other times she hated me with a fury I didn't understand."

Why didn't I protect him better? "I shouldn't have left you with her."

"You always loved me, no matter what." He hugs me tight. "Even after you found out?"

"Yes. It didn't make me feel any differently toward you."

He pulls away, holding me at arm's length. "You still let me live here. Brought me into your biker family cult."

We both indulge in the kind of dark laughter only the most fucked-up situations can inspire.

"Does Rock know?" he asks.

"I don't think so. Chuck told us when we were alone with him." My mind returns to the basement of the Wolf Knights' clubhouse. The dank scent. The stone walls. The truth about my past shattering around me. "I can't think of a reason Marcel would've told Rock."

"No?" He tilts his head. "Not even when they found out about *their* relationship?"

"Maybe." I admit it's possible. "I'm not privy to their every conversation. But if he did, he never told me. Would it bother you if Rock knew?"

He cocks his head. "No," he says as if he's reaching that conclusion as he speaks. "Like you said, it's not my fault. And I don't think he'd treat me any differently even if he knew."

"True."

"Rock always says blood doesn't matter. It's character and loyalty that earns your place in *this* family."

"He means it." I think over the conversation I had with the girls not that long ago. "Almost everyone—the brothers and ol' ladies—have little or no blood family in their lives for one reason or another. But we don't need them, because we have the club. *That's* our family."

"Thank you for letting me be part of your life."

I hug him again. "Always."

"You deserve a loving family, Charlotte." His voice cracks. "I like how close you are to the girls. Hope and Lilly, especially. You've always been such a good sister to me. You need a good big sister too."

I don't know if I really *was* that good of a sister to him. There sure seem to be a lot of things I missed.

"I remember how hard Mom was on you," he continues, touching one of the long curls spilling over my shoulder. "It drove her nuts that you were so pretty. She'd say the meanest things right to your face. Even when I was a kid, I thought she sounded jealous. But it felt weird. What kind of mother is jealous of her own daughter?"

I swallow hard, embarrassed he remembers those cruel details. "A vain, immature one."

He nods once. "That fits." He presses his lips together like he's debating his next words. "Chuck's gross the way he talks about women but I remember him trying to stick up for you sometimes when Mom got out of control."

Even I have to admit that's true. "I don't think it was easy for him to contradict her, though."

"She and Chuck had a thing before Dad," he says matter-of-factly.

"You knew?"

"Heard them argue about it. Talk about immature." He rolls his eyes in a dramatic fashion. "The two of them never evolved past senior year."

I snort.

"But when you changed, they did too," he continues. "Her addictions got worse. Their relationship more volatile." He stares at his pants and brushes at a loose thread. "I wondered if Chuck made a pass at you or something gross."

I sigh. "Our family's that fucked up, huh?"

He shrugs.

"This is hard for me to talk about. But you're right. I'd rather tell you everything now, so I can start my new life as Marcel's wife." I press my hand to my stomach. "And as a mother who will always do better for her children."

"I know you will, Charlotte. You were always so good, so patient with me. And I know I was demanding and annoying sometimes."

"No you weren't." I smooth my hands over my dress. If we're doing this, I better get it out now before I lose my nerve. "You remember I originally wanted to be a criminal lawyer?"

"Kind of."

"Well, I did. I thought I'd prove myself useful to the club, you know?"

"God, why?"

I shrug. "We all seek approval from our parents in different ways, I guess."

"Yikes." He presses his fist into his gut. "That's deep."

I tilt my head, but realize he's serious, not teasing me.

"Second year of law school, I went to the Christmas party at the clubhouse. You were sick." I squeeze my eyes shut. "I wish to God I'd stayed home to take care of you."

"You don't have to tell me if you don't want to, Charlotte." Anxiety creeps into his voice.

"Something bad happened to me that night," I confirm, uncomfortable sharing more details than that with my little brother. "It wasn't Chuck," I hurry to add. "It was a guy Mom owed money to." I leave it at that.

But Carter's too smart not to put the pieces together.

"No," he whispers. "She…" his voice trails off and he stares out the window.

"Well, she was kind enough to drug me first, so I wouldn't remember any pesky details." Anger sharp as acid burns my throat. "Then gaslight me afterward."

"Why didn't you tell me?"

"I couldn't tell you something so ugly." I blow out a breath wanting to just get this over with. "It happened at Chuck's clubhouse, so after all the family first loyalty bullshit we'd heard all our lives, I thought he'd take care of it. But he didn't. At least at the time, I didn't think he did. He was…awful to me. But he put two and two together and realized Mom had set me up."

"Jesus," he breathes out, but he doesn't question me or argue with what I'm sharing.

"He flipped when Marcel and I started seeing each other," I explain. "Not because of club stuff, but because he was afraid if I told Marcel what happened to me, he'd dig deeper. Chuck couldn't have that because all those years, he was covering up what *Mom* had done."

He sits back and stares at me. "I can't decide if that's better or worse than him trying to fight over you like a territorial dog with a patch of grass."

"Better, I suppose. He always had some sort of twisted love or loyalty to Mom, I guess. But he said once he knew what she did to me, it soured how he saw her."

He nods slowly and seems to ponder all of that. "I always wondered why they turned so vicious toward each other."

I lift one shoulder, not really caring to examine their toxic relationship much closer.

"No wonder Chuck went nomad these last few years. Teller's all the things Chuck claims to be. Must make him feel two feet tall to be around him."

I never quite thought about it in those terms. "You're probably right."

"Men who *think* they're alpha get super intimidated and defensive when they're in the presence of real alpha men," he explains like a professor of male psychology.

"I think Chuck *wants* to do better by us but he doesn't know how." I shrug.

"The few times I've seen him since the rescue, he hasn't called me any names." He lifts his eyebrows in a teasing way. "So I guess old dogs can learn new tricks, after all."

"I'm glad, but be careful. I'll never trust him completely."

"Same." He flicks his gaze toward the door. "Teller doesn't trust him either. At first, I thought it was that biker-territorial-claimed-my-woman thing. Now, I understand it's much deeper than that."

My nose stings. "Yes."

He takes both my hands in his. "I'm so, so sorry that happened to you, Charlotte."

"Thanks."

"And just so you know, you didn't ruin my memory of Mom, or anything." He pauses and seems to search for the right words. "I'd rather know the truth about the kind of person she was, than have you suffer in silence, trying to protect me from the truth."

That's it. I'm done. I burst into tears.

"Damn." He swipes a tissue and dabs at my cheeks. "Don't make me get Serena to come back in here and fix all your makeup stuff. I don't want to piss off a woman about to go into labor any day."

"I'll be fine. Come here." I gather him in my arms and hug him tight.

After a few beats, he gently pushes me away. "You need to go marry that ultra-alpha man of yours with a big smile on your face."

"Ultra-alpha, huh?" I sniffle and laugh at the same time. "Alpha isn't enough?"

"Not for him." He purses his lips. Thoughtful. "He loves you so much. He really would do anything for you."

"He would."

"And you'd do anything for him." He side-eyes me. "The two of you together are *terrifying*."

"Aw, what a romantic thing to say on my wedding day." I lean into him, bumping him with my shoulder.

Someone knocks on the door, then pushes it open. Hope peers inside. "It's dress time, Charlotte."

Trinity follows Hope inside and snaps a few pictures. A sweet one of Carter handing me his drawing, a few light-hearted shots, and a few traditional bride pictures.

Lilly joins us, and Carter leans in to give me a hug. "You have sisters now who will be a hell of a lot more supportive on your wedding day than our mother ever would've been," he whispers.

I hug him back as his words repeat in my head. My mother would've found some way to ruin my wedding or make it all about her. "You're right."

The truth may hurt but that doesn't make it any less true.

TELLER

"Charlotte's on board with the ink." Carter grins as he joins Blake and me in the backyard. "She was *not* thrilled about the ax-throwing."

"Why'd you tell her, then?" Blake asks.

"I told you she'd love the drawing," I say. "You were up there an awfully long time. Is she feeling okay?"

This whole can't see the bride before the wedding rule is bullshit.

Carter slides his gaze to Blake, then back to me. "We had a brother-sister heart-to-heart."

I throw a teasing glance Blake's way. "Why isn't *my* sister having one of those with me?"

Blake chuckles and sets his ax on a wide tree stump. He glances at Carter, then me. "She's a little busy."

"Everything okay?" I ask Carter when we're alone.

"Yeah. She can tell you what we talked about, later." His face perks up. "She looks really pretty."

"Of course she does." My gaze strays to the back of the house, to our bedroom window. From this angle and distance, I can't see more than a few shapes moving around. One of them has to be my soon-to-be-wife.

"Hey." Carter taps my arm, drawing my attention away from the window. "Thanks for…well, everything you do for her."

I cock my head, and almost ask what the hell they talked about, but he looks so serious, I decide not to tease him. "Hey, before everyone starts arriving, come into the house with me. I have something for you."

He eyes me with his usual skeptical head tilt but follows. "Should I be concerned?"

I catch sight of Wrath and point to the house. The girls chased me out of the upstairs so Charlotte could get ready. They graciously allowed me the use of my living room, for now. I enter through the kitchen and find Rock and Grace in the kitchen. "Is Hope upstairs with Charlotte?" I ask.

"Yup. Gettin' close."

Grace throws me a floppy hand wave and I scoop her into my arms. "You being good?"

"Yef," she says, carefully sounding out the word.

I pop a kiss on her forehead and set her down.

The door opens behind me. "We doing this?" Wrath asks. "Running out of time."

"Doing what?" Carter asks, backing away from us.

"Nothing bad," I assure him. "Stay here."

I nod at Rock as I walk past him into the hall closet where I open the safe and pull out the package for Carter.

"I wanted you to have something to wear to the wedding," I say as I return to the kitchen.

His gaze drops to my hands. "Brown paper bag wrapping? I don't even get a bow or something on it?"

I blow out an annoyed breath.

Wrath rumbles with laughter. "Never stop irritating him, Scribbles."

Rock circles his fingers in the air in a hurry-it-up motion. "Let's get to it, knucklehead."

I hand Carter the package and he takes it to the table, sitting across from Rock.

Curious, Grace toddles over, pressing her little hand against Carter's leg and standing on tippy-toes.

"Come here, Grace." He lifts her and sets her in his lap. "Let's see what your big brother has in here."

She helps him tear the paper off, joyfully throwing each scrap on the floor.

Carter pulls out the black leather and holds it up, staring at the back patch.

Protected by Lost Kings MC

"Uh, are you claiming me, Teller? I mean, I like you and I'm happy you're marrying my sister and all, but…"

"No, wiseass."

"Wait a second." Carter glances down at Grace and the little black vest she's wearing over her purple sparkling dress. "This is like the ones Wrath got for the kids."

"Those are 'product of.' You're 'protected by,'" I say.

"Just for club events," Rock explains.

"No one should fuck with you. But we still want to make it clear, if someone does, then they fuck with all of us," I add.

"Wow. Really?"

"Look at the front," Wrath prompts.

"Scribbles!" Carter grins. "Thank you." He looks at each one of us. "I'll do you proud, I promise."

"I know you will."

"Yay!" Grace yells, throwing her little arms in the air.

"Keep that energy, wee one," Wrath says, picking her up. "You've got a long day of festivities ahead."

She slaps his cheeks and plants a kiss on his nose.

Blake opens the kitchen door and walks in, holding Alexa's hand. Alexa immediately runs over to Wrath and jumps up, either to get his attention or to see Grace. He leans over and picks her up too.

Blake's gaze lands on Carter. "Looks good."

"You were in on it too, Murphy?" Carter asks.

"Yeah." He slaps Carter's shoulders. "We've got your back."

"Thanks."

Heidi wanders into the kitchen from the direction of the living room, carrying baby Bit-bit.

"Have you been here the whole time?" I ask.

"I wanted her to nap now," she whispers. "But maybe I should've waited. I don't want her to cry during the ceremony."

"It'll be fine," I assure her.

Grinder and Dex join us next. Z follows with his son, who hangs back until Wrath sets the girls down.

Rav pokes his head in the door. "Is this the nursery?"

"Yeah, jackass," Rock says.

"Come in, it's not contagious." I wave him closer. "I swear."

"Don't worry, you're not in danger of impregnating anyone with that attitude," Dex adds, cracking everyone but Rav up.

"Awful lot of kidlets here now," Rav says.

"Yes." Rock gives him a pointed look. "There are."

Rav leans down and ruffles Chance's head. "At least you won't be outnumbered for long, little man."

Grinder crosses his arms over his chest and leans back on the counter. "Your math off? Serena and I are only having *one*." He nods to Alexa and Grace, then points to Heidi holding Bit-bit.

Rav actually does the math on his fingers, then looks at me. "Wait, what are you having? Do you know?"

"A boy and a girl."

"Lord." Ravage raises his eyes to the ceiling.

"You want a calculator, bro?" Dex asks.

Rav wags his finger in Wrath's face. "You and Trin better be sticking to your no-baby pact."

Wrath slaps Rav's hand away. "Or what?"

Z glances at the door. "Where's Sparky when we need him to explain the balancing of harmonies to us?"

"He and Stash volunteered to meet people at the end of the driveway and escort them in," I say.

"Seriously?" Wrath raises one blond eyebrow. "You realize Sparky will hand out pot brownies to all your guests, right?"

I glance at Rock and shrug. "Wouldn't be a wedding without 'em, I guess."

CHAPTER FIFTY-FOUR

Charlotte

"THIS IS IT." HOPE SQUEEZES MY HANDS. "HOW DO YOU FEEL?"

"Nauseous. Excited."

"Perfect."

Someone knocks on the door.

Mercy hurries to answer it.

"I'm here for the bride." Rock's rumbling voice somehow calms my nerves.

"That means I need to get downstairs," Mercy says. She kisses my cheek. "I'll see you in a few."

"Thanks."

"I need to get Grace down there, too," Hope says.

"I've got her," Shelby offers, holding her hand out for Grace.

Grace eagerly runs to Shelby, smiling wide.

"Aw," I sigh.

"Thanks, Shelby."

"No problem."

Rock curls his arm around Hope's waist, kissing her cheek and murmuring a few words in her ear. Then he sweeps his gaze over Lilly, Serena, and me.

"Lilly, Z's in the kitchen waiting for you."

"Let's get this party started, Charlotte." Lilly claps her hands.

"Serena, Gray's waiting for you at the bottom of the stairs."

She struggles to push herself off the bed and Rock hurries to help her up.

"I got you." Lilly grips Serena's arm and guides her out.

Rock focuses on me. "How do you feel?"

"Eager to see Marcel. How's he doing?"

His mouth curls up at the corners. "Same as you." He takes both of my hands in his. "You've both overcome a lot of obstacles in life. And I'm so happy you found each other to face the rest of what life throws at us, together."

"Thank you," I whisper.

"There's no one else who's more perfect for…my son. And I'm proud to have you as my daughter, Charlotte. You can always come to me for anything you need. No matter what."

Rock's words touch me deeply. I'd never felt the same level of love or acceptance from my own parents. Hot wetness stings my eyes and I open them wide, hoping to dry any tears before they fall. "I know you had doubts about me in the beginning, so that means a lot to me."

"I don't have any doubts about you now." He hugs me tight, then offers me his arm. "Ready?"

"Yes."

Hope gives me a quick hug and I have a twinge of guilt for not asking her to be a bridesmaid after all.

"Trinity wants to get some pictures," she says.

Rock is surprisingly patient with the mini-photo shoot.

Hope hurries out of the room and Trinity follows her, running ahead to grab photos of us coming down the stairs.

Outside, I'm grateful for the cool air that coasts over my skin. Big, fluffy white clouds float against a perfectly blue sky. The long sweeping branches and lush leaves of the huge weeping willow tree at the back of the property have been shaped into a canopy. Clusters of sunflowers and red roses designate the arch where we'll exchange our vows. Once the sun goes down, the entire back yard will be lit with thousands of tiny yellow lights, strung through the trees and swaths of gauzy white fabric Marcel had painstakingly woven through the trees over the last couple of days.

It's beautiful.

Neat rows of simple white folding chairs had been set up for our guests. But everyone stands and faces us as we approach. My gaze pings through the crowd, landing on members from our downstate New York, Everhart Virginia, and Deadbranch Tennessee charters. My steps falter as I recognize the National president and his wife. No good comes from Priest visiting New York. Rock squeezes my arm and keeps us moving. More familiar faces. Members of the Devil Demons MC from Western New York. The president's wife, Mallory, flashes a big smile as we pass her. The members who will form a support club for the Lost Kings take up one row to themselves. Remy nods at me as we pass. His little sister, Molly, wiggles her fingers at me and I can't help smiling back. Hope and her friend Mara are seated up front. Lilly and Z sit next to an empty chair on Hope's left. Shelby and Rooster sit in the space directly behind them. Shelby ended up with Grace sitting on her lap, while Lilly's cradling baby Bit-bit in her arms. Wrath warned me earlier that the tiny chairs "wouldn't hold his big ass" so he's standing at the end of the first row, looking very much like a bouncer at an exclusive nightclub with his arms folded over his chest and his serious gaze sweeping over our guests. He catches my eye and nods, one corner of his mouth turning up. Grinder's standing in a similar position opposite from Wrath. Is his excuse related to comfort? Or were the two enforcers concerned about having a mix of bikers and civilians in one place?

My uncle gives me a tight nod and smile. He hadn't expressed an opinion on Rock's role in the wedding, but his thoughts are written in his scowl. My earlier conversation with Carter left me feeling a bit raw and forgiving toward Uncle Chuck. I reach out as we pass him and squeeze his hand.

"I'm happy you made it," I whisper.

His scowl softens. "You look beautiful, Char."

Mercy and Heidi beam at us as we approach.

Blake holds out his fist and whispers "ginger power" to me. A giggle escapes my lips as I tap my knuckles against his. My gaze lands on Carter, proudly standing next to Marcel wearing his cut.

If someone had told me five years ago that Judge Damon Oak would officiate my wedding, I would've thought they were nuts. He smiles when Rock and I stop in front of him. Rock kisses my cheek and stops to hug Marcel, before taking his seat next to Hope.

Finally, my nervous eyes land on Marcel and my breath catches. He steps forward and reaches for my hands.

"You're beautiful." His gaze roams over my face, then dips down to my dress. His mouth quirks as he leans in. "Can't even tell," he whispers.

The skirt of my long white dress falls over my growing baby bump, providing adequate camouflage. It still feels two sizes too small. "Thank you. Makes the corset I'm stuffed into worth all the struggle." I side-eye him. "Also, you're full of shit. Shelby could barely get the back of this dress laced up."

Amusement sparks in his teal eyes.

"You…" I sweep my gaze over his sharply tailored suit that fits every inch of him to perfection. "Take my breath away."

He curls his fingers around mine and turns us to face Damon.

Damon's lips quirk, as if he'd heard our brief exchange, and my skin flushes. Thank goodness for all the makeup Serena spackled on me. Hopefully, it's hiding that my cheeks now match the roses.

"Welcome, everyone," Damon begins. "I'm honored to be here to celebrate the union of Charlotte and Marcel."

There's a rustling behind us as those who had been standing take their seats.

"Love isn't always perfect," Damon continues without the aid of any notes. "Love is difficult to find and impossible to live without. There are no fairy tales in life, only harsh reality. Love doesn't always come easy. When you find love, treasure it, protect it with your entire being. You no longer have to face life's hardships alone. Hold on to each other and don't let go. Above all, remember every moment is worth it because you survived together."

It's almost as if someone gave Damon a CliffsNotes version of our lives.

TELLER

Charlotte's glowing. More beautiful than I have a right to spend my life with. The love I have for her and our children that she's carrying already burns in my chest hotter than the sun.

Damon's words sound nice. Charlotte seems pleased. I'm too focused on her for anything else to penetrate.

Damon clears his throat and I tear my gaze away from Charlotte. Are we done? Can I kiss my bride now?

"Do you, Marcel John North, take Charlotte Corinne Clark as your wife? Do you promise to love, comfort, honor, and protect her, in sickness and health, be faithful to her as long as you both shall live?"

"I do."

"Charlotte, do you take Marcel as your husband?" Damon turns her way. "Do you promise to love, comfort, honor, and protect him, in sickness and health, to be faithful as long as you both shall live?"

"I do."

"Do you have rings to exchange?"

"We do." Charlotte turns, searching for Chance.

Z walks his son to us.

"I do!" Chance holds out two small boxes to us. "I do!"

I pluck one out of his hand. "Thanks, buddy." I give him a little high five and he grins.

"Thank you," Charlotte says, smiling down at Chance and nodding to Z.

Baby Bit-bit lets out a scream loud enough to rip open the Earth.

Heidi's desperate eyes zip from me to Lilly, who's trying to comfort Bit-bit.

Our guests murmur "Aww," as Heidi scurries over to collect her daughter from Lilly. She freezes as if she's scared to return. But Charlotte motions her over to us. Heidi stops next to Charlotte and Charlotte leans in, whispering in Heidi's ear. She coos at Bit-bit, who's quiet now that she's in her mother's arms. Heidi's cheeks flush an impossible shade of red.

"It's okay," I whisper to her but I'm not sure if she hears me.

Alexa runs up to stand next to Heidi and the crowd titters with laughter.

Blake holds out his hand, encouraging Alexa to come stand next to him.

Charlotte beams at me, not one bit flustered by the brief interruption.

Damon waits with a patient smile. When we're focused on the ceremony again, he continues. "You may now exchange your rings as a symbol of your endless commitment to and love for one another."

I slip the thin, gold diamond band out of the box and take Charlotte's hand. She bites her lip, studying the ring as if she's worried it won't fit. We'd picked them out long before she found out she was pregnant.

"With this ring, I pledge my love and loyalty to you for the rest of my life," I say as I slip it on her finger.

She releases a relieved breath, then takes my hand.

My heart beats impossibly faster as she repeats the same words and slides the ring on my finger.

"By the power vested in me by the State of New York, I pronounce you husband and wife." Damon holds up his hands. "You may kiss the bride."

Charlotte throws her arms around my neck and I lift her, crushing my mouth against hers.

"I love you," she whispers against my lips. "I love you."

"I love you too, Sunshine. Want to spend the rest of my life making you smile."

I set her down and we turn toward our family and friends, lifting our linked hands in the air.

"Let's celebrate!" Blake shouts.

People cheer or run up to hug and congratulate us. Through all of the chaos, Charlotte and I hold tight to each other.

CHAPTER FIFTY-FIVE

Charlotte

As the sun sets, lights twinkle to life overhead and all around us, transforming our backyard into a magical wonderland. I tip my head back, staring up at Marcel. "Can we keep the lights up?"

"We can do anything you want, wife."

"Thank you, husband."

He presses his forehead to mine, staring into my eyes with affection. "Is this how you wanted our day to be?"

"Yes."

Heidi approaches us, wringing her hands. "I'm so sorry—"

"Stop it." I pull her toward us and hug her to my side. "I loved having both our nieces up there with us. It's okay."

Her shoulders drop and she lets out a breath. "Thanks. I know I kept saying how much I wanted another one, but I'm exhausted."

"You always have us when you need a break."

Her lips quirk. "You're going to have your own hands full soon."

Wrath sneaks up behind Marcel and curls his arm around Marcel's neck, yanking him closer. "Mom and Dad are looking for you."

Marcel scowls. Even though things are out in the open, he's still sensitive about rubbing Heidi's nose in it. Something Heidi seems to realize.

She rolls her eyes and shoves her brother. "What'd I tell you about those overprotective vibes?"

"What'd I tell *you*?" he fires back with a smile.

While they bicker, I lift my chin to Wrath. "Were you really uncomfortable with the chairs? Or were you and Grinder worried about a biker shoot-out?" I'm kidding. Sort of.

He frowns.

"You and Grinder were both standing like bouncers worried about a brawl," I explain, crossing my arms over my chest and flipping on my version of Wrath's mean bouncer face.

"Oh." He nods once. "Nothing that dramatic. G was worried about Serena going into labor and wanted to be able to whisk her away if needed."

"Shoot. Is she okay?" My gaze scans the area and finds them at one of the tables, next to Z and Lilly.

"She's fine. He's just overprotective." He taps his knuckles against the side of Marcel's head. "You're familiar with the type."

I burst into laughter. "Yes, I am."

Shelby slowly approaches us, holding Grace's hand to help her navigate over the grass.

"Got yourself a little shadow, huh?" Marcel nods to his little sister.

"Sure do." Shelby smiles down at Grace, then shifts her gaze to Bit-bit, sound asleep in Murphy's arms. "Although, I think Brittany's got a singing career in her future. She might be going out on tour with me one day."

Heidi ducks her head. "Maybe."

Grace drops Shelby's hand, turns to Wrath, and holds up her arms.

"You need a lift, Gracie?" he asks, scooping her up.

"I see how it is," Shelby teases.

Rooster joins us, curling his arm around Shelby's waist. "You tell Heidi you're going to nab Brittany for your record label one day?"

"Sure did." Shelby smiles up at him.

Heidi finally seems to relax.

When we have a moment alone, Marcel leans down and brushes his cheek against mine. "Thanks for not making Heidi feel bad about the interruption."

"It didn't bother me. I'd rather have her here, than Heidi worried about having someone watch the baby or miss the ceremony."

He squeezes me tight. "I can't wait to wake up next to you every day for the rest of our lives."

"The world could burn around us, and I wouldn't even notice as long as I'm in your arms."

Teller

Club and family obligations mean I can't duck out of our wedding and have my way with my wife—*fuck it feels good to finally call her that*—the way I want.

I still enjoy spending time with our guests. I'm able to introduce Charlotte to Margot and her father. Steer returned from Tennessee for the wedding and regales us with stories about how fucked up things are at our Deadbranch charter. Ice and his crew rode up from Virginia to spend the week. Chaser and Mallory, and a few other members of the Devil Demons, also made the trip. Priest congratulates us. I'm dreading a sit-down with him at some point, even though Rock told me not to worry about it today. Liam and Bree from my old neighborhood also came.

People we've known throughout different phases of our lives fill the loose, airy tents the guys helped me put together this week.

"Are you enjoying the day?" Hope stops and curls her hand around mine, then Charlotte's. "Do you need anything?"

"No, Mom, we're good." I grin at her as she shakes her head.

"I'll allow it since it's your wedding day." She sighs.

Rock joins us, holding Grace in his arms.

"What do you think, little sister?" I tease my finger over one of the puffy sleeves of her dress. "Are you having fun?"

"Yeth." She grins at me.

"Hard to believe she'll be an aunt in a few months," Hope says, a smile flickering over her lips.

I catch Rock's eye. "Nah, seems about right."

Charlotte and I continue circulating through our guests, but as the night goes on, we're drawn to hanging out with my New York brothers.

"You look spiffy." I run my gaze over Dex's tailored pants and button-up shirt under his cut. "I'm honored you dressed up for us."

"I'm not a total heathen."

Grinder walks over and holds out his hand, giving mine a quick shake. "Never thought I'd see this day, Teller. Congratulations." He leans in to give Charlotte a quick kiss on the cheek and they step away to talk for a bit.

Murphy joins us, holding a now sleepy baby Brittany. Dex reaches out and traces his fingertip over my niece's cheek with a fond smile curving his lips. "Tire yourself out, little one?"

"It was like she was waiting for the right moment to let loose," I say.

"True story," Murphy says. He turns to me. "You mind if I take her inside?"

"Of course not," Charlotte says, returning to my side. "Things are still all set up in Alexa's room if you want to chill there."

"Thanks, ginger twinny." He leans in and kisses Charlotte's cheek before leaving.

"You don't have to be the hostess on your wedding day," I whisper to Charlotte.

She flicks her eyes skyward. "Don't meddle in the affairs of gingers, husband dear."

Dex cough-laughs and pounds on his chest. "You're something else, Charlotte."

"Thank you."

An arm curls over my shoulders, tugging me backward. *Wrath.* He pulls Charlotte closer in a much gentler manner. "That's what I love about Charlotte. Knowing she's calling Teller out on his shit twenty-four seven gives me endless joy."

"*Endless joy,*" Grinder mutters, shaking his head. "You sound like a hippie."

Charlotte sputters with laughter. "That's not true. You didn't like me at first."

The amusement slides off Wrath's face and he releases us. "I didn't *know* you. Now I do. You've proven yourself. *And* you sass Teller relentlessly. What's not to love?"

"Thanks, big guy." Charlotte pats his arm. "The feeling's mutual."

He gives Charlotte another affectionate squeeze, then walks off to talk to Chaser and Mallory over at their table.

"He made your life miserable at first, didn't he?" Grinder asks Charlotte.

"I wouldn't say *miserable*," Charlotte answers as if she's trying to come up with a nicer word.

"He definitely tortured Hope more," Dex says.

"Hope?" Grinder's eyebrows shoot up.

"Charlotte grew up around an MC." I nod to Merlin who's standing on our patio talking to a few of the guys from Downstate. "Hope didn't."

"Merlin," Grinder grumbles, sliding a stink eye in his direction.

Charlotte half-shrugs. "We can't help the families we're born into." She tilts her head back to shine her smile on me. "It's the family you *choose* to love and make a life with, that matters."

"Without a doubt," I agree.

We seem to have lost Dex's attention. I turn and follow his line of sight straight to Serena, her friend Emily, and Emily's younger sister Libby.

"Why don't you go talk to Emily instead of eye-fucking her from all the way over here?" I ask.

Dex scowls at me.

"Marcel," Charlotte scolds.

"Still got that famous tact, I see," Grinder says.

"What?" I shrug. "It's my wedding day. Charlotte said I don't have to be polite."

Charlotte steps away from me, shaking her head. "I said *no* such thing."

I pull her back against my side. "No? I swore I heard that somewhere."

Dex chuckles. "That's for the *bride*. Not you."

"Hey," Charlotte protests.

"Forget Teller," Grinder says, slapping Dex's chest. "What do *you* want to do?"

"I want to not be having this conversation right now," Dex answers in a flatter tone than usual.

"She'd want you to move on, don't you think?"

For fuck's sake, I can't believe Grinder's bringing up Dex's dead wife at my wedding. I can't let Grinder keep on emotionally torturing Dex. I place a hand in front of Grinder in a "back off" gesture. "Ease up, old man. Let's let everyone enjoy the evening."

Grinder looks at me, then Dex. "You're right. I just want to pass on whatever wisdom I've picked up. No matter how small."

"Thank you, Father Time," Dex sneers.

In a gentler tone—well, gentle for Grinder—he adds, "Since I've been out, all I've seen you do is work and help your brothers, Dex. It's admirable. But you need more. Don't let guilt rust you up so tight, you never move forward. Take chances. Move forward. *Rust or ride.*"

Dex and I both groan. In the early days of the club, Grinder and Lucky had used that phrase often. Then Lucky died, and prison stole fifteen years of Grinder's life.

"I was wondering when you'd bust that one out," Dex says.

"Laugh all you want," Grinder says. "Those are the only two options for a biker. Rust or ride. Which one you wanna do?"

"Neither right now," Dex says with a smirk. "But I *am* going to *run* away from this conversation."

He claps my shoulder. "I'll catch up with *you* later."

"You got it, brother." I grab onto his arm. "Sorry I started that," I say in a lower voice.

He tilts his head, accepting the apology. "It's all good, brother."

Then Dex does exactly what he said, and hurries away from us.

"Happy now?" I ask Grinder.

"What did you do?" Serena's soft voice as she cautiously approaches us wipes the agitated scowl off Grinder's face.

"Nothing, buttercup." He slides one arm around her waist and rests his free hand on her stomach.

"Your ol' man was just handing out some wise—if not ill-timed—life advice," Charlotte says.

Grinder's not offended. If anything, the half-smirk on his face says he's amused. "Firecracker, I told you." He points at me. "Glad you finally got your act together."

Charlotte chuckles. "Everything fell into place."

Grinder smiles wider. "She's gonna hold your feet to the fire for the rest of your life."

I hug Charlotte to me tighter. "I'm looking forward to it."

Grinder turns, searching the backyard until his gaze lands on Dex. "That's all I want for him." He presses a kiss to Serena's cheek and she leans into his side.

"I'm sure Dex knows it's coming from a good place," Charlotte says.

"If not an annoying one," I add.

Serena winces and moves her hand over her stomach. Grinder forgets all about rusting, riding, or anything but Serena. "What's wrong? Are you okay?"

"I'm fine." She squeezes her eyes shut, then opens them. "All good."

"Let's sit down." Grinder whisks her away without another word to us.

As the sun slips away, the hundreds of tiny white lights I strung up around the yard flicker to life. Music flows from speakers set up around the patio. I curl my arms around Charlotte and draw her close, gently swaying—not quite dancing—to the rhythm.

"This is nice," she sighs.

"I don't ever want to be without you," I whisper, leaning down to kiss her lips.

Charlotte melts against me. "Then you won't," she promises.

For most of my life, I was convinced happily ever after was a myth only found in the books I read to my little sister.

Now, I know I want to spend the rest of my life making this woman happy.

Ever after isn't enough. I want her for eternity.

EPILOGUE

Grace

YEARS LATER...

"*DAAAD.*" I hate the whiny note in my voice. "It's not fair. Alexa and I don't need Chance to babysit us all summer."

Chance—the smug jerk—kicks back in one of our dining room chairs, laces his hands behind his head, and shoots me a shit-eating grin, complete with his adorable dimples that absolutely do *not* work on me.

"Grace," Dad rumbles in a similar tone he uses to lay down the law to the club, "Chance has his own job lined up working for Dawson. It has nothing to do with you."

Chance sticks his tongue out at me.

"Mom!" I protest, turning her way. Surely, she's not going to allow this patriarchal bullshit.

"It'll be nice for the three of you to be together. You can all look out for each other." She pins me with her serious mom stare. "Honestly, it's the only reason I'm allowing you to go. I still think you're too young to be out on the road all summer."

No. *Oh no.* Nope. Alexa and I fought too hard for Mom to yank her permission away now. "Aunt Shelby will be watching out for us," I sputter.

453

"Aunt Shelby is busy performing," she argues. Having a lawyer for a mom is the *worst*.

"Yeah, but Alexa and I will be her assistants so we'll be by her side twenty-four seven." *Ha ha,* having a lawyer for a sister-in-law is the *best*. I've learned the *art of persuasion* from Charlotte.

I shoot a look at Alexa. *Jump in and help any time now.* But she remains silent and continues watching with an amused expression.

"Bet Uncle Rooster's gonna love *that*," Chance mutters, reminding me of his annoying presence. "You two constantly pestering him."

"Aunt Heidi, are you really allowing this? It's insulting."

She flicks her gaze to my dad then to Chance's dad. "Uncle Z, are you sure you don't need your son at home this summer?" Aunt Heidi asks.

I knew she'd be on our side.

"Sorry, Heidi-girl." Z walks behind Chance's chair and squeezes his shoulders. "Gotta let the bird outta the nest sometime. Besides, he wants to gain experience doing whatever the hell it is he's doing for Dawson."

"Sorry, I tried." Aunt Heidi gives me a helpless shrug. Too bad she can barely hide her laughter.

So much for being on our side.

Alexa rolls her eyes at me. "Saw that coming. My mom's in on this too. I overheard her talking to Dad about it." She slides a stink eye at her mom. "Otherwise he wasn't going to let me go."

"There's still time to change our minds," Aunt Heidi says.

"Great," I grumble. "Glad everyone finds this so amusing."

Heidi nudges her oldest daughter. "Go home and finish packing, smart-ass."

"Toodles!" Alexa waves at us over her shoulder as she hurries out the front door.

Aunt Trinity's been sipping coffee in our kitchen, where she could quietly watch the drama but not be part of it. Now, she sets her mug down with a hard thump. "I *am* outraged on your behalf, Grace," she says. "Absolutely outraged."

She's also not trying hard to hide her giggles.

"No you're not," I grouch, crossing my arms over my chest.

"Aw, come here." She pulls me in for a hug. "You're going to have a great time."

I hug her tight and rest my head on her shoulder. "We're not babies."

"I know," she says in a soothing voice. "You're a big girl. About to go out into the big bad world."

Sheesh, no respect from anyone.

"All right." I push her away.

"Rock, you sure this is a good idea?" Trinity asks.

"I'm having second thoughts every minute, Trinny," he answers.

"You guys are the worst," I mutter.

Someone knocks on our front door and pushes it open without waiting for an answer. My big brother strides into the living room and I rush toward him. "Marcel, please be the voice of reason."

He takes one look at all the assembled members of our family. "What's wrong?"

"Grace thinks I give a crap about whatever dumb stuff she and Alexa want to do while we're on tour," Chance answers.

"Watch your mouth. *Your* permission can be revoked at any time too," Z warns his son.

Chance shoots a crap-laced grin at his dad. "No, it can't."

"See! I knew it!" I explode, throwing my arms in the air.

"Where are Charlotte and the kids?" my dad asks Marcel.

"Charlotte and Ivy are still at the house. Ivan stopped at the clubhouse to talk to Lincoln."

"When'd Grinder get up here?" Dad stands.

"How should I know?" Marcel shrugs.

Dad mutters something at my brother that isn't kid appropriate.

"Come here, kid." Marcel wraps his arm around my shoulders and pulls me outside onto the deck.

"Marcel, it's not fair." I hurry to explain my side of the story. "Alexa and I are the ones who came up with the plan to work for Aunt Shelby and—"

"If you think there's any way you two are going on this tour without someone else looking out for you, you're out of your mind."

"But Uncle Jiggy will be there and—"

"Doesn't matter. Be thankful we're all not riding along."

Oh, yikes. That would be worse. "Grrr."

"Quit being a brat." *Geez, he sounds just like Dad when he uses that tone.*

This is the problem with having a much older brother. He sides with my parents way too often.

I blow out an exasperated breath.

Shaking his head, he pulls an envelope out of his cut. "Take this."

I peek inside. "What's that?"

"Cash. People used that in the olden days to buy things," he explains in a slow, mocking tone.

I roll my eyes at him. "I know that. Dad already gave me some."

"Good. Hide that in a different place so in case you lose it, you won't be stuck."

I give him a quick hug. "Thank you."

"You're going to listen to everything Rooster and Shelby tell you to do, right?"

I heave out a long, dramatic sigh. "Yes, Marcel."

"You're going to be careful. Pay attention to your surroundings, and not go off with anyone for any reason, right? Don't trust anyone."

"Oh my God! How dumb do you think I am?"

He drills me with his blue-green eyes until I relent. "Okay fine. You know Dad, Uncle Murphy, and Uncle Wrath already gave me this speech, right?"

"You, Alexa, and Chance stick together," he continues, ignoring my protest. "Don't let her sneaky ass out of your sight."

I smother my laughter with a hand over my mouth.

"I'm serious. If either of you get so much as a scratch, you know Chance will get his ass kicked. Is that what you want?"

As much as Chance annoys the ever-loving cupcakes out of me, no, I don't want him to get in trouble. I still think the club's archaic "protect the women" stuff is stupid, though.

"What about us? Will *we* get in trouble if something happens to Chance?"

He snort-laughs and stares at the ground for a second or two. "Yeah," he finally answers. "You will."

"Well, at least that's fair."

Because he has radar for anyone talking about him, Chance sneaks up behind me and wraps his arm around my neck, rubbing his knuckles over the top of my head. "Nothing's gonna happen to me, Princess."

"Get off me!" I elbow him in the ribs until he lets go.

Marcel glares at him. "Keep your hands to yourself, Chance."

"It's fine." I lean into Chance. "I'll kick his ass later."

"You wish," Chance mutters.

"Where'd your sidekick go?" Marcel asks me.

"Aunt Heidi sent her home to finish packing."

"For real?" Chance groans. "We'll need a separate bus to carry all her shit."

Marcel hugs me one more time. "I'll see you again before you go."

After he leaves, I turn to Chance and push him around the side of the house, away from the prying eyes of our parents. "This is going to be a whole afternoon of every single person in the club saying goodbye and warning us to behave, isn't it?"

"One-thousand-percent yes." He laughs. "At least no one's threatening to kick *your* ass if you two get into trouble."

"Not true. Marcel said we're supposed to look out for you too."

He snorts. "Sure."

I bust out some self-defense moves. "We're trained assassins thanks to Uncle Jake."

He laughs a deep, rumbling belly laugh and catches my flying fist in mid-air with minimal effort. "You forget, Uncle Wrath's been training *me* since I was like three."

"Not fair. You're already twice my size."

As if that was a compliment, he puffs up his chest.

"Geez." I roll my eyes.

"Okay, Princess." He loses his playful grin. "For real, though, I'm not going to be watching your every move. But you two better stay out of trouble or we'll never be allowed to do anything ever again. Neither will Bit-bit and you know she's dying to tour with Shelby."

A bit of jealousy prickles at me but I push it away. Even if every single one of my cousins were to tag along, Aunt Shelby will always make time for me.

THE BABYISH TREATMENT continues with Chance being designated as the one to drive us to where we're meeting Aunt Shelby's tour bus.

"Why did I bother getting my license if I'm never allowed to drive?" I grumble.

"I'm the oldest." Chance smirks at me in the rearview mirror.

We're not alone on the highway. No, the entire club—about thirty bikes and a minivan or two—are riding in front and behind us. Our own personal, overprotective caravan of cavemen.

Alexa stretches her arms up and over her head. "I'm just thrilled to get away from Bit-bit and Connor for a few weeks. You don't know how lucky you are to be an only child, Grace." She kicks the back of Chance's seat. "Aren't you excited you won't have Raven tagging along everywhere you go?"

From where I'm sitting, I spot the solemn expression on Chance's face. "Nah, I'm gonna miss her." He flicks his gaze to the mirror. "You're not gonna miss B & C even a little?"

"Maybe Bit-bit," Alexa says.

I turn and peer out the back window. I swear the line of motorcycles behind us looks longer every time I turn around. "This is ridiculous. We're going on tour, not to the moon."

"Please." Alexa waves away my concerns with a flick of her wrist. "We'll ditch Chance in no time. He'll be busy working or chasing groupies and we'll have our own fun."

Chance snort-laughs. "Keep telling yourself that, Duchess." He catches my eye in the mirror. "Grace won't let me down, right?"

"I'm not doing anything to disrespect or embarrass Aunt Shelby. It has nothing to do with *you*, Chance Frazier."

A RUSH of excitement floods me as I spot Shelby's tour bus in the parking lot of the restaurant owned by the Lost Kings MC. *Phew.* For a minute, I was worried someone might've called this off and told Shelby not to come.

Then a wave of sadness hits me.

I've never been away from my parents for this long. Dad goes on runs with the club all the time but for anything longer than a couple of days, Mom and I have always gone with him.

Chance barely has the SUV in park when I jump out. Alexa follows.

Aunt Shelby and Aunt Lilly are talking but Shelby turns as soon as she sees Alexa and me.

She welcomes us with open arms and we grab her in a fierce hug.

"Here're my favorite nieces," Shelby whispers to us. "Don't let yer cousins hear me sayin' that." She presses her finger to her lips as if it's a big secret.

I hug her tighter. "I know I'm really your favorite," I whisper in her ear.

She shakes with laughter but doesn't deny it.

"Are you excited, Aunt Shelby?" I ask, pulling away.

"I am. We have a lot of dates lined up."

I think the last time she toured was when I was twelve or thirteen. Aunt Trinity and Uncle Wrath had taken us to a bunch of shows. That's sorta how Alexa and I hatched the plan to work as Shelby's assistants when we were old enough.

We just didn't plan on Chance crashing our party. *Grrr.*

I hug Aunt Lilly. "Are you sure you don't need Chance at home this summer?" I ask.

Lilly doesn't smile. If anything, she seems sad. Then she shakes it off. "I can't believe I'm letting him do this."

"You know we'll take good care of 'em," Shelby says.

Uncle Rooster comes up behind Shelby. "Don't worry, Lilly, I've got so much work for him to do, he won't have time to get into trouble."

"Wait a minute," Chance hollers. "I didn't sign up for that."

"Ha-ha!" I laugh in his face.

It's going to be an epic summer.

AUTHOR NOTES

I feel like crying as I finish *Reckless Truths*. Every book is hard to write but this one felt so much different for some reason. Almost like I was wrapping up the original five officers of Upstate (I'm not done with the series!) and saying goodbye to them.

I've wanted to write *Reckless Truths* for a while. But I kept telling myself no one wants to read *another* book about Teller and Charlotte. Then I kept getting messages and questions about when everyone would find out about Teller and Rock. Some people just assumed it came out in a different book and they missed it—don't you know me at all?—*of course* a secret this big would have an entire book dedicated to it! Some suggested I could "just write a novella" about it. I assume they've never written a book, let alone a book series as long as mine. Besides, whenever I write novellas I get complaints that it's "too short."

This year has been a *lot*. In many ways it feels like an extension of the never-ending yuck of 2020. While I was trying to finish and launch *Throne of Scars*, we also closed on our new house and sold our old house —a goal Mr. Lake and I had been working toward for the last six years and were starting to think would *never* happen. We both got *the* plague, which thankfully was not as bad as some have had it but still took time to shake off. Moving to the new house was a painful *chore*. Literally painful. I don't remember it hurting this much 15 years ago. We're currently living out of boxes and trying to acclimate ourselves to the new place. Have I mentioned I don't adapt well to change? Well, I don't. I've spent weeks roaming around, trying to find just the right place where I could write and be comfortable enough to turn all my ideas into words on a page.

And I still had this book to write! I've been thinking about it for years. Years! But every time I thought about it, the next thought was, wow, that's going to be a tricky one to write one day. Good luck with that, future Autumn!

But the future was here.

Reckless Truths needed to be written. I was still shy about announcing *what* or *who* it was about (although, I did feel the title and tagline were giant clues) because I just didn't want to hear, "I already read Charlotte and Teller's books" or "What about Jigsaw?" "What about Dex?" "Why is it taking so long?" "I hope they're brothers instead because it's so gross if they're father and son." The book was hard enough to write without that negativity.

Then the messages and comments about how *excited* people were that Rock and Teller were *finally* going to tell the club—and especially Heidi—that they were father and son. The speculation, the fear I would do something awful to our beloved characters, people telling me they were re-reading specific books to "prepare." I was *floored,* humbled, and so grateful. Rock and Teller moved to the top of the list (sorry Dex and Jigsaw, your turns are coming!) While I can look at my numbers and see plain as day that the *overall* interest isn't there for this book, those who did want this story, *really, really* wanted this story. I thank you so much for that. It gave me life when I was feeling very out of sorts. I poured everything I have into telling their story in the way I thought it deserved to be told. Let's be honest, I've been writing about how I prioritize artistic happiness over financial success for years anyway.

Reckless Truths couldn't only be about *the* secret. Since Rock and Teller took so long to tell everyone, it would have been odd to have a story that only focused on that. If I just picked up where *Throne of Scars* left off, it would've been jarring and weird. But if I re-wrote the last *eleven* books from Teller and Charlotte's points of view, that was going to be mighty long and probably quite boring for everyone involved. And I was very committed to tying up this story in one book. One. Just one book. Not two. Or three. One. So, I tried to pick the highlights and weave them into their story in a way that felt as natural as possible. I didn't want anyone to feel "lost" while reading *Reckless Truths*, but I also wasn't going to info dump big chunks of information that wouldn't make sense for the characters in the moment as a way to "catch up." I feel so strongly about this, probably because I write in first person point of view, and present tense. I'm always stopping to think—is that normal? Would I think that way? Would I look at someone and flashback to their entire history for no reason? No. It's also a personal peeve of mine when I'm reading a series—if each book takes time to rehash previous books with no new perspective on the same situation, it feels forced, and I hate it. If you're wondering why some things were shown, and other things were not, that's why!

I realized the expectation was for this book to be about the secret and maybe a wedding for Teller and Charlotte. But I had plans to torture Carter and bring Merlin back into their lives. I don't know why. I love Carter and I love the relationship he's developed with Teller and the club. Why his toe of all things? I'll admit, that was mean. I also wanted Carter and Charlotte to move into a more adult brother/sister relationship by opening up and talking about the past. And, yes, Carter letting her know that he's known for years the truth about *his* father.

I knew a lot of people expected Heidi to be the one who would be upset about Rock being Teller's father (and not hers.) But I knew it was *Murphy* who would take it the hardest at first. That's why it was so important for me to show Heidi and Murphy as their own family unit. I don't think they'll ever move to Deadbranch, but I liked them *thinking* about something so extreme (for them) without any input from Teller or the club, even if it was only a revenge fantasy of sorts. Who hasn't thought about saying "fuck it all" and running away at least once (a week) in their lives? I can't be the only one.

Anyway, I liked Heidi and Murphy taking time to cool off together, coming to the realization of *why* Teller had such a hard time telling them, and finding compassion for everyone's actions, *together.*

I had three epilogues in mind but ended up going with Grace because it just felt like a fun thing to do, I hope you thought so too! One thing that became obvious while writing *Reckless Truths* is that there are a lot of characters in my world to write about! I feel like Trinity hauling out her binder (mine would be blue, though) to write lists of all these people who live in my head. Some I have nothing in mind for, others I could write dozens of books for and can't wait to get to their stories. Anyone who has reached out to ask me if certain characters will be getting a book one day—*thank you*! Even if I don't have plans for them, I'm honored that you care about my characters enough to ask.

Now, I'm looking forward to doing a little more unpacking and then digging into Dex's story and so many others. I'm excited to settle into my new space and finally turn all the ideas that have been running through my mind loose on the world.

Thank you for reading *Reckless Truths* and if you made it to the bottom of this note, thank you! I am grateful that I have such wonderful readers who care about the stories I want to tell as passionately as I do. *Thank you.* If this was a Facebook post, I would punctuate this with a thousand heart emojis as my way to virtually "hug" each one of you.

xo

Autumn

7-15-22

ACKNOWLEDGMENTS

Thank you for asking me to write this book. I loved every second I spent with Teller and Charlotte, Rock and Hope, and Heidi and Murphy, even when they were being difficult. I hope you enjoy it too!

I especially want to thank Jan B for the countdown updates in our Facebook Group. I had so much fun with all the snippets she posted leading up to release day! I'm hesitant to ever name too many people for fear I'll leave someone out and hurt feelings. But I need to thank Jennifer Stewart, Nanci Cardwell, Ethel Jackson, Michelle Stezewski, Lorraine Irvine, Kim Brown, Jennifer Godwin, Brandi Wiley, Ready Snodgrass, Mia Stewart-Robinson, Roz Butler, Jenny Matisie, Deborah-Lee, Allison G. Cynthia Rendall, Rosemary K. Ashley J. Alexis Marre, and Erin Rockel for their kindness, and generosity. These ladies help make our Facebook groups such a fun and interesting place and I thank you so much for being part of it!

Thank you Liz for all of your beautiful notes.

My editor for trying so hard to keep me on track! She is such a kind and patient person and I appreciate it so much!

Julie, thank you for catching those pesky mistakes I looooove to introduce at the last minute when I go fuck around with all the words.

Author LK Shaw, thanks for letting me be salty every day. I appreciate you so much!

Sophie, Laura, Shawna, Tanisha, Shawna, Heather, Jessica, Athena, and Brittany thank you for recognizing how bad I am at promoting myself and helping to signal boost my social media posts even though I always forget to ask for help.

The anxiety that I'm leaving someone out is real here!

Thank you for buying and reading Reckless Truths!

A

THE LOST KINGS MC® WORLD

By Autumn Jones Lake

Sometimes I'm asked where the stand alone books fit into the Lost Kings MC World. This is a loose, chronological reading order that might help!

Suggested Chronological Reading Order

1. Kickstart My Heart (Hollywood Demons #1)
2. Blow My Fuse (Hollywood Demons #2)
3. Wheels of Fire (Hollywood Demons #3)
4. Renegade Path
5. Slow Burn (Lost Kings MC #1)
6. Corrupting Cinderella (Lost Kings MC #2)
7. Three Kings, One Night (Lost Kings MC #2.5)
8. Strength From Loyalty (Lost Kings MC #3)
9. Tattered on My Sleeve (Lost Kings MC #4)
10. White Heat (Lost Kings MC #5)
11. Between Embers (Lost Kings MC #5.5)
12. Bullets & Bonfires (Standalone)
13. More Than Miles (Lost Kings MC #6)
14. Warnings & Wildfires (Standalone)
15. White Knuckles (Lost Kings MC #7)
16. Beyond Reckless (Lost Kings MC #8)
17. Beyond Reason (Lost Kings MC #9)
18. One Empire Night (Lost Kings MC #9.5)
19. After Burn (Lost Kings MC #10)
20. After Glow (Lost Kings MC #11)
21. Zero Hour (Lost Kings MC #11.5)
22. Zero Tolerance (Lost Kings MC #12)
23. Zero Regret (Lost Kings MC #13)
24. Zero Apologies (Lost Kings MC #14)
25. Swagger and Sass (Lost Kings MC #14.5)
26. White Lies (Lost Kings MC #15)
27. Rhythm of the Road (Lost Kings MC #16)

ABOUT THE AUTHOR

Autumn Jones Lake is the *USA Today* and *Wall Street Journal* bestselling author of over twenty-five novels, including the popular Lost Kings MC series. She believes true love stories never end.

Her past lives include baking cookies, bagging groceries, selling cheap shoes, and practicing law. Playing with her imaginary friends all day is by far her favorite job yet!

Autumn lives in upstate New York with her own alpha hero.

www.autumnjoneslake.com

www.ingramcontent.com/pod-product-compliance
Lightning Source LLC
Chambersburg PA
CBHW072015020726
47501CB00006B/1823